Outstanding praise for the novels of Viqui Litman

MIDNIGHT PEACHES

"*Midnight Peaches* has all the makings of an eccentric small-town Texas screwball comedy . . . a lot of fun . . . enjoyable."
—*The Free Lance-Star* (Fredericksburg, Virginia)

"Full of heartwarming emotion served with a healthy dose of humor."
—*Romantic Times*

GENERATIONS OF THE HEART

"An entertaining read."
—*Booklist*

"There are enough simmering relational issues to keep pages turning."
—*Dallas Morning News*

THE LADIES FARM

"Litman's comic pitch is true and her intentions just."
—*The New York Times Book Review*

"Get ready for a good time, but get out your handkerchiefs . . . funny and tender . . . Never healed-hurts and the importance of hair, good men and bad boys, the meaning of work and the meaning of meaning—it's all here along with raucous laughter and more than one good cry."
—*Booklist*

"Female friendship overcomes all obstacles in this sweet, sometimes sassy first novel. A touching tribute to the bonds among women."
—*Library Journal*

"An intelligent debut novel and a nicely astringent take on love, friendship and Texas foibles."
—*Kirkus Reviews*

"Brisk and chatty . . . Litman keeps her story upbeat and on track."
—*Publisher's Weekly*

"Readers will feel right at home . . . Litman has a nice way of giving her characters voice."
—*Fort Worth Telegram*

Books by Viqui Litman

THE LADIES FARM

GENERATIONS OF THE HEART

MIDNIGHT PEACHES

Published by Kensington Publishing Corporation

MIDNIGHT PEACHES

Viqui Litman

KENSINGTON BOOKS
http://www.kensingtonbooks.com

KENSINGTON BOOKS are published by

Kensington Publishing Corp.
850 Third Avenue
New York, NY 10022

Copyright © 2003 by Viqui Litman

All Kensington titles, imprints, and distributed lines are available at special quantity discounts for bulk purchases for sales promotion, premiums, fund-raising, educational or institutional use.

Special book excerpts or customized printings can also be created to fit specific needs. For details, write or phone the office of the Kensington Special Sales Manager: Kensington Publishing Corp., 850 Third Avenue, New York, NY 10022, Attn. Special Sales Department. Phone: 1-800-221-2647.

Kensington and the K logo Reg. U.S. Pat. & TM Off.

ISBN 0-7582-0166-4

First Hardcover Printing: October 2003
First Trade Paperback Printing: December 2004
10 9 8 7 6 5 4 3 2 1

Printed in the United States of America

For Sue and Aaron and Ian the Magnificent

Chapter 1

When the storm hit, Della was indulging Tony's penchant for sex in risky places with a session in the fitness shed. Though the thrill lay primarily in the danger of discovery—Melissa Freschatte Warringale and her two boys were due at the Ladies Farm any second—Della also found challenge in balancing on the narrow benches and mustering her upper body strength to lever into stimulating angles. Plus, she liked the split-second maneuvering from one station to another, which demanded the kind of communication achieved only in a partnership honed through years of practice.

They ended, as they always did, in a modified missionary on the ab board, her heels braced in the elevated foot rests, blood rushing to her head on the sloped bench. The rain crashed down on the metal roof to announce *STORM*, as opposed to rain, in which drops might start plinking randomly. Like most of their violent weather, this deluge attacked decidedly southwest-to-northeast. Then, in a thrilling coincidence, the tempest delivered hail that exactly matched the peak of their passion.

"There!" Tony exulted, as pleased as if he himself had fired the barrage onto the fitness shed.

Even while they pushed against each other to test the limits of the ab board, their Texas ears had registered the moment when the forceful drops turned to hail. Now, struggling to sit up as she unhooked her feet, Della gauged the stuff as pea-size, but growing. It could disappear in a second, she thought, leaning around Tony for the towel draped over the shoulder press. She hugged her ex-husband, who straddled the bench and faced her. "Score one for fitness," she whispered into his ear, rubbing his sweaty back with the towel.

Her legs were draped over his, and he supported her back with his arms as he smiled at her. "I meant what I said," he told her, kissing the side of her face. Then he jerked back and cocked his head to one side to listen.

"Jesus Christ!" said Della, hearing what he heard. She grabbed a few more towels and the clothes scattered over the shoulder press, then jammed her bare feet into her shoes and dove toward the door. This shed wouldn't stand a chance if that siren was more than a warning.

Melissa added Texas hail to the litany of trauma she had inflicted on her boys.

"What's hail?" Garrett asked from behind her. Melissa could hear him working at the seat belt.

"You stupid!" Trey sneered. "Mom, he's—"

"Honey, I need us to all stay buckled up right now. Hail is ice."

"From the sky? Ice from the sky?"

"Stupid!" Trey chided his brother, yelling to be heard above the barrage. "What if it breaks the glass?" His seven-year-old bravado had fled.

"It's just a spring storm," Melissa assured her boys loudly. Daddy, she was certain, would never subject them to such dangers. "Just spring in Texas." She struggled to sound airily dismissive as she shouted.

In the second of vision that followed the sweep of the windshield wipers, she saw an overpass. Bless the railroad trestle, she thought. Quarter-size balls of ice were bouncing across the hood, and the noise had risen from tattoo to roar.

"Mom?" Trey was calling. "Mom?!"

Swish. The viaduct loomed closer. Swish. Roar. Swish. Closer. Swish. Pow!

The thing that crashed through the passenger's windshield was the size of a softball.

"Mom!" Both boys screamed, but Melissa forced herself to picture them safely buckled into the back as she jammed the brakes to activate the ABS and shuddered to a stop under the railroad bridge.

* * *

Gladys Hutto had never once been sorry for having sex with her husband Ray, but she puzzled to herself that, even in pain and often unable to complete the act, Ray still wanted it so badly. "It shouldn't hurt," she had said to him not long ago.

"It only hurts when I stop," he had replied, but she doubted it. Even though they had left Sydonia and opted for the drier climate of the Big Bend, his arthritis had progressed to the point that some days he couldn't get his clothes on, or turn a key to start the truck. Gladys sat at an interior table in the Sydonia Dairy Queen, licking a Dilly Bar, thinking about Ray and their marriage, and watching hail pound hell out of her Avalon.

The sky to the west had lightened since she had swerved into the parking lot and nosed the car up to the overhang that protected the entrance. The hail had grown larger. But now the lightning that crackled across the purple sky had paled slightly, and there was a beat before the crash of thunder. Must be petering out, thought Gladys, though it was too late for her back window.

She wondered if she would be able to drive the car back to the Big Bend. Fix it with plastic, she thought. Then when they get the window in at the dealer's, bring it back to Fort Worth to fix the dents. Or maybe try the dealer in Midland. I should have backed in, she thought. You could get front windshields; rear windows took forever.

Gladys hadn't planned to stay long. Just talk to those women at the Ladies Farm, then get back to Ray. He had their nephew, Earl, to look after him, but Earl also had Darlene and their new baby, not to mention Darlene's little daughter, Tiffany. Earl was trying to build a house on the back of their lot, and Ray would stay busy doing what he could to help, but Gladys worried about his meals. She doubted he could take more than a day or two of the convenience-store pizza and burgers favored by Darlene and Earl.

Maybe she could leave the car with the dealer in Fort Worth and take the train back to Alpine. Or hitch a ride on someone's plane. She and Ray could make do with the truck at home.

The Avalon was a silly car anyway, she thought, watching a few remnants of hail bounce indifferently off the car roof and onto the wet asphalt. Expensive, and too low-slung for the unpaved road to the house where she and Ray had retired south of Alpine. But the car had a blaster of an air conditioner, and floated along the highway for these trips back to North Central Texas. It was silly, but it was the perfect fit as far as Gladys was concerned. It gave her the matronly look she wanted to cultivate, ferrying illegal substances back and forth along the roads of West Texas.

Chapter 2

The electricity went out before Della made her way to the trunk in the corner of the storm closet. "It's better this way," she grunted, wading through the blackness with her hands before her. "This way I don't see the critters scattering." Thunder crashed above them, and she was glad she couldn't see the lightning.

"Just get the lantern," Tony instructed. "Here." He opened the closet door to let in a little light.

"Tony!"

"What? We're just as safe with the door open."

The door had muffled the roar of the storm and the siren's wail, but she didn't want to admit that the noise frightened her. "I'd like to pull my jeans on before we welcome the world." She opened the trunk and withdrew the battery-powered lantern. "Here." She flipped the thing on and hung it from a hook as Flops, their mostly-retriever, nosed into the closet. "All the comforts of home." She knelt down to hug the dog, who had probably sought safety by pushing nose and face beneath the sofa in the Ladies Farm office.

Della stood back up and handed Tony a towel, then pulled one out for herself. Pauline Freschatte, her late partner and founder of Sydon House, the bed and breakfast that had morphed into the Ladies Farm, had equipped the storm closet as logically and thoroughly as she had done everything else. Her handwritten inventory, tucked neatly inside the top of the trunk, had guided them in restocking the sheltered space under the staircase during the last two years, and they had not amended the flowing script of the list by a single item. Of course, Della and her two remaining part-ners—Rita and Kat—hadn't really used the closet in those two years, but there was a certain pride in maintaining Pauline's stan-dards of preparedness.

Della kept her back to Tony and Flops while she wiped mud off her legs and hopped into her jeans, which were only slightly drier than the T-shirt she had donned in the dash up to the house. "There's a bunch of dry socks and shirts," Della offered, but Tony had found the weather radio and was fiddling with the dials.

"It's probably just a little hail," Tony muttered. He grazed his fingers over Flops's head while the weather service advised that several funnels had been sighted, though none had touched down. "That they know of," Tony amended. Flops looked up, but re-mained settled at his feet.

Della stepped up behind him and leaned her head against the center of his back. It was an incongruous moment to think that there was nothing like a tall man, but that was what she thought. After a second more of weather—the storm was heading, pre-dictably, for southwest Fort Worth—Tony turned and guided her to the back of the closet. "We'd better break out the blanket, just in case. This lull would be the center; there's bound to be more in a minute."

Della knew his concern wasn't for their safety; the two of them would be fine in the closet. Even his truck was parked under the carport. But Tony owned two copy shops in Fort Worth, and who knew what they were in for? Not to mention the house they had lived in together when they were married. Tony still lived there, and he wouldn't be able to check it till after he had helped out here in Sydonia and then swung by both Fort Worth stores.

He pulled out his cell phone but didn't dial, using it instead to emphasize his point. "This is what I meant before," he said, ges-turing to the gloom of the lantern-lit closet. "Here we are in peril, and if we died in this storm, we'd just be two unrelated people in a closet. They might not even bury us together."

Just then another barrage of hail hit the house, which enabled Della to restrain her laugh. Instinctively, they both crouched as the noise pounded the roof over the second story. "Rita couldn't stand separating us," Della whispered as they settled on the floor. Even with the guest rooms above them, the noise on the creased metal roof was deafening.

Hail doesn't fall, thought Della. It's hurled down. Della just hoped the roof held. She didn't mind replacing it so much as she minded the idea of water pouring all over their guest rooms. It would take forever to undo the damage and get the rooms ready again.

And where was Rita? Della imagined her for a second at the convenience store and service station owned by Rita's husband, Dave. She tried to picture them safe in the walk-in refrigerator and not staring bleakly at the barrage of hail through panes of storefront window.

"Oh my God!" Della said as the radio crackled with wind velocity and warnings to take shelter. "Melissa!"

"You don't think she's on the road in this?"

"I hope not!" Della shook her head. "She didn't sound like she was thinking too clearly. She's got those boys with her, too."

"Well," Tony said, "I'm sure once she heard on the radio—"

"Tony! She's a Silicon Valley yuppie who's probably got on earphones while her kids watch the TV in the back, and she's been driving all night because she's run off from her husband!"

"She seemed like a pretty level-headed girl when she was growing up," Tony insisted. "I mean, Della, she's Pauline's daughter. You'd think when the sky turned black, she'd at least pull off the road."

This obtuseness was one of the reasons Della didn't want to talk about getting married again. "Tony! Did that storm make us stop fucking?"

Even in the weak light, she could see his grin. "Well, speaking purely for myself, it did hasten the conclusion." He frowned. "Not too hasty, I hope."

"Right on target," she said lightly. And she meant it. But this recent need for reassurance exhausted her. Guiltily she leaned into him and breathed deep against his chest. She focused on the session in the workout room. And how glad she was that he was with her here now. "Nothing like the Tony Brewer special."

"So why do you think Melissa's leaving her husband . . . what's his name?"

"Greg. Who knows? Must be another woman. Why would she just up and leave like that?"

"Criminal activity," Tony replied. "Child abuse. Spouse abuse. Failure to pick up his socks."

"Well, there's that," she said. She thought a second. "Maybe it's another man."

"Maybe."

They sat shoulder to shoulder on the floor, listening to the storm and drawing comfort from someone else's marital distress. Her own breakup with Tony seemed ages ago now, tied to the death of their teenage son and the heartache she had drowned in her affair with Richard Morrison. Now she did sigh.

"What?"

Della shrugged. "Nothing. Just thinking how complicated it all is. And how the things you think are so important turn out to be just stupid when you look back on them."

"Are we still talking about Melissa?"

"That and how much shit we'll have to go through before we get the roof replaced."

"You're mighty optimistic. What makes you so sure you're getting a new roof?" No one in their part of Texas voluntarily replaced a roof. With any luck, hail and high winds delivered insurance benefits before the property owner had to pay for it.

"Believe it or not, I'm not looking forward to it. Cleaning up that mess. Thank God we're empty right now. But we've got two couples coming in tomorrow."

"Well, it sounds like it's letting up."

"We're not moving till the all-clear," Della warned.

"I'm not arguing," he said in an agreeable tone. "You think we've got a few minutes before Rita barges in?"

Melissa had pulled as far onto the shoulder as she could without slipping into the ditch. Once under the bridge, she barely looked at the windshield, just dove into the back and examined the screaming boys with her hands, stroking their faces and murmuring reassurances as she unbuckled them and pushed them down on the car floor. If it was a tornado, they would be safer outside, on the ground. But more people died in flooding that followed heavy storms, so she played the odds. The lightning crackled and the thunder crashed around them as she silently defended herself to Greg. She draped herself over the whimpering boys and pulled a car blanket around them all.

"We could suffocate," Trey pointed out in a suddenly controlled and objective voice that made the thunder seem far away.

He sounded so like Greg that Melissa started, then gave a little laugh to reassure him. "Here," she whispered, shifting around. "Is that better?"

"There still might not be enough air."

"Honey," she said with a sigh, "there's a hole in the windshield the size of a grapefruit. I think there'll be plenty of air."

"We could be drownded," Garrett said. "When the ice melts."

"We're going to be okay," she whispered, then caught herself and tried to speak in a normal voice. "Once this ol' storm passes, we'll just head on over to Aunt Della's and all those ladies are gonna make such a fuss over you!"

"How come you're talking like that?" Trey asked.

"Like what?"

"Like a hick!"

"A hick!" Garrett repeated, giggling.

Melissa could hear the relief in his voice as he drew comfort from the familiarity of his brother's sarcasm.

"I guess I'm just talking Texan," she said, annoyed at Greg, who often scolded her for her diction. The kids' California cool was Greg's doing. Melissa lifted her head. "I think it's letting up," she said, looking out the back of the SUV. The rain was still falling, but Melissa could see light at the far edges of the sky, and the hail had passed. At least nothing was bouncing on the hail-dotted asphalt beyond the overpass.

"Okay," she said calmly, "let's slide out Trey's side and stretch our legs while I get all that glass cleaned up."

She did the best she could with one eye on the two of them. She used a magazine to sweep the loose glass off the seat and into a McDonald's sack, and a beach towel to blot the water from the upholstery. Trey was showing Garrett the rainbows made by motor oil in the roadside puddles, and picking up melting balls of ice at the edge of the bridge cover. It wasn't until the truck rolled up behind her that she realized they hadn't seen another car since they'd pulled over.

The boys backed up almost against her knees as the pickup driver, brandishing a cell phone, walked around to her and asked if he could help. "You folks okay?" He was older, maybe in his sixties or seventies, heavyset, in dusty khakis and a blue work shirt. He squinted at her and the boys, then nodded at the Lexus. "Get hit?"

Melissa nodded, held up the magazine and paper sack as if they were self-explanatory. "Just one big one, before I could get under the overpass."

He walked over to the windshield, winking at the boys as he passed. "That there's about seven inches!" he said.

Melissa nodded.

"You boys in the back?" he asked them, and both nodded solemnly.

"It was ice," Garrett said. "Ice from the sky!"

"He means hail," Trey confided. Melissa hoped he didn't comment on the man's twang.

"Well, it looks driveable, but I'll be glad to give you a lift if you'd rather. Are you going far?"

Melissa shook her head. "We're staying here, actually. Sydonia."

"The Ladies Farm," Trey said. He was looking at the man's boots, but the man was studying Melissa.

"I'm Melissa Warringale—Melissa Freschatte Warringale. You might have known—"

"Oh, those folks who bought the old Sydon House: Pauline and Hugh, was it?" He nodded. "I remember them. I'm Webb Dyer. I'll bet you knew my boys, if you grew up here. One or another of 'em. Wade. Tommy. Clark. Steve. Ethan." He paused after each name, giving her time to consider, and, indeed, she knew one well.

"Ethan Dyer," Melissa said, grinning. "We used to take the canoe up to the Brazos."

"That would be Ethan," said Mr. Dyer. He waved the phone. "Just talked to him, he's driving up tomorrow, from Austin. Help me sort out what's left of the peaches."

"Oh, Mr. Dyer!" Melissa said, appalled at her stupidity. "I didn't even think about . . . did it hit your orchard?"

He shook his head. "Well, we got two up near the house that look pretty bad, I was just driving over to look at the one off four seventy-three."

"I guess you've added a few fields," Melissa said.

"I've got two that back all the way down to the river, on the other side. Back up against Castleburg. I don't imagine there's much left there."

"Oh, Mr. Dyer, I'm so sorry. Here I am worried about my windshield—"

"Well, it's lucky you got to the overpass. So far, sounds like the only thing's hurt is peach trees and that's bad enough. Do you want to call those ladies, let 'em know you're all right?"

Melissa shook her head. "No. I mean, I've got a phone, but I think I'll just head on over. You're right, there's no reason not to drive the thing."

"Just like getting back on the horse."

"You have a horse?" Trey asked.

"No more horses," said Mr. Dyer. "I told my kids, you take those horses with you when you go." He looked down at the disappointed boys. "I imagine those gals know someone with horses you could take for a ride, though. Don't you worry." He paused for a second to let the reassurance sink in. "I got some plastic in the car, let me tape a little over that hole, get you where you're going."

In a few minutes, Melissa was rolling onto the roadway, knowing he would sit there in his truck and watch until they were underway, the plastic billowing inward but holding. "Aunt Della and Aunt Kat and Aunt Rita are going to be so glad to see us. And you know what else?"

"What?"

"I'll bet Uncle Dave can fix our window, too!"

"Does Uncle Dave have horses?" asked Trey.

But Melissa didn't answer. She concentrated, instead, on her satisfaction that she had taken refuge from marital disaster in a place where neighbors stopped to offer roadside assistance, and her girlhood love was due in town the next day.

Tony and Della emerged from the closet and blinked at the serenity of the entry hall. Nothing shattered, nothing flooded. Tony, shoes still in hand, padded to the kitchen to check the back of the house, while Della took the stairs. She took a moment to peel off her clothes and pull on a stretchy pantsuit. Flashlight in hand, she unfolded the attic steps and climbed up to see what had happened. She braced herself for melting blobs of ice and gaping holes to the clearing sky. Instead she found two puddles where rain had run along damaged seams. She poked carefully into the corners, trying not to rouse any mice, whose presence she had learned to tolerate in exchange for their staying hidden most of the time.

When she bent low to check the screen on the eaves that faced the river, she saw movement on the other side, on the top of the hill where they had added the old Hutto place to the Ladies Farm. I'll have to check over there too, Della thought, squinting at what looked like a big sedan through the trees.

They had been remodeling the place bit by bit, renting it out in-between to families and small groups in search of a nice view and a rustic setting. That roof, composition shingles on a shallow peak, would certainly be a total loss if it got hit. They'd have to refinish the floor—again—thought Della, but the next group wasn't due in for a week or so. Hopefully, they could patch the roof to hold till then, and get the floors done in an afternoon.

Passersby on the county road sometimes ignored the sign directing inquiries to the Ladies Farm and walked up to peer in the windows of the Hutto house. It was disconcerting to guests, but otherwise did little damage. Occasionally drifters, or maybe illegals, would camp there, breaking the door latch when the house was unoccupied, heating cans of food directly on the electric burners of the stove, and dragging the bare mattresses into the big room with the fireplace.

Kat favored an alarm system, and Rita a shotgun, but Della couldn't bring herself to do anything. "Is it so terrible," she would ask, "that someone with nowhere else to go spends the night in an empty house? Maybe we should just leave it unlocked."

"You won't say that when they burn the place down," Rita would grumble, but they hadn't caught anyone yet.

Homeless people didn't usually drive up in the middle of the day, though, and it irked Della that she'd have to drive over there to see what was going on. I'll take Tony, she thought in response to Rita's warnings about reckless endangerment. She clumped downstairs to the second-floor closet where they kept cleaning supplies, then back up to the attic again with buckets to place under the two leaks.

She heard the phone ringing, but knew she couldn't get to it. It was either Kat, who had heard the weather while calling on clients in Dallas, or Rita, checking in to exchange damage reports.

When she returned downstairs, Tony was examining the kitchen doorway where water had seeped in under the jamb. He nodded toward the back, which faced the river. "That shed looks fine. We probably could have had an encore in there and lived to tell the tale."

"It's like washing your car to make it rain, Tony. If you stay in the shed, it draws the tornado away from the trailer park."

Then Della gave him her assessment of the attic and her survey of the second floor. "The rooms are all fine."

"Lucky," Tony said. He motioned toward the door. "Call Kirk Hilgon for this."

Della nodded. She was thinking about Rita. "Why haven't we . . . I need to—" She stared at the door. "The water backed up—"

"Well, it pools around that little concrete step . . . Dell? What's the matter?"

She was looking out the back windows at a jungle of downed limbs. The river was running only a little higher, but a tangle of debris coursed between its banks. Midway down the backyard, the little resin table that normally sat between two slung chairs had been split in two, with one piece tangled in a crape myrtle. "Oh my God," she whispered. "It's . . . there's so much . . . we could have . . . everything's such a mess!"

"Dell, we're okay. The house is fine, no one's hurt so far—"

"I have to call Rita," she said.

"Hello?" It came from the front. "Aunt Dell?"

"Melissa!" Della rushed to the front.

"It's us," a child called. "The Warringales. Three Warringales!"

"Three!" It was the younger one—Garrett—trying his hardest to hold up three fingers on his right hand.

She held her arms wide and the boys came into them. "We got hailed!" said Garrett.

"It broke the windshield," Trey said, "and Mom had to drive the car and we were like, swerving? And then when we got under the bridge? Then we were skidding—"

"My God!" Della cried. "Melissa!" She stood up as Melissa moved into her arms.

"Oh, Aunt Dell, first it was just rain, and then it got so black and then the hail started, all so fast, I could barely think, and then the windshield—"

They were all out front, marveling at the size of the hole in the windshield and exclaiming over Webb Dyer's fortuitous appearance when the Avalon pulled up, followed by Rita's Lincoln.

"Tarps," Rita explained the Lincoln's pristine appearance. "First warning, Dave got all the customer cars into the bays, threw tarps over everything else. Like a drill: one, two, three. Then he puts us all in the back, with the weather radio. He wanted us to get in the fridge, but I wasn't having any of that. When'd you get in, Gladys?"

"Just now," Gladys said. "Minus a stop at the Dairy Queen, and then borrowing their whisk broom to get all that glass cleaned up." Gladys, with her gray curls, open gaze, and faded jeans, made a perfect contrast to Rita, who was vividly made-up and dressed in purple Lycra.

Della guessed that to Melissa they were all variations of her mother's generation. She just sees us as extensions of Pauline, thought Della, glad that she at least had lined her eyes and restrained her own brown hair with a half-dozen of the newer-styled small clips.

"Well," Tony drawled as he stepped up behind Della, "I'm suspecting you ladies will be all right for a while. I'll just get your bags in, Melissa—yours too, Gladys—and let you catch up. I've got to go see what's happening in Fort Worth."

"Oh, I dropped mine across the way," Gladys said. "Thanks, though."

"Did you get an answer?" Della asked Tony, nodding and smiling to Gladys to let her know it was fine if she wanted to stay in her old place. She wondered when Tony had pulled the denim shirt on over his tee.

Tony shook his head. "They may just be taking cover somewhere," he said. "Disconnect everything and get under the counter. Maybe they actually followed instructions."

Della doubted it, but she gave him a quick peck before he disappeared with the suitcases from the back of Melissa's SUV.

"He looks good, Aunt Dell." Melissa looked almost wistful as she watched him.

"He's just pining away after Della," Rita cracked as they migrated inside. "He looks healthy 'cause we all feed him, but inside he's existing on crumbs she doles out in those mid-morning love sessions." She pronounced it *luuuuuuuv*, a succession of rolling syllables.

"She wants me to make an honest man out of him," Della said.

Melissa looked pained, and Gladys just shrugged. "Hard to know what difference it would make," she said. "Better for insurance and estate planning, I guess."

"Well, Kat's still going strong with that doctor up in Colleyville," Rita filled them in, "and she'll be moving up there before we know it. So it's going to get mighty lonely for you-know-who if her luggage shlepper finds he can get home-cooked meals in Fort Worth as easily as he can out here."

The incongruity of Rita's drawling about *shlepping* was not lost on Melissa, who grinned at Della.

"Excuse me, Miss Rita," Della said, rolling her eyes, "I'll just say good-bye to poor suffering Tony, sprinkle a few crumbs of affection, if that's okay."

She walked Tony to the carport, stepping around Trey and Garrett, who were performing feats of strength on the porch railing.

"I got hold of Lisa," he told her, patting the pocket where he kept the phone. "On her cell. They haven't had hail yet, just rain."

"So why are you leaving?" Della said.

"Well, I've still got a business to run," Tony said. "I imagine I'll be there late."

Della nodded. She hadn't expected Tony back tonight and looked forward to hearing Melissa's story, with all the breathless questions and asides it no doubt deserved.

"Don't forget to call Kirk about that door," Tony cautioned. "He's bound to be busy now."

Della nodded, looked up at him. "I'm glad you were here," she told him now. "For the storm."

He smiled. "I'm glad I was here before the storm."

"That too. But Tony, you know, I mean . . ."

"What?"

"Not because it made me feel safer. I mean, it did." She thought for a second. "Because I wanted you to be safe. With me."

This wasn't what she had meant to say, and now she wasn't

sure why she'd said it, but Tony, as usual, listened without comment.

She nudged him, reached up to kiss him.

"I'll call later," he said before he got in the truck. "Tell Dave I'll come back down if he needs help. There's bound to be more damage, storm like this."

Chapter 3

If there was one tree in one orchard that had not been hit, Webb Dyer had not found it. The rows were strewn with broken branches. The young fruit, barely past blossom, that remained on the trees had all been bruised. He lifted his beer and drank, then set the can down on the porch floor and looked toward the river.

Webb knew that the Nolan River Valley was a narrow, unremarkable thing; but, seen from his porch, his own small crook in the wide elbow that defined Sydon County offered modest pleasure to a man willing to watch closely. Even so, the shallow undulations that rose from the Nolan delivered little comfort as he rested in his porch chair after surveying his orchards.

From here, the river glowed metallic—now silver, now gold, now bronze—and the slope of his fields obscured whatever debris had been placed there by the storm. Part of his mind turned to the practical: reduce irrigation, knock the bruised fruit from the two orchards most heavily damaged, contract with a wholesaler for the remaining, to be processed for preserves or chopped for flavoring. Put tomatoes into that field he had planned to let lie.

The rest of him concentrated on the curves of the orchard, green waves rising from the river. Before peaches, there had been peanuts, and before peanuts there had been a few cows, a few sheep, a horse or a mule grazing on the pale grass produced by that slim layer of soil covering the granite and limestone hill. No one had ever really made a living off this land. Not Webb, nor the peanut farmer who had sold it to him, nor the fellow with his cows and sheep who had sold it to the peanut farmer. There was always something else: harness-making, carpentry; in Webb's case, a TV repair service and, when his wife was alive, a roadside stand all summer long.

There were strawberries. Tomatoes. Pole beans. Drought. Flood. Borers. Locusts. It didn't matter. For Webb Dyer, reared as an orphaned cousin in a Chicago walkup, it was land he could finance through the Texas Veterans Affairs Office when he walked out of Fort Hood. It was a place where he and Alice could build a house that lent itself to adding on. Bedrooms, family room, even a second floor the boys turned into their own clubhouse.

Webb sipped a little more, smiled out at his kingdom. You want a year off? Webb thought. You could take it. The boys are grown, through school, on their own. Alice is in the ground. You could take five years, he told the curves of peach trees hugging the gentle rise. Just not this year.

Johnny Urquardt nudged the truck along the muddy ruts toward the river.

"Mom said you're not supposed to—"

"I'm not doing anything," Johnny told his son. He looked over at the boy, then glanced at the girls in the back. "Just checking out the storm damage, that's all."

"Pee yew," said Celine. "It stinks."

"That's Castleburg's," Junior said with authority. "Cow shit."

In the back, Celine and her sister, Cindy, dissolved in giggles. Junior eyed his father.

"Tell you what," Johnny proposed, still inching forward. "You keep this to yourself, you can say *shit* all you want in the truck."

"Whenever I want?"

"As long as it's just us," Johnny spelled out. "So it stays just between us."

Junior gloated toward the back seat, where his sisters had fallen silent. "Well, shit," Junior said. "That's a shit-good idea. Shit. Shit. Shit."

"You girls keep this to yourselves, you hear?" Johnny called to the back.

"Yes sir," Cindy said. She knew better than to say the bad word herself.

When he got close enough to see the far side of the river,

Johnny stopped the truck. He opened the door and considered the mud below the step pad, then closed the door again. In the dusk, the Nolan looked almost chocolate, filled with branches and debris.

Be here, Johnny started to pray. Be here, be here, be here. He tried to see upriver a little, to the cottonwoods from which Freddy usually emerged. Johnny studied the trees, trying to gauge how high the water had been. Freddy's shack had probably flooded. But a little water never stopped him before.

"Shit, shit, shit," Junior sang in a low voice. "Shit for breakfast, shit for lunch, shit for dinner."

Johnny squinted. He couldn't keep the children out much longer, Siggie got really pissed when he held up dinner.

"Is that man coming?" Celine asked from the back. "The one . . . the one with . . . you know, the hair."

Johnny shook his head, fired the engine. "No man tonight, sweetie-pie. Daddy just wanted to look at the river."

"The river!" Cindy popped up between the two front seats. "I want to see!"

"It's flooding," Junior informed her. "Flooding like shit. People's houses, floating away."

"Cut it out," Johnny said automatically. "Don't scare your sister." He put the car in reverse, gunned the engine and let up on the clutch. Cindy fell back against Celine.

"It sounded like bombing," Junior informed him. "We had to go to the cafeteria and get under the tables."

Johnny felt traction, backed the truck back to where he could get turned around. "We're all okay," Johnny said. "Right, girls?"

"Yes," said Celine.

"Except that man," Cindy said. "That hair man. He could drowned."

"He's fine," Johnny told her. "Freddy's fine." Somewhere.

Shit. Shit. Shit.

"Women's clothes?" Rita brought the recliner to an upright position with a crack.

"You mean he's a transvestite?"

Melissa could hear Della's struggle to control her voice and it irritated her more than Rita's astonishment. "If a transvestite is someone who likes parading around in lacy negligees on caribou mules." She blinked hard. "Peach-colored," she added. "Brings out the bloom in his skin."

"He told you that, did he?" At least Gladys saw some humor in it. She had turned a little on the sofa to get a better look at Melissa, who had curled up against the other arm. "Ray and I knew a Cuban, once, who did that. Played the clubs in Havana. Retired rich in Miami."

"I'm so sick of *Bird Cage* references I want to puke!" Melissa said. Suddenly, the tension from her ponytail felt as if it would make her head explode. In one motion, she ripped the elastic band away and pushed her widespread fingers along her scalp.

"What does *Bird Cage* mean?" Gladys asked, dumbfounded.

"Honey," Rita told Melissa, "Gladys and Ray really did live in Cuba before Castro, and the way I hear it, it was a pretty wild life."

"In Havana," Gladys said. "We were more in Santiago. But I still don't—"

"*Bird Cage* was a movie," Della jumped in. "About two gay men. In South Beach. One directs a revue by transvestites. The other *is* a transvestite."

"Greg is not gay," Melissa said, trying not to scream. "Transvestites are not necessarily gay." This was a mistake, she thought. She didn't know why she just now realized it. Two thousand miles worth of mistake, and the closest job was probably in Dallas. No matter. She could stay here a while, let the boys get used to life without their father, scout out possibilities back in California. Maybe Chicago. Or New York. She massaged her scalp some more.

"Well, obviously not," Della enthused.

"Well, obviously not anything," Rita argued. "Though that has nothing to do with Greg. But if I had a dollar for every customer of mine who thought her guy was straight—or every one who said she was straight, now that—"

"Oh, stop!" Della said. "Melissa, she had one customer— one!—who was bi, and one whose husband was cheating on her with a guy!"

Melissa smiled weakly and ordered herself not to scream.

"And that has nothing to do with Greg!" Della said. "We know that."

"We just really don't know what to say," Gladys told her. "Truth is, other than old Raul, I've never met a, ah—"

"Transvestite," Melissa said. "Cross dresser. A man in touch with his inner woman." She managed a smile for Gladys. Until this moment, she had never pictured the woman as stepping outside of Texas. "My bet is, you have. We've all met plenty of them." She gave a short laugh. "Until now, though, we just didn't know it."

She shifted up, then settled back on her curled legs. "You know what he told me? Everyone does it! Everyone! Do you believe that?" She looked at Gladys, who, she knew, was about to assure her that Ray didn't wear women's underwear. "He meant everyone we know! All these guys he worked with at Enertec . . . all our friends."

"You mean, there's a whole company of them?" Rita had dropped her blasé act.

"Well, till the dot-com bust. That kind of put an end to the party." Melissa shook her head, pressed her fingers hard into her scalp.

"Well, sure," Rita said. "That catalog stuff's expensive. Now they can't afford that, all that Lycra and all."

"I mean, Greg moved us up to Portland. Sold the house."

"Oh my God!" Della cried. "Melissa! That beautiful house! I had no idea!"

"Greg was smart that way. We sold that thing a month before everything really tumbled."

"So how'd you find out?" Rita prompted.

Melissa started to tell them about the middle of the night. About waking up and finding him draped over the couch. About the boys asleep in their room. About his insistence that he had never tried this before. About the sneaking: not his, hers. Going through his dresser. The duffel bag in the trunk of his car. Following him to the post office box, watching him pick up the bills and the special catalogs. All this over Lycra and silk! Feathers and lace!

But the tears spilled over, and Rita rushed to her side. "Oh, honey, it's okay." Rita stroked her hair and pulled her forward. "You're home now."

Melissa buried her head against Rita's shoulder, letting the spangles on Rita's top scratch her face and inhaling deeply the combination of Shalimar and Aqua Net. These women are loyal, Melissa thought, luxuriating in Rita's warmth. Once they find a scent, they stay with it.

"I don't know, Tony. This one's new to me." Della was sitting on the bed in her nightgown, and held the phone between her ear and shoulder while she rubbed cream into her legs.

"Me too. I promise," Tony said. "No matter what Melissa tells you! No duffel bags, no hidden credit cards."

"Alone in that house by yourself," she teased, "night after night?" She grew serious. "It's hard to know what to say to her."

"I imagine she's just glad to be home, right now."

"I guess," Della said. "Let's go back to the stores." He had called her to check in, and she had launched right into the saga of Melissa and her transvestite husband. "Anything besides the ceiling at Camp Bowie?"

"It's barely a trickle. That storm left its heart in Sydonia." He had checked the west-side store on Camp Bowie, the downtown store, and the house before he reported to her. "They're saying the peaches are shot. I saw Castleburg on the news."

Della snorted. "They're dairy farmers!"

"I know. But they lost a cow . . . some old shed collapsed. Evidently the cow had wandered in. It showed them trying to move the cow up away from the river so the remains wouldn't, you know—"

"You mean, wash into the river along with all the cow shit?" Eli Castleburg had an ongoing battle with local authorities about compliance with runoff regulations.

"Something like that. And"—Tony's voice filled with amusement—"some enterprising chemist evidently lost his meth lab to the water. They say they found most of it floating down the Nolan."

"My, my, my." Della clucked. "Sin in Sydonia."

"Did Kat check in?" he asked.

"Oh, of course. She and Nick were all cozy up in Colleyville. Out of harm's way."

"Meow!"

"You think I envy Kat? Honey, I've got you!" She knew it was a mistake the second she said it.

"Not so's you'd notice."

"Look, let's not do this tonight." She smiled at the phone. "Let's save the morose discussions for when you're here, so we can waste that time too! You know what's weird?" she hurried on. "It's that I don't feel any different now than I did when we were young. I mean, it's stupid, isn't it? We're grandparents, married and divorced, and we can't even have a relationship without it really affecting me as if we were teenagers! I mean, Tony, you know what I'm doing right now?"

"Uh, does it involve anything with batteries?"

"Uh, no. What I mean is, I'm rubbing cream into my legs, because boys like soft skin. Don't you think there's a time when I could be less preoccupied with what boys like?"

"Yeah. After you're married. Isn't that worth the chance?"

When Della sat straight up in her bed, she could study her reflection in the dresser mirror. At this distance, her face was unlined and the green of her eyes still vivid. What had become fleshiness was mere fullness, and the wide yoke and billowing folds of her cotton gown looked soft, but hardly as if they disguised far too much body. "You know, Tony, you ought to try someone younger," Della suggested. "I've kind of run to fat."

"I think you just like to hear me say that doesn't matter."

"True."

"And, no matter what silly things I said when we were younger, you truly, truly, truly are beautiful. You are the one I love, Della."

"And you're the one I love, Tony. Then and now. The difference isn't love. It's that now, maybe love isn't enough. I mean, we loved each other before—"

"Della, that was one thing. One bad thing: our son died—"

"And we fell apart. Tony, I never loved anyone more than I love you, and we still fell apart."

"Except that we're still together. Think about that, Della."

Gladys was glad to leave the others and drive back over to her old house. She hadn't meant to stay so long, but first they traded storm stories and she brought Rita up-to-date on Darlene and Earl and the kids, since Darlene was Rita's daughter. After that, it would have seemed ungracious not to help with dinner and getting Melissa's boys to bed, and then she felt it only polite to spend a few minutes listening to Melissa.

But, she reflected, once Melissa started, it would have been hard to stop her. No matter, Gladys thought, slinging the backpack onto one shoulder and grabbing the cooler with both hands. Later's better anyway.

She peered into the brush that fell away from the back of her old house, letting her eyes adjust to the dim light of the quarter moon until she could make out the little trail down to the river. She took a deep breath and stepped forward. Once she was under the trees, though, the pitch of the trail coupled with the darkness convinced her she would topple forward, if not slide, in the mud. She set the cooler down. Then she slipped the backpack off her shoulder and fastened the shoulder harness around the handle of the cooler.

Let's try it this way, she thought, lifting the handle and moving forward with the backpack balanced atop the cooler. It wasn't perfect, but gravity helped, and she stepped and slipped her way down to the sunset landing, where Ray had built a bench out of rocks he had dragged up from the river.

Gladys rested on the bench, which was chipped off on one corner but still wonderful. Even in the dark, the smoothed sydonite seat gleamed testament to Ray's masonry. And his persistence. Ray had always worked home improvement projects to his lumbering internal schedule.

Despite the cool night, Gladys was sweating, She stripped off her long-sleeved work shirt and set it on the bench. Then she sat for a second, letting the breeze dry her forearms while she strained to hear the movement of the Nolan. Halfway down her hill, she was still looking down on the Ladies Farm and its gently sloping lawn on the far bank. A light or two burned, but Gladys figured they were too busy with their own problems to be studying the hill.

This side of the river was mostly stony cliff covered with scrubby trees. It gave them a fine vantage for sunsets, both from the house and this natural terrace, but didn't leave much boasting for either water pressure or garden space.

Gladys stood and stretched, hunching her shoulders and rolling her head to one side and then the other. Long car trips took their toll, even in a comfortable car, and it annoyed Gladys that it took so long to work out the kinks. She sighed and started along the tiny path that hugged the side of the hill. She moved tentatively, stumbling a little, mindful that the hill fell off steeply to her right. It took longer than she had guessed to get herself and the cooler to the downed cedar that signaled the entrance to Earl's fort.

Smiling, she worked her way over the first barrier to her nephew's boyhood fortress. We must have been crazy, she thought, letting that boy swing an ax. But he had been a big, angry child the first time Ray's sister had asked if they could take him for the summer. Ray placing an ax in Earl's hands was probably the first time anyone had ever demonstrated any faith in the boy's abilities. Together, Ray and Earl had cleared a small patch, stacking the branches into a cavalry post/medieval castle/postnuclear encampment/other-galaxy settlement/campground. The passing summers had seen supply chests, campfires, tents, two-way radios and, eventually, heralding the survivalist summer, a vegetable garden.

Once she got the cooler over the barriers and picked her way to the clearing, Gladys rested again, and took a few minutes to study her surroundings. Things had grown back, of course. Even in the dark she could make out the silhouettes of short trees and see that the ground over the garden was covered with long grasses. It didn't matter. Even the inevitable prickly pear wouldn't get in the way, provided she watched her step.

There would be four hours of bright sunlight. There would be warm temperatures and, unless there was a drought, sufficient rain. The soil was deep enough to hold, and the drainage good. She'd sprinkle fox urine to keep the deer out, and fertilize a little, and she'd be back every few weeks. If she had to, she could even resurrect the drip irrigation that had been Ray's pride.

Gladys wished she could sit for a while and marvel at the sky, as clear now as it had been black before. But she stood up and started rooting through her backpack for her claw tool. She wasn't planting a lot, just a dozen seedlings. Just enough, she thought. Just a steady, supplemental supply to help Ray smoke his way through the pain. Not enough to cause anybody any trouble.

She couldn't wear a nightgown. On the road with the boys, she had just kept her clothes on, unhooking her bra and sleeping in her jeans and a T-shirt. Now that she had tucked the boys into the small room next door, Melissa pulled off her clothes and looked at herself in the mirror on the back of the door. Nothing had changed. Her hair still hung down her back, she was still slim and small-breasted, her eyes a little close together, her feet high-arched but turned out.

Everything was the same, except that it made her sick to see her own lingerie because she kept picturing her husband in it. He denied touching her things, of course.

Too plain for you?

Yes. No. You don't understand, Mel. It wasn't . . . it isn't about you.

Right. Not about me, or my plain-Jane undies. Just about my husband and his affinity for satin and lace.

Melissa took a hairbrush and started brushing her hair. She brushed furiously, forehead to crown and down to the nape. Then her right side. Then left. It's just brown hair, Melissa thought. Brown hair, brown eyes. Medium skin, leaning toward olive. Smooth. Neat.

It was her first moment alone, with the boys in the next room and the Ladies Farm crew distributed throughout the house. She thought about the white eyelet gown in her suitcase, and the shorts and teddy she had thrown into her carry-on. Then she brushed some more.

There was a torch lamp next to the bed, and Melissa leaned forward and switched it off. Then she brushed her hair some more in the dark, until she could see it spark in the mirror: flares of soft light and the crackle as the brush passed through. Someone wants this, she told herself. She felt her way to the bed and set the brush down on the night table. The sheets felt cool for the first second after she slid into bed, then felt like nothing at all. It was a comfort just to feel the smooth cloth without having to wear anything. Anything that made her look any way at all.

Chapter 4

Della guessed guys like Kirk Hilgon didn't register on Melissa's radar. Sporting overalls, a too-tight tee, and hair that grazed his neckline, Kirk was a leftover fortyish hippie. When Della saw the way Melissa stepped over Kirk as he knelt at the kitchen doorway to pry up the doorplate, Della wanted to drag the girl back to apologize.

"You only caught the last act," Kirk assured her when Della offered him a compensatory coffee. "Her two boys hit a beeline for the river, and she was taking them somewhere all dressed and clean."

"Well, she's got a lot on her mind," Della conceded. She slid a plate of muffins across the counter toward him. "She promised the boys breakfast at the lunch counter. I guess she wanted them to look nice."

Kirk shook his head at the muffins. "I had breakfast," he said. Then, "Aren't they in school?"

"Oh, she'll get to that, I'm sure," Della said. "They're just settling in."

"Hard on kids," Kirk said. "Divorce." His hair dipped over his brow and he shook his head impatiently to clear his eyes.

"Do you have kids?" Della asked.

"No. No kids." He sat the coffee cup down on the counter. "Divorced, though."

"I'm surprised you're still single," Della said. She grinned to show him her interest was purely friendly encouragement. "Nice-looking guy like you. I'd think the girls would be all over you."

He looked a little confused, but grinned back. "Me? Too ornery." He swiveled atop the wooden stool at the counter and headed back toward the doorway. "I'll be back with the door-plate," Kirk promised.

"I'll be here," Della replied. She liked men who could fix things. She understood why Rita had remarried Dave, who repaired cars, and why Kat was so wrapped up in Nick Lantinatta, who was an ob-gyn. That was part of her affection for Tony: even after they divorced, he had been willing to straighten out her tax records and update her succession of computers. A man who could install software was as helpful as a man who could replace a doorplate.

So many things can go wrong, she thought. You need someone to repair some corner of your life. Della tried to explain that to Melissa when she returned, but Melissa wasn't interested. "Stuff's torn down all over town," Della said. "Kirk's got all the work he can handle; it was a special kindness for him to drop by here."

"It's probably just the fuss you-all make over anything in pants," Melissa said, watching the boys through the kitchen window. She shook her head as if that sounded harsher than she intended. "Next time he's here, I'll apologize. It's just . . . I was talking to Randi at the lunch counter and she said everyone's so busy fixing up, no one's even thought about Peach Fest."

"I imagine once we fix our doors so the rain can't pour in, we'll tackle Peach Fest," Della said.

Melissa shook her head. "According to Randi, next item is the trial of Frederick Parker. Turns out it was his meth lab that got washed away. Downwind of Castleburg's."

"That's one way to hide the stink," Della said. "Frederick Parker's been heading for jail since he cracked someone's head open two years ago in a Fort Worth bar."

"Well, Randi says they've been watching him ever since; they caught him dragging a case of batteries and a sack of diet pills out of this shack before it floated away."

"It might have been nice," Della said, "if they were helping protect people from the storm." She squinted. "Why batteries?"

Melissa shrugged. "Something about lithium. Anyway, Peach Fest is in trouble."

Della waved a hand in assent. Then she nodded at the boys, who were tossing stones into the river. "Are you enrolling them in school, or what?"

"I suppose."

"You know, if you want Fort Worth, or private school, we'd help with the car pool. There's probably someone else in town—"

"They don't need private school," Melissa said, then shook her head. "I mean, that's not why I haven't done anything. Besides, we can't go private in the middle of the semester, or even make a transfer from their old school." She leaned over and gave Della a quick peck. "Give me a few more days," Melissa said. And just like that she was out the door and calling the boys.

"Well," Kirk said when Della related the conversation by way of apology, "she's got more than schools to worry about." He wiped the newly installed wood subplate with a clean cloth. "I imagine she'll be looking for a job. What does she do?"

"Event planning." Della shrugged. "Races, concerts, auctions . . . you know: fundraisers, awards pageants."

"People get paid for that?" Kirk was sitting on the back step, balancing the new doorplate on his lap.

"I got paid for it," Della confessed. "For a while. Till the novelty wore off and I went back to newsletters and press releases." She grinned at him as he swiveled around to measure the doorplate against the opening. "People get paid for that, too."

As he grinned back, Della thought that Kirk must do mostly indoor work, for he was not at all weather-beaten and his hands, readying the drill, were smooth and sinewy. "Do you work out?" she found herself asking.

"Free weights, every now and then," he confirmed. "Yoga."

"Yoga!"

"Yeah." He grinned again, shrugged. "Think she'll find a job in Sydonia?"

"Sydonia?"

"Melissa," Kirk reminded her.

"Oh! No." Della frowned. "Maybe not in Fort Worth, depending on what she wants."

"So Sydonia might just be a rest stop," Kirk said.

The whine of the electric drill prevented any response.

The peach growers met at the fire hall. Della figured it saved a lot of trouble the few times an alarm sounded during the monthly meeting. Besides, the coffee was the kind these farmers had grown up with. Now, though, since this was the joint quarterly meeting with the chamber of commerce committee for the Sydonia Peach Fest, a coffee urn replaced the battered Mr. Coffee on the Formica-topped table, accompanied by a basket of strawberry-peach muffins and peach-flavored creamer.

Della's primary responsibility was selling ads for this year's cookbook. She had already collected the recipes and, in a burst of quality control, tested them in her own kitchen and submitted them to her guests to rate. Even the copy—her own chirpy notes about which family's tradition and whose grandmother had originated each recipe—was written and formatted and ready to go.

Randi Buckler, who ran the fountain at the drugstore and chaired this year's Peach Fest, started the meeting by asking for a moment's silence. Now that she was dating the Bahai optometrist she had met at the withholding workshop sponsored by the community college, Randi insisted that the customary prayer at these quasi-public events be truly nondenominational. If you could see things through Ahmed's eyes, she said, you'd never pray in Jesus' name again.

Of course, except for the meetings led by Randi herself, Sydonians persisted in the traditional bless-our-works-and-bring-us-good-fortune-in-Jesus'-name variety of prayer. Ahmed himself, a shy, soft-spoken Iranian who had opened an eyewear clinic in the professional center next to the county hospital, almost never attended meetings, and rarely spoke to anyone other than Randi, except when he was fitting people for glasses.

The silence gave Della a chance to survey the attendance, counting someone from each of the five big orchards, plus a variety of smaller growers and retailers. She herself would have skipped the meeting, except that it gave her a chance to tackle a few advertisers and, oddly, that Melissa had exhibited such interest in accompanying her. "I just feel so sorry for the growers," Melissa had said over dinner. "If you could have seen Mr. Dyer the other day . . ." her voice had trailed off.

Della supposed Melissa's emotions were displaced. She's really grieving for her marriage, Della told herself. Randi had resumed the meeting, and they were going through the committee reports. A farmer—Harry Ochs, one of the old guard—interrupted. "What's the use of getting all these folks here? There's nothing to sell them."

"Speak for yourself," retorted Cassie Ellers, who sold antiques and collectibles on the square. "I've got a shop full of—"

"There's no peaches," old man Ochs said. "Not a one!"

"Well, now," Eli Castleburg said, "some of us've got a few left, Harry." He grinned. "Not to mention a little peach-flavored ice cream."

"You siphoning cow shit into your ice cream?" someone called into the angry buzz.

"Just stop it!" Randi ordered, but they ignored her. Eli Castleburg was not a member of the peach growers. He maintained only a small grove of trees around the back garden. He was a dairy farmer with an ice cream stand, and the anger grew as much from the knowledge that he imported California peaches for his ice cream as it did from resentment of his current swagger.

Della did not know the man who stood up and waved a hand to quiet the others, but she loved his voice. "We can spit on Mr. Castleburg all night, but once folks realize we've got no peaches, no one's coming to Peach Fest. No one's eating at the diner, no one's shopping on the square, no one's buying antique trinkets"— here he bowed slightly toward Cassie Ellers—"no one's buying peach ice cream." Now he had their attention. "No one's bidding at the auction."

"We haven't got a single reason for anyone to come to Sydonia," he concluded. "So we'd better think of something." Then he sat down.

"Why, he must be one of those Dyer boys," Della said as the young man sat down next to Webb Dyer. "Where's he been?"

"Austin," Melissa whispered, eyes shining. "He's just come back to help his father."

To Melissa, Ethan remained untouched by Sydonia, as separate from the town as his earring and affection for REM had once separated him from his contemporaries. His hair had darkened to a medium brown and his voice had edged still lower, but that had nothing to do with his separateness. It was the way he didn't seem to care about what people thought about him, even while he was trying to sway their opinion. She bit her lip while debate raged around her: cancel! change the name! sell tomatoes! bring in a rodeo! Even the way he sat now, next to his father, listening as if every word here counted, made him different.

"No rodeos," Della was murmuring. "No one ever stays overnight for a rodeo except the cowboys, and they sleep in their trucks."

Melissa chuckled. She doubted there was time enough to book a rodeo anyway. She was still looking at Ethan, but the event-planner part of her brain ran through the possibilities for short-turnaround, high-yield, high-crowd festivals. Contests. Galas. Auctions. Sporting events.

She wondered if Tiger Woods would play a round at Sydonia Municipal, or if Britney Spears could trill a few tunes out at the football stadium.

"What are you grinning at?" Della whispered.

Melissa frowned, sat up straight. "By the time they figure out what to do," she muttered, "it'll be over."

Della raised an eyebrow and smiled in challenge. "Why don't you tell them that?"

Melissa waited while Randi pointed out the value of repeat attendees nurtured through years of Peach Fests. Then Melissa stood.

"Have y'all ever tried a run?" she asked. "Or a bike ride?"

"It's the last weekend in June," someone called out. "You want to kill people?"

"Well, other towns do it," she pointed out. "Some of them are even famous," she added. "Like the Hotter 'N' Hell in Wichita Falls. Even so, it wouldn't have to be so bad."

"We could run at sunrise," Randi said, but the whole room groaned before she got it out. "C'mon, guys," she defended herself. "Y'all are farmers!"

"Or at night?" Melissa said.

"Say it again," Ethan said from two rows away. "They didn't hear you."

"We could run at night," Melissa said, this time with enthusiasm. "Midnight, even. It would be cooler—less hot, anyway—and it would be different. Fun. We could light the way with luminarias, hand out peach-flavored water, peach-shaped trophies." She stopped to breathe. "Midnight peaches: a cool run through a hot town," she proposed.

"Hire that girl!" called out Shane Castleburg. He grinned, winked at Melissa, who recognized him by his Castleburg girth. His voice sounded exactly like his father's.

"If we have a race we need a race director," Randi offered. "Long hours, surly volunteers, and all the bruised peaches you can scrounge off the damaged trees."

Melissa turned to Della, who was smiling up at her. "Someone's got to do it," Della advised.

"You should have seen her," Della reported to Kat and Rita. "She couldn't stop staring at him." She held out her cup for Rita to pour a little more decaf. "And he couldn't take his eyes off her, either."

Della was explaining how it happened that Melissa was still out and had left them to put Trey and Garrett to bed.

"Not that I mind," Rita said. She put the carafe back in the coffeemaker and joined them at the oak table that ran along the windows at the back of the kitchen. "I'm always willing to do my part for true love."

"Or rebound attraction," Kat said.

"You can find true love on the rebound," said Rita, whose marriage to Dave was their second marriage, following her second divorce from her second husband. She smiled. "What I like about those kids is how they said their prayers. On their own, without a word from us."

"Sucker prayer," Della said. "Got us to tiptoe right out of the room. They're probably up there right now with their flashlights."

"They are well-behaved boys," said Kat. She squinted. "Didn't that older one used to be—"

"Taylor," Della supplied.

"But he had a second-grade classmate who told him Taylor's a girl's name," Rita said. "And he's actually Gregory Taylor the third."

"So: Trey," Della said.

Kat nodded to show she followed.

"Though, he's still worried," Rita said. "That's how he came to tell us. When we tucked him in, he asked us if we thought Trey's a girl's name."

"I imagine they're uncertain of everything right now," Kat said. "Kids sense stuff, even when they don't know the particulars." She sipped her tea.

"You think she's really planning on staying?" Rita asked. "I hate to think of her dragging those children all over the country. Particularly after we get attached to them." Rita's daughter and granddaughter, Darlene and Tiffany, had spent a season at the Ladies Farm, but had resettled with Earl Westerman near Gladys and Ray—his aunt and uncle—in the Big Bend.

Kat gave a practiced shake to her head, allowing her taffy-colored hair to fluff out, then settle back to a perfect, chin-length edge. "Doubtful," Kat said. "I mean, she's obviously panicked, or she wouldn't have fled with the boys before the end of school, even if we are just talking about kindergarten and second grade. And"— Kat shot a wry look toward Della—"this does put her closer to her brother."

"Slime!" Rita said. "Why would she want to be closer to him?"

"Because he's her brother," Della said. When Pauline, former owner of the Ladies Farm, had died, Melissa had derailed her younger brother's attempt to turn the property into a gravel pit. "Actually, it makes me feel a little better, knowing they're talking to each other."

"A few hundred thousand makes it a little easier to forgive," Kat observed, referring to the money they had paid to buy their bed and breakfast from Pauline's children.

"Plus," Della continued as if she hadn't heard, "I'm glad that when she had to flee, she thought of us as family."

"I think she'll move on, though," Kat said.

"That's what Kirk—Hilgon—said," Della said. "I guess because she—what?" She stared at Rita, who had held up a hand to stop her.

"You boys need anything?" Rita called. "Garrett? Trey?"

All three women looked toward the ceiling as if to see the scampering bodies that matched the footsteps running above them from the upstairs landing.

Rita beamed. "I've still got it."

Della and Kat nodded in admiration.

"Who's Kirk Hilgon?" Kat asked, lowering her voice to a whisper.

"He's the hottie who does home repairs," Rita whispered in response. "Looks deep in your eyes while he rewires your thermostat or primes your drywall."

Della felt herself grow warm, then grinned in surrender.

"My customers rave about Kirk." Rita kept the volume at a murmur, but an urgent murmur. "Anyway, I want to know about Ethan Dyer. He was the shyest thing, and then he got to high school and just ..." she shook her head. "I don't know ... turned into the anti-prep."

Gladys and Alice Dyer had cochaired the Friends of the Sydonia Library from its storefront days through the building campaign for the second addition at the municipal center. Ray had helped Webb figure an irrigation system when Webb planted the orchard on the high side of the river. Webb's boys had provided most of the labor for building the Huttos' deck and later their garage.

"It was different then," Webb observed when Gladys reminded him of those times. He pushed a plastic spoon into a small bowl of ice cream topped with chocolate. "We were more isolated out here then. More dependent on one another."

Gladys nodded. "We're not as isolated in Alpine as Sydonia was then," she said. "You more than us, of course. At least we were here in town. You-all were on the farm. There were times," she recalled, "I couldn't even reach Alice by phone, because of the party line."

Webb nodded, remembering. Then he patted his shirt pocket. "I guess we're all on call now." He told her that he had skipped out of the peach growers' meeting early, since it involved Peach Fest. "Leave that to the young ones," he said. "I know my part in all that: tractor for the float in the parade, ad in the program book. I even gave a recipe to that woman—Della—for the cookbook." He sampled the ice cream. "How's the old man?"

"He doesn't say much. But he's hurting."

"I thought those shots would've helped."

"The cortisone? They helped a little, but it wears off." She bit off a longer explanation. Even when Alice was dying, Webb had let Gladys explain the nuances of treatment to the boys. Webb was like Ray: he didn't care much for medical details.

"He lives on anti-inflammatories," Gladys said, provoked by his silence. "And pot."

Now she had his attention.

"It helps," she told him.

"I've heard of that," Webb said slowly. "But for cancer."

"Antinausea," Gladys confirmed. "But it's pain relief, too. Doesn't tear up your stomach like the anti-inflammatories."

A thousand questions flickered across his face, but he just stared at her and twirled his spoon around in the ice cream.

"And he smokes it?" he asked finally.

"Every day. Usually in the afternoon."

"I guess . . . down there on the border . . ."

Gladys shook her head firmly. "You buy regularly, sooner or later someone who's never been interested leans on you to give up your source. And then he leans on your source for his source."

Webb waited.

"We're growing our own."

She could see the struggle: reticence warring with agriculture. How much water? How many hours of sunlight? Yield per plant. Yield per acre. Which pests? What fertilizer? She imagined him walking the small plot with Ray, the two of them fingering the spiky leaves, kneeling to test the moisture in the soil. She could feel the sun on her face, the sweat trickling down her sides under her blouse as she watched them, comparing Webb's easy stride to her husband's stiff gait.

"Mighty dry there."

Gladys nodded, suppressed her smile.

"Of course, indoors—"

She shook her head. "You had it right the first time."

"But aren't you afraid?" Webb asked. "Doesn't it worry you?"

"Every day," Gladys said. "What would worry me more is if I could do something and didn't. Besides, I figure, sweet little old lady, tiny amount, personal use: I get busted, no one's sending me to jail."

He smiled. "Not for long, anyways. Do you—"

Now she smiled. "Only now and then. Did you—"

"Hell, in Chicago, it was the only way to be cool."

"Well, you ought to come out. Ray'd be glad for the company."

"Sort of a senior commune, huh?"

"He doesn't really get high, Webb."

"I know." He shook his head. "I'm sure sorry."

"I know." Gladys was tired of sympathy. Even from old friends. She had brightened when Webb walked into the Dairy Queen, but now she wished she was back in the Big Bend, sitting on the porch with Ray. "It's just arthritis," she said, recalling Alice's struggle with heart failure. "It's not fatal."

Webb nodded.

"I'm heading back tomorrow. Dave managed to find me a window in Midland, so he's taped me up with plastic and I'll stop the night there." She tilted her head. "I wish you would think about a visit."

"Maybe in the fall," he said. "You need any help?" He looked around. "Packing up, that sort of thing?"

"You want to check my little garden for me?" Gladys asked.

"Your—"

"You remember that patch—"

"On the hill?"

Gladys nodded. "It's just a few plants in a sunny spot, Webb. Backup. I'm just thinking—you know—if the weather turns dry."

"You need anything else?" Webb drawled. "Pest control? Fertilizer? You want me to enter any of that at Peach Fest? Tallest stalk? Biggest bud?"

"It's okay, Webb, if you'd rather not. Ray would kill me if he knew I even told you—you know, got you involved in it."

Webb pressed his lips together. "It's little enough," he said.

"A run is a simple event," Melissa insisted.

"I didn't disagree," Ethan said. They were standing outside the firehouse, watching the newly formed run committee—Randi, Shane, Cassie, and Orrin Bell from the chamber—vacate the parking lot.

"But you didn't agree, either." She meant it as an accusation, but she smiled recklessly.

He put a hand on the door of the pickup and looked at her. He was only a little taller than she was, and it was easy to meet his gaze, even in the glare from the mercury-vapor light. She supposed Greg was better looking—taller, with broader shoulders and more even features—but there was something about Ethan's longish face and quiet eyes.

"Where's your car?" he asked abruptly, looking around.

"I'm afoot," she said. "I rode with Della and she had to get back." Melissa grinned. "Someone has to tuck the boys in." Her regret at the comment preceded by at least one second the shock that registered in his eyes, but she didn't know how to explain the comment.

Finally, he said, "Well, hop up and let me drop you off."

Melissa shook her head. "Walk me home." She laughed a little, her recklessness returning. "It's only a few blocks, and it will give us a chance to catch up. You barely said a word in our impromptu committee meeting."

"This is very un-Texan," he observed, stepping back from the truck. "Walking instead of riding in a pickup. Pretty Left Coast."

"Aw, take a risk," she teased.

They walked toward the courthouse, skipping over a block to get away from the bright lights of the state road. Ethan told her that he was in real estate in Austin.

"Sales?" she asked.

"Development, more. I'm a developer. Project manager. Office parks. Multiuse campuses."

"I shouldn't have said that, before, about someone tucking the boys in," Melissa said. They were walking a short block of single-story houses with indifferent yards, most boasting repair shops and home offices. Dogs barked as they passed, and one ran at a wooden fence but stopped short. "I was trying to sound clever," she said. "But we left Portland two weeks ago, now, and this is the first night I haven't tucked them in."

"You don't have to explain," he said. "I'm sure you're a good . . . a great mother."

"Yeah, well, the jury's still out." She exhaled, hard. The street ended at the courthouse square, where they crossed and looked up at the turreted building.

It had been difficult, on the West Coast, to explain about the courthouse, and the way her mother and father had led the vanguard of a preservation movement that seemed to arise simultaneously around most of the turn-of-the-century county seats that dotted Texas. "We have two hundred and fifty-four counties in Texas," she would recite, "and almost every one has a court house built between 1836 and 1920. And each one is different. Ours is built of a local granite called sydonite," and she would watch as her listeners' eyes glazed over and their smiles froze.

"Did you ever tell anyone about this courthouse?" she asked Ethan.

"The courthouse?" He slowed and they looked at the pinkish stone, glowing in the light of the lamps placed strategically among the live oaks. He shook his head, then nodded abruptly as if he caught on. "Oh! No. I mean, I've been in Austin six years, so they all know, sort of. And in Philadelphia, I don't know, you would explain—"

"About the sydonite," she prompted. "And the additions. And the fights about tearing it down."

He nodded, kicked a little at the grass, motioned her over to one of the benches that the Rotary had installed as part of the Sydon County Centennial. "Well, you know, you say something like: there are trees, huge live oaks whose branches almost touch the ground. And they . . . they've had trees all their lives, they don't know what a tree like that means. Or water."

Melissa laughed as she seated herself. "Well, they did appreciate water in California. But you're right, they don't quite get it."

"You can't, really," he said, sitting down next to her, "unless you grew up here."

"And then you just want to leave."

Ethan chuckled. He leaned his head back and looked straight up.

"Are you thinking about the orchard?"

He shook his head. "Nah. Hail's hail. We've had a string of good years. When we were little, a storm like this would put us under. Now?" Ethan shrugged. "The peach trees will recover."

"How come you're here, then?"

Another shrug. "One of us gets here every few weeks. Check on Dad."

"Where are your brothers?"

He gave her the rundown: Steve in the Air Force, Wade a pilot out of Houston, Clark a produce buyer in Dallas, Tommy still struggling as an investment counselor in New York.

"Tommy's in New York?"

Ethan nodded, glanced over at her. "Still." He grinned. "You know Tommy. After the World Trade Center, he dug in. It's a point of pride with him now. Economy's in the toilet, but he's slugging it out."

"Well, you were all like that, weren't you?" Now she smiled. "Tough guys. Lots of back. No retreat."

He didn't answer.

"You know, your dad was my knight in shining armor the day of the storm. He performed a roadside rescue."

"Dad's definitely the tough one."

"How's he doing?"

Another shrug. "Hard to tell, with dad. He mentioned you were in town, staying with *those ladies.*"

"Thank God for those ladies." Melissa laughed. "Nice to have a place that will take you in."

"Yeah." Ethan frowned. "What happened to your marriage?"

She hadn't expected it this quickly, but never mind. She could hardly wait to tell it. She wanted to unload the whole thing, tell it all to someone who knew what she had been, someone her own age, who would understand how her expectations had been betrayed.

She stretched her legs out so that they were parallel with his, four denim stalks at an oblique angle to the walk from the street to the courthouse door. In the dark she could make out only the outlines of his pointed-toe boots, swanlike next to the stubby profiles of her hiking shoes.

Melissa closed her eyes, then opened them wide and stared straight ahead at the dark lawn. "It's hard to say, really. We just drifted apart, I guess. Ordinary. Horribly ordinary."

"Was there . . . you know . . . someone else?"

She shook her head. "Nope. Nothing that dramatic." Then she laughed. "Why? What have you heard?"

"Nothing, really. Just that you were here, alone with the boys. And, of course, since the ladies are so tight-lipped, even Rita, that there must be some scandal." They laughed together. "Are you divorced yet?" he asked.

"Not yet. I've barely spoken with a lawyer, but neither one of us will drag out the process."

"Amicable's better, I'm sure." If he was disappointed that she was not yet single, his voice did not reveal it. "Though we might appreciate a good fight just for the amusement value. It's so quiet here. And it would fulfill our expectations, you going so far away to school and marrying a Californian like that. Perfect makings of a domestic disaster."

"Well, sorry to disappoint. No major eruptions."

"Just your plain old everyday breakup, huh?"

Relief flooded her, stinging her eyes so that she had to turn her head. Everyday breakup, she thought, resisting the impulse to hop around and hug herself. Plain. Everyday. Breakup.

"Humdrum," Melissa confirmed when her head stopped spinning. "Are you married?"

"Nope."

"Living with someone?"

"Actual real live single guy." He motioned with his hands out. "No domestic partner, no live-in lover."

"In all this time?" Melissa couldn't imagine it.

"Well, yeah. I just meant—"

"Oh, you mean, right now, you're *between* women."

"You and you," he muttered. "Can't we talk some more about your breakup?"

"Can't we fill in the blanks about your personal life?"

He had lived with a woman for five years in Philadelphia, and when they split up he had bunked with his brother in New York for a while, then retreated to Texas. He switched from insurance to real estate when he moved back, and it had taken all his time and energy for a while. Real estate. An MBA in urban development. Building a house for himself. Twice.

"Tiny things," he assured her. "Lots recovered out of parcels we were subdividing, kind of salvage."

Melissa pictured slivered lots graced by limestone jewels, a pair of neat open-plan homes with oak floors and twelve-pane windows. She was filling in the live oaks (maybe just one, considering the minuscule lot), watching the play of the deep-green foliage as it shifted in the hill-country breeze that blessed Austin in its fortunate moments.

"Sold them," Ethan continued the tale. "Now I'm in a garage apartment behind a friend's place. I had to bail when the market tanked."

"That's what took us to Portland: the market."

"Did you take a big loss?"

Melissa thought about the solid house in the Portland mist and shook her head. "Greg, my husband, got us out early. With everything—you know, with the boys, and their school and so on—we always stayed out of the high flyers. And the rest—I mean, don't get me wrong, it was a big hit—but we don't have to pay for college next month, or retire this year or anything. Greg managed to stay employed. And he says . . . I'm sure by the time we need to cash out, it will have recovered."

"I hope Greg's right," Ethan said. "I'd hate to grow old in the garage apartment."

"Well, you can always come back to the farm."

They sat some more, watching the occasional car speed through the blinking stoplight, talking about where they had been and what they had done. It was less awkward than she had supposed, talking about her life with Greg as if it had all happened to her alone. What did Ethan know about the intricacies of teacher conferences and dental appointments arranged over the phone, dropoffs and pickups coordinated around two office schedules, two sets of meetings, two intersecting circles of friends and coworkers?

The sprinklers came on, driving them from the bench. Less chatty now, they wandered the two remaining blocks to the Ladies Farm. "If you ever need to steal a car," Melissa whispered after he declined a late dessert, "now you know where." She motioned him off the porch where the ladies had left the light burning and around to the canopied parking area.

They took the Accord, because it made less noise than the Suburban, and because her own SUV was at the Fort Worth Lexus dealer awaiting a windshield and dent repair. Melissa showed him how the ladies didn't even bother to hide the key, leaving it in the ignition so the next driver wouldn't have to hunt for it. Melissa dropped him back at his truck, putting a hand on his shoulder to express her thanks for the walk home as well as to forestall any closer embrace.

"It's good to have someone to talk to," she said. "I hope I wasn't too . . . effusive. It's just so odd, in some ways, being back."

"I know what you mean." He grinned, slipped out of the car, then leaned back in for a second. "I'll call you."

She raised an eyebrow, then smiled back at him. "Do that," she said. "Besides, we've got some work ahead of us."

He looked confused, then caught it. "I almost forgot. Committee work! My favorite thing!"

It was as much a relief when he left as it had been to talk with him. She found herself sighing when he pulled onto the highway and turned in the opposite direction. Melissa had stopped trying to second-guess her emotions; merely controlling her wilder impulses took all her energy. She wondered what Ethan's reaction would be if she told him the truth about Greg, then wondered how she could trust a former boyfriend whom she barely knew when she herself could not assimilate the facts.

It's important not to feel ridiculous, Melissa assured herself, pulling the Accord back under the canopy and leaving it unlocked. Not to be the joke of the day at Randi Buckler's lunch counter. From the Ladies Farm porch, Melissa could see the outline of the courthouse and the lights through the trees. She stood for a second, looking at the courthouse and remembering her anger toward her parents when they moved from Fort Worth to Sydonia.

Her parents' involvement in the fight over the courthouse had only heightened the differences between Melissa and the kids who had grown up here. Snobby daughter of counterculture parents. Locals had pronounced the word *preservationists* the same way they might earlier have hissed *communists* or *hippies*. Melissa had insisted on continuing high school in Fort Worth, and couldn't wait to graduate and head for the West Coast.

But here I am, she thought. Back in Sydonia. She turned and headed inside. Just trying not to look ridiculous.

Chapter 5

"When I left, they were debating whether car sex was better than yard sex."

Ray set down his *Roads and Bridges,* looked over at Gladys. "And what was the verdict?"

"Well, Kat won't vote; likes them both." Gladys looked with satisfaction at the peaks of the Big Bend that were just now turning from purple to gray in the morning light. "Della takes the yard side. The danger of being discovered makes it more exciting, plus it feels nice to be outside. Then Rita asks Della if she's ever done it in a car up on the lift in a garage."

Ray hooted.

It's good to be home, she thought.

"And you didn't want to stay for more of that?"

Gladys bit back her observation that she had no hope of either car sex or yard sex ever again. Reaching over to wiggle his bare toe, she winked. "I just wanted to hurry back to you." He grimaced and she released his toe. "Did you take the Vioxx?" she asked.

He lifted his head from the arm of the sofa where he lay with his ankles hanging over the other arm. "Yes, dear. With milk." He lifted his head slightly to catch her eye. "And I did my stretches."

This porch is too cool to be out here without shoes, Gladys thought. And if he stretched before his coffee it means that his back pained him too much to fix the coffee.

Before them, the hill sloped away from the house in shades of gray-green, dotted with clumps of creosote. Where the hill rose on the opposite side of the graded road, sunlight had begun to illuminate the metal roofs of their neighbors. We only did it once, Gladys thought. Slowly.

"Nice of Dave to get the windshield," he said.

"They're—Rita and Dave—they're thinking we're in-laws now. You know, with Darlene and Earl. And the baby."

"Seems reasonable."

"Rita asked me about throwing a party for Darlene and Earl. Up there." She peered carefully at him. "Be a nice thing, since they got married at the JP."

Ray nodded slightly. "Up there," he repeated.

Eight hours in the car, thought Gladys. Unless we break it up, spend the night in Midland, or San Angelo. Or squish into a plane.

"How's the place look?"

"You'll have to see for yourself," Gladys said. "I got all the seedlings planted. As long as it doesn't hail, we'll be okay. But come the middle of June, we'll have to get that rig of yours dripping." She thought that now was the time to mention Webb, but she did not.

He narrowed his eyes. "We don't have to do anything, honey. The rain stores in the rock piles. It filters down through the stones to the gravel, and then channels into the tubing. It's been working the whole time. That's why it's so green there."

"And if it doesn't rain?"

"If it doesn't rain at all, we'll need someone to run the hose to the tanks," Ray conceded. "But that's only if there's no rain at all."

"Maybe you should puff now," Gladys said. I'll just tell him about Webb later.

Ray pushed himself to a sitting position. "I'm okay, baby. Just stiff. I like to wait till afternoon. I managed on that schedule the whole time you were gone."

"Did you get over to the springs?" she asked him.

"Twice," he said. "Sun's good over there. Drainage. They're popping up."

"You didn't see any—"

"No one. No tracks. No nothing. It's a seeping spring, Glad.

No place to skinny-dip, no road in, and it's off the desert floor in a national park full of warning signs about the dangers. I don't know why you even bothered about the other."

"You're the one who thought of it. Your secret plot."

"I know. I guess I only meant it would be good if we still lived there." He stood up and hobbled forward.

She stood and walked over to him, slipping an arm around him. "It gives us a little backup, that's all. The weather's different than here, the pests are different, even the law's different. If we lose a crop, we'll still have the other. It's what that gal from California told me. Letty."

Gladys had met Letty at a tour of the hydroponics center near Fort Davis. The high desert had proved a perfect place to grow tomatoes indoors; Letty wanted to convert her Marin garage to her own hydroponics center, if she could figure out how to conceal her electricity use. Meanwhile, she worked a communal plot for a co-op that had officially disbanded when the Supreme Court negated California's approval of marijuana use for medical purposes.

"Of course, down here," Letty had said, "you can buy it as it comes across the border. The way I hear it"—she had lowered her voice—"they bring so much across it doesn't even bother them when they lose a truckload."

Gladys leaned her head against Ray's arm, thankful that she wasn't dependent on people who could afford to lose a truckload of marijuana and the driver who transported it. "It just makes me feel safer," she told him. "A little back."

"Was there someone else," Hugh asked. "Because if he was seeing someone else, you can still—"

Melissa glared at the phone. "Hugh," she said to her brother, "I told you there's no one else, it's an amicable split, I just need a lawyer in Portland. Surely someone in that big, high-dollar Dallas firm of yours knows one reputable divorce attorney in Portland."

"I still don't understand why you went straight there. Why didn't you come here first? You should be staying with us, not them."

"I told you: I needed someplace where I could get away with the kids. Think things through. Figure out what to do with the rest of my life." She knew none of this made sense to Hugh. He had sued the ladies in a dispute over their share of their mother's

claim to the Ladies Farm. Even though things were settled, he regarded the ladies as enemies and Melissa's allegiance as traitor-
ous. "We'll come over in the next week or so. The boys really
want to see you and Carrie."

"Well, yeah. I'll tell Carrie."

Melissa imagined her sister-in-law's relief that she and the boys
were residing elsewhere.

"The woman down the hall does domestic," Hugh continued
after a silence. "Let me see what she says."

In the gray light, Ethan watched the four men gather around
the thermos on the tail of the pickup. They had pulled their truck
next to his father's in the center of the orchard's highest row, and
the two from the cab and the two from the back slid silently onto
the dry ground. He knew Manny from his teens, when they had
both labored under the direction of their respective fathers.
Manny's crew were strangers: one boy in his teens, two guys perhaps in their twenties.

From Webb's greeting, Ethan gathered his father knew them
all, that they had harvested last year, pruned in the fall, sprayed in
the spring.

"Where you been?" Manny asked, grasping Ethan's hand in
both of his. "Off in the big city, making money!"

"Making trouble, mostly," Ethan replied.

The men poured coffee into plastic mugs grown dark through
years of bouncing out to fields and being handed 'round early-
morning deployments. Last vestige of the cowboy breakfast,
Ethan thought. Crouched around the campfire, tracing the trail in
the dirt.

Webb nodded at the men, sipped his own coffee. "How's your
family?"

Ethan started and stood frozen as he listened to Manny's almost unaccented description of his children's antics. When
Manny switched gears to describe his father's supervision of the
family ranch on the Rio Conchos near Monterrey, Ethan reminded himself that he had plenty of contemporaries who were
heads of households. There's nothing surprising, he thought,
about a Mexican farmworker with a wife and a bunch of kids.
Webb's conversation with Manny's father had been the same
twenty years ago.

Now Webb motioned with his empty cup toward the hill that sloped down to the river. "We have to pull 'em all off," he instructed. "Whatever's left, this field and one other. The two other fields, we'll wait and just pull the worst ones."

Manny turned and motioned with his head to the three others as he spoke in Spanish. The kid—a nephew, Ethan thought—asked a question. Waving off Manny's translation, Webb shook his head. "No broom. Pull 'em off by hand."

Manny nodded and caught Ethan's eye. Old man's the same, his expression said.

Two hours later, wringing sweat from his bandana and rubbing his sticky, peachy hands on his jeans, Ethan thought the old man was right. The trees, cropped to a man's reach, were trimmed out in the center to let in light. The few remaining peaches—tiny, hard, bruised things—would take a lot of whacking for minimal results. Hard storm, Ethan thought, retying the scarf around his neck and plodding fifteen feet to the next tree in his row. Pain streaked through his upper body as he raised his arms to yank the gumball peaches off their branches.

His right hand moved quickly, thumb and fingers gripping, pulling, rolling the peach into his palm as his hand moved to the next one. Five in hand, discard to the bucket, back to the thicket. These bitter little things didn't yield the way ripe fruit did; he jerked them off, snapping them from branches whose leaves had been stripped by wind and hail. Memories of a ripe, firm peach mocked him: the way it resisted for a second, then slipped free into your cradling hand. You could grasp a peach like that and feel its flesh, warm from the sun, pushing back at you. But if you pressed hard with your fingers, the skin would split, the flesh would bruise, and the peach would be ruined.

The pickup rumbled toward the row, rolling as deliberately as if his father were its engine. "How's it coming?" Webb asked when he slowed to a stop.

Ethan backed away from the tree, turned. "It's bad," he said. "Nothing left here at all." He hoisted the bucket and emptied it over the side into a tub. "Headed for the pig trough?"

Webb shook his head. "Not many of those here. Make good compost though, for that couple down at the organic." He put the truck in gear.

"Is that the Motts? Fred? Karen?"

"Nah. Now it's some other couple. He's an engineer, she's a programmer."

"I guess no one's a full-time farmer anymore," said Ethan.

"Who ever was?" his father asked. "Can't stay the way you want us so you have a place to come back to."

Ethan felt himself color. "I just meant, we're pretty typical, none of us staying on the farm."

Webb nodded. "I'm not sure I should stay on the farm."

"Well, I can always find you a good place in Austin." They had been through this several thousand times. Ethan motioned to the rest of the orchard, over which Manny's crew had dispersed. "How're they coming?"

Webb, elbow on the lowered window, looked out over the orchard. "No faster than you," he said. The transmission groaned as he eased the truck forward, then turned around and headed back out to the road.

Melissa listed tasks on the white board in the meeting room of the Sydonia Chamber of Commerce. She wrote the broad categories in red: *promotion, registration, run, sponsorships,* and *volunteers.* Orrin Bell, the chamber director, had volunteered to take minutes, and labored over a lined pad. The others—Ethan, Randi, Shane, and Cassie—pushed at their soda cans and avoided eye contact. Everyone looked tired, and Melissa wished they had met during the day instead of after work.

"Look, we'll all help get sponsorships," Melissa said. "But somebody's got to be in charge. Otherwise, we'll be pestering the same people, and they'll just hate us."

"Well, I don't mind doing the calling," Cassie said. "But I don't have any idea what kind of sponsors we need. I mean food and drink, that's obvious. But the race stuff—"

"I can give you all that," Melissa assured her. "I've done dozens of these . . . well, really, the agency I worked for . . . we specialized in nonprofits, fundraising—"

"Nonprofit's the right word for us," Shane cracked.

Ignore him, Melissa ordered herself, but it was difficult. His family's—meaning his father's—participation was critical. Eli Castleburg sat on boards at the bank, local cable, and the electrical co-op. A bad word from Shane to his dad . . . Shane would have to be handled.

Melissa beamed at him. "We're counting on you to turn that around, help with promotion, soliciting sponsors."

Shane's eyeteeth gave his lazy grin a wolfish cast. "I'll solicit with you." He eyed her up and down. "Maybe Castleburg Dairy could be the drink sponsor."

"Water, not milk," Randi counseled.

"We need to sit down and talk about this," Shane said. Another grin. "You could tell me how much water we need. Or sports drink."

Melissa took a breath. "Good. I'll do that." She looked at the others. "Now, I've asked Della Brewer to work up a logo and posters for us. She does all that for the Ladies Farm and her newsletter, and she's real good."

"What about a race manager?" Ethan asked.

"Who's paying for that?" Cassie said. "It's just a fun run. I already talked to Rotary; they'll lay out the course for us."

"The thing is," Melissa said, "a timed race would bring in a lot more runners."

"Rotary could figure out the timing," Randi said.

"I should have said certified. Plus"—Melissa forced herself to speak slowly—"a race manager could handle online registration, free us to promote team participation, aid station sponsorship, that kind of thing."

"You want to sink how much into this?" Shane asked. "Ten, twenty thousand?"

"What?" That was Randi. "Twenty thousand dollars into this . . . fundraiser?"

Melissa's mouth went dry. It was that high school feeling: the outsider who commuted to private school. Like approaching the table of gigglers at the Dairy Queen only to find herself mystified by their references, terrified by their dismissal of her clothes, her hair, her vocabulary.

Think about what you're doing, Melissa reminded herself. You don't have to tell them you've never planned a race without a professional director. She took a breath. "It's more like five thousand," she said. "And we can't hire anyone if we're not sure we'll get enough registration to cover the additional cost. But normally you do, even in the first year."

"I might know someone who could help us," Ethan said.

The others turned to him.

"Someone I worked with in Austin does this, sort of a weekend business. She might help us. Cut us a deal." Ethan grinned. "If I lean on her a little."

"Sounds like work I can help with," Shane said.

"So your pal has done a lot of races?" Melissa hated friends of friends. On the other hand, she knew no race directors in Texas.

"I don't know exactly," Ethan said. "I'll just call and ask." He gestured toward her. "Maybe we could do a conference call."

"Let's do that," Melissa said. She fought the warmth in her face, ignored the flicker in Randi's eye.

"Well, what about Rotary?" Cassie asked.

"We need Rotary," Melissa said. "There's plenty for them to do. Including helping a race director figure the course. And, Orrin, if it's okay with you, they could handle getting the aid stations sponsored and staffed."

"Less work for me," Orrin said. "Rotary's lunch tomorrow. Come on by, say a few words, get someone to offer to chair the thing."

"Oh, I don't . . . speaking . . ." Melissa bit her lip.

"Come on," Randi said. "It's Sydonia Rotary. I'll swing by and pick you up."

It was like the gang waving you over at the Dairy Queen, Melissa thought.

"I could pick you up," Shane said. "Then Randi won't have to leave the lunch counter so early."

"No, I'll pick *you* up," Melissa told Randi. She turned to Shane. "And we'll meet you there."

Predictably, Melissa had no trouble getting Orrin to oversee race registration with the help of a race director, and Randi to work on volunteers. Cassie wasted no time assigning who should contact which potential sponsors, as well as assuring them that they wouldn't have to act until she had delineated a dollar amount for sponsorship levels.

"Maybe we could sit down after Rotary, back at my shop," she told Melissa.

Melissa nodded. "Sure." She could put off visiting Hugh for at least another day or two.

"You give good meeting," Ethan quipped after they had adjourned.

"Well, you give good support." Melissa raised an eraser and

began to wipe away her own colorful scribbles as the others filed out.

"I'll get these typed up and e-mail them tomorrow morning," Orrin said over his shoulder.

"Thanks, Orrin." Melissa looked at Ethan, nodded at the phone. "You want to try your friend now?"

Ethan smiled. "Nope. I've got to get back to the farm and my friend will keep till tomorrow. How 'bout I come by tomorrow evening, we call from the Ladies Farm? They've got a speaker phone, don't they?"

Melissa laughed, resumed wiping the board. "Everything at the Ladies Farm is set up for communal use. Of course," she turned, "you realize they'll want to chime in . . . not to mention interrogate you about your intentions!"

"It's a little early, but I can handle it," Ethan assured her.

He stood for a second, hands in his pockets, gaze steady and mild. Why should that render her speechless? Melissa couldn't find anything clever enough to speak, couldn't find a reason to stop basking in his unwavering acceptance.

Finally came a lopsided grin and an incline of his head. "The farm beckons. And," he motioned toward the window through which Shane was grinding out his cigarette stub on the chamber walk, "you've got a meeting with your drink sponsor."

"I knew that was too easy," Melissa muttered.

Chapter 6

"What do you think?" Della asked, nodding at the color prints Tony had pinned up over his desk.

She had e-mailed the logo designs earlier, then driven to Fort Worth for a morning of appointments. Tony's print shop was her last stop.

"Nice design. Hard to get the smooth blends on the peach."

"I've already had this fight with the screen printer, and he can manage it on the T-shirts." She smiled. "And before you tell me how tough it is, remember who's doing the copy for the *Barbecue Boys* catalog and just tell me you can do this job."

"We can do it. Especially with barbecue hanging in the balance." He studied the figures, running forward as they reached for the perfect peach dangling before them in the moonlight.

To Della, the contrast between the abstract, brush-stroked figures and the photographically exact, delicately shaded peach animated the design.

"It's really good, Dell."

"Thanks."

"What do you need? Entry forms? Programs?"

"Entry forms. Programs. Counter signs with ripoff entries. Posters. An estimate."

"An estimate? Who else is bidding?"

"No one. It's . . . there's a committee, and Melissa—"

His eyebrows lifted.

"—Melissa's chairing it. She'll have to report back to them. I'm working on *Barbecue Boys;* I'll have something next week."

Barbecue Boys was the mail-order barbecue venture run by Tony, Dave, Kat's friend Nick Lantinatta, and Earl Westerman, Gladys and Ray's nephew, and Rita's new son-in-law. Earl, who lived with Rita's daughter Darlene, near Gladys and Ray in the Big Bend, smoked the briskets with sauces developed by the others. They also bottled four kinds of sauces, gathering monthly at the Ladies Farm kitchen to concoct their specialties.

"Is Melissa staying?"

Della shrugged. "At least through the peach festival."

"How's she going to make a living?"

"Dunno. Doesn't matter. She can stay with us till she figures it out."

Tony stepped closer, kissed the top of her head. Della knew that he was sniffing the perfume in her hair; she listened to him breathing deeply and it made her smile. Years ago, they had spent an afternoon visiting perfume counters, spraying her bare arms and inhaling. They had settled on Halston, because it was citrus-y and light and likely to stay on the market for a long time. Of course, she and Tony had split up, but she had continued using the perfume.

"I miss Pauline," Della said. She closed her eyes and leaned her head back, stretching her neck. She tried to recall if Richard, with whom she had carried on an affair for several years after her divorce, had liked the Halston, but she couldn't remember.

"I know." Tony continued the conversation without noticing that she had jumped. "But there's nothing for Melissa in Sydonia."

"What?" There's nothing stupider than rubbing up against Tony and daydreaming about Richard, Della lectured herself. She straightened a little.

"There's nothing—"

"The Ladies Farm is in Sydonia," Della countered, willing herself to relax. "We're all there, we can help her. And maybe she could find a job in Fort Worth."

"Maybe she could," he said mildly.

She could hear him inhaling and she guessed the perfume had intoxicated him to the point that he couldn't read her thoughts. Or maybe he could never read her thoughts.

Della turned and smiled up at him. "Thanks," she said, stroking his tie.

He didn't ask for what.

* * *

Ethan insisted on helping with dinner. It fit, Melissa thought, since Della had insisted that Ethan stay for dinner after they completed their phone call, and Rita had insisted that Trey and Garrett let her help them wash up for dinner, and Kat had insisted that Ethan provide full financial disclosure before she allowed him access to a salad bowl and a head of romaine.

"Caesar?" Ethan asked, picking up the romaine.

"Vinaigrette," Della sang out.

"Well," said Melissa. "I'll just"—she motioned toward the dining room—"set the table."

From the dining room she listened to Della inviting Ethan to work out in the shed any time he wanted. Provided there was no aerobics class or other ladies' activity, Kat amended. Melissa pulled crockery off the cart the ladies used to move tableware. They had three guests, one couple and a single, and the ratio of residents to guests gave her déjà vu. She could see her mother's mouth tightening as she struggled with the cost of feeding a family of four who regularly outnumbered paying diners. Of course, Melissa realized, plunking the cream-colored plates and bowls directly down onto the oak table, the ladies counted on weekend trade; weekday guests were a bonus.

Through the doorway, she could see Ethan's back, his shoulder blades and upper arms moving slightly, his head bent over his task even as he enlightened Kat on the vagaries of Austin real estate. She tried to imagine a camisole or lacy hi-cuts under the knit shirt and khakis, but thankfully failed. Even so, she bet he had his own secrets.

Stainless steel flatware lived in the drawer on the cart—really a small cherry server Dave had mounted on casters—and Melissa pulled out knives, forks, and spoons and laid them atop the folded cloth napkins. The woven splotches of primary colors enlivened the table, but Melissa wished that the ladies would at least let her substitute paper napkins where the boys sat.

When they finally assembled, Melissa tried to position herself between Trey and Garrett, but Rita insisted on doing the honors. "Y'all want Aunt Rita to cut your meat, don't you?" she encouraged.

Trey shot her a skeptical look, but Garrett smiled and wriggled onto his booster seat.

"Auntie Rita's gonna make yellow hair," Garrett announced. "On me!"

"He means blond," Trey said.

"You look pretty blond to me already," observed one of the guests. The woman, Janice, plopped herself down on Garrett's free side and winked up at Melissa.

"Oh, we were just talking about highlights," Rita said.

Janice, who was headed to Arkansas for a rafting trip, smiled indulgently at the notion of bleaching a child's hair.

"Make him look more Californian," Rita said, smiling at Ethan, who took the chair to which Della directed him. "Of course, everything about Melissa's all natural."

Melissa rolled her eyes and seated herself next to Trey, which put her across the table from Ethan and out of eye contact with her younger son. Just the way Rita had planned, Melissa figured.

Ethan grinned. "So that tough-woman thing on the phone with Erica, that was all you, no act?"

Della, who took the head of the table with no challenges or hesitation, arched an eyebrow but said nothing, reaching for the salad bowl and handing it to the guest on her right.

"She's donating her services," Melissa explained, "but then she tells us we have to pick up her expenses on a per diem."

"How much?" That was Kat.

"Five," Melissa answered.

"Five days?" Rita asked, looking up from a discussion with Garrett about kindergarten.

"Five hundred a day," Kat corrected. She looked at Melissa. "Right?"

Melissa nodded.

"Well, now," Ethan defended his friend, "she was only talking about the whole days she'd be spending here, which would only be one visit plus the race weekend."

"But she can stay—"

"Here. Exactly," Melissa finished Kat's objection. "And I had already explained that. And she did have a point"—Melissa smiled at Ethan—"about how much time it takes to lay out a course—the politics about who wants which street closed for how long—and her crew."

"We could put together a crew," Della said.

"Well, she won me over on that one," Melissa replied, reaching

over Trey's head for the salad bowl. She looked at the greens Rita
had heaped on her son's plate. "Just try the salad," she encouraged. He nodded wordlessly, and she prayed Rita was less generous with the pasta and meat sauce. Trey had no sooner hit the
road than he had adopted a no-sauce, no-dressing, no-condiment
policy that exceeded any strictures his picky father had embraced.
Ethan took up the tale while Melissa served her own salad.

"What she said," he explained, "is that she has a whole list of
volunteer posts—she's done a lot of these—but certain key posi-
tions, particularly the monitors for the sensors, have to be done
by her people because you only get one chance to do it right."

Melissa helped Trey secure his napkin in the yoke of his shirt
and nodded as Ethan explained the tiny sensors that the runners
would lace to their shoes and how the electronic monitors at the
midway and finish lines would be staffed. She let her fingers fluff
the ends of Trey's unbleached hair and she smiled both at the soft-
ness and the sheen. Neither of her boys needed highlights, she
thought, and made up her mind to talk to Rita.

"Well," Melissa resumed her conversation, "it was a productive chat, once we got fees out of the way. Especially since Erica's
seen all the write-ups of the Ladies Farm and was really curious
about staying here." She smiled at Ethan. "Of course, the real
story may be why she owes Ethan so big-time, but he's not saying."

"You can't miss hearing about the Ladies Farm," the guest
named Pam chimed. She bumped shoulders with her husband.
"Even Tommy had heard of the place."

Tommy shrugged, kept chewing.

Rita was murmuring to Garrett, and Melissa could not keep
herself from glancing in their direction. "How about if Aunt Rita
gets some plain salad, without the dressing?" Rita was offering.

Melissa sighed. "Garrett?" She leaned forward so her younger
son could see her two places down at the table. "Isn't this salad
yummy? Trey's almost finished his, it's so good."

Garrett studied his plate, poked his fork unsuccessfully at some
lettuce. He looked back at his mother, who gave him an encouraging nod, then picked up a lettuce leaf with his fingers and
popped it in his mouth. "I like lettuce," he said, his soft voice
coming to her under the general conversation, which had moved
on to a comparison of the guests' itineraries.

"Me too," she said. She nibbled her own salad, then looked up to see Ethan studying her. "Beautifully torn."

His considering gaze hung only a second before he turned to Tommy and Pam to pursue the topic of their road trip across the southwest.

Later, after Kat had insisted on taking the boys up for their baths and Della and Rita insisted that they could handle cleanup, Melissa and Ethan moved out to the back lawn. The plastic chairs destroyed by the storm had been replaced by old metal ones, freshly enameled by Dave, and so white they gleamed in the dusk.

"Odd, seeing you with kids," Ethan said.

"I suspect so. But you must know . . . don't your brothers have kids?"

"Except for Tommy. Must know what?"

"Oh, nothing. I mean, we're in our thirties now; most of us that are married have children."

"True. And I've got lots of married friends with kids. Guys at work. I just meant . . . you know, seeing you, all these years later. I guess in my mind—"

"Oh! Tell me, please, I'm still eighteen in your eyes!"

They both laughed. "You are!" he said. "Of course, your hair's shorter. And I notice you've stopped ripping your jeans so your butt shows through."

"Uh, right on that one."

"And it's hard for me to think that you've been married, not having seen your husband."

"I'm still married," Melissa said.

"But you're still getting divorced, right?"

"I suppose so. I mean, nothing's changed since the other evening. My brother found me a lawyer. I talked to her this morning, she's e-mailing me a package of forms. I guess, even when it's uncontested, there's a lot of paperwork."

"That's what they tell me."

Melissa didn't want to talk about her divorce. She wanted to ask him why he was still single, wanted to hear him say he never got her off his mind, still dreamed of her eighteen-year-old butt peeping through her torn denims. "Listen," she said, attempting to take charge, "let's switch gears. Erica's terrific, thank you."

"You two didn't even need me. You have a private language: race night, timers, sensors, splits, comps."

Melissa sat up straighter. "I'm sure you do, too. Commercial real estate."

"That's the favor."

She shook her head.

"Erica. That's the favor: real estate. I got her out of this . . . I found someone to buy her out. She was in over her head."

"Ethan, that's really nice."

"Melissa, that's really illegal."

Melissa felt even more confused, which made it hard to know how to respond.

"Misrepresenting the value of an investment. Inflating its value. To the point of hinting at it in an e-mail. No one's arresting me, but if this joker didn't have so many skeletons in his own closet, he really could come after me. As it is, he sent a nasty letter to the chairman of my firm."

"Oh, Ethan . . . did you . . . you're not going to lose your license?"

"Nothing that dramatic. The guy could afford the loss, and he's ticked, but he's pulled a few slimy deals on his own. So we'll give it a few months and he'll lose a few more million, stop bad-mouthing me, and my stupidity won't even be a memory."

"That's a lot to do for a friend." Melissa didn't have to fake envy.

"Which is why Erica's so generous. And why I thought this might be a good time for an extended visit with Dad."

"So you saved Erica a few million dollars, really?"

"Not Erica. Her share was about two-fifty, most of which came from the sale of her mother's house."

"Then you are her knight in shining armor! I repeat: that's really nice! And," she hoped she had a teasing lilt to her voice, "not the kind of favor you'd do for just any friend."

"True. Erica and I were really close, hanging out on Saturday nights when we didn't have dates, that kind of thing. And now that she's married, she and her husband, Peter, still let me hang out on Saturday night."

"Well, you've been a good friend in return." Melissa hoped her relief wasn't audible.

"Funny," he said. "You're the first one outside the firm I've told the whole thing to."

"Your secret is safe with me," she promised.

*   *   *

"I don't want to talk about it." Melissa held up a hand to ward off Della, who had started a baking project in the cleaned-up kitchen. "I'm kissing the boys good night and then I'm getting on the computer."

"You can't avoid us forever," Della sang out, but Melissa headed straight upstairs.

The boys were sharing a double bed in the Janis Joplin. Melissa had the next room till Friday; then they would open the sleeper sofa in the boys' room for the weekend.

"You sleep with us," Garrett said when she opened the door and found the boys sitting up in bed while Rita told them a story.

Ordinarily, she would have snuggled down between them, a boy on each arm beneath the covers. When Trey and Garrett fell asleep, they would roll away, each to his own edge, and she could, with practiced stealth, slide beneath the covers down the center of the bed until she slipped off the foot. But now she grinned at Rita and clambered over Garrett to hug Trey until he protested; then she smothered Garrett in giggly kisses. Garrett protested too, a weak, imitation protest, and then she climbed off.

"Lights out after the story," she reminded. "Eyes closed."

Downstairs, she started a new database for her peach-run contacts, and fiddled through her bookmarked Web sites, looking for ways to promote the race quickly. The ladies had promised her that Rita's son-in-law Earl would get a race site fired up, but Melissa and Della would have to gin out the content. Melissa outlined the pages for the site, trying to shape the information, listing the links. There would have to be a links page, she determined, leading to the chamber, the sponsors, a guide to accommodations. Online registration would be the only link that showed throughout the site.

She looked at the outline—barely a list of topics—and sighed. There was a lot to do.

Melissa clicked back onto the Net and hit the search button. She keyed in *cross-dressing* and *transvestite* and *spouse* and excluded *purchase* and *hot*. She knew most of the sites that came up on the first page of the list, but she never bookmarked them. She went right to the bulletin board for significant others and lurked there, reading the updates from Jackie and Rhonda about their counseling sessions and their pain and their ongoing struggle with their husbands' special secret.

Some nights Melissa thought that these entries were penned by men desperately wishing for a wife with whom they could share. No woman could be this generous. But tonight Rhonda described getting ready for her mother's birthday dinner at a trendy restaurant and her dismay at turning to see her husband in his lacy thong and a camisole.

I knew no one would know but me. I knew he would wear his undershirt and boxers over them, and then his shirt and suit over that. He had even shown me how he could pee, how he could pull himself out of the thong (and through the front of his boxers) with no one ever guessing. (Besides, guys try NEVER to look!) It was stupid to get so upset. But I couldn't help it. First I turned away and told myself to forget it, but the thought of all of us—my parents, my kids, my sisters, and their families—sitting around the table in that restaurant with my husband in his lingerie . . . I just lost it. 'Do you have to wear that tonight?' I asked him. 'Couldn't you at least wait till we got home?' All he could talk about was how hot it made him, and how reassuring, too, being outnumbered by all my family. How overwhelming they are, and that's why he needs to be who he is inside, even if it's hidden, to keep in touch with his true self, blah, blah, blah, until I just stepped into the bathroom and cried—not too loud because the kids were already dressed and in the living room and I didn't want them to hear me—and then I thought: I could either call and cancel or I could accept this and go on. And when I came out, he already was dressed, but I knew he had them on, and I just smiled, and kissed him and apologized, and we were only a minute or two late. But I feel like my whole marriage, my whole LIFE is that way: either I have to cancel or I have to accept and go on, and I don't want to accept this. Why should I?

A number of SOs—Significant Others—had already responded, most commiserating with Rhonda. A few veterans advised her that these little episodes would get much less frequent. One woman, Cara, who defiantly signed herself "Cara, Significant to No Other," congratulated Rhonda on taking the first step—articulating the true choice—toward freeing herself from sexual coercion. "He may not have chosen this preference, but he chose to deceive you about it," wrote Cara, "leaving you only the choices of accepting it or freeing yourself. Good luck whichever way you choose."

Melissa stared at the part about taking the first step. She felt her eyes starting to burn, but she blinked the tears back. The first step is packing up the kids, she thought. The first step is getting out of there. She wondered what would happen if she logged on to the discussion, gave them some phony name and told them that the first step wasn't articulating a choice, it was not allowing your cross-dressing husband to join family events. Melissa kept reading.

Sexy Sadie did what she always did. She described a similar situation which required her to discipline her husband with the back of a wooden-handled hairbrush before snapping his panties back in place and ordering him to perform cunnilingus. "We arrived at the party late, breathless, and grinning from ear to ear," she concluded.

Melissa found Sexy Sadie particularly disturbing, but she ran into her on almost all these boards. Not that Sadie knew that, of course, since Melissa only lurked, never signed in. Melissa sometimes wondered about being spanked. But she never saw herself as the disciplinarian, schooling her mate when he dressed in frilly underthings. Not much comfort in that scenario.

Maybe, Melissa thought, returning to her home page and clicking on the *History* button, I do secretly yearn for a dominatrix as my partner. She accessed her browsing history and erased everything from her search through Sexy Sadie. Maybe I haven't opened my mind enough. She shut down the computer. Silly me, thought Melissa. Dreaming about Ozzie and Harriet Nelson, Donna Reed. Fantasizing that I'm Rachel on *Friends,* pursued by Ross, the klutzy, totally conventional paleontologist who would love Rachel forever.

Time for bed, she thought.

If Melissa wanted to fuck Ethan Dyer, Shane didn't care. He could do a lot better than that prim little package, especially now that she had two kids. He set down the night goggles and lifted his beer. He hadn't realized what a pleasant place the old shed occupied until that storm destroyed it and they had poured the foundation for the new prefab.

"A prefab?" the old man had exclaimed. "Why the hell do we want anything down there?"

Thank God for Linda, his stepmother. "Maybe you could store some of those old tractors down there. Get them out of the stable, anyway."

"Let you bring in more horses!" Old Eli had snorted, but he was already relenting. Linda had grinned at Shane. Eli could refuse either one of them, but not both.

"Maybe I'll spiff up those old pieces," Shane had offered, but no one believed him. It was enough for his father that the old equipment wasn't discarded. And that his young wife was happy with the way he accommodated her horses.

With the cottonwoods around him, Shane felt sheltered, almost like in a deer blind. He would move his hunting things down here once they got the building up. And it would be a perfect place to store bottled water for the race. Shane saw a future for himself in beverage service.

He picked up the binoculars and looked through the trees at the Ladies Farm. They weren't bad neighbors, for a bunch of dikey broads.

He focused on the rooms in the old house, where the women lived. It looked like lights out over there. I guess she's not sneaking out for Ethan tonight, Shane thought. Pity. He wouldn't mind a few photos of that meeting. Just in case he ever met her husband.

"How was your dinner?" his dad asked. They drank their coffee on the porch, illuminated only by the light through the kitchen window and the thin band on the horizon that preceded the sun.

"Pretty good," Ethan said. "You ever eat over there?"

"They invite me, now and then."

"Ever go?"

"Once or twice," said Webb. "They like for me to bring them peaches. That one—Della—she's the one's taken over the canning. Ice cream. Cobbler. Clove and ginger. Candied ginger." Webb shook his head. "Tasty, if you like that sort of thing."

Ethan sipped his coffee, looked toward the elbow in the river, well down from where the Ladies Farm sat behind the cottonwoods leading up from the low bank. He imagined Melissa sitting in the chair where he had left her last night. She was the kind of woman who wore clothes that looked like men's clothes: oxford-cloth shirts, boxers, hiking boots. If you looked closely, though, you could tell they were cut to reveal the delicate lines of her neck and along her shoulders. He pictured her on one of those white chairs, leaning her head back so that you could look straight down some blue cotton nightshirt, right down between those neat breasts and all that taut, smooth skin.

He sipped his coffee.

"I'm still wondering how dinner went."

"Well, dinner was just an afterthought, really. We had some committee business—"

"She staying?"

"At the Ladies . . . you mean staying here in Sydonia? To live?"

Webb said nothing.

Ethan set his coffee cup down on the porch floor, turned more toward his father. "I don't know. I don't think she knows right now. I think she just stumbled here, almost reflex, you know, back to the warm cave. Now she's got to figure out what to do."

"Did she say why she left her husband? He find someone else?"

"She's not talking about that. Not about anything, really." Ethan looked back out toward the river. "I think it's just too soon."

He could see his father's grin, even in the low light. "Y'all spent a lot of time not talking. Past midnight by the time you got back."

"You're not going to ground me, are you?"

"What did you talk about?"

"Nothing, really. The race. High school."

"Did you talk the whole time?"

"Jesus, Dad! We were just sitting out back—"

"I meant were you talking—actual sound, first her, then you—the whole time, or was there silence in between. Times when neither of you were talking?"

The growing light revealed his father's gaze to be as mild as always, his eyes sunk deep and his face seamed and dark.

"We had our silences, I guess."

"That's what I miss about your mother," Webb told his son. "Sitting and saying nothing."

"Dad, I wish you'd think about selling this place. Or at least lease the orchards. You could move down to Austin . . . or Houston, with Wade. Whatever you want. Get to know Wade's kids."

"I think now maybe I've talked enough for a lifetime, said everything I should say. Maybe the best way to make this world better's just to stop my own voice."

"Dad? What the hell are you—"

Ethan was stopped by the shake of his head, the turn of his shoulder. He drew a breath. "I hope you don't mean starting now."

Webb stood, walked to the end of the porch. "We've still got the small orchard to clear, and then we've got to spray the east field. Manny's needing to head back the end of the week." With that he picked his cup off the chair arm where it had rested and walked back into the house.

Chapter 7

"Tell me again why we're doing this?" Tony asked, following her across the threshold at the Hutto house.

Della strode through the modest living room and unlatched the glass door to the narrow balcony. "Here," she said, walking out to wave a hand at the river and the Ladies Farm on the opposite bank. "Don't lean," she warned. "It needs fixing."

Tony stood well back, against the house. "You want to move across for a view of the mighty Nolan River?"

"I told you," she said, turning to look at him. "I've got Pauline's old room. It's got a sitting room with a door to the hall. If I move out, Melissa can sleep in the sitting room and put the boys in the queen. Or vice versa. She'll have some privacy, and we can get the guest rooms back. And"—she moved closer to him—"if she thinks we're doing it for true love, she won't worry about moving me out of the house."

"Is this true love?"

His face was in shade and she could barely make out his eyes. Della stepped toward him and reached a hand out to touch the muscle in his arm. "Well it's true that it's love," she said.

Tony rested both hands on her hips and she leaned into him. "Why is it," he asked, "you'll move out of the Ladies Farm for Pauline's daughter, but you won't move back to Fort Worth with me?"

Della frowned. She had been expecting a kiss and a little fondling before the pickup with her things arrived. "This is still the Ladies Farm," she said with a gesture that encompassed the

Hutto house. "I'd move this far for you, too." She kissed him lightly, then pulled away.

"What are you saying?"

She had turned back to look at the river, but she knew he was still watching her. What *are* you saying? Della wondered. Oh, just say it without thinking about it. Just once.

She turned back to him fully determined. "I'm saying that I don't want to get married and I don't want to move back to Fort Worth but that I'm moving here for a while and you could . . . I mean, I want you to move here, too. With me. You could live here with me."

There.

Where's that truck, she wondered. It was stupid to hire those high school kids just to move boxes. Tony and I could have done it. I could have done it myself.

Say something. Anything.

But he stood, studying her.

"Are you measuring me for my coffin or what? Look, Tony, you've been after me for a year to move ·back to Fort Worth."

"And you wanted nothing to do with it."

She sighed. "I wasn't ready to move back to our old house and resume our marriage. But we've certainly developed a new relationship. And now we're taking it to a new level."

"A new level?"

"Oh, don't make fun of me. You know what I mean."

"Yes I do. You mean you've stopped mourning and now you want me to stick around for the next step in your grief recovery."

For a second she thought he was referring to Jamie, their son who had died in a car accident at sixteen. But he never ridiculed her feelings about Jamie. This was about Richard, with whom Della had carried on an affair after she and Tony divorced.

"Richard's been dead a few years," she said. "I don't know why you'd bring him up now."

"Richard may have died a while back, but you didn't stop loving him till after Barbara showed up and taught you a few things about her dead husband."

Della felt her face growing warm, but she stood where she was and held his gaze. "I'm not apologizing for Richard, Tony. Not to you and not to anyone else."

"I didn't ask for any apologies," Tony said. "You certainly

don't owe one to me for sleeping with someone after we were divorced and I was married to someone else."

She waited.

"I'm just saying you're still sad about it."

"And you don't want to be my therapy." Della didn't blame
him. Tony was accommodating, but he had his limits. "Fair
enough. Of course"—she smiled gently—"assuming you're right
and you don't want to be here while I overcome my grief, you
take the chance that someone else will be."

"Yes I do."

"And, it's strange, given my supposed grief, that you'd be willing for me to overcome it at our Fort Worth marital abode." Her
grin widened. "Of course, this might be less about my grief than it
is about your territory."

"Territory?"

She reached for his hand, tugged on it. "You know. Dragging
me back to your cave. Tell you what—" Della paused to listen to
the truck pulling up out front. "If you move in here with me, I'll
let you pee all along the perimeter of the property."

"Nice wheels," Melissa said. She gritted her teeth and ignored
Shane's leer as she hiked her skirt and climbed into his truck. The
bench seat offered an expanse of leather that stretched forever.
When she peered out the window, the distance to the ground
made her dizzy.

Rolling by the courthouse, Melissa comforted herself that no
one could see her through the heavily tinted windows.

Shane yawned, a great, wide-mouthed, noisy kind of yawn,
then winked at her. "Late night," he said. "Sorry."

"I thought you farmers were used to early morning," she said.
They had crossed the square and rumbled onto Crockett Street,
bouncing over railroad tracks before turning onto a side street
that followed a rail spur.

"I let my little brothers handle the early chores," Shane said.
He waved a hand to dismiss the responsibilities of operating a
dairy farm.

Melissa had a hard time recalling Castleburg brothers, but she
pictured a stairstep array of Shanes: pale hair, white eyelashes,
beefy necks, ham-hock hands made for pulling cow teats till they
squirted money. Not that Castleburg Dairy didn't boast gleaming

batteries of chrome milking stations, scientifically balanced feed, meticulously weighed, measured, and sanitized producers. But the Castleburg genetics were every bit as pure as the Texas guernseys that had built their bovine dynasty.

"Nice life," Melissa murmured as she shook her head to banish the vision of the brothers wagging their Castleburg tails as they filed into the barn. I've got to stop reading that crap on the net, she thought.

Despite the early hour, three cars were parked in front of Superior Feed, a cinderblock warehouse with a garage-door entrance opened to the cool morning. The wisps of straw on the concrete floor and the line of bright green implements ready for rental hinted of a slower time. Siggie Blanton Urquardt, who managed the franchise on behalf of her parents and grandparents, encouraged the link to yesteryear with artful displays of weathered implements. Wooden-handled rakes and hoes leaned against hundred-pound sacks of feed, and a rusted harrow was backed up to a gleaming tractor.

Siggie herself, sporting overalls and a knit cropped top, glanced anxiously at the angry on-hold lights of her countertop phone while Melissa and Shane suggested Superior Feed underwrite the runners' T-shirts. "Jeez, I don't know," she mumbled over and over. "I gotta talk to my folks, you know?" She stared at the list of sponsored activities.

"Y'all get your logo on every shirt, on every application, every counter sign," Shane said.

"We're already sponsoring the dance, you know. Saturday night."

"You and nine others," Shane scoffed.

Siggie glanced at the phones. "Jerry?" she bellowed. "Cathy from Central Irrigation's on two." She turned back and waved an arm at the store. "I've got to go."

"Why don't we stop back by when it slows down," Melissa suggested. "Say, around ten, when Johnny's here?"

Siggie rolled her eyes. "It never slows down," she warned. "I can't spend any more money without checking with my folks. They always sponsor the dance. Why are they doing a run, anyway?"

Melissa smiled her sweetest smile. "Shane tells me you always work the hospital booth at Peach Fest."

"Oh, yeah." Siggie smiled back. "You know, the auxiliary makes those cobblers, and little sock puppets."

"But we won't get those crowds, this year, with no peaches," Shane said.

"You think a run will bring the crowds in?"

"The right kind of run," Melissa assured her, wishing Shane would stop hovering. "With some novelty—a little . . . you know . . . buzz."

"I know what you mean," Siggie said. She held up the sponsor sheet. "C'mon back after I talk with Johnny and the folks, then we can sit down about it."

"What a bitch," Shane said as they retreated to the truck. "I have to ask Mommy and Daddy," he mimicked in falsetto. "We sponsor the dance."

"We should have thanked her for that," Melissa said. "That's the first thing we say when we go back: how much we appreciate how generous they've been. Her whole family. Then we go over the damage from the storm: how everyone's hurting, what it means to the groups who depend on their booths, blah, blah blah, how much it all means to everyone to get a crowd."

"How about if we just hold a gun to her head and make her an offer she can't refuse?"

"You know," Melissa said, "I promised you this morning and Thursday to hit these prospects. You might want to participate while I'm here."

"Whew! You're as touchy as you always were. Or don't-touchy. How about we drive down to the creek and rekindle our relationship."

"I don't recall a relationship," Melissa said. "I recall a struggle or two in your truck."

"Ah, c'mon Mel, every relationship is a struggle. Anyway, why—"

Mel, she thought. Mel! "Why don't we concentrate on how we can close Siggie and Johnny."

"You mean Siggie's folks."

"That was an excuse. She didn't want to tell us that she couldn't make the decision without Johnny. I think if Johnny wants it, she'll get the family to go along." Unlike your family, she thought. "Look, let's ride over to the co-op and hit them up for the race management. Then we'll sit at Randi's and you can tell me every-thing about Johnny."

Shane shook his head, grinned. "We can go to the co-op and over to Randi's. But we don't have to talk about Johnny. I'll han-dle Johnny."

"What do you mean?"

They were stopped at a light and Melissa registered a few peo-ple crossing toward the courthouse, but she studied Shane.

Shane wasn't looking at the intersection either. "Johnny and I party."

"You party," Melissa repeated. For a second she pictured a candlelit dinner with friends at her old house, the one they had sold in California. The wine. The muted voices. Grilled tuna and portabello with goat cheese.

"He don't want me talking to Siggie."

Melissa saw the dots connected. She nodded.

"Let's go to the co-op," Melissa said. "Then you go talk to your buddy Johnny."

"Don't you want to stop for a drink? Coffee?" Exasperated, he turned slightly and put the truck in gear, rolling forward, then jerking to a stop when he saw that there were still people in the intersection.

"Watch it!" Melissa said.

"What's the matter?" he asked. "Afraid you'll miss your date with Ethan?"

"I don't have any date," Melissa said, angry that she had re-sponded. "You didn't even look before you started."

"That's because you made me mad. I didn't hit anyone, did I?"

"Let's just get to the co-op," Melissa said. "Without killing anyone."

"How'd it go?" Kat asked when Shane finally dropped Melissa back at the Ladies Farm.

"The electric co-op said yes to half the race management, and Johnny and Siggie Urquardt will probably underwrite the tees." Melissa sprawled onto the old sofa in the Ladies Farm office. "And I have only one more morning to spend with Shane Castleburg."

"That's a pretty productive morning," Kat said. Since Melissa's last visit, following her mother's death, the ladies had moved Pauline's rolltop and upholstered chair to the other side of the office, and Kat had replaced them with a glass-topped table and Aeron chair. Now, swiveling and leaning back, she rested her feet atop a polished coffee table and smiled at Melissa. "Shane's no Ethan, huh?"

Melissa started. Of the ladies, Kat was the most strictly-business. Even Melissa's story of leaving Greg had elicited little response from Kat. "Well, Ethan's probably no Ethan," Melissa said. "I mean, in the sense that most of you seem to hope he'll rescue me from the mess that's my life."

Kat's blunt-cut hair shimmered with her slight toss of head, then fell back into place while she grinned. "You mean: you don't think any man can rescue you?"

"I don't even think a man *should* rescue me," Melissa said. "It's my mess, I'll clean it up. Meanwhile, we've got this run on our hands." She grimaced. "He called me Mel. He nearly ran someone down in an intersection. And," she recalled, "he dropped one other bombshell. I want to know one thing: Did Aunt Della really date Mr. Castleburg?"

Kat shook her head. "She went out with him once. Right after she moved out here. According to her, it was more like a job interview, or maybe the judging at the stock show. You know how they assess the potential yield?"

Melissa's stock-show experience consisted of nights in a private box at the indoor rodeo with her Fort Worth friends, but she nodded as if she had spent her winter afternoons enthralled by the grading of livestock. "Well, Aunt Della made a big impression on the Castleburgs. Shane says his stepmom's always comparing herself to Aunt Dell. Anyway," Melissa hurried on, "Shane's a jerk, but his dad controls a lot of money. Every town's like that, you know. It's just a question of whether or not you can liberate the cash." She leaned back. "And Shane promised me he'll get a commitment from his dad tonight."

"Sounds like you're the one making a commitment . . . to this project."

Melissa considered. "It's something I know how to do. It's like putting one foot in front of the other. And it's just till the end of June."

"What about Ethan? Is he staying in town?"

"Oh, maybe. I don't know. He's in a little hot water in Austin real estate—" She frowned. "He's pretty vague. You know, it's like he woke up one morning to find all his friends, not to mention his brothers, were married and had kids and homes and knew everything about preschools and baby seats, and now there's no one left to play with." Melissa threw up her hands. "Except, of course, those of us who got an early start and are heading into round two."

"Don't sound so cynical about yourself," Kat said, but even Melissa could tell she was just making an effort to be supportive.

"I'm okay, Aunt Kat," Melissa said. Then she looked around. "Did Aunt Dell say when she'd be back?"

"No telling." Della had taken the boys for the morning. "She'll call, but I think she's gone into Fort Worth. Needs to stock up the Hutto house." Kat smiled, and her eyes grew gentle. "I think Tony's really moving in."

Melissa nodded. "I'm going to use her office," she said. "I'll close the door so the phone doesn't disturb you."

"Well, here's a challenge," Ethan said as he settled into Rita's salon chair. "Nothing orange, okay?"

"And you say you're from Austin!" Rita draped him, then stood behind, studying the mirror and fingering his freshly washed locks. "Nice," she said. She ruffled his dark hair a little, just to enjoy the texture, then reached for her scissors. "I do love my work."

She started at the crown, lifting locks and snipping steadily, questioning as she worked.

He told her about Austin, about real estate, about his last two houses and the garage apartment where he lived now. He gave her the rundown on Wade, Tommy, Clark, and Steve, all of whose hair she had trimmed at one time or another, to their father's chagrin.

He asked about her daughters, and she filled him in on Carla and her three kids. She even shared a little about Darlene's adventure as a gestational carrier for a couple whose child had been sick.

"So she ended up married in the Big Bend, with a new baby."

"What happened to the kid, after all that?" Ethan asked.

"Seems to be doing okay, so far." Rita shook her head. She still hadn't adjusted to Darlene as the mother of two. Particularly not as Mrs. Earl Westerman. "How is your dad?" she asked. "We don't see him much."

"Working, most of the time. He said he's had dinner here."

Rita stepped back, then turned him to work on his right side. "Once or twice." She switched scissors.

"How'd he seem to you?"

She stopped clipping. "Okay. Quiet. Missing your mom."

"It's four years," Ethan said. "He told me how you came over to do her hair, when she was sick."

"We must look like a very small town to you," Rita said.

"But a hotbed of big-city hair." His face was longish, drawn down to a squarely defined chin, and even mock-serious conversation conveyed a certain weight. In the mirror, she saw his half-grin fade. "Has he ever said anything . . . you know, indicated . . . he's just so quiet."

"You think he's depressed?" Even the half of Rita's customers who weren't taking Paxil, Prozac, or Zoloft themselves stood watch for signs of depression among family and friends. "How's he sleeping? And eating?" She knew all the symptoms.

"Who knows? He seems all right that way, but I doubt I'd know what's normal for him. I think the person I remember may have never existed. He towered over all of us, even my mom. He forced his opinions—you know, about hard work, clean living, all that—on us, made us walk the straight and narrow. So it's hard to say, now, which one of us has changed."

Rita laughed a little. She had pumped the chair up and bent from the waist to work on his sideburns. "You mean he was indomitable and now he seems puny?"

"Not puny, exactly." Ethan gave a short laugh. "He's still working the orchards. Every day. It's more—"

"Hold still," Rita commanded, clipping at his sideburns with the tiny scissors, then brushing his cheek with her finger. "There." She turned him away from the mirror to work on the other side. "Well, if he's working with gusto, it's not like he's going to, you know—"

"He's not suicidal. Too much like quitting. But he's silent."

"Silent?"

"Yeah. But it's more like: less sure. Almost that he doesn't say anything because he doesn't want to sound like a fool."

"That's no problem," Rita muttered, focusing on the left sideburn. "Most of us, the less we have to say, the more we jabber. You ought to spend a morning in here sometime. Especially when my manicurist and shampoo girl are here, and we've got four or five heads going."

"This is more than fear of foolishness, though. He said, the other night, he figures he's talked enough. What does that mean?"

"There!" She straightened up, mortified by the cracking sound from her joints. "Maybe he's taking a vow of silence," Rita said. "I wish my knees would do that." She caught the sorrow in Ethan's gaze. "Ethan, your dad's lonely. He misses your mom. If there's no immediate danger, maybe what your dad needs most is your company. He's not likely to ask you for it."

"True."

"Stick around," she advised. "Listen to what little he does say."

"You know," said Ethan, "Melissa told me you're easy to talk to."

"Comes with the territory," Rita told him. "No extra charge." She picked up a cylindrical brush and started styling his hair. "You might chat up Gladys Hutto next time she's here. She and your folks go way back."

"I don't know, Greg. What do you think we should tell the boys?" Melissa shifted the phone to her other ear and leaned forward over Della's desk. She hated her own sarcasm, but it was either that or shrill accusations.

"I guess," he said, "I'm just saying that someday, I'd like it all out in the open. When they're older, of course."

"And I'm dead," said Melissa. They had scheduled this conversation for midday Portland time so that he could close his office door while most of his coworkers had gone to lunch. Somehow she had thought that picturing him in a business setting would encourage her to conduct the business that remained between them: lawyers' names, health insurance, readying the house for sale.

"Let's talk about the house," he said.

Melissa saw it: two stories of dun frame, hidden by trees whose names she had never learned. The boys' dormers facing the street, allowing them to signal neighboring children with their flashlights. Even Silicon Valley had not prepared her prairie soul for moist, shadowed Portland.

"Just hire someone to box up my stuff," Melissa said. "I took all the important things; get someone in there to get all the rest boxed and rent a storage place. That's the first thing they'll tell you: get rid of the clutter." And the lingerie. "You can take it out of my share."

"I told you, I'm not pulling that crap, charging every nickel to your share or my share. We are not going down that road. We'll keep track of the expenses, we'll sell the house, we'll pay the costs of getting it ready, and we'll split the proceeds. Finito."

"I'm only saying, Greg, we've got to get the house ready, and that's the first step. Clearing out all the junk. I don't want to wait on the lawyers to get that resolved." She reached over and opened the blinds on Della's window, which faced the unproductive Castleburg gravel pit, soon to be a lake around which Shane planned to build tract homes. "I'm trying to be fair, too. You shouldn't have to clean up my mess, just because I'm in Texas."

"And, anyway, who wants a cross-dressing creep handling your personal belongings."

"Stop it! I didn't say anything like that. Anyway," she hurried on before he accused her of thinking it, "you haven't changed your mind about staying in the house, have you?"

"Would you and the boys move back if I did?"

"No."

"Then I'd just as soon burn it down."

"Selling it will do," said Melissa. Then, "Do you know where you're moving?"

"I'll get the house listed, then I'll look. Probably an apartment first. I don't want to rush. You're still sending the boys to me this summer, right? That's what we agreed."

"I know what we agreed, Greg." She sighed. "But don't push me, okay? Who knows where I'll be this summer." For a second, Melissa considered the chances that rioting Sydonians would pursue her to the city limits after the run fizzled, but she shook it off. She couldn't afford terror. "I'm the one who's quit my job, remember? I'm the one who's got to start over somewhere else."

"I offered to move out."

His mild tone infuriated her. "Yeah. I think that was right after you offered to swap undies."

"I've got your lawyer's name. You've got my lawyer's name. I'll get the house cleared of clutter. Boys and girls, I think we're done with today's lesson."

"I'm sorry," she said. "I tell myself I'm just going to deal with the facts—"

"But you're too angry. I'm sorry too. We're two sorry people. Mel, let's just let it go for today. Maybe we can talk at the end of the week."

"Yeah. You're right." She was exhausted. As she set the phone down, she realized that what had bothered her earlier, with Shane, was that he had called her Mel. I should have told him not to do that, she thought. That's what my husband calls me.

Chapter 8

When the phone rang, Ray wondered how arthritics had managed before portable phones. He'd been contemplating his graywater runoff, thinking that the outdoor shower needed a deeper gravel filter below it, and there was no way he could have hobbled inside to get the phone before it stopped ringing. Straightening up and reaching into his pocket took two rings, and then a third to punch the green button before he could say hello.

"This is Webb . . . Webb Dyer, in Sydonia," as if Ray knew a bunch of Webbs.

"What the hell 'you doing in Sydonia?" Ray shot back. "How come you're not out here in the high desert with the rest of us cranky bastards?"

"I'm sweeping peaches off trees all day. What're you doing out there?"

"Contemplating water. Hell of a thing, how much time I've spent thinking about water." Ray stared at the rocky slope that led away from the shower to where the ground leveled off. "Bridges. Dams. Sewers. I'm thinking about plum trees, Webb. How much water you think I'd need for a plum tree?"

"No telling," Webb said. "I'll look it up for you in the water book."

"You do that," Ray said.

"How you feeling?"

"Fine. I'm just fine. Why'd you ask? What'd Gladys tell you?"

"That you're in pain all the time. And that you're full of crap."

"Yeah. Well. Hell getting old." Ray thought about the storm.

"Sorry to hear about the hail." He wanted to tell Webb that he and Gladys could lend him money, but Webb would just turn it down. He's got plenty of family, Ray told himself. All those boys'll pitch in.

"Act of God," Webb said. "Funny that we're sorry about an act of God."

Ray squinted at where the ground leveled out and wondered if five trees were too many. Maybe three, he thought. Three good ones, well-spaced. "God works in mighty mysterious ways, if you're thinking that's who sent the hail."

"Well, I just wanted to say the Good Lord's been smiling on us all lately. Good sun, two more soaking rains. Things growing right along. Everything growing, leafy green, if you can picture that."

Ray held the phone out and stared at it a second. *The Good Lord's been smiling on us all???? Leafy*—"Oh, I can picture it," Ray reassured his friend, jerking the phone back to position.

"It's like medicine," Webb said. "Medicine for the soul, seeing everything growing just the way—"

"*Just the way* what?" Ray couldn't contain himself. "The way the Good Lord wanted to overtax that miserable layer of soil in Sydon County? The way the Good Lord wanted those thieving Castleburgs to overgraze, as long as everything's so blooming green? Or the way you and Gladys knock heads over who can grow the biggest sunflower?"

Webb didn't miss a beat. "You should see the sunflowers now. You know, Ray, I do believe the Good Lord does have something to do with this. Hail. Rain. Sunshine. Leafy plants. Heals the soul."

"Why don't you cart your soul out here to heal?" Ray barked at his old friend. "It's clear the Good Lord's replaced your mind with oatmeal. At least out here, we can get some of Gladys's good cooking into you."

"Damn it, I'm just trying to tell you—"

"I know just what you're trying to tell me, and I'm telling you to sweep your peaches off the trees and get on out here. Whatever you're growing'll take care of itself, for a week. Besides, Gladys says you got your boy there: Ethan."

"Now you're the one with mush for brains. I still got one orchard in peaches. Late crop. I'm not going anywhere."

"Well," Ray said, straining not to plead, "after you pick them, then."

Della couldn't wait to get the boys back to Melissa. By the time they had jumped from the car and run full-speed into the kitchen, Della felt terminally depleted of open-arm hugs and cooing reassurance. "Those are the neediest children I have ever encountered," she muttered to Tony.

He pulled the emergency brake, then shook his head. "They're okay. They're just confused."

They both slid out of the car and walked slowly toward the door, which the two boys had left open. "They need sports or something," Tony observed. "Other kids. They'll come 'round." He took her hand. "You were great with them."

"Yeah. That's why they couldn't wait to get back to Mommy."

As they stepped into the kitchen, Della heard Trey telling Melissa about the helicopter film at the IMAX theatre.

"He hid in Aunt Della!" Garrett giggled.

"We were snuggling," Trey insisted, and Della laughed.

"We sure were," Della backed him up. "But it was very scary," she assured Melissa and Ethan, who was evidently visiting. "Just like we were flying. Huh?"

She addressed this last to Garrett, who nodded while he giggled, safe in his mother's encircling arms. His older brother stood uncertainly between table and door, eyeing Garrett's position with envy. "Then we ate barbecue," Trey continued his report.

"Checking out the competition," Tony confirmed.

"And then we made copies. On colored paper. Eight thousand!" said Trey.

"Eight thousand," repeated Melissa. She rolled her eyes at Ethan, who lifted an eyebrow.

"Well, they had to work off their lunch," Della explained. "Tony keeps claiming that new machine's so simple—"

"I could do it!" Garrett crowed. "I could make eight thousand. Or a billion," he exploded, dancing away from his mother and pushing a little against his older brother.

The two tussled a little in some familiar dance, then tumbled back toward Melissa, who gathered them to her, oblivious to unwashed hands and T-shirts sticky with barbecue sauce. She looked over their heads at Ethan. "Welcome to family life," she said, laughing.

Della thought Ethan did a good job of resisting the impulse to scrape back his chair and beat a retreat. She saw the flicker in his brown eyes, caught a little tightening around the mouth. Then he smiled, as beguiled as Della by Melissa's laugh.

"Family life's not so bad," he drawled. "You ought to bring them over to the orchards, we'll put them to work picking peaches."

"There are no peaches," Trey informed them all, slipping free once again. "The hail got them. So my mom's putting together a race."

Flops, who had settled at Tony's feet the moment he had appeared, raised her head when Trey hopped a little on the wood floor for emphasis.

"And we're all helping," Della assured the eight-year-old. "But your mom's definitely in charge."

Melissa smiled her appreciation, gave a little squeeze to Garrett, who remained in her arms.

Della stepped over Flops and into the working part of the kitchen. "You're staying for dinner, I hope," she addressed Ethan.

"Uh"—he glanced at Melissa—"no thanks." He grinned, ran his hand through his hair. "Believe it or not, I just came over for a haircut. But then I stopped by to visit Melissa and now I've got to get back to Dad's before he sends out the sheriff."

"How's he doing?" Della asked.

Ethan shot a quick look at Melissa, then shook his head slowly. "Hard to tell, really. I mean, in some ways, he's amazing, working a full day, strong as a bull. He just seems, I don't know—"

"Older?" suggested Tony. He grinned at the younger man. "It happens."

"More like lonely, I'd imagine," said Della. She, too, smiled at Ethan. "That comes with older. So it's good you're here. And maybe you'll bring him with you to dinner." Della smiled some more, mostly because she liked looking at Ethan and Melissa and the kids, all of them flushed and happy, with not a clue about what would happen next.

Ethan nodded his thanks, let Melissa and the boys walk him outside.

"It's the unpredictability I miss," Della explained to Tony after dinner. He had waited on her while she finished her part of the cleanup, then they drove over the bridge and up to the Hutto house. Now they sat in the living room on the tacky pseudo-Mediterranean leather sofa with the wood and cane arms. "You know," she clued him in. "Relationships. When we're older."

Tony laughed. "Oh, that again. Well, I'm sure if you asked Melissa, she'd prefer fewer surprises in her life."

"Oh, I don't mean it that way." Della set down her magazine. "It's that rush of optimistic uncertainty, not nasty surprises. You know: I'm a good-looking woman with two gorgeous kids; is the handsome, sophisticated son-of-a-farmer-turned-real-estate-tycoon falling in love with me? Is he going to ask me out? Will it be an afternoon at the zoo with the kids? Will there be a great night at some plush hotel in Fort Worth? Is he going to take me over to see his dad?"

"So there's no excitement in our relationship? No great nights?"

"It's not the same." She looked at him fondly. "You're wonderful. I love you. But we've been through those things: the fights, the make-up sex, meeting the in-laws. We know what comes next. And that's comforting. But it's a different kind of anticipation." She thought about Jamie. "We know all the ways surprises can hurt us, Tony. When we look forward, even when we're optimistic, we know how many ways things might not work out."

He smiled a little and she felt a rush of gratitude that he had understood, that he didn't take it as a criticism.

"Anyway, all I'm—"

He put his hand up to stop her, and she guessed she had overestimated his patience with her feelings. Then she realized he was listening to something else, and as he stood up, she heard the rustling, then the whining at the door.

By the time Tony reached the entrance, they had both recognized Flops' whining, who was now barking. Tony opened the door, and the retriever padded into the center of the room. Della was still trying to figure out how the dog, whose mixed heritage evidently included a forebear who avoided water above all, had made it across the river when Flops shook herself off. Water flew everywhere, and Della headed for the towels.

Tony, oblivious to the mess, had slid to the floor to hug Flops. "Did you follow us home? Huh? Did you ford the mighty Nolan?"

"More likely she picked her way over the spillway and slipped in," Della said. "She hates water."

"Not as much as she loves us. Huh, girl?" Flops's tags made a rattling sound that merged with Tony's laughter as she shook some more. From the floor, Tony accepted Della's towel and looked up imploringly. "She followed me home. Can I keep her?"

"Well, if you ask me, and I know you didn't, that boy's just falling all over himself for you," Rita said. She and Melissa had walked out to the salon to refill Melissa's bottle of no-tears shampoo. "Here." Rita took the empty container from Melissa and held it under the dispenser of the larger bottle she kept near the sinks.

"Well, *falling all over*'s a little strong," Melissa said. "It's more like he's pleasantly amused by me, since he's here in Sydonia and there's no one else he's interested in right now. Not"—she grinned, taking the refilled bottle back from Rita—"that he might not get some encouragement."

"Well, go for it!"

Melissa grew more serious. "Oh, I don't know." She shook her head and looked at Rita, whose fluffy blond curls gave her the look of a protecting angel. "It's exciting to have someone interested. I mean, it's just what I need when I feel like I've been run over by a truck. But I'm not ready." She locked on Rita's eyes. "Not ready at all."

"Well, honey," said Rita in the voice Melissa remembered from the kitchen conversations of her youth, "you don't want to make him wait too long. I mean, I'm always thinking two minutes might be too long, and you . . . you should take your time and all that . . . but that Ethan: it'd be a shame to lose a boy like that."

Melissa put an arm around Rita's bony shoulder and pulled her close. She could still picture Rita and her mother huddling over coffee in the kitchen after her dad's death. "Be patient, okay?"

"You better tell that to Ethan," Rita advised.

Upstairs, the boys were trying to stop up the overflow drain to see if they could fill the tub to the rim. "Hand me another wash-cloth!" Trey ordered his younger brother. "Quick, before this one soaks through!"

"Hold it right there!" Melissa ordered. "You!" she pointed at Garrett. "Into the tub by order of the bath police. And you!" She regarded Trey severely. "Start scrubbing. Yourself, not your brother. And stop splashing!"

She kicked off her sandals and knelt by the side of the tub. "We need to wash that hair, both of you."

"I can do mine," Trey said.

"I can do mine," Garrett repeated.

"I know. Both of you can wash your own hair, I'll just help you rinse." She nodded at the spray attachment on the shower head.

"How come you kiss?" Trey said. He was rubbing a bar of soap over his belly and frowning at the lack of lather. Her boys liked a lot of suds.

"Because I love you," Melissa told him.

"No, him," Trey said, rubbing harder. "Ethan."

"We didn't really—I mean, we're just friends, honey; some-times friends kiss each other." She thought a second. "The way Daddy kisses Aunt Christie when he sees her."

Trey looked up, shook his head. "That's his sister. You *have* to kiss your sister. Or your brother."

"Well," said Melissa, seizing the opportunity, "you don't have to kiss anyone, ever. You should never let anyone force you to kiss him, or her. But," she hurried on, "a lot of friends, especially old ones, kiss when they see each other. That's what Ethan and I were doing."

His stood up to soap his lower body and she watched him as he moved down, thorough about his genitals, studiously covering his bruised knees and scraped shins, then seating himself once more to lift his feet above the water line and soap between his toes.

"Here," Melissa offered Garrett, "Trey's getting way ahead of you, let me help with your back." Trey handed her the sponge.

"Anyway, that's—that kind of little, friendly kiss—that's what they call a peck on the cheek. Like this." She half stood, leaning over the side of the tub to kiss both boys. "Okay?" They nodded. "Everyone's really friendly here in Sydonia, aren't they?"

Both boys nodded again, watching her.

"Aunt Rita and Uncle Dave. Aunt Della and Uncle Tony. Aunt Kat. Ethan."

She studied Garrett's soapy back, helped him to stand. "I like Sydonia a lot. So tomorrow," said Melissa, smiling brightly, looking from son to son, "let's go visit the school. It's time to get you back in school, don't you think?"

Neither child answered. They knew this was one of those questions adults asked that you were not supposed to answer.

"I thought we agreed about this," Ray said. "No telling anyone!"

"But it's Webb!" Gladys said. "And once I saw the place, once I thought about water, I thought we might need help. And I didn't want to be talking about it long-distance!"

"No," said Ray. "So instead he's calling and blabbing on about the Good Lord making things nice and leafy. Like someone tapping the line wouldn't know what that meant!"

They were outside, walking down their drive toward the road to the highway. Gladys had checked for mail when she drove in, but it hadn't arrived, so they walked to the mailbox because sometimes walking helped ease Ray's pain. And because they thought it was safer to discuss growing marijuana only when they were outside. They stuck to the road because Gladys was wearing running shoes and Ray had on hiking boots with shock-absorbing inserts.

"What's all that with the Good Lord?" Gladys queried. "Is he born again?"

"Don't try to change the subject," Ray said. "We're talking about why you told Webb when you agreed not to tell anyone."

"Well, I think we're talking about Webb," Gladys responded. "Maybe all that God reference is some kind of code, did you ever think of that?"

Ray glared at her for a second, then returned his attention to the rutted drive. "We need to blade this thing," he muttered.

"Now who's changing the subject?"

He hated when she teased him while he was irritated. He didn't like his irritation dismissed that way. "Gladys, what if he tells someone? One of his boys, say, or one of those peach growers at those meetings."

"Ray, it's Webb. Webb doesn't tell anybody anything! Listen to me." She put her hands on his shoulders to stop his walking and make him look at her, and she stood there even though his eyes narrowed and he looked down: first to the hand on his right shoulder then to the hand on his left. "I was scared," she said. "When I finally put the plants in the ground, I got scared that there wouldn't be enough rain, or the drainage irrigation wouldn't work after all this time—"

"One year."

"One year we've been here, but how many since we planted anything out there? And if we needed help, who would we call? Wouldn't it be Webb?"

He looked away, and she dropped her hands. "We agreed," he said. "We wouldn't tell anyone. Ever. Because you never know who might have trouble with the law, or need to put pressure on us or something. Gladys"—and now he looked directly at her— "what would happen if we had real trouble, if one of us had to go to jail?" He was sorry the second he said it, seeing the fear in her eyes. They had discussed it often, but it remained a nightmare.

"Well, I guess in prison you'll have to trade sex for pot to relieve your pain." She gave a short laugh. "But you won't have to worry about rainfall."

If she could force a joke, he could force a chuckle. "No one else. Promise me."

"I promise," she said. "And Webb promised, too. But honey, I'll tell you something else." They resumed their walking.

"He misses you. That's why he called. You boys are going to have to figure out how to say you care about each other, or he's never going to shut up about the leafy goodness of the Lord."

Chapter 9

"C'mon, Christie, I know you're holding the page." Melissa tossed her pencil onto the pile of papers that covered the rolltop and glared at the logo proofs stuck to the wall. "I can send the art today, we're all set."

"I can't promise anything," Christie said. "We can put it on the calendar, but the writer's already submitted the story, I don't know if they'll rework it to include your race. That's editorial's call."

"Yeah. I want it boxed."

"Boxed?"

"The sidebar," Melissa said. "You can print the release verbatim. It's chatty and ends with our phone and e-mail."

"I can promise you that I'll talk to editorial."

"I'm sending separations," Melissa said. "Electronically. And I'll e-mail the release again. That way you can print it out and walk it over to your editor."

"They asked about you at the Ladies Farm," Ethan told Webb. "Told me to bring you over for supper."

His father grimaced. "I'm not much for socializing."

"Really? I never guessed." Ethan shook his head, reached for his soda. His father lunched primarily on hard-boiled eggs and sandwiches thick with lunch meat and cheese. Dinner was almost identical. Ethan drank slowly, then set the can back on the table. "They asked how you were doing. I didn't know what to say."

Webb looked around, then shrugged.

"Dad, look at you. You're living on junk, you're locked away on this farm. And now you're talking about not talking anymore. What's that about?"

His father shrugged again, and for a moment Ethan thought he wasn't going to answer.

"I don't have much to say anymore. That's all."

"Maybe you're just grieving for Mom."

"Oh, will you—the TV's right there if you want to watch Oprah."

For a second, Ethan recalled his friends' complaints that their parents never turned off the television. Old people ran the thing without stop, according to those friends. They watched CNN, the Weather Channel, and Oprah. They watched *Nightline* from bed. They watched the *Today Show* and *Good Morning America* and the noon news. According to Ethan's friends, it saved their parents from talking to each other. But his dad was sitting in silence.

"I wanted to win best bushel," Webb said.

"Best bushel?"

"You know. At Peach Fest."

"But you've won that before," Ethan said. "And you've got one orchard. You still could. The hail hit everyone."

Webb nodded, offered no argument. "I figured I'd sell."

"Sell the bushel? Sell the orchard," Ethan said. "Sell the orchards. Well, hell, why didn't you say that? You could sell. I'd help you. So would the others." He looked around. "Though it might be nice to keep the house. If you could." He had no idea of his father's finances, other than that there had never been any money, and there was no indication of any now.

"Then you could move on down to Austin," Ethan continued. "Or to Houston. With Wade." He grinned. "Go fishing down in the gulf. Take one of those cruises through the Panama Canal."

"I was thinking I'd give you all the money. You boys."

"Gee, Dad, we were thinking we'd have to kill you for the Dyer fortune!" His father raised an eyebrow. At least he still knows a joke, Ethan thought. "Dad, you're not . . . I mean, you're okay, aren't you?"

Now his father actually laughed. Ethan didn't know how anxious he'd been until his father's laughter released the knot in his stomach.

"I'm old and slow," Webb said. "Not much good on a farm. Not without a family to help out."

"Dad, you never . . . you and Mom said you wanted us to go to school. To go—"

Webb nodded. "I'm just saying, this is a family business, it belongs in the hands of some family." He shook his head. "Not my family. Not many, if you look at what's happening around here: quarter horses, subdivisions."

"Okay, so you want to sell," Ethan said. There was an odd letdown in his father not pressuring him to return to the family farm, but he let that pass. No future in that disappointment, Ethan was sure. "Uh, Dad?" Webb looked at him. "Did anyone tell you I'm in the real estate business?"

Webb inclined his head. "I'm talking to you, aren't I?"

"I believe this is the most we've ever talked," Ethan said. "I mean, I can help you, or we can list this thing with someone local. But, Dad," Ethan leaned forward, avoiding contact with his sandwich, "what are you planning?" He studied his father. "You got a girlfriend?"

"One of us should," Webb replied.

"Hey, Dad, that would be great. Is it—"

Webb was already shaking his head in disgust at his son's gullibility.

"Well, then"—Ethan felt himself coloring—"what the hell's going on? Where are you going?"

His father nodded toward a stack of fliers and magazines piled on one corner of the table. Ethan saw nothing at first, then pulled the pamphlet that sat on top. "Brothers in Trust?" He unfolded the pamphlet. "What is this?"

"It's where I'm heading." For the first time that afternoon, his father smiled. "I always wanted real brothers."

"The way we're doing this," Melissa told the vendor, "I need a vendor who stocks enough shirts that if we up the quantity by two-thirds the week of, you can handle it."

"How many?"

"I think this will go to six thousand," Melissa said. "But I want a commitment for ten if we get it."

"I can't do it," the vendor said. "Not and get them to you for Friday morning."

"What about Saturday morning?" Melissa asked.

"Nah. Not at that price."

"Even if we did all extra-large for the overage?"

"Look—what'd you say your name is?"

"Melissa."

"Look, Melissa, I don't know anyone in Fort Worth who can do that kind of turnaround at that price. Unless you've got some guy in a garage who's got access to a big setup and a big family."

Melissa had heard this part before. She had already called Dallas and Austin, assuming no one in Fort Worth could handle the order. Then she'd switched gears and started looking for someone who'd be excited by the size of the order.

She took a breath.

"What if we pay for the six thousand in advance?"

"The whole thing? Shirts and printing?"

"Shirts."

"And half the printing."

"Half the printing." Melissa smiled. I still got it, she thought. She fumbled through her notes till she found Shane's number. "Hi!" she said when he answered. "Go lean on your friend Johnny."

Della looked from the stack of boxed parts to Kirk Hilgon's assessing gaze. "How long do you think this is going to take?" she asked.

"You mean, how much will this cost?"

She grinned. "No. I mean, will you be joining us for lunch or lunch and dinner?"

"All day, then." He motioned with the instruction package in his hand. "You mind if I set up my worktable on that patio?"

"No problem," Della said, thinking that he flattered the concrete apron that bordered the sliding glass doors of the workout shed. "There's an outlet behind those bushes."

"Listen," he said, "I'll come find you once I get these parts put together. Then we can set the thing down exactly the way you want it." He looked around. "Kind of odd, working in a place with all these mirrors."

"Takes a lot of confidence," Della said, putting a hand to her hair and smiling at him in their reflection. "You must work out, the shape you're in."

He grinned. "Every now and then."

His face was lopsided, craggy-looking, with a square chin and a wide bottom lip that repeated the shape.

"You know," she invited, "we've got a yoga teacher who's starting a power yoga class next month. You might want to check it out."

"Power yoga." Kirk shook his head. "Sounds mighty cerebral."

"Disciplined strength," Della advised.

"And do you do power yoga?" His eyes seemed to take in everything and Della found herself growing warm.

"Not yet."

"Too bad," Kirk said. "You almost had me sold."

"I'll be in my office," she told him, shaking her head.

"I know you get the hots for anything that wears a tool belt," Rita advised when Della wandered back to the salon. "But don't you think you better let that boy work?"

Della grinned. "Caught me."

Rita stared at her. "You having a hot flash or what? You are really red!"

Della walked over to Rita's station. "Anyone coming in?"

"Nah. Not for another twenty minutes."

Della seated herself in the chair. "Why don't you trim my hair?"

"You're not serious."

"About trimming my hair?"

Rita shook her head, then snapped out the smock and wrapped it around her friend. "He's at least ten years younger than you."

"Thirteen," Della said. "It's just for fun."

"Doesn't sound like fun for Tony," Rita said from behind her. Della smiled but didn't reply. She had never thought about it before, but it was funny how many mirrored walls adorned the Ladies Farm. Rita snipped and scolded, reminding her about Tony's fragile ego and his eager devotion.

Della, meanwhile, thought how odd it was that she and Tony sneaked off to the workout room frequently but never met each other here in the salon. We'll have to try that, she thought, watching Rita work. These chairs.

*   *   *

Melissa remembered Earl Westerman, Gladys's nephew, as a moony middle-schooler who lived with his aunt and uncle across the river and communicated with her brother Hugh via notes clipped to a cable-and-pulley rig the two boys strung across the Nolan. It didn't surprise her that he had turned into a computer jockey, but she had a hard time picturing him as a self-appointed king of tchotchkes.

"Congratulations," she said to him. "A new wife and a new baby."

"Yeah." She thought she could hear him blush. "He's a pretty good boy. We're renting a small place in town, but we're planning to build out near Aunt Gladys and Uncle Ray so they can spend time with him."

"That's nice," Melissa said. She had already heard several versions of the story, how Darlene had contracted to be a gestational carrier but conceived Earl's child instead, then gotten in a trick because the intended parents needed a stem-cell donor for their sick child. She couldn't imagine Darlene, who had always been the talk of Sydonia, with Earl.

"Listen, Earl, I hear you're the master of getting things," she said.

"Some things. Imported stuff, mostly. What can I do for you?"

"You know what a luminaria is?"

"Well, sure, but you just put those together, you know. Paper bags, a little sand, candles. I can get you all that. Y'all having a par—"

"I need ten thousand of them. Already assembled. And no paper bags. Tin cans or something."

"Tin cans."

"You know," said Melissa. "Punched out with holes so the light comes through in a pattern. But really cheap, Earl."

"Is this for that run?"

"Midnight Peaches. That's what we're calling it."

"Ten thousand?"

"One every other meter, both sides of the course."

"It'd be a lot cheaper with paper sacks," Earl said in his affable way.

"Recent weather notwithstanding, we'll be setting these burning candles on roads lining fields of tinder. We don't really want five thousand candles in paper sacks."

"You might not want candles."

"We haven't placed any orders, Earl. But if there's a flat enough bottom and weighty enough tin and they don't cost more than a penny or two—"

"Whoa!"

"Well, three pennies, then."

"Not likely," Earl said. "But let me see what I can find."

Chapter 10

"We'll bring you a tray," Kat offered when Melissa said she was stuck on the phone through lunch.

Melissa hadn't given much thought to communal dining when she headed for the Ladies Farm. At first, breakfast, lunch, and dinner had charmed her; then the frequently voiced opinions about the boys' diet and table manners started getting to her. Now, a soggy burger and fries in her car at the Dairy Queen sounded like heaven. Lunch on a tray, by contrast, sounded like homage to her late mother conceived by her misguided friends.

"Oh, thanks," said Melissa. "I think I'll get something when I go get the boys from school."

Kat nodded, headed to the kitchen. Melissa, feeling like an ingrate, turned back to the phone. She told herself she'd be especially patient at dinner, let Rita cut Garrett's meat, let Kat show Trey how to wash his hands, as if they really needed that help. She studied her planner, wondered how long she could ignore the call from her lawyer, picked up the phone and called Erica Lynch. They worked up a schedule for Erica's day in Sydonia, adding five more tasks to Melissa's list. "I'm glad we'll get to meet," Erica said. "Ethan called last night and he jabbered on and on about you."

"I hope that's a good thing," Melissa responded with a laugh.

"I don't know anyone who doesn't think Ethan's a good thing," Erica said.

Melissa ended with more assurances of how much she was looking forward to Erica's arrival, then leaned back in her chair and closed her eyes. I'm so stupid, thought Melissa. As if marriage would take Erica out of the picture. What's marriage anyway? She balanced there, half reclined, and listened to herself breathe.

"Knock knock."

Melissa jerked around, fearing one of the ladies bearing the dreaded tray. Instead, it was Ethan. She pointed to the phone. "That was Erica. She's coming in next week."

"Great," he said. He stood in the doorway, inclined his head toward the living room behind him. "They said you were skipping lunch, but I'm on my way to get a sandwich. C'mon with me."

She started to shake her head, then changed her mind. "Could we just swing through the Dairy Queen and eat in the truck?"

They ate in the kitchen, Kirk sliding in next to Rita, Kat and Della facing them over the pasta.

"Penne," Della said to Kirk as he handed his plate to her.

"That's my favorite pasta," he said. "Tricolor penne."

Rita handed him the basket of crostini. "Not many men have a favorite pasta," she said. "Usually, it's a favorite beer. Favorite barbecue."

"Favorite *Terminator* movie," Kat chimed in.

"Uh. Let's see: Shiner Bock, Barbecue Boys, and *Terminator II*." Kirk grinned at Kat. "But I still love my tricolor penne. Especially like this."

Della beamed. It had been her idea to skip the red and dress the pasta with garlic, oil, and cheese.

"Well," said Rita, "we'll have to pass the compliment along to the Barbecue Boys. Won't we?" She smirked at Della.

Kat turned to Kirk. "How're we coming on that chin dip?"

He looked startled for a second, then smiled. "Is that what you call that contraption?"

"Assisted chin dip," Della corrected. Purchase of workout equipment was her specialty and usually involved a struggle with Kat, who kept the books.

"Well, I got it assembled," Kirk said. "Soon as we're done here, Della's going to show me exactly where to place it, and then I'll start drilling holes. Should be a few more hours." He grinned at Della. "Assisted chin dip! Sounds like party food."

Della grinned back. He had dark eyes that warmed with his smile.

"Expensive party food," Kat grumbled.

"Here," Rita said, passing the pasta bowl to Kirk once again. "You need your strength."

"It'll pay off," Della promised, turning reluctantly to Kat. The assisted chin was the last piece they needed to complete the workout center at the shed. Della took some satisfaction that the shed, once Pauline's domain for ceramics and crafts classes, had maintained profitability. They had brought in a series of crafts teachers, settling finally on a woman who commuted from Keene, nearby; but the center of activity had shifted to fitness.

"That's a good thing," Kat rejoined. "We're still paying on the loan for the shed," she told Kirk.

He nodded. Della watched him taking it all in. He's quick, she thought. He's been in business for himself for a long time; he understands finance.

She studied his hands, scrubbed clean before he sat down for lunch. As his fingers raised and lowered his fork, wrapped around his glass, rested lightly on the oak tabletop, Della found herself imagining his touch: the authority of his strength, the gentle certainty of his grasp. Get a grip! she ordered herself, then giggled at her own pun.

Rita looked up. Della felt herself grow warm for the hundredth time, but Kat and Kirk continued to exchange opinions about depreciation of work vehicles. Sheepishly, Della picked up her own fork and unenthusiastically speared the penne. One more benefit for Tony, she told herself. Maybe I'll lose a few pounds.

"He's joining a monastery?" Melissa asked. They were eating cheeseburgers in the truck's front seat, watching the river in the city park.

"It's not exactly a monastery. I mean, they're not Catholics."

"But they take a vow of silence?" She swished a fry through the plastic thimble of ketchup and popped it into her mouth. "Why would they do that?"

"To cleanse the universe of hateful sound."

When Ethan shook his head, his dark hair lifted lightly, then settled back. A little girly, Melissa thought, if he weren't so wiry. "You do anything to your hair to make it that glossy?" she asked.

"My hair?" The shake again. "Nah." He grinned. "If you were

me, would you leave mousse in the bathroom for your father to find?"

"Not if my father was your father. Or something." She shrugged, looked out the open window at the municipal boat ramp. "Hateful sound?"

"It's sort of a speak-no-evil commune," Ethan said. "They farm. They teach. They build houses. They just don't talk unless they have to."

"But . . . is it all men?"

"Uh, I think that's what *brothers* refers to."

"Very funny. I mean, are they all single?"

"No. They're all widowed or divorced."

"I think that's single. Oh!" She threw her head back and laughed. "Oh!"

"You want to share that?"

"It's the Ladies Farm! For men!"

He cocked his head to one side. "You know, I think . . . I mean . . . you're right!" He gulped his soda. "That makes it sound almost harmless."

"Well, Ethan, what's harmful about it? Basically it sounds as if he distributes his earthly goods a little early, takes a vow of silence—or less noise—and spends his time helping others and praying. They do pray, don't they?"

He nodded.

"Then why are you so worried?"

"It's like he's giving up. I mean, why does he want to go off and take care of strangers? Doesn't he think he does enough good here?"

"Ethan! He's lonely."

"Well, then, why doesn't he go live with Wade and his family? They've got plenty of room!"

"I notice you didn't say he should come to Austin and live with you."

"Because there's no one to take care of him," Ethan said. "Nothing for him to do. He'd just go crazy, living with me." He grimaced. "Even if I moved out of my garage apartment."

"Might interfere with your action," Melissa suggested. She smiled gently, to make sure he knew she was teasing.

Ethan gave a short laugh. "More like my no-action. You know

how many women are attracted to guys who've gone broke before they're thirty?"

She pictured the dark house in Portland, the big one in California. "We've all gone broke, Ethan!"

"Is that what happened?"

"What?"

"Between you and Greg? He lost his job, went broke, made you poor and miserable?"

"You think I'd leave him over money?" The remainder of her cheeseburger sat on greasy paper in her lap; the drink in her hand sweated onto the floorboard.

"No. That's the thing. I don't think you left him over money, and you said there was no other woman. So what happened? Did you fall in love?"

She shook her head. "I told you—"

"You told me it was ordinary. But Melissa"—he set his drink in the holder, turned toward her—"you know there's nothing ordinary about you."

"I . . . it's just a little soon to talk about, Ethan." She felt her eyes filling.

"Soon how?" he pressed. "Too soon since you left him? Too soon since we've started . . . become friends again."

"We never stopped being friends," she said lightly. "We just resumed where we left off. At least I hope so."

"Yeah." Now he looked out the window.

"You okay? I wish I had better insight about your dad."

He straightened up, turned the key to start the engine. "It's okay."

"You don't sound okay." Bewildered, she stared at him. "Did I miss something?"

He glanced at her a second, then looked over his shoulder as he backed the truck onto the pavement. "I don't expect you to solve my problems with my dad." He drove forward on the road out of the park. "I just figured you'd trust me back."

Rita, who had run her own shop for years at the Ladies Farm, had been the last to realize the joy of turning the budget and accounting over to Kat. Actually, she had turned over only the accounting. There had never been any budgeting until Kat started reviewing her finances.

For her part, Kat found her monthly meeting with Rita a reassuring ritual. Week in, week out, no matter the season, no matter the economy, no matter the state of the world, women visited Rita. They came from Sydonia, from all over Sydon County, from Fort Worth, even from Arlington and Dallas. Some returned yearly, for a facial and a new style; others appeared quarterly. Even when the rooms at the Ladies Farm were empty, the salon, like the classes, was full.

Now, though, even revenues didn't assuage Rita's gloom. "They get so close, so close," said Rita, shaking her head. "They finally move in together. And she finds a way to screw it up. With a tool belt!"

Kat turned from the computer, where she had revised the annualized projections for the salon by product and by provider, since Rita maintained an army of part-timers. "She's just enjoying a little flirtation. He's cute. I thought you'd approve."

"And I thought you'd stop her!" Rita, whose appearance over the past year had evolved from punk black spikes to shoulder-length blond in a Farah Fawcett update, tossed her head and fluffed her hair. "Anyway, I agree he's cute. I've just never been one to stop at flirtation. I had dozens of them, and I'm telling you she's just a moonlight stroll away from hopping into bed with that boy."

Kat arched an eyebrow at Rita. "She's not you. I've known Della for years." Kat shook her head to clear the memories. "She's not serious."

"Serious has nothing to do with it. Serious fun, maybe."

Kat supposed Rita, since daughter Darlene had fled to the Big Bend, had been forced out of managing her children's lives. Now there's no one left, figured Kat. "This doesn't sound like you," Kat said.

"I've grown up." Rita asserted. "Well, Dave made me grow up," she conceded to Kat's skeptical expression. "Anyway, I wouldn't risk what Dave and I have now for some boy, no matter how handy he is. And no matter what I might have done when I was single. Or married to Dave the first time. You talk to her."

"Della? About Kirk Hilgon? I don't think so. We need to get back to the books."

Rita shook her head. "Don't blow me off. I'm telling you, she's trying to drive Tony away. She's scared."

"Of what?"

Rita grinned. "She marries Tony, she's never going to fuck anyone else ever again."

Now Kat was the one who laughed. "So instead of remarrying
Tony and living forever with the one she loves—the father of her
surviving son, the man who would do anything for her—you
think she's going to sleep with Sydonia's favorite handyman?"

Rita nodded. Then she played her best card.

"Of course, after Tony stomps off to Fort Worth, it'll take
months to get Della's attention back to this place." Rita waved a
hand toward Della's office. "She'll be too busy, between riding her
boy toy and agonizing over Tony's departure. You know." She
grinned. "The agony and the ecstasy."

First he stretched. Rolling silently off the edge of the bed, he
knelt on the floor on all fours and pushed his hips back, trying to
visualize himself as a cat. Sometimes that was all it took, but Ray
could tell this night would take more. And now he had to pee.
Ray had found that Gladys would sleep through his rolling off the
bed and most floor stretches, but she jerked awake the second he
stood and walked. Not that he could stand now, anyway.

He held the stretch for as long as he could, forcing himself to
breathe normally. Then, taking care to follow the path of the
woven runner, he crawled to the bedroom door on all floors,
thankful that they had never been a couple who slept with the
bedroom door closed.

Why would we, he asked himself, crawling through the hall-
way. No kids. No live-ins. He tried the cat stretch again. Ray recalled waking to the breeze on the porch in Cuba, reaching over
and stroking up under those cotton shirts Gladys used to sleep in.

Kids would have brought their own rewards, but Ray secretly
didn't regret childlessness. He just hated it for Gladys's sake. He
hadn't realized the deprivation until Earl had shown up, sent by
Ray's exasperated sister and her bewildered husband. I guess we
closed the bedroom door then, Ray thought, but he didn't recall
that. Must have been automatic.

He needed heavy furniture to help him stand, so he crawled all
the way to the living room sofa before he got himself to a kneeling
position. Ray braced himself there, both hands clutching the sofa
arm while he caught his breath and stretched from the hips some

more. He placed his left foot, then his right, flat on the floor and pulled with his hands.

"Oooof!" he grunted, low as possible, while he straightened. Thankfully, he remembered to pull the afghan off the couch before he padded softly to the door. He gave himself credit for keeping latch and hinges working soundlessly as he slipped onto the porch.

Ray had taken to keeping some medication in a wooden box nailed atop the wide porch rail where it met the house. He could take the painkiller, which would let him sleep now but keep him fuzzy till noon. He could take more anti-inflammatory, but he had already exceeded a day's dosage. There was a muscle relaxant, but it never did much, which confirmed his suspicion that it had little effect on his joints, or the nerves pinched by his collapsing spine. Then there was the fatty, safe in a green jar that used to hold liniment. He glanced back at the closed door. If he smoked it off the end of the porch, it wouldn't get to the bedroom at the back of the other end of the house.

He stumbled forward, an old man wrapped in an afghan over his shorts and T-shirt, shivering in the high-desert air. A cripple causing endless pain to his wife. When he got to the corner of the porch, he reached down and opened his shorts, aiming for the little stone spill below the outside spigot. An old man who could barely take a piss in the middle of the night.

Chapter 11

The ladies talked about giving Erica Lynch the Babe Didrikson Zaharias room, but it was the only handicap-access one, and they needed to keep it free for the weekend. So they put her upstairs in the Governor Ann, from which she could see across the river to the hill and the Hutto house.

"This is gorgeous," she exclaimed to Melissa and Ethan, who had escorted her upstairs. Erica, her red hair gleaming in sunlight, stood profiled at the window as Ethan slipped her suitcase onto the luggage rack and Melissa stared from the doorway. "So green, down by the water."

"Yeah," Melissa said. "We water it with hail." She caught the look between them, but Melissa didn't care. "Look, get settled, I'll be downstairs whenever you're ready." She said it with an impartial smile, without indicating whether she expected Ethan to stay or to accompany her downstairs.

"Oh! I'm ready now," Erica said. "Just let me get my maps, and I'm good to go."

"I'm leaving it to the two of you," Ethan said as they clattered back downstairs. "I'm meeting Dad over at the real estate office—they're listing his house with me as broker. Courtesy."

"Your dad's selling his farm?" Erica asked.

Melissa knew her rush of superiority was petty, but she needed the boost.

"Orchard," Ethan said. "It'll take at least a sixpack to explain it."

"We can do margaritas out back," Melissa offered. "After we get back tonight."

"I'll have to take a rain check." Erica looked back up the staircase at Melissa, then down at Ethan. "But I expect the whole saga once you get back to Austin."

"It's a date," Ethan promised. "After Peach Fest." The three stood on the landing. "Till then I'm dividing my time between the orchard, the peaches, and the run." He leaned forward and gave Erica a quick kiss on the cheek. "See you in town," he promised.

He smiled impartially at Melissa, touched her shoulder, and was gone. Tag, you're it, she thought.

Erica and her husband, Peter, did not have children. Peter traveled. Erica traveled. Erica and Ethan had hung out all through their time at the University of Texas, sharing a house one time with three other guys. Erica, Melissa decided, was a guy's girl. A beautiful, beer-swilling tomboy who, in her mesmerizing, hip-slinging stride, made her own way and made no demands.

Erica would never order her husband to stop wearing lace panties, Melissa thought. Erica would laugh about it with her friends. And her friends, Ethan among them, would judge her generous of spirit. A good sport.

Melissa concluded these things in the time it took to drive to the start/finish line in front of the courthouse.

"Why this side?" Erica asked after they drove, then walked, around the courthouse. Melissa had filled her in on where the booths for Peach Fest would cover the generous, tree-shaded square and three of the four rerouted, bordering streets.

Melissa shrugged. "This is the front. Why?"

Erica pointed. "If we start there, at the back, route them through the park along the river"—she pointed to her map—"we can bring them back along that long, shallow rise, and as they finish they dump directly into the center of the food court."

"It'll be midnight," Melissa said.

"Exactly. And your other booths will be shut down. But if there's a party all evening, the food vendors might find it worth their while."

"Well, we've got the stage on that side, so there'll be entertainment till almost midnight."

"So why separate your runners from the action?"

"You ought to do this for a living," Melissa said.

As they drove to the park, Melissa told Erica about the luminarias. "That's pretty ambitious," Erica said.

"But it's the deal: you know, the contract with the runners. You pay your money, you come in droves, we give you a memorable, enjoyable experience. And a T-shirt."

"Fanny packs don't work," Erica said.

"Nor wristbands."

"Or gimme caps."

"Or athletic socks."

"Or shoelaces."

"You gave out shoelaces?" Melissa asked.

"Well, you gave out socks!"

"Nothing like a T-shirt," Melissa assured Erica.

"Nothing," Erica confirmed.

They walked through the park to the footbridge that crossed to the ball fields on the other side of the Nolan. Erica knelt, studied her watch, looked at the bridge. "This'll look great with lights," she said. Then she stood, pointed to the parking loop. "We'll break the five K off here, so they'll get the full effect of the bridge. The ten K will cross, they'll loop along that commercial strip there"—she pointed—"then cross back on the highway bridge."

"We don't have any permits for closing the highway," Melissa said.

"Just one lane. At midnight."

Melissa nodded.

"I'll get them." They headed back to the car. "And line up police escort, if you want."

"Our sheriff's kind of counting on the honor," Melissa said.

"Oh, that's great. He can ride in the pace car with the race director; I'll line up troopers for the highway part." Erica started the car and they rode toward the highway bridge.

"We don't really have a race director," Melissa said. "Unless you—"

"Oh no!" Erica said. "I've got too much to do. You should do it; or someone from the committee." She smiled a little, watching the road. Her hands on the wheel looked tan and strong, almost mannish, but her nails sported a French manicure, with white tips glinting in the sunlight. "Give it to someone who's worked hard or paid a lot; it's an honor."

Seeing Erica's rings, yellow gold, a plain band and a solitaire of some authority, Melissa twisted her own bare fingers. "Sure," she said, unable even to take offense at Erica's assumption that she didn't know that the race-director title was an honor.

"Once we've mapped this, I'll go back and measure. I'll make my adjustments, give you the course tonight. That way, you can go over it, I'll stick around tomorrow morning and make whatever changes you want." She grinned. "Then we're done till race day."

"That's it?"

"This part of it," Erica said. "Why?"

"Oh. I don't know," Melissa mumbled. "I guess . . . I mean I've done plenty of races, I know you can do most of it from Austin. I just hadn't thought it through. Let's get lunch, huh? I'll take you over to the lunch counter at the pharmacy. That's the local hot spot."

Erika wrinkled her nose. "Any chance we could get Mexican? I was in Nebraska all last week, and I'm just craving it."

"I know. I lived in Portland for a year, and I thought I would die for decent chips."

They went to Miguel's, where they ordered the special—one enchilada, one soft taco, beans, rice—at the counter, then sat at a picnic table on a patio adorned with chili-pepper lights and papier-mâché parrots. A waitress—Miguel's niece—brought them iced tea, salsa, and chips in a red plastic basket. They dove into the chips without a word.

Finally Erica spoke. "What were you doing in Portland?"

Melissa, on the theory that Erica would know whatever Ethan knew, gave her all the details of the crash in Silicon Valley. She talked about how Greg lost his job and found something in Portland; how they sold their house in California and moved to a smaller one, where she became a full-time events planner and the boys went to public school.

"Big change," said Erica. "We've gone through something like that in Austin. Makes you feel lucky not to have kids yet."

Melissa nodded.

"It's hard to hold a marriage together with all that," Erica said.

"Yeah." Melissa took another chip and dipped it in the salsa. "No."

"No what?"

"No. My husband and I did not split up over money. Or the kids. Or another woman. Or another man." She bit into the chip.

"Hey!" Erica held up a hand. "I wasn't trying—"

"No, I know you weren't. But you're . . . I mean, tell me what you would do if this happened to you."

The niece returned with their orders and a warmer filled with flour tortillas.

Melissa reached for her fork, realized she was still holding the half-eaten chip, and dropped it on her plate. Erica sat calmly, alert, watching her.

"One day I drove Trey to soccer. The weather was warm, for Portland, and it was almost sunny, which meant that contractors were working furiously, trying to get as much done as they could before the next rain," she recited. "So, close to the soccer field, there were two or three homes getting new roofs, and a bunch of us ran over roofing nails, which must have been scattered in the street. No one realized at first, of course; this is something we figured out later, comparing notes. When it turned out no one could drive car pool the next morning, because everyone had flats." Melissa smiled weakly. "An epidemic of crippled SUVs."

Erica smiled, picked up her fork, and sampled the enchilada.

Melissa took a flour tortilla and slathered it with refried beans and pico de gallo. The combination of searing pico and warm, mild refritos strengthened her resolve. "No problem, I assured my friends. I'll just take Greg's car. Because Greg, good citizen that he is, thought it was his duty to bike to work whenever the weather cleared."

"I had Trey and Garrett. And Susie Robinson from next door. And the Rubenstein kids from down the block. And Seth Rubenstein's model space station, anchored on a plywood board that had to sit flat for the perilous journey to Lewis and Clark Elementary School."

Now she moved to the enchilada: chicken, sour cream, and white cheese. She was sweating, despite the shade over the patio.

"This is so good," said Erica, who managed the burrito with elegant efficiency, as well as both hands.

"So I rearranged the trunk," Melissa said. "Mostly just pushed the stuff to the back. But we couldn't have that big duffel bouncing onto the landing module, crunching off an energy spoke." Melissa grinned. "Solar energy, of course. Power for eternity."

Melissa sampled more of the enchilada, spearing a bite of chicken and tortilla, swishing it around in the cheese and sour cream before popping it into her mouth. "Oooh," she said. "And I was ready to settle for tuna salad on crustless white."

"I notice the Ladies Farm said they have a workout room," Erica said. "So I figure I'll atone this evening."

Melissa nodded.

"So there was a duffel."

"A duffel," Melissa confirmed. "A sports bag. And it was a modest, but entirely safe neighborhood, so I set it by the side of the driveway, secured the space station in Greg's trunk, and drove off. When I got back, the Triple A was there to change the tire, so I put Greg's car in the garage and let them change my tire in the driveway. Then I was late for work, so I just threw the duffel into the back of the Lexus and drove off."

"And that's when you learned he was an ax murderer?" Erica prompted. "By the head in the duffel bag?"

"Good wife that I was, I took it inside when I got home. Greg was working late. It was laundry night. I was determined that my boys learn how to do household chores. So they helped me sort the laundry into stacks on the floor: whites, lights, darks."

" 'Go get Daddy's sports bag,' I said. 'Let's get his smelly old socks and put them in the wash.' Only, the next thing I saw was Trey, lifting out garters and a silk teddy. 'This must be yours,' he said. 'Where's Daddy's?' "

"What a nightmare!" Erica shook her head.

This is key, thought Melissa. She's always on your side. Instantly.

Melissa loved this part of the story. The twist, the shock. Not that she had told many people. But there was always shock.

"So I laughed, and told Trey he was right, and took it all from Trey. Later I put the stuff back in the duffel. And back in the trunk. And then"—she smiled faintly—"I followed him."

"I don't blame you."

"No, of course not," Melissa said. "We would all do the same thing, follow our husbands because we found sexy women's clothing. Only," she paused, "there was no woman." She held Erica's gaze.

"Oh my God!"

Melissa nodded. "There was a post office box, which he checked every few days. There were bookmarked Web sites that took only a second to find once I figured out his password. And at the very back of our closet, the closet in our home, behind the trunk where he stored his hunting rifles, was a second trunk. Full of clothes. Silky, sexy, virginally white. More ruffles than I could wear in a lifetime."

"What did you do?"

"Made the boys a picnic for the tree house. Told Trey to try doing his math homework there, by the light of the battery-powered lantern, just like Abe Lincoln. And then I climbed down from the tree and asked my husband how long he had been a cross-dresser."

Erica shook her head. The burrito was gone and she had a free hand with which to gesture, but she could only lift it uncertainly, then drop it back to the table.

Melissa nodded to show she got the meaning. "So there we were, alone in the house while he told me how he'd been doing this since his teens, fascinated by women's clothing—stockings, panties, nighties—all his life. That he had never told anyone, ever. So he didn't see why he needed to tell me. Ever."

"What'd he do with the duffel?"

"Turns out that he did meet a few buddies in Silicon Valley. They'd dress up, get together."

"Did they . . . you know, were they gay?"

Melissa shook her head. "Not Greg. At least that's what he said. One guy, Lee, was, but even his partner didn't know about this little hobby."

"What?"

Melissa nodded. "I know. But that's what he said, anyway. And I believe him, mostly because he told me so much. I don't think he hid anything, because he knew it didn't matter anymore. And I could hear the boys, outside—you know, everything's screened up there, and you can leave the windows open and not bother with air conditioning—and all I could think . . ." Melissa took a big gulp of tea, letting the wedge of lime bump against her lips as she slid the ice into her mouth. She crunched, swallowed.

"All I could think was that I wish I had never opened the duffel bag. Or that, if I had opened it, the clothes had turned out to be his girlfriend's. Because then he would have just been unfaithful. Infidelity: that happens all the time. We could have gotten over that."

Chapter 12

"This is your new fitness shrine?" Tony walked around the assisted chin machine, touching the cushioned handles and gazing up at the overhead bar. "I can't believe this took a day to assemble."

"Well, we had to drill holes through the floor and into the concrete to anchor it."

"You let someone drill into your precious floor?" Tony asked. The special, shock-absorbing floor in the workout room had been the subject of a long battle between Kat and Della.

"Well, that's the thing," bragged Della. "This floor is specially designed to fill in around the bolts, even when you're anchoring into the concrete underneath. And you have to be careful when you drill," Della advised. "Kirk says if you do it wrong, you can crack the whole floor."

"Kirk should know," muttered Tony. He touched the lift, which was controlled by placing a pin in a set of weights that acted as ballast. Then he turned, grinning. "Show me how this contraption works."

"Wait!" she commanded, reaching for the pin. "Okay, grab the overhead and step onto the lift."

He obeyed.

"Now chin," she said.

"Too easy," he commented, pulling himself up as the lift assisted him.

"You adjust it," Della said. She pointed to the pin. "Step off, adjust it, get back on."

He followed her instructions, cutting the support by half, and chinned himself easily. Then he stepped off, lowered the lift entirely, and chinned himself without support. As he slid back down to the floor, he looked at Della. "Like that?"

"Show-off."

They heard Flops, who guarded the doorway, rise and stir. "Put your clothes on!" Rita called, pushing Flops back outside as she entered.

"We lock the door when we're doing it in the gym," Tony advised. He looked at Della. "Don't we?"

She leaned over, patted his cheek. "You just keep believing that," she told him, pursing her lips in a kiss.

"It's no wonder we keep running out of towels," Rita drawled. She stopped in front of the assisted chin. "This it?"

Della nodded.

Rita stepped onto the platform, reached for the high bar, lifted herself with no support, and dropped off. "This is great," she said.

Della whirled toward Tony. "Did you guys plan this?"

He shrugged toward Rita. "She gets like this sometimes. Hey," he told Della, "it's not our fault if your zillion-dollar machine has a lift we don't need."

"You need it," said Della. "At least most people do. Very few of us are in your shape." She glanced at both of them. "And it helps you do more reps. Plus," she insisted, "you can do other things."

"I'll bet," said Rita.

"Did you come in just to ridicule?"

"No," said Rita. "I came to see how we're spending all our money. Also to see if you've heard from Melissa."

Della shrugged. "Nope. You want help putting the boys to bed?"

"She put them to bed. Then she went out with that Erica."

"Well she's got the key and the alarm code." Della checked the wall clock. "It's not even ten. They probably just met Ethan somewhere for a beer. Call her cell if you're worried."

"No answer."

Tony, bored with the exchange, made his way to the ab board and started doing crunches. It annoyed Della that he could do hundreds of crunches without breaking a sweat, while she struggled eternally with her midsection. She turned back to Rita. "What's up?"

"Greg called."

"Well, they talk. They're putting the house up for sale. And I'm sure there are things about the boys to discuss. Is that why you were calling her?"

"Something's not right."

Della waited.

"I can tell these things, there was something not right."

"So you want to track down Melissa and tell her her husband called and that something's not right? I think she already knows that part."

"Was he wearing his nightie when he called?" Tony asked, grunting as he continued sitting up and lying back on the board, his feet elevated well above his head.

"Did you tell him?" Rita asked.

"Of course I told him. Didn't you tell Dave?"

"I guess. Anyway, he never calls at night, he always calls during the day. Even when he wants to talk with the boys, he calls her first to find out what time he should call them."

"I'm sure it's okay," Della said.

"Yeah. Well, I'd feel better if she returned the call and told us what's going on."

"I suspect keeping us posted is not top of Melissa's list."

"I think he's found out she put the kids in school."

"I'm sure she told him that," Della said. "Did he say anything about school?"

"No. But I have this feeling."

Della shook her head. "You'd be the first one to tell me to stop worrying. Take your own advice."

"You want me to leave now so you two can go at it, don't you?"

"Lock the door," suggested Tony, as he completed his last crunch. Rita shook her head and left. He swung his legs to the ground and stood up. "One thing about living around here," he told Della, "it's a whole lot easier to work out."

That was exactly what Kirk had said to her just a few hours earlier. He had grabbed the overhead bar on the assisted chin; then, facing the room and suspended full length, he had lifted and lowered his straightened legs. " 'Lot easier to work out, living in a place like this," he had said, suspended in midair with his legs held out in front of him at a right angle.

Now Della studied the device, imagining how strong a man would have to be to have sex while suspended by his arms. Could she straddle him in midair, lifting and lowering herself by pulling on that same upper bar? Could she rest her ankles on the set of handles that protruded from midway down? How, exactly, could the lift be used in that position? she wondered. How strong would I have to be?

"I'm sorry," Melissa told Rita the second time she called. "We're at the Dairy Queen, and by the time I dug the thing out of my purse, it had stopped ringing. I knew you'd call back if there was something about the boys."

"Well, it might be," Rita said.

Melissa snapped her head up and turned away from Erica. "What is it?"

"Your ex called."

"You mean Greg?"

"He's your ex, isn't he?"

"Not quite," Melissa said. "What did he say?"

"Nothing. Just to call," Rita replied.

"He wanted me to call him now?"

"Actually, he said when you get a chance. Call on his cell."

"When I get a chance? What else did he say?"

"Oh, you know, the usual: how am I doing, congratulations on my marriage to Dave and my new grandson, how are Della and Kat, that kind of thing."

Now Melissa turned back to the table and shook her head and rolled her eyes at Erica. "So Greg called, had a pleasant conversation with you, asked that I call him back when I got the chance." Erica chuckled. "Anything else?"

"Nope, that's the full report," said Rita.

"Well, thanks," said Melissa, shaking her head.

"You going to call him?"

"Of course," said Melissa. "I'll give him a call in the morning."

"They're two hours behind us," Rita reminded. "It's just dinnertime there."

"I know," said Melissa. "But Erica and I are going over this map right now. I'll call him tomorrow. Thanks, though. For letting me know."

"Oh, honey, that's the least we can do for you now. If not for your mama, you know I'd still be struggling in someone else's shop."

"I just want you to know I appreciate it," Melissa said quickly, trying to avoid the history of her mother's patronage. "I'll see you in the morning, okay?"

"Sure," Rita said. "Have a good time."

"Thanks. Bye."

Melissa switched the phone off, still shaking her head. "It's as if it's an emergency that Greg called."

Erica grinned. "It's nice that they care about you. Have you told them the whole story?"

"Yes." Melissa frowned. "They're sworn to secrecy, which I think means that they don't tell anyone except their significant others. I was going crazy thinking about it. I had to tell someone."

"It's great that you have them," Erica said. "Three surrogate mothers."

Melissa nodded. "We should get back to the map."

"You know, I won't tell anyone, either," Erica assured her. "Not even Ethan."

"Thanks," Melissa said. "I'm not sure that I even want to keep it secret. I mean, except for the boys, of course. But it's hard to explain why we split up."

"That's crap," Erica said. "You don't owe anyone any explanations."

"Thanks," Melissa said again.

"Except me, of course, if you do anything to Ethan. Then I have to hunt you down and kill you."

"Things here are great," Webb said with a heartiness he didn't feel. "A little dry, these days. That storm was almost the last of our rain."

"Funny," said Gladys. "It's been nice and green out here. Sometimes I think that's what's bugging Ray; just a touch of rain, and he aches all over."

"You ought to see your old place," Webb said. "That Della's

put out pots of geraniums on the balcony, had Kirk Hilgon over to shore up that railing. She—Della—says they sit out on that balcony almost every morning, have a cup of coffee. Can you imagine?"

He heard Gladys sigh. "I guess I can imagine. Ray and I used to do that, now and again. Of course, he was a much earlier riser than I was. Still. We used to sit out in the evenings, before Earl came to live with us. Of course," she said, enunciating very clearly, "once Earl showed up, we had to keep an eye on him, and we couldn't see that much of our lot from the balcony. Pretty much treetops from up there," Gladys assured him. "Not like the view we have here."

"Well that's good to know," Webb said. "About the view being so good out there, I mean."

"I wish you'd come see it for yourself," Gladys said. "Do Ray some good."

"I know what you mean. When Alice took sick, it did her a world of good whenever you showed up. Even just sending Earl over with those cobblers. I mean, she didn't eat much toward the last, but that boy was always real polite, it just cheered her to see someone like that."

"Yes. I know."

Gladys could be short when she wanted, according to Ray. Webb smiled. "I've got the crop," he said. "What's left of it."

"Oh, I know that," Gladys assured him. "It's just . . . I don't know Webb—"

"I'd have to figure out . . . I mean, once the crop's in, I guess." He remembered something else. "Of course, there are other things that need looking after, up here. Around my place, if you get my drift."

"The whole world gets your drift," she teased.

She was quiet for a minute, and Webb imagined her there, thinking. She would be standing in a kitchen, wearing stretch pants, and some sort of flowered top, just the way Alice dressed. He missed having someone to count on like that; he used to close his eyes and picture Alice, and when he'd get back to the house she looked exactly the way he had pictured.

"You know, you couldn't find someone more responsible than Della and Tony. Except maybe Dave, of course."

Webb shook his head. Ray must really be bad, he thought. "I don't know," he said slowly. "I get the feeling those women tell each other everything; no secrets in that group."

"You're probably right," said Gladys.

"My boy Ethan's been staying with me," he mentioned. "It might be a treat for him, looking after everything while I'm away."

"You think Ethan's up to that? Running the orchard? Isn't he in business in Austin?"

"He's taking a break from all that," Webb said. "He'd be glad to get the old man out of the way."

Chapter 13

"Ethan!" Shane called to him across the lot at Dave's shop. "How's tricks? Anything new?"

Ethan shrugged. "Just rolling right along. How about you?"

Shane nodded at a truck, which was up on the lift. "Not rolling anywhere. How long's this going to take?" he called to Dave.

To Ethan's satisfaction, Dave ignored the question. Ethan, stopping for gas on his way to the appraiser's office, felt the need to greet Dave and go inside to pay, even though he could swipe his card at the pump. For his part, Dave seemed willing to handle the transaction personally rather than leave it to his cashier.

Shane wandered behind, hovering over the candy bars and eyeing the two of them.

"Nice haircut," Dave said, handing credit card and receipt to Ethan.

Ethan grinned. "You're married to a talented woman."

Dave, leathery and worn, grinned back. "Tell me something I don't know." He eyed Shane. "How you boys coming on that race?"

"Just great!" Ethan said. "Shane and Melissa have the sponsors lined up, Melissa and Erica, from Austin, have the race under control. There's a mailing going out. Posters. Ads. Gonna happen."

Dave nodded.

"Sure is," chimed Shane. "Melissa and I are corralling sponsors left and right."

Dave looked down at the counter. "I guess I better get your

wheels balanced, then." He looked up, nodded at Ethan. "Thanks for stopping by," Dave said.

Ethan got himself to the appraiser's office and walked through the business of comparables and a friendly exchange about what the orchards might bring with a zoning change.

"A lot of cutting-horse folks moving in from California," the appraiser told him. "That's about the only buyer who wouldn't change the zoning."

"Life was easier a year ago," Ethan said.

"You mean, some dot-com billionaire or bond trader looking for a ranch away from Dallas or Austin would sweep the place up in a heartbeat?"

"Something like that," Ethan replied. He thanked the appraiser and asked him to call when the report was ready.

Outside, the sun glinted off the cars parked around the square. The bench where he and Melissa had sat the night after the peach growers' meeting was obscured by a cluster of clerks and bailiffs enjoying their morning cigarettes. Their conversational laughter drifted across the narrow street beneath the occasional engine rumble or shouted greeting. He imagined the barbs at coworkers, the exchange of weekend reports, the updates on activities of spouse and kids. He connected the desultory conversation to the badges on chains around their necks, the guts overlapping belt buckles, the thinning hair and the sagging chins. It's more than the toll of smoking, thought Ethan. It's the cost of house and job, wife and kids.

He climbed into his father's truck and fired the engine. Then he thought about Melissa and the shock on her face when he'd left her with Erica. And Erica's enthusiastic call, telling him what a fool he'd be to let her get away. Not everyone ends up a bald, smoking, county employee, he reassured himself. He put the car in gear.

"We haven't even done the cleanup," Melissa told Greg over the phone. She glared at Trey, who should have been dressed, and motioned to him to return to his room and don the shirt he held in his hand.

"I know. But they think they've got a hot one and they want to list the house to show it to this one couple. They're from California, and they're just in for the weekend."

"Poor fools," muttered Melissa.

"We haven't got anything to lose," Greg urged. "We list for just this one weekend, we set a minimum price, and if it doesn't sell, then we go ahead and do all the cleanup. What have we got to lose?"

"It makes sense," she agreed. "Tell you what, fax me the contract and to my lawyer at the same time. I'll talk to her today, sign it, and overnight it back. Unless they'll take a faxed signature if they know I'm mailing an original?"

"I'll call them."

"You know what—"

From the next room came Garrett's squeal, followed by Trey's angry command, "Give that to me! You asshole! That's mine."

"Wait, hold on." Melissa put her hand over the phone, hurried to the doorway. "Cut it out! Garrett, give your brother his sock."

Garrett wiggled the sock on his hand. "I'm sockie," he said, leaning his head behind his nipping fingers. "Sockie eats boys!" The sock-clad hand lunged at Trey, who took advantage of it by ripping the sock away and pushing his little brother onto the bed.

"Stupid!" Trey shouted. "Ass—"

Melissa stepped forward and grabbed her older son by the arm that held the sock. "All right!" she said. She looked at Garrett, who half lay on the bed, howling. "Garrett," she said softly. "Sit up, please." She looked down at Trey and shook the arm she held. "Apologize to your brother for calling him names. Now."

"He took my sock!"

Melissa gave another shake.

"I'm sorry I called you an asshole," said Trey.

She released the arm. "Now go get dressed." She turned back to Garrett. "You need to get dressed, too," she advised. "And you are not to touch your brother's things without permission. Got it?"

Garrett, who had not taken his eyes off his mother, nodded. Melissa reached into her robe pocket and handed him a tissue. "Here," she said. "Blow."

She addressed the room. "Twenty minutes. We're leaving in twenty minutes, breakfast or not." Melissa held the phone back to her ear as she turned and walked into her own room. "Just fax the thing," she told Greg, hoping he was still there.

"Couldn't I talk to them?" he asked.

"Greg, they're really late," she warned. "Could they call you after school? Around four?"

"I've got a meeting," he said. "How about if I call, around four-thirty? Should I call your cell?"

"No, try the phone here. If I'm out, they'll still be able to talk. That's one thing you'd love, these three grandmas are always ready to baby-sit."

"Sounds like heaven," he said dryly.

"Look, just fax the thing to me, I'll call my lawyer and then I'll fax back. House or office?"

"House," he said.

"Greg! Have you not told them?"

"I will," he promised.

"Greg," Melissa reminded her husband, "our neighbors know. My friends know. My former coworkers know. Portland's not that big."

"Everyone here knows, too," he said dully. "They're just waiting for me to announce it so they can tell me how long they've known."

"Just fax me," she repeated. "And call the boys this afternoon."

She tossed the phone on the bed, peeled off her robe, and threw on yesterday's jeans and shirt. "Come on," she urged the boys. "If we hurry, we can get toast and peanut butter."

They clambered down the stairs, then she and Garrett proceeded to the kitchen while Trey ran back upstairs for his backpack. Rita, as had become her custom, had spread toast with peanut butter and filled two glasses with two-percent milk, as well as a travel mug with black coffee. "Thanks," Melissa said, taking up the plastic mug and sipping gingerly through the hole in its cover.

Rita took a quick look from Garrett to his mother. "My pleasure." She grinned at the child. "Eat up, Garrett." She smiled at Trey, who appeared with the backpack. "Here," she offered. "You too."

"Thanks," Trey said, and Melissa's eyes filled at the joy of her son's good manners.

Rita pulled a small brush from her pocket and knelt before Garrett. "Would you let me brush your hair?" she asked. "It might bring me luck."

Garrett nodded without ceasing his chewing.

"You could brush mine," Trey said.

Rita nodded, smiling as she concentrated on Garrett. "I will," she promised. "This is going to be such a lucky day for me." She swept her brush through Garrett's hair and chucked him under the chin, then turned to Trey. "You've done a pretty good job here," she assured the older brother. She brushed quickly. "Here. Let's get that shirt tucked in, too."

"I like it out," Trey said.

"Okay," Rita said. "Let's get it all pulled out."

"All right, boys," Melissa said, taking a breath and sliding off the stool at the outside of the kitchen island. "Let's get going."

She took her keys off the peg at the back door. "Aunt Rita," she said. "You're a miracle worker. Thank you. I'll be right back." And then I might get to brush my own hair, she thought. She imagined the oil on her unwashed face, the puffed-up skin around her eyes.

Then she looked up and saw Ethan.

"Hi there," he said. "Good morning! I thought maybe . . ." he glanced down at the boys.

"We're on our way to school," she said brightly. "But Rita has coffee on."

"Uh, I've got you blocked in."

Melissa breathed out hard, then waved Ethan back to his truck. "Let's go," she ordered. "You're driving. Come on, we're late," she told the boys. "We're squeezing in. Four across."

"Mom! No seat belts."

"It's okay," Ethan assured Trey. "It's a special law, here in Texas. Only on the way to school and only if you go less than forty the whole way and only if it's two adults and two boys."

"What if it's girls?" Trey asked, climbing into the truck.

"Oh, they're included by virtue of the equal-protection clause of the Constitution," Ethan said.

Melissa snorted, crowded in after Trey so that they were sitting four across on the truck's bench seat. "Here," she said, pulling the lap belt out from under Trey. As Ethan pulled out, she buckled both boys together.

"Ow! Mom!" Trey protested. He wiggled around. "I can't move."

"Just deal with it," she ordered. "If you boys had dressed on time, we would have left in the Lexus before Ethan even showed up."

She looked at Trey, next to her, but he was studying his feet. Garrett, on the other hand, busied himself by shaking his head back and forth and mimicking her voice without words in a squeaky singsong.

If you boys had dressed on time, she could hear in his high-pitched hum, *if you boys had dressed on time, if you boys had dressed on time.*

"Cut it out, Garrett."

Cut it out, Garrett. He kept up the hum.

"You have to turn," Trey said. "This is where you turn."

"Oh! They moved it," Ethan said. He turned right and they joined the line of cars in front of the new elementary building. "Doesn't anyone walk?"

"Did you?" Melissa asked.

"Three miles through the snow."

"There's no snow in Texas," said Trey.

"C'mon," said Melissa, unbuckling the boys. "Let's walk from here." She unlatched the door and slid unto the street. "Meet you on the other side," she told Ethan.

"How come you did that?" Trey said as they walked the short half-block to the front door.

Melissa smiled at a teacher on duty out front. "Did what?"

"Because you didn't want us to see you kissing?" Trey said. "What?"

"You didn't want us to see you kissing," Trey said. They were at the flagpole, near the school entrance.

"Kissing," Garrett repeated. "Kissing. Kissing."

Melissa looked around, but no one seemed to notice; the stream of children flowed around them toward the open entrance. She knelt down. "Let's have some kissing here," she said. She wound her arms around both of them and kissed both on the cheek, leaning in to sniff a day's worth of little boy. "No more grumbly mornings, okay?" she asked.

"Was that Daddy?" Trey asked. "On the phone."

"Yes," said Melissa. "And he's going to call you this afternoon, just to talk to the two of you." She smiled brightly. "Okay?"

They nodded. She kissed them again, Trey pulling away as he took in the glances of the other kids. Melissa let them go, watched them until they walked inside. She stood, dusted off her jeans, and ran a hand through her hair. Oh, God! She'd forgotten about the shiny nose and uncombed hair. She saw Ethan's truck inching along the curb, and turned a second to dab the corner of her eyes, in case she had sleep in them.

"How about getting a real cup of coffee?" Ethan invited when she climbed back into the truck.

She shook her head, reached for the commuter cup she had set in his cup holder. "This is Rita's finest," Melissa told him. "How real can it get?"

"Well, you think we could talk a second?"

"Let's get you a cup of coffee," she suggested. "Kat's in Dallas, Della rolls in around ten, Rita's already snipping hair. Kitchen's ours." She glanced sideways. "It's my secret morning time. The moment I become human instead of the overbearing mom."

"You talked me into it," he said.

At the Ladies Farm, Melissa made two cups of fresh ground Colombian, set them down on the oak table. "Wait a second," she said, holding her mug up so that she could see the bottom.

"Is it leaking?"

Melissa stared at the initials under the glaze of the bright red mug. She set it down gently, then smiled as she sat next to Ethan. "My mother made these," she said. "Here, in the shed. She used to teach ceramics."

Ethan looked at the mugs. "They're pretty," he said.

"Yeah. Pretty."

"I'm not sure what you're getting at," said Ethan.

"What do you mean?"

"I mean, you said that—about your mother—and I felt like I was supposed to have some response, but I don't know what you want me to say. I barely remember your parents."

"Sorry," said Melissa. "I guess I'm just—it hit me, this is the first time I've really stayed here since she died. I mean, I was here after the funeral, but I stayed in Dallas, with my brother. And it just hit me that she's not here, that she's never going to see the boys. And I don't want you to say anything." She smiled weakly, fumbled at the chair before she sat next to him.

He sat back a little to look at her.

"I'm sorry about this morning," said Melissa. "Greg called; it always throws me off."

"What'd he want?"

"Nothing. Just some stuff about the house." She shook her head. "It's just, you know—"

He waited.

"Hard. That's all." She shook her head again, tried to sip the coffee, but it was too hot. Everything was hot, her face felt like flames, and the tears in her eyes were boiling. "Oh! God!" She groped around for a tissue, dragged one from her jeans. "Perils of being a mom," she muttered at the shredded thing, then dabbed at her eyes and nose. She couldn't look at him. "I'm such a mess. Such a mess."

"Here." Ethan leaned toward her, took her in his arms, helped her bury her face in his shirt and cry onto the fresh oxford cloth. He smelled of a commercial laundry, a quality, city place that brought it all back to you on hangers or in boxes, according to your preference. It didn't help Melissa that Greg's closet was full of this smell. Full of this smell and women's lingerie.

She sobbed harder.

"And the boys," she said, pulling away from him and gulping as she spoke, "the boys don't even know—"

"They don't know you're getting divorced?" Alarm flooded Ethan's face.

"No. No. They know that. I mean, they don't know what's happening . . . what's happening to them!" She cried hard, harder than she had cried into any pillow, in Oregon or at any motel on the highway to Sydonia. It was just the two of them in the kitchen, and Ethan was obviously bewildered, but even if she had to write him off it didn't matter. She wanted to cry, to sob and sob into this nice, fresh shirt.

It's a good thing I didn't do my makeup, she thought, but he couldn't read her thoughts or see the little smile she buried against his shirt before she sobbed again.

Ethan sat there, holding her, but couldn't think of a thing to say. You ought to comfort her, he thought. First you comfort her, let her know how much you care. Then she'll like you.

But he knew that was stupid. She already liked him. Liking him was a touchy business when you were dealing with a woman in the middle of a divorce. A woman getting a divorce would always be glad to have a new man around, but later, in Ethan's view, she might resent that you knew her when she was so vulnerable. Worse, she could blame you for the split.

Ethan had only dated one divorcing woman himself, and that one had had no children, but his friends had shared their experiences, and he had concluded that it was a situation to avoid. That avoidance only made sense, though, when you were considering a roomful of equally attractive single women in which only a few might be undergoing divorce. It was useless in considering Melissa, whose sobs were subsiding, presumably due to the comfort of his arms.

Tentatively, he stroked her hair, which was tangled but soft. She didn't pull away, and he tried rubbing her shoulder and back. Ethan kept formulating things to say, but none of them seemed to fit, which left him cursing his own conversational lack.

Finally, she pulled back a little, turning her head so he couldn't see her face. "Sorry," she whispered, standing up and making her way over to the box of tissues on top of a counter.

She wiped her eyes and blew her nose, all with her face averted as if Ethan had never seen snot. When she turned, her face was blotchy but dry. "Some cup of coffee, huh?" she said. "I'm sorry."

"Stop it," Ethan said. "Stop apologizing." He surprised himself with his vehemence. He pushed the chair out for her and she sat next to him again. "We're friends. We were friends when we were the Sydonia oddballs, and we're friends now. What would you do if it were me in a marriage shot to hell? Wouldn't you let me talk? Wouldn't you tell me you were sure I would work it out as best as possible? Wouldn't you try to show me that I'm a good parent, that the kids would be okay?"

Melissa pushed back from the table and looked at him. "You think the kids'll be okay?"

"Of course they will!" Ethan enthused. "Kids are more resilient than we think." He struggled to recall things his friends' wives had told him. "They'll adjust. As long as they know you both love them."

Melissa regarded him skeptically. "This from your vast reserve of child-rearing experience." She started off sarcastic but ended gently.

"Good to see a smile, even that little one." He leaned toward her, took both her hands. "Look, Melissa, I don't really know if things will turn out fine, but they'll turn out. I mean, your kids might struggle, and you might struggle with them, but you'd struggle if you were still with Greg, wouldn't you?" He took her nod as encouragement. "Look, I don't know what I'm supposed to do here. I mean, no matter what, I want to be a friend, Melissa."

"You are a friend."

He shook his head. "You know what I mean. I want to stay a friend even if we start—ah, you know—dating."

Melissa gave a laugh, but it wasn't reassuring. "You mean dating as in nekkid dating? Dating as in swapping body fluids and tangled sheets? That kind of dating?"

He gave a little laugh, let go of her hand to stroke her cheek. "I thought we might start with a movie. Dinner in Fort Worth. Maybe take the boys to the zoo, or a museum." He grinned. "You know: safe, afternoon dates. Then maybe we'll progress to necking in the truck. Hot passionate kisses. Hickeys. I'll put my hand down your blouse."

Now her laugh grew musical and her color deepened.

"You could put your hand in my clothes, too!" He smiled, relieved that she voiced no objection. "By then, my dad will have gathered his entry for the best bushel contest at Peach Fest. He'll head to the Big Bend, to visit Gladys and Ray, and you can tuck your boys in bed and head on over to the house with me. And we," he wiggled his eyebrows, "can fulfill my fondest boyhood dreams in my narrow adolescent bed." He kissed her lightly, on the side of her face. Once, twice, several more times while he stroked her hair a little more. "Hell, I might even reassemble the bunk beds, just to set the scene."

Her giggle made his heart pump.

"Come on, Shane, let's do some cooking."

"What's the matter?" Shane asked his friend. "Didn't Siggie give you your allowance this week?"

Johnny glowered, but Shane ignored him. He took a long drink from the bottle sitting next to him on the concrete step, and then picked up his night glasses and looked across the river. "Look at that stupid bitch! Some retriever! She slides down that damn hill and then she stands there on the other side, whining."

"Why's she over there, anyway?" Johnny asked. "I thought she belonged to that B and B."

"They've got the Hutto house," Shane answered. "Della—the brunette's—got a boyfriend; they're up there full time. Here, look at that dog, pissing into the water." He passed the scopes to Johnny, reached for his rifle. "They must be over on this side, she's going to sit there all night, pissing and moaning." He sighted through the rifle scope.

"Jesus! Your cows piss all up and down this river."

Shane lowered the rifle. "My father's cows," he said. He looked at his friend. "You worried I'd fire? No one fires anything down here, buddy. Nobody even drives down here with his lights on."

"If we're not cooking, I've got to go," Johnny said. "Siggie's got the kids and she needs me to pick up milk on the way."

"Not tonight," Shane said. "I'm reevaluating."

"What does that mean?"

"I've been thinking about old Freddy Parker. I thought it might be a business opportunity, going out on our own. But there might be a sweeter deal." Shane tipped his chair back on two legs. "Not so risky."

"I thought you had his list," Johnny said.

Shane nodded, tapped the side of his head. "I do. But it turns out everyone's got to change with the times."

"What does that mean?"

"It means maybe we don't have to boil up batteries and diet pills anymore. It means that storm, and pretty little Melissa, might be giving us a new business."

Johnny shook his head, gestured with his beer in hand. "What the hell are you talking about?"

"Just hold on, buddy, I'm still checking things out." Shane grinned up at him as Johnny stood. "You don't want to know more than you have to, do you?"

Johnny shook his head in frustration. "She'll be paging me if I don't get started."

"Just keep it on vibrate, Buddy," Shane advised, laughing at his own joke.

Chapter 14

The county road ran alongside the Nolan River on a ridge that rose up opposite the town side. Webb's orchard, on the far side of the road, faced the back way into Gladys's plot, as he thought of it. Webb felt safe leaving his truck at the orchard gate. But he worried about someone seeing him cross the road and slip through the brush that led down to the river. He had to order himself not to duck as he crunched across the graded gravel.

Webb slid his way down the rocky slope, doing his best to avoid steadying himself on the prickly pear and mesquite. Once he got into the shade of the cottonwoods, the ground leveled off a little, and he moved along the side of the hill, about halfway up from the river. The brush concealed him from the top and the cottonwoods screened him on the river side.

He pushed into the clearing. He had dragged a rock to the incline above the plants, and he seated himself there for a moment, just to catch his breath. There wasn't much to do. Gladys had spaced the plants well apart, and mulched around each of them. Ray's irrigation tube stayed steady, feeding a lateral cross Webb had brought over so he could move the whole rig a little closer to the plants.

No sense watering that much ground, he intended to tell Ray when he saw him. Ray had run the tube down to a crescent-shaped head. It probably worked fine when they had a garden right under it, but now the target was too far down the hill, and it worked better Webb's way.

The hose itself ran from a little cistern Ray had dug into the apex of a wide triangle of piled-up stone, channeling rainwater that ran down the hill. Webb chuckled at the setup. It was like Ray to waste his time with rainwater, storing it in a pit full of rocks when there was a river just down the hill. Ray never siphoned or pumped when he could do without mechanical gear.

Pushing himself up from the rock, Webb stepped over to the plants and pulled up the few weeds that had sprouted through the mulch. The plants themselves were already knee high, dark and ferny-looking to Webb's view. He felt stupid on his knees, weeding as if it were some vegetable garden. They sprayed in the orchards, but he didn't feel comfortable spraying something that might be rolled up and smoked as opposed to washed and eaten. It made no sense, but spraying the ground around a tree seemed less dangerous.

Webb walked over to the bramble where an overgrown path led back to a bench and the walk up to the Hutto house. Ray picked a good spot for a house, thought Webb. You couldn't plant much here, but it was the kind of overlook women liked, and men too. Sitting up on that back deck, or standing with a drink in your hand just inside that sliding glass door, you could look out over the treetops and feel that you owned the world.

Not just that, Webb corrected his own thoughts. It was as if you owned a good world, a leafy green one full of good friends and no greed. As high up as that house sat, you still couldn't see Castleburg's place on the other side of the river. For a second he squatted and glanced down through the cottonwoods. You could make out the Ladies Farm if you knew it was there. From downriver came a metallic glint; that would be the new shed young Shane was putting up so he could move out from under the roof of his father and stepmother.

Standing, Webb toed up a network of vines that overlay the path entrance. Shane, Eli's oldest, grew up banging on his younger brothers and anything else smaller. Webb might have worried about Ethan, who had been much smaller than Shane through most of their school years, except that Ethan was well-protected by four older brothers. Shane, recalled Webb, had kept his frustrated distance, though it had pained Alice, who thought the boy just needed some friends.

Webb smiled and returned to the plants, recalling Alice. He had dropped a tablet into Ray's cistern yesterday, and now he studied the water flowing out to make sure it looked bluish. Alice perfected the art of raising boys. She could get them washed and dressed and ready for school or church without raising her voice or her hand. Even from the orchard, Webb would look back toward the house and see the line of them marching to the truck. They had driven around with the boys in the truck bed back then, at least around Sydonia.

Watching the water drip into the mounded mulch, Webb thought how glad he was that two of the boys had married before she died, so that Alice at least enjoyed daughters-in-law. And two granddaughters.

Alice had loved sonograms, which alerted them that a girl was on the way. With the advance warning, she maximized her trips to Fort Worth with forays to Baby Gap and Babies "R" Us. "Don't ever tell the boys," she had admonished. "But girl clothes are much more fun." Once she had granddaughters, Alice had even set aside her quilting. "What's a gold ribbon compared to stitching up ruffly baby dresses?"

Webb rose and stretched. He doubted Ray knew, the last time he had stood here, or sat with Gladys on that little bench below his house, that he wouldn't visit this place again. Even if Ray visited Sydonia, Webb doubted Ray would try the hike down this hill.

It grieved Webb that he couldn't remember the last time he and Alice had been intimate. Her heart disease had progressed so gradually that they hadn't known it would be the last time, and it was probably just one of their ordinary married times, at night, in their own bed. Not like the time in the orchard, or that hotel in Chicago after his aunt's funeral. It had probably been good. *Just fine for both of us,* was how he liked to think of it. But he regretted that he hadn't known how precious *just fine* had been.

"Why's Kirk Hilgon pulling into our driveway?" Rita asked. She was peering through the window in the kitchen door. Melissa, nursing her coffee, said nothing, but it was Della whom Rita addressed.

"He's bringing me the bill," Della said, getting up from the table and heading over to the sink to rinse her cup. "For the door, and setting up the chin." She wished Kirk had waited a little, till the kitchen emptied out, but he was a morning type. "He still needs to adjust something on the chin, balance it. I'll just talk to him out in the shed," Della said.

Wordlessly, Rita stepped back and let her go outside.

His hair was still wet at the neck from his shower, and his green T-shirt looked freshly pressed. She motioned him toward the shed, glanced back to make sure he followed, then stopped. Nodding toward his truck, she grinned. "You better bring your tools," she advised.

Della waited until he joined her, and they walked along together, her giggling and him silent. From the kitchen, Rita shook her head and pulled back from the window over the table, where she had moved when she couldn't watch them from the doorway. "Well," she told Melissa, "let's go back to speculating about your future."

Out in the shed, Della pointed at the chin. "It's not rocking, exactly. But I can feel something, just a tiny . . . shiver . . . like a little shake . . . toward the back there. You know?"

Kirk reached up and shook the frame with his right hand. "Can't feel anything," he said. "Tell you what: let's go over the bill and then I'll run a little more of that vinyl cushion around that back leg. Let you get back to work."

Della smiled. "This is my work."

He squatted down to examine the base. His shirt had ridden up a little, but rather than the nasty butt-crack standard to repair types, his rear view offered a smooth expanse of browned lower back and a line of fine hair disappearing below his leather belt.

Della edged closer, squatted down next to him to see where his hand touched the base. "You think that will steady it?" she asked. She herself felt surprisingly unsteady, and she touched his back lightly to keep her balance. Abruptly, he straightened, grasping her upper arm and pulling her up.

Della gasped.

"You okay?" he asked, releasing her as she settled on her feet.

"Just fine." She looked up at him, but he was turning, retrieving an envelope folded into his back pocket. Della stepped back, allowing him out of the narrow place between the wall and the assisted chin.

Once free, he smiled gently and held out the envelope. "Why don't you take a look at that bill?" he asked. He nodded slightly at the table they kept near the door for small groups in nutrition and workout programs. "I'll get this fixed in a second, and then you and I can be done."

"They've got it all figured out," Melissa told Erica over the phone. She sat at the rolltop and kept glancing around, expecting Della's return at any moment, or Kat somehow back from Fort Worth in the middle of the morning. She could have made this call from her cell, in her room, or out near the river. But she had planned to talk about the race, and it made more sense to do that at her desk, with her laptop open.

Erica was laughing. "Well, that doesn't mean you have to do it their way. I mean, Ethan may not want to marry you. Your sons may decide they don't want to live in the Hutto house. Anyway," Erica strategized, "Ethan says his dad's house is pretty big. Built for a big family. Why wouldn't you live there, with a real parent, instead of three parent surrogates?"

Melissa shrugged, realizing that Erica couldn't see her, but needing the moment. "Rita was just speculating, about the Hutto place." She gave a little laugh. "She's thinking Della's doing the handyman and when Tony finds out, he'll split. Della'll move back in her room, the boys and I can move across the river, Ethan can come a-courting, tra-la-la."

"And he'll move from Austin to Sydonia?"

"They all did. Why wouldn't we? Instead of selling the orchard, Ethan and I could become peach growers while his dad goes off to the monastery. Or whatever that is." Melissa shook her head. "I wish I knew what I was doing here."

"Directing a race, for one thing," Erica replied. "I hope you're sending me some of those posters."

"Packet of fifty." Melissa launched a briefing on promotional activities, listings and ads in surrounding newspapers and regional running publications. She talked about Earl's completion of the Web site's first edition, as well as the more important placement of embedded links in other, high-traffic sites.

Erica and a partner operated a racing utility service that would handle registration through the Midnight Peaches site. "Elegant transparency," Erica bragged, and Melissa agreed.

"How did people do this before technology?"

"It was a pitiful existence," Erica assured her. "How's the luminaria project?"

"Not so good," Melissa admitted. "I may have been overly ambitious."

"No such thing. How about just the bridges, the start and finish? Pretty good effect. And you wouldn't have to worry about fires where you couldn't see them."

"Oh, that part's covered," Melissa said. "We've got every person over fifty who ever bought a raffle ticket for the fire department volunteering to man the water buckets. And, that same group of fire bugs wants to do the lighting. Though they may have to fight the kids in Young Life. They're convinced that lighting thousands of candles is a spiritual experience. So far, Earl's come up lacking."

"Well, tin may be cheap, but it's not free. Sure you can't do paper sacks?"

"I can. I just don't want to."

"You could put the logo on the sack," Erica said.

"Yeah. But I'm thinking about the long term. They'll be able to use the tin ones year after year. And . . . sell them. You know, official knockoffs at a festival booth."

"That's starting to sound like next year's project."

"Next year's and the next director's, hopefully."

"You really are in the next stage, aren't you?" asked Erica.

"What do you mean?"

"You know. Accepting that you've split with Greg, figuring out where you go next. You've stopped running, started to think."

"I like to think I've been thinking all along," Melissa muttered. "Not clearly, mind you."

"Welllll," drawled Erica. "What are you thinking now? Ladies Farm aside, what would be tough about life with Ethan?"

"Pardon my reserve, but I'd like to shed one man before I snag the next one."

"Why? You'd look for a job before you left the one you're at, wouldn't you?"

Melissa wasn't certain Erica was kidding. "But this isn't a job. This is a life. Anyway, it doesn't matter. We've got the divorce in the works, and I told Ethan I'd go out with him while he's still in town."

"Well, here's something to add to the mix: Ethan or not, if you decide to move to Austin, we might want another partner."

"Oh yeah? To manage races?"

"To help us expand," Erica said. "We could do more events, with you on board. Races and bike rides, for sure. But also newer stuff: skateboard and scooter competitions, road rallies, and regular fundraisers. Auctions, galas, street fairs. All that."

"I always thought there was a bigger market there, in fundraisers. You've got nonprofits cutting staff, and a shrinking pool of volunteers. A good management team could pick up the slack, get the volunteers assigned, handle the logistics."

"Austin's a lot sunnier than Portland."

"A lot more crowded, too. Anyway, I'm flattered. Seriously."

"I figured you screwed each other to death," Rita told Della, "and that we'd find your bodies tangled in that chin-up thing and we'd have to bury you all together. Or have the whole thing bronzed and set it out in the square as a memorial to the fucking fitness fools."

Della doubted that she could brazen this out, but she didn't want to slink back to her office and have to worry about facing Rita later. Thankfully, she could see the salon from the shed and had confirmed departure of all customers before she headed back into the house.

Della flopped into one of the chairs and pushed herself into a spin with her toe. "This is my death spiral," she said.

"Arch your back," Rita advised.

Della closed her eyes, spun around.

"I'd give you a six-point-four on form, but maybe a little higher on level of difficulty. Spinning after sex and all that."

"There was no sex," Della said, her eyes still closed.

"Spinning before sex, then."

Della stuck out her foot, caught a cabinet door with her toe and slowed herself to a stop. "There won't be any sex. Not now. Not ever."

"For any of us?"

"Well, I can't speak for you, but I intend to have some this evening." Della brought the chair upright. "Just not with Mr. Toolbelt."

"That was quick."

"Yeah."

Rita plopped herself down in the next chair. Though she usually had another stylist on Friday and Saturday, Rita herself often had three heads going at one time, not to mention the phone crammed between ear and shoulder while she scheduled new customers. Della had talked it over with Kat, and they had identified that skill as Rita's secret of success: she maximized and exploited her peak times instead of trying to force customers into less desirable grooming schedules.

In between, Rita rested, lying on the sofa in the back and flipping through trade magazines, or trying new styles on the wigs she kept mounted on Styrofoam heads.

Della recounted Kirk's indifference. "It was just a flirtation," she said. "I mean, for me, obviously not for him. But I never thought we were going anywhere serious."

"I've had a lot of fun going nowhere serious."

"Anyway," said Della, "it's no great loss."

"Except to your ego." Rita leaned forward and picked up a slender styling brush. She started fiddling with her hair, twirling it around the brush and holding the strand out from her head.

Della sighed. "It's just . . . I've told Tony about this. I tell him about it all the time. I miss the excitement. I get jealous just seeing Ethan and Melissa, even with the kids around . . . all that nervousness, uncertainty."

"What about Dave and me? Don't we just give you goose bumps?"

"Nope." Della glanced over at her partner. "Well, you're scary, but that's a different deal." She grinned.

"Kat and Nick."

"We don't even get to see them, they spend so much time in Colleyville. They barely exist as a couple."

"Darlene and Earl?" Rita asked, putting down the comb. She was always pumping Della and Kat for their views of her relationship with her daughter.

"Now, that makes me jealous. Not of Darlene. But, I mean, Earl . . . Earl would do anything for Darlene! He's done almost anything! I can't remember the last time I felt that passionate. Who would I ever do anything for?"

"Jamie," Rita said.

"Jamie's dead. And we're talking about men, not children."

"We were talking about love. And if you'd be honest about it for once, you'd admit that—"

"I'd admit that I'd do anything to get Jamie back. But I didn't do anything for him while he was alive. And I don't do anything at all for Robbie and his family. Except send them checks."

"You go visit them," Rita said. "And you don't stay too long. That's something every daughter-in-law appreciates!"

"Well, they live near her mom, so they get enough parental attention."

"And if anything happened to them," Rita said, "you'd take your granddaughter, wouldn't you? And raise her?"

"That's duty," Della countered. "Not passion. How'd we get from a hot guy in a tight T-shirt to this morbid—"

"Because you go from Jamie to hot guys as quick as you can. Jamie to Richard, Jamie to Kirk. The only thing that interrupted you was Pauline up and dying. And then Barbara!"

"Hot guy interruptis."

"You can joke all you want," Rita told her, "but this Kirk's giving you another chance with Tony. You ought to take it. You know you love him."

"I think I'm just grateful to Tony. For loving me, no matter what." Della looked at her own reflection in the salon mirror. "I guess I'm his passion."

Chapter 15

Cara, Significant to No Other, listed the steps to getting back to a normal life. She emphasized the importance of attending a support group to her Net readers. *Even if it's not specifically for the wives of cross-dressers,* Cara advised, *if they understand your estrangement, they'll keep you from backsliding into decisions based on sentimentality and your wish for a life that really existed only in your imagination. You will not recover by surfing the web or watching TV confessions. Recovery lies outside, where you can relate to real people.*

Nevertheless, Melissa drew comfort from reading accounts of women who had managed to stitch their lives back together. *The first time a man kissed me,* wrote Michigan Mom, *it started out wonderful and ended as a nightmare. We had just started dating, and I liked this guy. Ed seemed really decent, and kind. I was to the point that I wanted him to pick me up at home, so I could introduce him to my little girl, instead of just meeting him somewhere after work. But when we met for drinks one night, we set a real date. Then he walked me back to my car and he leaned forward to kiss me on the cheek. I turned my head to kiss back, and I got so excited, feeling his warm lips, his hunger for me. But as soon as I started responding, standing right out there in the parking lot, it was like an alarm went off in my head, and a drum pounding.*

And I thought: Sean kissed you just this way too, and his feelings were a lie! He pretended it was you he was excited about, when really it was the feel of panties under his jeans. And I jerked away from him, and it was months before Ed even tried to kiss me again. I just broke into tears and all I could do was cry and say you don't understand, and he wanted me to tell him, but I couldn't. It was awful. I was sure he'd never call me again. But I just couldn't tell him.

Melissa kept reading because she knew how this story ended. Ed was patient and loving, and after a lot more dates and a lot of talking, Michigan Mom learned to trust Ed. It wasn't perfect but, as her friends assured her, no relationship is. Now she and Ed were discussing marriage, and thoughts of Sean rarely intruded.

Scrolling down through the now familiar tale, Melissa skipped through the travails of single-mom dating. At least, thought Melissa, I've got the ladies to look after the boys. And Erica for support. She liked what Michigan Mom had concluded.

I believe honesty is the most important thing in a relationship. But I also believe the past is the past. I wasn't ever going to live with Sean again. He wasn't part of my life. So I leveled with Ed that I would never lie to him, but that our relationship had nothing to do with Sean, and that I did not want to discuss Sean with him. We do not have to live in the shadow of my first marriage. We agreed to let the past stay past as we endeavor to live in the present.

"You said we didn't need it all up front," Johnny said to Shane.

"We don't. But we need it all before we start printing your logo on six thousand T-shirts."

"I never said we'd do it," Johnny muttered, kicking at the ground with his toe.

"You said you'd get Siggie to say yes." Shane shook his head. He keyed the code onto the pad at the door, pushed it open. "And now farmer boy wants his cash."

"You pay him, then."

They stepped inside and Shane closed the door. He led Johnny through the newly furnished living area and into the kitchen, then opened the broom closet and inclined his head toward a mop and bucket. Without a word, Johnny leaned down and cleared the way, then followed Shane, who slipped between the wall and the hot-water heater and opened another door.

There was a sink and a propane-fueled burner. There was a supply cabinet. There was even a scale.

"You like being a partner?" Shane asked.

"What's not to like?"

"Then pay for the goddamn T-shirts. Take it if you have to; you can put it back after the festival. Siggie'll never know, if you do it right." Shane pulled open a drawer and withdrew a magazine.

Johnny watched, but said nothing.

"Take it out of your savings. You'll have it back before Siggie sees."

"Siggie'd see it in a second."

Shane took a step toward him, touching his chest with what Johnny saw now was a catalog. Shane's voice was low. Friendly. "You and I are heading toward a very successful Peach Fest. It'd be stupid to risk it over a few thousand dollars for the shirts."

"But I don't have the money." Johnny exhaled loudly. "Look, just spot me on this." He gestured at the counter. "You know I'm good for it."

"I know you are," Shane said, "and I, my friend, will be happy to cover it for you." With a flourish, he laid the catalog on the counter. "All you need to do is order one canister for me."

Johnny stared at the page of specs. "What . . . what the hell? GHB?"

"I told you, we've got to change with the times, buddy."

"But we . . . I thought we were going to cook tonight? You want—"

"Just a canister," Shane instructed. "Tell them you're private-labeling a little cleaner. Or insecticide. That'd be better."

"I can't do that," Johnny said. "Siggie'd—"

"Screw Siggie!" Shane shook his head. "She wouldn't be such a bitch if you did screw her." He clasped Johnny's shoulder, and gave it a little shake. "Come on, buddy, we may never have to cook again. Just mix, and watch the money roll in."

Johnny nodded toward the page on the counter. "I can't order direct from the manufacturer," he said.

"But that's the beauty of it. You've got a distributor, don't you? It's legit. We mix in a little lye—"

"Lye?"

"Better than stripping out batteries." Shane tapped the catalog. "Who's the distributor for these people?"

"I guess Wilson handles—"

"Then let's just call Wilson. Tomorrow."

Johnny shook his head. "I don't know. They must keep track—"

"That's the beauty of it. They keep track, and you're a legitimate customer."

"But what if someone . . . someone comes and asks—"

Shane leaned close, spoke into Johnny's ear. In the cramped space, Johnny felt his breath, heard each word. "We take what we need. You keep the rest of the canister at the store. When they ask, you tell them you were messing around with it, looking for a better insecticide. Tell them you're working on a project to kill mosquitoes. Eradicate West Nile."

Johnny closed his eyes, pictured himself on the phone. Just one canister. Shane was right, it wasn't much.

"So we're not going to cook anymore?" He was sweating.

"What's the matter?" Shane crooned. "You run out of Freddy's finest?"

Johnny managed a laugh. "Not me, buddy." He braced himself.

"Here," Shane said. "This'll get you through it."

Johnny turned and took the water bottle Shane held out to him. "D'you mix this up?"

"Nah. This is Freddy's."

"I thought he just did meth."

"Turns out," Shane said, "Freddy had more than one business. Quite a chemist, Freddy. Knows the whole alphabet." Shane gave a short laugh. "Lot of good that'll do him now."

"He cut a deal, Siggie said."

"Well what do you know?" Shane replied. "Siggie's right about something." Shane nodded at the bottle. "You take that home with you. When you get to feeling bad, you sip a little. See what you think."

Johnny grinned. "Maybe I'll slip a little to Siggie."

"You do that," Shane advised. "Slip her a little and slip her a little."

They both snorted.

"Freddy's canister ended up in the Nolan. All I've got is five bottles. We've got a big chance coming up, thousands of people here for the race, and my job is to deliver cases of bottled water all over town." Shane picked up the catalog, swatted at Johnny's shoulder. "You place that order."

Johnny swallowed hard, grasped the bottle. Shane was right, he knew that. GHB was a whole lot safer than meth. No smell. No explosions. No crazed users beating on your door or going off on you in front of your families. Johnny pictured himself hoisting a case of bottled water, bearing it in to a bunch of dancing white kids, spoiled party boys slipping hundreds into his pocket.

It was all good. Except that Freddy had pleaded, and if Shane wasn't cooking, Johnny had to find himself a new dealer. Or learn to love the water.

"You ever grow marijuana?" Webb asked Ethan. He had stayed up late until Ethan got home.

"You're not wearing a wire, are you?"

"I'm asking for a reason."

"Well, in college I had a grow light for a plant I kept in the closet. Personal use only, not for distribution. And," Ethan smiled, seating himself on the plaid sofa in the big room, "it didn't provide that much personal use. Spindly thing, really."

"Ever try outside? In a vegetable garden, or some such?"

"I never had a vegetable garden, Dad."

Webb nodded. "I've got to go to the Big Bend. Gladys needs a hand with Ray."

Ethan waited.

"I got six plants up on the hill at Huttos, where they used to grow vegetables with that nephew. It was some sort of hideout or something."

"I know the place," Ethan said. "We used to raid it, his fort. Little path over from a bench below the house?"

Webb nodded.

"You have six plants? You're growing weed?"

"I don't mind if you call it pot," Webb advised. "But it's a little insulting for a farmer to get accused of growing weed."

"Why, exactly—" Ethan leaned forward, regarded his father. "Are you smoking this pot?"

"I've got my reasons," Webb replied.

"You're telling me you're growing six marijuana plants on your neighbors' hill, but you don't want to tell me why?"

Webb nodded. "That's about it. I'm asking you to trust me when I say it's for a good reason."

"Just what . . . is this what those brothers want you to do? Is that what they mean, when they say they'll always have a place for a good gardener?"

"I'm not going to get into a big uproar over this," Webb said.

"Then why are you telling me? Why'd you even bring it up?"

"Because I've got to go to the Big Bend. Those plants are pretty much okay up there, but I'd feel better knowing someone was checking on them."

"You want me to check on them?" Ethan gave a laugh. "I don't believe this. You—who took the truck because you found a pack of Marlboros under my mattress; who grounded Wade because you caught his friends with beer when they came to pick him up—you're telling me that you're growing pot, you don't have to answer any of my questions, but you'd appreciate it if I'd look in on your stash on the stem up there on the hill."

"Without the sarcasm," Webb said mildly, "that's what I'm asking. Yes."

"How long are you planning to be gone?"

"You mean, do you get to harvest?"

"Now who's being sarcastic?" Ethan shot back. He thought of something else. "Didn't those women buy that property?"

Webb nodded.

"Don't you think they should have a say in whether or not you grow pot on their property?"

Webb thought exactly that, but there was no sense going into that with Ethan. He comforted himself with thinking that the ladies could rightfully claim no knowledge if anything happened, and that's what he told Ethan. "Anything happens, they're better off not knowing. None of them have a thing to do with it."

"Anything happens," Ethan repeated.

"It's pretty well concealed," Webb said. "And we're not exactly the type . . . I hear they just look for excess electricity use, or water. It's six plants." He stopped, having said more than he had planned.

Ethan could enter the Brothers without preparation, thought Webb. He sat without moving, without challenging his father, without even the appearance of thinking. Webb studied him, but Ethan met his gaze without seeming to see his father. I'm a stranger to him, thought Webb. He's thinking he doesn't know me at all.

We could just leave things be, thought Webb. That's how Gladys planned it originally. But he intended to show her, with the growth chart he had kept, the importance of just a little care, a little chemistry, the difference between growing and thriving.

Webb stirred. Ethan was still staring at him. "Just think about it. Let me know." Standing, Webb stretched and yawned. "It's way past my bedtime. Good night, son."

"Good night," Ethan replied, but Webb doubted Ethan even realized he had spoken.

Melissa crept down the back stairs and found Della and Tony sitting in the kitchen. "Oh! Hi!"

"Hi!" Della said. She exchanged a look with Tony. "Everything okay?"

"Yeah." Melissa pulled the tie on her robe a little tighter. "I thought I'd make a little cocoa." She squinted. "What time is it?"

"Five-thirty," Tony said. "Almost time to get up."

"Couldn't you sleep?" Della asked.

Melissa shrugged, headed for the cabinet with the cocoa. She doubted she could describe her dream. "I don't know . . . I just woke up and couldn't get back to sleep. How come you're up?"

"You mean, how come we're here?" Tony asked. "I've got an early meeting in Dallas, and we needed to check something—I needed Della's computer."

"We should move over there," Melissa muttered. "At least you could have your own room back. And your Internet connection." She had filled her cup with milk and measured in the cocoa and sugar, but she stopped as she was putting it in the microwave. "Maybe I should have coffee."

"We're as connected as we want to be," Della said.

Melissa looked over at the two of them, noticed that they were holding hands on the tabletop. "We probably shouldn't even be staying here," Melissa said, wanting Tony to hear her explanation. "It would make more sense to settle in Dallas, or Austin. But once I got started with the race—"

"Well, we're glad you're here," Della said. "And if you want some advice you'll stay put, at least till the race."

"I think Rita's gotten attached to your boys," Tony said.

"She . . . all of you have been great. It's just, I think I need to stand on my own two feet now. Not be so dependent." She stared down at the cup in her hand, still undecided about coffee or cocoa.

"You know," Tony offered, "if you still feel that way after the race, you might want to think about our house, in Fort Worth. I've been trying to get my nephew to say he'll look after it—he's at TCU—but you and the boys are welcome to it. It would be a favor to us."

"Oh, that's sweet," Melissa said. "Impossible, but sweet. I can't imagine moving back to Fort Worth." She shook her head, took her cup to the sink. "I guess I'd better switch to coffee."

"Honey," Della said, "why don't you just drink your cocoa, go back to bed, and sleep in. Rita and I can get the boys to school for you. Tony's leaving in a bit, and I'm already up."

Melissa took in Della's makeup, her clean blouse, her watch and earrings. She turned again and put the cup in the microwave.

Tony returned to the house discussion. "You don't have to decide right now. It just gives you an option if you find a job in Fort Worth."

"Thanks," Melissa said. She leaned against the counter, watching the digital display count down. If she closed her eyes, she could still see Ethan in her dream, his bare chest and tight butt both visible in the way things could be in dreams. Only she hadn't been alone in seeing him. Everyone—his father, Erica, the ladies, the boys, Shane, the race committee—everyone had been there. It was some sort of finish line, with huge phallic torches blazing down both sides, and her chasing him, just ahead of the pack. And then, instead, they were carrying torches, she and Ethan, and they were looking for the canoe in which the two of them used to explore the Brazos up near Possum Kingdom Lake.

"Trey can pick his own clothes. I think I got Garrett's approval on the outfit I put out for him last night," she said dully.

"We'll manage," Della assured her. "Just close the door between your room and theirs, so you can sleep."

"Better let them come in," Melissa said. "Trey the policeman might not get in the car with you otherwise."

"He does enforce the rules," Della said.

"He's a good kid," Tony assured them.

"He likes order," Melissa said. She opened the microwave before it could buzz and wake everyone else in the house. They had two guests, and the ladies hated guests in the kitchen before seven.

Tony stood. "I've got to hit the road," he said. Della walked him to the door.

They kissed good-bye, a sweet morning kind of kiss in Melissa's eyes, and she could not restrain a sigh.

"I know," said Della, walking back to the table. "How could I want Kirk Hilgon when I have Tony. It's insane, isn't it?"

Melissa sipped, shook her head. "He's pretty nice. Tony, I mean."

"I know."

"Have you ever tried, you know . . . counseling?" Melissa felt silly suggesting counseling to her mother's friends, but she couldn't imagine what Della thought she would find with the handyman that she couldn't find with her husband of years and years. "How long have you been married, anyway?"

"We're not married," Della said. "Remember? We're divorced. It would be thirty-two years. But we've been divorced for ten."

"Greg and I weren't even married for ten," Melissa said. She sipped her cocoa, trying to let the sugar and milk make her sleepy.

"You should take that upstairs with you," Della suggested. "That way you'll be in bed and you can just set it down and doze off."

Melissa nodded obediently and took the cup from the table as she stood. It was too weird, offering relationship advice to her mother's friend. It was the canoe part of the dream that had disturbed her. They had been on the water, in the canoe, with those stupid torches, and there was Shane, leering as he reminded them that in high school, the boys had called it Pussy Kingdom Lake. Melissa recalled that, even dreaming, she had willed Shane out of the picture and he had disappeared.

She spilled a little cocoa going up the steps, but most of it landed on her robe, a practical white cotton, standard Ladies Farm issue, that would bleach clean for the next user. Melissa sipped only a little more, safe in her bed, with the boys breathing steadily in the next room, and the blinds pulled hard against the imminent arrival of morning light. She and Ethan had rocked the boat, she recalled with pleasure, drifting off again. They had dumped themselves into the bath-warm lake on the Brazos, their torches blazing above them and then extinguished as they fell into the water with a final fiery sizzle. Even falling asleep, Melissa could appreciate the warm, sexual comfort of the dream and she smiled before she lost all awareness.

To her surprise it was Garrett, not Trey, who woke her. At first she assumed her younger wanted a morning snuggle, curling himself up against her. But that was only for access to her ear, into which he whispered "Mom," and to which she replied, "Mmmmm." They rehearsed the exchange several times before she roused herself to mumble, "Aunt Della and Aunt Rita are going to take you to school." She turned, and closed her eyes a little tighter. "Give Mommy a kiss," she told the pillow.

"Mom!" It didn't sound stuck-with-pin, strangling, or bleeding urgent, but it did jerk her awake.

"What?" she said without turning. If he couldn't get his shirt on frontward, there was still a chance his brother or the ladies might show up to help.

"Daddy's here," Garrett said, leaning over her so she could feel his warm breath on her face. "Daddy's going to take us to school."

Chapter 16

Her cocoon rent, Melissa jerked upright, nearly sweeping Garrett off the bed.

"Daddy's here?"

Garrett slid on his stomach to a standing position and nodded cheerfully.

Melissa told herself to respond calmly. She dispatched Garrett for his clothes before she whipped off her sleep-shirt and threw on shirt and shorts. She brushed hair and teeth, washed sleep from her eyes, swiped her face with powder and blush. Then—slowly, regally, decisively—she followed Garrett down the stairs.

The tableau that presented itself—Greg, at the counter, spreading peanut butter on toast as Trey sat happily on a stool and directed his father in the particulars of breakfast at the Ladies Farm—loosed a fierce wave of hatred, drowning all longing for lost family life. "Hi, Daddy," she said brightly. "What brings you to the Ladies Farm?"

In one movement he turned, scooped up Garrett, and smiled at Melissa with a gaze that took in both boys. "Do I need a reason to get these hugs?" He jostled Garrett, who wrapped his arms around his father's neck in response. From his perch, Trey watched Garrett and Greg, then turned to Melissa.

"We're making breakfast," he said. "Just the way Rita does it. I'm showing him."

Rita stood by the back door, set to flee, or too shocked to step back into the kitchen drama. Della, similarly posed, stood at the other end of the kitchen.

"Well, I'll pour the milk," offered Melissa. She moved toward the refrigerator. "What time did you get in?"

Rita sprang to life. "He just got here, didn't you, Greg? We sent Garrett up to tell you just as soon as he got here."

"Just got here," Greg confirmed, still holding Garrett as he labored over the peanut butter and toast.

"Well, that's great," Melissa enthused. She pulled the milk from the refrigerator. "We'll have breakfast together and then we'll all drive to school in Daddy's car."

"Can I sit in the front?" Garrett asked.

"That's not fair!" Trey protested. "He always gets everything because he's the baby. It's not even legal."

Greg looked to her.

"You know what?" Melissa proposed. *You know what? I hate you!* "You both can sit in the front. I'll sit in the back."

"He's too short," Trey said.

You've got no right to step into the state of Texas while I'm here with my boys.

Greg set his younger son on his feet and eyed him up and down. "He'll pass."

Melissa thought the boys did well, considering. They ate their toast and drank their milk and brushed their teeth in the half-bath off the living room lobby. They climbed all over their father, who half-dragged, half-carried them to the car; they chattered about their trip to Sydonia, and at school, they got out of the car without too much anxiety, obviously torn between hanging onto Greg and telling their new friends about their father's appearance.

Melissa herself got out of the car to kiss them, then slid into the front seat. "Now let's you and me talk," she said. She directed him to the Hutto house. "Just come around down here," she instructed, once they left the car. She led the way around the house and down the path, grateful that there were some steps left on the trail the Huttos had built to what they called the sunset bench.

This early in the day, the bench sat in shade, and she seated herself on one side, leaving the other clear for her husband.

"Why are you here?"

"Kiplinger went to Finland."

"The moon rises over a purple dawn. What the fuck are you talking about?"

"Sorry."

Greg hadn't looked at her since that first greeting in the kitchen, and now he hung his head and studied his hands. She wanted to slap him.

"Kiplinger is project leader, and he went to Finland to consult with one of the customers, so there's a three-week lag in the project."

"And you didn't have back correspondence? No one needed your help on some other project?"

"Oh, of course they did!" He raised his head. "But I missed my boys. I wanted to see them. And I missed my wife. I wanted to see her." He gestured with his hands, but he didn't lift his gaze.

"You are pathetic," she told him. "Oh, I missed my kids," she mimicked. "Oh, I missed my wife. You didn't think about missing me when you were slinking around in your little panties, did you? You didn't care about your boys then, did you?"

"We've already been through that." He stood up and paced a little way down the path along the hillside, then turned back toward her.

He looked directly at her, his hazel eyes large in the shade.

"We have been through that," she conceded, thinking that he looked almost gaunt, though still impossibly square-shouldered. Wholesome. It infuriated her, and she gripped the stone bench to stay calm. "I've accepted who you are. Your secret life. Now it's time for us to go on with our lives. You have to leave the boys alone, let them get used to living with me."

"You promised I'd be able to see them," said Greg.

"I know." She looked straight ahead. "You will. I just don't want them believing some fairy tale about our getting back together."

"Together or not, we're a family, Mel."

She hated the word *family*. "Oh, yeah: just the four of us and Daddy's little secret!"

He winced, but stood steady on the path.

She imagined punching him, the way you'd punch one of those weighted, inflatable dolls, knocking him down, then watching him bounce back up again. Then she pictured diving at his knees, tackling him with a twist so that he jerked sideways off the hill, tumbling uncontrollably until he cracked his skull on the point of a well-placed boulder. There would be insurance money. Proceeds from the house in Portland. Greg dead and buried.

Dream all you want, she taunted herself.

"I'm not part of your nasty little world anymore, Greg."

"You were never part of that; that was separate."

"Yeah, well, your separate panties managed to find their way to our very shared closet. Deal with it."

"Dealing with it is what I'm trying to do," Greg said.

He was getting counseling. She could tell by his objective tone, his refusal to engage in argument. When she had first confronted him, he'd cried. Now he stood dry-eyed.

"The boys and I are not part of your rehab," she said. "I—we—are not obligated to help you overcome this compulsion."

"I don't want to overcome it," Greg said. "I just want to live my life without having to battle you over my children."

"Battle me? Listen, asshole, if this were a battle, I'd have you wrapped so tight in restraining orders you'd need a tube to breathe." Melissa took a breath of her own. "If this is just about the kids, why didn't you call? Why the surprise? I'll tell you why," she hurried forward. "You want forgiveness. Absolution. My blessing!" she spat.

"Hey, I never asked—"

"No, you never asked, you chickenshit! You just showed up here looking hangdog. Poor, pitiful Greg. Meanie Melissa won't even be nice to you. Well, fuck off."

She had run out of breath and inhaled sharply, only to find herself sobbing. "Unnnh!" she grunted, stunned and furious.

"Come on, Mel," he urged, taking a seat on the bench.

She let him talk as she struggled to regain her composure.

"We can't keep arguing about how guilty I am. We reach the same place every time: you hate me, you want a divorce, I'm a good father, and you want the kids to have a father. Save us this uproar. I'm only here for a few weeks. I want to spend time with the boys. It's not what you planned, but it's their summer vacation. I didn't tell you I was coming because you'd just tell me not to. You know how my job is; I might not get this much time again. Can't we work this out?"

Melissa felt betrayed by her own resolve. Even her anger hadn't been enough to strengthen her in his presence. Now she was the one who stared at the ground.

Coming to Sydonia was stupid, she thought. *As if I could leave it all behind.* "It's all right for you to see the boys," she said quietly. *But I don't want to see you. Ever.* "But we have to have some order to it. A schedule. We can't keep disrupting their lives."

"I didn't drag them off to Texas."

"But you agreed it would be better if I took them somewhere else, somewhere to start over."

"You could have gone back to California," he said. "It wouldn't have been as far."

"I can't afford California," she told him. "We couldn't afford one household there between us, let alone two. There's no job there for you, and probably not one for me. Besides, I'm sick of pretentious places where there's no place to park."

"You told me you hated it here."

"I did, growing up. And I already told you that I'm probably not staying here anyway." She sighed. "Are you thinking that you'll find a job down here, maybe move here?"

He shrugged. "I haven't thought that far. All I thought was . . . I mean, they told me I needed to be out of the house Sunday afternoon for them to show it, and Kiplinger called to tell me he had to take off for Finland, and the next thing I knew I was booking a flight and getting a rental car."

"I know the impulse," she said, then remembered that she was still angry. "Just where are you planning to stay?"

"Well, I thought maybe I could rent a room here for the next three weeks." He looked back up the hill. "Maybe over on this side. Della told me she and Tony are staying over here, but they still have two other rooms."

So much for canoeing through pleasant waters with Ethan, she thought. Put that on hold.

"Or I could stay at a motel," Greg offered. "I saw two out on the highway."

Melissa considered. Fort Worth. Dallas. Houston. Oklahoma. She kept hitting the same wall. If he stayed out of her sight, she couldn't watch him. Embrace your enemies, she thought. If he took over some of the parenting, she could work on putting together a résumé, find a job. Get through the race. Get some place where she could make a living.

The sun had climbed up over the hill, lighting the river below and warming beyond comfort. Melissa had pulled off her sunglasses when she and Greg had got into the shade, but now she unhooked them from her buttonhole and put them back on. She sat there, sweating, glad that Greg had no more to say.

From this point, she could see clearly across to the Ladies Farm. The tree from which her brother had draped the communications line up to Earl lay just below here. There actually had been two lines, Melissa recalled: one up to the balcony, and one to a fort the boys had built somewhere down the little path. As she remembered it, Hugh hadn't considered Earl to be a suitable friend, but he had sufficed for the summer, when Hugh's Fort Worth friends weren't handy.

Sometimes, now, when Trey and his friends climbed into the car after soccer, their hot, sweaty, boy smell transported Melissa back to those summers. Angry at the move from Fort Worth, she had wandered alone along the Nolan, climbing fences, stirring up Castleburg cows, and sulking. Resentfully joining her brother and parents for meals, forced to help remodel the old Sydon house; lining shelves, scrubbing woodwork, sanding and painting corners and edges. She smiled, convinced she would never tolerate that kind of sulking from her own sons.

"What are you thinking?" Greg asked. It was the way he used to ask after sex, when they would lie side by side, still warm, hearts still racing. She had never known what to say. It wasn't a time for talking, she thought now, resentment rising.

"I'm thinking that if you drag one lacy . . . one pair of . . . one little thing, I swear to you, Greg—"

"I didn't pack any of it," he told her. "It's three weeks. I can live without it for three weeks."

Sydonia was a small town, and Della expected to run into Kirk Hilgon sooner or later. She just had not expected to see him at Central Market in Fort Worth. "Though, I always thought this would be a great place to pick up guys," she assured him.

They stood before the sausage case. "I was debating between hot Italian and chicken feta," he said.

Della checked her inclination to lean into him as she shared her preference for the pork and apple with sage. "If you cook it with spinach and rice, a little garlic . . ." She rolled her eyes toward heaven and was rewarded with a smile. We have to get back to normal, she thought.

"Come share some hummus," she invited.

He checked his watch.

"Just an appetizer," she insisted. "Come on. We'll get some coffee—or a beer—while they put together your order. And some bread."

The caution with which he regarded her tugged at her conscience. She took a step back from her basket and held both hands up. "No touching. I promise."

It was good to see his shrug, and hear his laugh.

They took the shortcut from wines through the coffee and bulk grains and on to the bakery. She plucked fresh tortillas, then led the way to the deli for both hummus and eggplant spread, along with a few large, black olives, and finally through the carryout with a ginger ale for him and a lemon tea for her.

They sat outside at an umbrella table, a safe distance from an earnest young man who accompanied his reedy voice on an acoustic guitar. It was warm and still light, and Della sat opposite Kirk, handing him a small stack of paper napkins and urging him to tear the warm tortillas and pluck an olive.

He had worked a job on the west side of Fort Worth, he told her, and this was his first visit to the palace of gourmet organic. Della tagged her feelings as safely maternal, and she listened attentively but not raptly while he described the bungalow at which he was restoring the mantel. "This mantel's been painted white who knows how many times, enough that there's almost no depth between this great beadwork—sort of a garland—and the background. And then, some designer had the brilliant idea of trying green—"

"They painted the mantel green?" She tore off more tortilla and swiped at the eggplant.

"I think they were going for an antique effect; you know, brush it on, then wipe enough away that you can see the grain. But of course, all you could see on this thing was sticky white semigloss. It's a mess."

"And you're going to restore it?"

He nodded. "I'm going to try." He tilted the soda and drank.

An Adam's apple is just a secondary sex characteristic; she reminded herself, trying not to stare at his throat. This is what got you in trouble to begin with. Think about Tony and his Adam's apple. She drank her tea, which scalded her back to her senses.

"I'm glad," said Della, "that we can be friendly. I didn't want anything to be awkward."

"You've got to be friendly to live in a place like Sydonia," Kirk said. "I meant you no offense."

"None taken. But—"

"You know, I built a lot of counters at the copy store. When Tony was expanding."

"And we were getting divorced, you mean."

"I was just starting on my own, Tony kept me fed."

"And you know all the gory details about how badly I treated Tony."

Kirk looked away. "Pretty standard stuff. Long-term marriage goes stale, hits a pretty rough spot, bingo! You hit middle age and you're all by yourself."

Middle age.

"It happens to a lot of people I've seen, people who go through a whole lot less than losing a son." Kirk ran a hand through his hair. "You should see how many couples split up over remodeling."

"That's not much of a recommendation for your services."

"No." He grinned. "But people go a little crazy. They move to the sleep-sofa while I work on the bedroom, and all of a sudden one of them wants to be making love on the floor, or in the bathtub. Stuff like that."

"That doesn't sound so bad."

"Well, maybe it's okay for young folks starting out, but after you're settled, and you've got a house and family, it's just the kind of thing that gets you in trouble."

"Sex in odd places?"

He didn't exactly blush. It was more like his bronze tone deepened. But you could see it. "All I'm saying is, a lot of folks can't even handle the challenge of remodeling the house. Let alone tougher situations."

Della nodded, to show she got his point.

He was right about one thing, she decided on the way home, her fresh sausage and exotic veggies safely in the car trunk. If you don't do the wildest things when you're young, you probably have missed your chance. Even Tony, remarkably fit, could not manage the gymnastics of the assisted chin.

Middle age. Della had heard the term. She had used the term.

Even about herself. Even knowing that if this was middle, she'd have to live beyond a hundred. Strip away all the kind concern, all the warm understanding, Della thought, and Kirk Hilgon just told you you're too old for him. Never mind. Who wants someone with no interest in sex on the assisted chin?

"He's just here because of the kids," Ethan repeated. He had been repeating it for a week: to his dad; to Randi behind the fountain at the drugstore; to Shane when Shane recounted his own introduction to Greg; and now to Ray Hutto, who was calling to talk with his dad.

"How much wardrobe'd he bring?" Ray asked.

Ethan sighed. Who cared? "A few weeks' worth, I guess."

"Nothing too exotic, huh?" Ray's chuckle came through with a little static. No doubt he used a wireless, as much time as he liked to spend outdoors.

"I guess not," Ethan replied, impatient to get back to the appraiser's report. "I'm sorry Dad's not here," he repeated. "Most days he's out watching what's left of the peaches."

"Well, I thought I might catch him at lunch," Ray said. "Let him know I called."

Ethan regretted that he had let his impatience creep into his voice. "Better tell me how you're feeling," he said, "so I can give the old man a full report."

"What's that?" Ray asked, the static resembling a giggle. "Here"—Ethan could hear him talking to someone else—"let me have another handful."

"I said, how are you doing?" Ethan spoke loudly this time.

Now there was a definite laugh, followed by chewing sounds. "You tell that father of yours we're just sailing along out here," Ray said. Ethan heard comment from someone—probably Gladys—in the background, but Ray evidently ignored her. "Feeling no pain. No pain at all."

"Sure thing," Ethan promised.

It was dinner before he delivered the message. They were sharing a tinfoil pan of lasagna, the kind that came frozen from the grocery and required only heating up. To their delight, Ethan and his father had discovered they shared a fondness for the dish, and Webb had stocked the freezer, bottom to top, with the delicacy.

"He sounded almost giddy," Ethan reported. "If he was aching, he sure didn't sound it."

His father nodded, scooped a little more tomato sauce and noodles onto his fork. "He always says he feels fine," he advised his son. "You've got to get the real story from Gladys. She calls late at night, when he's snoring over his journals." He guided the fork to his mouth.

"He keeps a journal?"

"Magazines," his father corrected after he swallowed. "Engineering. Geology. You know Ray: spends a lot of time worrying over raw materials, natural movements. Rock, water, soil."

"I guess I don't remember him that well," Ethan said. He pushed his lasagna around on his plate, creating swirl patterns. "Even he knew Greg was here."

"That his name? Greg?"

Ethan nodded.

"I guess it's him I should thank then: Greg." His father gave a half-smile. "He's the one's made you pay attention to the orchard."

Ethan started to protest, then conceded with a laugh. "Hanging out at the Ladies Farm's not too cool these days."

"But you're still working on that run?"

"It's mostly done. At least my part. I asked a few sponsors. Got Erica to come in. Now I'm just helping with the accounting. Following up to make sure people pay their pledges." He studied the swirls. "That's another reason not to be hanging out over there. It's mostly Melissa, now, flogging the press, as she calls it. Calling reporters, pitching features about participants. I suspect she's hit her stride, just wants to be let alone. Kind of like Erica, now that I think of it."

"How are they doing? Erica and her husband?"

It surprised Ethan that his father remembered his friends, but he filled him in about their lives and promised to bring Erica over when she came back for the race.

His father shook his head. "I'll be out in the high desert, by then. With Ray and Gladys."

"I forgot," said Ethan, rolling the term *high desert* around in his mind. He thought of the area as the Big Bend, but *high desert* connoted something a little more mystical. While his father ate, Ethan mulled over the contrast between high desert and the stolid, methodical personality of Ray Hutto, an engineer of life-long—

He let go of his fork and it clattered onto his plate, splashing specks of tomato sauce onto the oak table. "Sorry," he muttered. Ethan thought about the long friendship between his parents and the Huttos, and remembered Gladys's steadfast tending of his own dying mother.

"I've been thinking," Ethan said. "About your garden plot."

His father looked up from his dinner.

"There's no need for me to get back to Austin anytime soon. And," he said grinning, "I do want to keep an eye on the Ladies Farm. There's no reason why I can't check that little garden. I mean," said Ethan, "that's nothing compared to the orchards, anyway."

Chapter 17

Spying Greg on the balcony of the Hutto house, Tony headed to the bedroom to change, hoping a walk with Flops would help him avoid the sad young man. Tony admired the guy's persistence, but he hated having so little encouragement to offer. Plus, no matter how hard he tried, Tony couldn't keep himself from imagining Greg's underthings.

I'll just get into shorts and shoes and hit the road, Tony plotted. Give him a wave on my way out the door.

But Greg was a miserable, lonely guy who had no friends in Sydonia. He wouldn't miss a chance to walk with Tony. I'm slowing down, Tony thought when he emerged from the bedroom to find Greg in the kitchen, petting Flops and pulling two bottles of water from the fridge. At Tony's appearance, Flops hustled to the door and sat, whining.

"Mind if I join you?" Greg asked, holding a bottle out to Tony.

"I don't set much of a pace," Tony said. Had Greg been wearing running clothes out on the balcony? How could he have laced up his shoes that fast? Tony did not want to speculate about how Greg had acquired his quick-change skills.

Greg just stood there, holding out the bottle.

"C'mon, if you'd like."

Walking the county road, Tony tossed a stick into the Dyer orchards, and they watched the foliage shudder as Flops tore between the trees. The hard-packed road curved away from the river, winding between orchards for almost two miles until it rejoined the state highway. They walked down the smooth center, heading for the first curve, where the heat shimmered in ribbons of pinkish gold.

"She'll retrieve anything useless," Tony said as he tossed the stick into the next orchard.

"If you're the one to throw it," Greg said. "I tried a little earlier today, when I had the boys at the house; it was pretty unimpressive." He kicked at the rocks embedded in the dirt road. "She moves pretty smoothly for a big dog."

Tony nodded, concentrating on his walking. He was a head taller than Greg, but Greg had an intense, well-packed energy, almost a spring in his step.

"She's good with the boys, though," Greg said. "Garrett practically rides her, and she puts up with it."

"Boys okay?"

Greg gave a short laugh. "What do you think?"

Tony kept walking, glancing sideways at Greg and holding on to the stick once Flops brought it back so she could slow down.

"It's easier on Garrett. He's more outgoing, plus he wasn't so dug in. But first we move them up to Portland, then one day they come home from school and Melissa puts them in a car and drives them to Texas."

"They're good kids," Tony said, trying to make Greg feel better about his failure without encouraging him to confide much.

"Yeah, they are."

Tony believed that most divorced fathers, himself included, agreed that their children were good and generously regarded the admission as praise of their ex-wives. We have no shame, Tony thought. Men. We make no pretense of taking credit.

Flops nipped at the stick in his hand and Tony tugged on it, pulling till the dog gave it up. "Let's walk," he told her. "That's a good girl."

Her panting made the only sound for a few steps, and Tony let himself feel the heat, feel the day's air-conditioned stiffness melting out of him. Then Greg spoke again.

"I don't wear it all the time."

Tony started to feign ignorance. Then he got annoyed that he felt obligated to make Greg feel better by pretending that they hadn't all discussed it in merry detail. Instead, he humored his own curiosity. "When do you wear it?"

"Just . . . not that often, really. Just times I want . . . you know . . . to jerk off."

Keep walking, Tony told himself. We're two men walking down an empty road with a big dog. "C'mon, Flops," he said and clucked to the dog, who was keeping pace through the peaches while she routed out birds. Tony tossed the stick with what he hoped was manly strength.

Flops leapt in the air, pursued the stick, repeated the act two more times. They had reached the first curve. Tony let Flops keep the stick, which she dropped in the middle of the road. Then she ran to the bar ditch to pee.

"You know how sometimes you just have to . . . uh, you know . . . it's not exactly having sex, with a woman, I mean, it's . . . there's this urgency, and you can't wait till she's in the mood, or the kids are in bed . . . and if you can . . . take care of it, quick . . . just step into the bathroom. You know what I mean?"

Tony wished he could say no.

"But they . . . at least Melissa . . . it's like you're having sex without them, but really, really—"

"But really, really, it is having sex without them," Tony said. Surprised by his own vehemence, Tony strode forward, eyes fixed on the next curve in the road.

"So you nev—"

"Hey! I'm not the one we're talking about!" Get a grip, Tony ordered himself, but he was outraged that the kid would cross-examine him about this. What man didn't know that you never, ever tell your wife she isn't all you need? "That's private," Tony blurted, before he even realized he had spoken aloud.

"That's my point," Greg said, matching Tony stride for stride. "When you jerk off, it's your business."

Tony had not participated in this sort of discussion since high school, and even then he had only listened to the confessions of others, never volunteering his own secrets. He supposed there were as many techniques as there were guys; and it made sense that most guys, particularly the ones with wives, stuck with whatever scenario worked best. They saved the variety for their wives. At least Tony always had.

"Look, I didn't mean to dump all this on you," Greg said. "It's just that, it's obvious Melissa told the ladies, and you're married to Della, or living with her, or something, so I know you must be wondering. I would be wondering."

"Yeah. I think we'd better turn around here," Tony said. He gave a whistle for Flops, who had gone ahead, and she raced back to them and on toward the house.

Tony remembered the bottle in his hand and took a long sip, squeezing hard to get a steady stream through the sports cap.

"I figure whatever you do, that's your business," Tony said.

"I envy you," Greg said.

"Because I don't need women's lingerie to jerk off?" Tony kept walking, but he prayed the kid took it the way he intended.

"Well, that too," Greg said.

Tony relaxed. He'd have to watch his mouth, though. He could probably defend himself if he had to, but Greg definitely could make it hurt. Tony was glad Greg wasn't one of those guys who exploded over an insult.

"What I envy, really, is that you got a second chance. With Della."

Tony slowed. "Is that what you'd call this?"

"Well, you were divorced, right? And you married someone else. And she had an affair. And here you are together."

Ahead of them, Flops sat in the middle of the road, her tail thumping. Tony frowned. "It's not exactly the same."

"I know that. Nothing is the same as Melissa and me. Nothing comes close to Melissa and the cross-dressing freak." Greg kicked at the dirt.

Tony agreed. Nothing in his experience, among any of his friends and acquaintances, resembled Melissa and Greg.

"But I do wonder how you got Della back. What you told her. What you did."

Tony stifled a bitter laugh. What made Greg think he'd gotten Della back? There were times when the tenuous relationship made him sick to his stomach. "They tell me jewelry works," was all Tony said. It was too humiliating to explain to Greg that he would leave Della if he had any self-respect. "Jewelry and flowers."

Tony kept walking, looking at Flops waiting for him in the middle of the road. Greg should get a dog, he thought.

He was about to voice that idea when Greg turned around,

looking back toward where they'd been. "Maybe I'll run a while," he said, running backward as he spoke.

"See you later," Tony said. "Thanks for the company."

Greg shot him a look, then took off, raising a small trail of dust and pebbles.

Flops stood, shook herself out, and Tony smiled. "Come on!" he said. She jumped, she sniffed, and then she started toward him. He figured he'd throw the stick one more time, then brush her out on the front steps, maybe have a beer. But Flops took a right, heading into the brush on the river side of the road.

Damn it! thought Tony. She'd run down to the river and he'd have to dry her and check for ticks before Della made it home.

"Flops!" he yelled. "Get back here!" But she was after something or someone. It was just as well, Tony thought, jogging over to the edge of the road, I didn't tell Greg he needed a dog like this.

Melissa knew men who waited until their wives were under maximum pressure at work before they launched unreasonable demands for attention and support. Sometimes they disguised their efforts as devotion, presenting their beloveds with special dinners and surprise concert tickets at the exact moment these women needed total attention and energy for their project. It looked like love but it was really sabotage.

In this regard, Ethan had passed his first test. Even after Greg showed up, Ethan stayed cool. He e-mailed her every day, passing along jokes and bits of gossip about the race, and called her every few days. According to Erica, he had reported that Greg looked clinically depressed, and not interested in anything except Melissa and working out.

"He's pretty patient," Erica said.

"Well, he's got you to plead his case." They were on the phone, going over the registrations, which were trickling into the Web site and in the mail.

"He honestly hasn't said much," Erica told her. "Just that you and Greg seem to be taking the high road, very civil."

"Actually, with school letting out, I'm kind of glad Greg's here. I'm thinking maybe I'll suggest a road trip with the kids: Austin, San Antonio, Houston. The Capitol. The Alamo. The space center."

"Sea World. Six Flags. Schlitterbahn."

"That too." Melissa failed to imagine a world in which Greg could take the children anywhere, but it comforted her to know that Erica and Ethan believed she had married a man who could be divorced amicably. She turned to her expenditures spreadsheet. "How's Ethan coming on flushing out the deadbeats?"

"Coming along. Why?"

"We're down to the luminarias."

"You found them?"

"Yes and no."

"What does that mean?" Erica asked.

"It means I can have them here in a week."

"From Mexico?"

Melissa gave a little laugh. "From China. Tin, candles, whimsical outline of a peach and stem punched into the side. Suitable for resale."

"And?"

"And it's seventy-five hundred for ten thousand."

"And you don't have a sponsor."

"No," said Melissa. "But it's a one-time investment."

"What does that mean?"

Melissa took a breath. "The run is Saturday night. There's a half day left of the festival, including the judging of the peaches and the auction. Vendors out in full force."

"So, you're thinking you can gather them up, turn 'round and sell them on Sunday?"

"Say we sell them for two-fifty. We only have to sell three thousand of them to break even."

"Why sell them at all?" Erica asked. "You can just keep them, use them again next year. Order new ones to sell next year."

"I just thought we might want to recoup something now," Melissa said. "Plus we can leave the Web site up all year, sell shirts and luminarias all year, sell them at chamber events."

"Who needs to okay the purchase?"

"Just Randi, Ethan. And they already have. But it'd be better if I had a sponsor."

"I'd go ahead and order. You're running out of time," Erica said.

"I know. I ran through the whole thing last night with Kat. She agreed."

"Who would disagree? It's the equivalent of three hundred and fifty runners. You'll get that many just by dummying up a picture of the course."

"Huh?"

"Talk to that guy, Della's . . . the quick-print guy."

"Tony?" Melissa frowned into the phone.

"He's got an artist. Or get Della to do it. All she has to do is lay the candles in over a shot of the bridge. Post it."

Melissa tried to conjure a reason to ignore Erica's suggestion. But there was only the obvious: Erica was a logistics expert. Melissa was supposed to do the marketing. Melissa sighed. "That's a great idea," she said.

Tony spun the chair around so he faced the salon mirror and held his arms out to his ex-wife. "Climb aboard," he invited.

"Tony!" she scolded. "Whatever happened to foreplay?" She moved one of Rita's scented candles to the center of the work counter and struck a match. "There!" Della walked over to the salon entrance and switched off the overhead lights. "Let's try a little romance here."

"Come here, then," he said. She stood near the chair and he slipped his hand under her skirt. "Ah," he said, feeling her bare skin. "This is romantic."

She reached down, helped him undo his pants and slip them off before she straddled him. They kissed some more. In the candlelight, she could make out his grin as he popped the front-close bra. "Another favorite thing," he said. "It's not my birthday, is it?"

"Nope."

"Well, is it yours?"

She laughed, leaned down to kiss him again. Della thought it would be one more of those ordinary places in her life transformed by a little sweat and semen.

The salon chair was not as accommodating as the equipment in the fitness room. The sides of the chair were rigid, and once Della accepted Tony's invitation to climb on, they couldn't shift position much. They found a rhythm, though, and eventually generated the excitement they needed to forget the restrictions of their surroundings.

In that sense, thought Della as they clung to each other afterward, it almost didn't matter where they coupled, as long as they did. She smiled down at him, her arms still tight around his neck and her legs over the sides of the chair.

"Not as good as the ab board," Tony said, smiling. "But I do like the mirrors."

"Me too," she assured him. "Since I don't have to face them."

"Something for both of us then."

They laughed together and began, slowly, to rearrange themselves. Rita had gone somewhere with her courthouse friends, and Melissa and the boys were with Ethan on some race-related task, which meant they could take their time. "Where's Kat?" he asked after Della ran this all down for him.

Della cocked her head to one side. "You know, I think she's around somewhere. Nick was working late, and she had lots to do here, so she's home for a change. But she never comes down here."

"There goes the fear of discovery!"

"I figured we were past that," Della said. "This session, anyway."

Tony grinned. "I'm always working on next time."

"No doubt." Della helped herself to a brush from Rita's supplies, and began to brush her hair in light from the candle. "Anyway," she said, "it's nice not to have Flops whining outside the door, wondering what I'm doing to you."

Tony laughed. "You want the lights?" he asked. She nodded, and he walked over and flipped on the overheads. "That dog's just addled," he said. "She a retriever, but she's afraid of water. And she should be attached to you, or Kat, since you're the only original owners left. But instead, she guards me."

"Well, she attached to Barbara, too," Della reminded him. "Almost from the second she walked in. It took her months after Barbara died to start noticing any of us again."

Tony stood at the salon entrance, watching Della brush her hair. "We dogs have to stick together," he said. "She just recognizes her own kin."

"Kin or kind," Della shot back.

Later, after she locked up the salon and they drove around to the Hutto house, they found Flops on the step, waiting outside in the warm night. "She's been down to the water," Tony said, taking the towel off the railing to dry Flops's paws. "Were you listening to us?" he asked the dog, rubbing the towel beneath her belly. "Huh? Eavesdropping across the Rio Nolan?"

Della swallowed hard, watching the affection Tony lavished on Flops. Some people are just more generous, emotionally, she thought. I'm a miser, and Tony's a philanthropist. She hated the comparison, but was pleased with the analogy. I'm not investing without a guaranteed return, she thought. Tony's always willing to gamble.

But he wants a different kind of return, she thought. He's happy if you just love him back. He doesn't expect fireworks.

She debated sharing this line of thought with Tony, but she feared it would hurt his feelings. Then, after they were in bed, and she was almost asleep, something else occurred to her. "Hey, Tone, you asleep?" she asked.

"Not anymore."

"What do you think about this? All that excitement and passion you get when you're first in love?"

"Yeah."

"Maybe after you have it the first time, the only way you can get it again with someone you love is just to forget about it, write it off. And then you could be surprised again, because you've written it off."

"Or," he mumbled, "you could just keep running after new men until you run yourself into the grave."

"Or new women. It's mostly men who do that. Perpetual adolescence." She poked his shoulder gently.

"You're reading too many relationship books," he muttered. "Men are from Sears. Women are from Saks." He snuggled deeper into the mattress.

Della pushed herself up on her elbows, wedging the pillow behind her head, and peered into the darkness. Tony groaned a little, which she took as a warning not to disturb him further with her insights, but she didn't see how he could sleep. The difficulty, she thought, is that once you've had a new-love kind of excitement, how could you ever forget it?

They took Webb to the seeping spring. First they parked the car at the edge of a day-use lot, and followed a marked trail along the desert floor. Then they moved to an unmarked trail, a little path that headed through the creosote and acacia until it disappeared over a tiny ridge. Below the ridge lay a gully that they followed downward, until they rounded a bend into darkness.

"Jesus," Webb whispered as the cool air hit them.

"I know," Gladys said.

"How did you—"

"Rock hounding," Ray said. "Out here with a pick. Trick is finding your way out of the gully onto that little path. And not getting stuck here in the rain."

The pink bark of the madrone—lady's limb—stood out against the juniper and pine. Webb took Gladys's cue and let Ray set the pace. "Climb up," Ray instructed, leading the way up along the rocky slope that circled the water. He moved slowly, testing his footing with each step.

The plants—several dozen—sat in a sunny spot beyond the juniper, on the far side below the spring, surrounded by tall grasses.

"Just enough soil," Webb noted, scratching the dirt with a boot heel. He squatted, rolled a dark leaf between his thumb and forefinger. He looked up at Ray.

"You were out here by yourself?"

"The two of us," Ray said. "She used to sit back toward the river, wait on me there." He shrugged. "Days I could move around."

Webb crumbled a little dirt in his hand, noted the mulch. "You dragged all this out here, Gladys?"

Ray looked annoyed, but Gladys laughed. "Dragged it out here myself," she said. "Crime's no picnic."

Webb glanced back over his own shoulder to take in the backpack of cold drinks and sandwiches.

She laughed again. "No matter what you think."

Webb straightened, nodded toward the plants. "Have you tried any of this?"

"We're waiting on buds," Ray assured him. "Seeds." He took off his hat, and wiped his sweaty face with his neckerchief.

They seated themselves on the rocks, kicking first for snakes. Then they opened new water bottles and shared sandwiches.

"You're risking everything, and you don't even know if it's any good?"

Gladys shot him an annoyed look, but Ray remained cheerful, inclined his head toward his wife. "This keeps her busy, makes her feel like she's doing something for her sick old man."

"Where are you buying it now?" Webb asked.

"We got a kid or two in town," Ray said.

"Couldn't you just—"

"Sooner or later someone tells someone," Gladys said. "Someone always does. There are no secrets. And maybe no one does anything. Maybe for a long time. Maybe never. But what if something changes? What if they need a witness, just to threaten our contact enough to give up someone higher on the food chain? Or some politician makes a big stand about guarding the border?" She motioned at Ray. "This is something we won't outgrow. We need a steady supply. And a therapeutic dose, no variation in quality."

To Webb, it was like knowing that even without cash he could put ripe tomatoes and fresh eggs on the table.

Their silence was amiable, first while they ate, and afterward while they studied the purplish-green peaks of mountains that marked both sides of the Rio Grande in the Big Bend. Every few minutes, Ray shifted position, moving into the sunlight and lying on the rocks to warm his back, then standing and stretching, balancing with one boot on the ground, the other braced atop a stump.

Webb guessed the spot stayed deserted because it remained unmarked on the park guides and because the spring created a marsh around a pool too small even for wading. The mosquitoes would discourage most hikers, thought Webb, appreciating Gladys's emphatic warnings both to grease up and cover up.

Webb had heard that the park and surrounding ranches were honeycombed with secluded springs, where you could frolic naked and never hear another human voice. Locals kept those places to themselves, even the ones on public park land. And custom dictated that even on private property such springs remain open to those who could find them.

Maybe, Webb thought, instead of a spring that watered a marijuana plot, Ray should find a hot spring and soak his back and hips in that. Webb left the suggestion unspoken, though. He found that when he thought about things long enough, he usually found abundant reason not to speak them. Certainly Ray was smart enough to think of a hot spring. So either he hadn't found a good one yet, or that wasn't enough, and he still needed the drugs.

Gladys had smoothed a blanket on the rocks and she lay on her back, with her straw hat over her face. Webb could hear a light snore, and Ray winked at him when he caught Webb studying her.

"Tomorrow she goes to town for water workout at the college," Ray said as he and Webb skirted the edge of the seep. "We'll stay at the house, have ourselves a real smoker after lunch." They stepped back into the shade. "I meant what I've been saying. I never wanted you to take on this risk. Let alone your boy."

"It'd be a first offense, all around," Webb replied. "Feels good to do something useful."

"Is that what that brotherly order is about? Doing something useful?"

"It's not that exalted," Webb replied. "I just wanted to find myself a brother or two." He grinned at Ray, who, unlike Webb, had both brothers and sisters.

Ray looked back at Gladys and smiled a little. "Something happens to me, you'll come take care of Gladys?"

"Well, sure," Webb said. "She looked after Alice, you know." There was no path, and they were climbing over dead limbs on a soft floor of brown leaves and pine needles. "Y'all got Earl and— what's her name? Her mama's at the Ladies Farm."

"Darlene. They're busy, Webb. That barbecue catalog. Two kids, who knows how many more."

Webb nodded. It was the same with his boys. They'd come if called. But you hated to call.

"The way it is now," Ray said, "it's Gladys looking after them, when she's not taking care of me. She goes over there one or two afternoons a week to watch the kids, lets Darlene take a class at the college. Business math, or some such."

"Do they know? Earl and Darlene?"

"That'd be all we need! She'd get on the phone to her mama, Earl'd be on the Net finding some extra-power, arthritis-fighting magic weed."

"I'm going to mix you up a little fertilizer," Webb said. "Something to counter the alkali. Add a little magic of my own."

"It's not much of a crime, when you think about it."

"No," Webb agreed. "It's not."

"But I'd feel like a fool, everyone knowing. Plus, it's one thing for Gladys and me, something else for you. Hell, you end up in jail, neither one of us can look after Gladys."

"No one'd go to jail for this. Probation, maybe." Webb wondered where Ray was taking him, but he kept his eyes on the ground ahead of him and followed. "Mostly it would be embarrassment, wouldn't it? That and an end to your medication."

Ray had stopped, and they stood on the edge of a sharp drop. He nodded toward the vista without comment.

"You're looking pretty hearty," Webb continued, peering out. "Anything you're not telling me?"

Ray shook his head and grinned. "I'm feeling just fine. This stuff . . . it only gets worse, you know."

"But it's not fatal."

"No." Ray laughed. "Though there are times I wish I were dead." He touched his friend's shoulder. "We don't know what's ahead, that's all." He waved his hand at the space before them. "Just when you think you're as low as it gets here, it falls off lower."

They balanced over the slope. Webb was so turned around, he didn't know whether the river was before him or behind him, but another dry plain of creosote and yucca stretched into the distance. The sun glinted off the mineral-streaked ground, and Webb wondered if there was another dip out there concealing another oasis. Someone else's stash, he thought.

Chapter 18

This time, Tony didn't call Flops, he followed her. When she dove off the county road, Tony conjectured that the little trail through the mesquite hooked up with the path that led from the bench below the house. The ladies considered the bench a prime asset on an otherwise unusable steep hill. If the paths met where it was level, maybe he and Dave could clear a space, make a little picnic spot.

Then again, maybe it was just some hideaway where he could take Della.

Tony half-slid down the hill, bracing himself on the spindly trees and skirting the prickly pear. He could hear Flops snort and crunch below him, barking as she heard him approach. She reached him as he braced himself on the edge of a cleared space, knocking him against a stump, then racing away again. Wishing he had on boots, Tony stepped into the sunlight and took in what must have been a garden, at one end of which sat the remains of a wooden shed.

Flops kept barking. Maybe a deer, maybe a rabbit, maybe a snake. She raced at the far corner of the plot and Tony followed through knee-high weeds. The path must come in there, he thought. From where he stood, he could see a corner of the Hutto house, but it disappeared as he strode forward.

"What are you hunting?" he asked the retriever. "Hmmm?" Her tags jingled to her yelping and jumping, and Tony wondered if this dog had ever located fallen prey, let alone carried it back to a hunter. The slope leveled out, and it was then he saw the half-dozen plants, leafy and green, mulched and well-tended.

"Hello!" he said. Tony had gone to college. He knew what he was looking at. Now he noticed the hose that ran down from behind the wooden remains, and he followed the hose back up the hill. He had just about reached the structure, which he saw was some sort of barrier, when Flops ran up from behind. Tony turned, and that was when he saw Ethan.

"Found my stuff," Ethan said.

"This is yours?"

Ethan nodded. "Farmer's son. Chip off the old block."

Tony looked around at the clearing, then walked over to the old wood. Behind it he saw the cistern, picked out the line of rocks that channeled water.

"Pretty elaborate."

Ethan nodded.

Tony stood there, the hum of insects rising as he felt the heat from his walk congeal on his bare arms and legs. Robbie, his son, was close to Ethan's age, but Tony couldn't imagine Robbie working this hard to grow pot. He couldn't imagine why anyone would.

"Is this your business now?"

"Nah. Six plants. Private stock." Ethan shrugged, walked over to the barrier and sat on it. "Couldn't let the old man find it."

"Well, it is still illegal."

"Oh, that's not why." Ethan grinned. "I just couldn't stand to let him know I'm conducting botanical research. See him gloat."

"So what do you do with this?" Tony seated himself next to Ethan. "If you're not selling it?"

"I'm not sure. I just . . . I mean, I'm sure I'll smoke some of it. Give some of it to friends. Private stock and all that. Mostly, though, it's curiosity. What yield, how strong, et cetera. You know, past the dorm-room stuff, no one ever pays much attention to it. Despite what you may have heard, I do care about growing things."

"So, you're here to help out your dad, and things seem a little slow, so you plant marijuana over at your neighbors' place, experiment with fertilizers, light, water. You're a regular Brother Mendel."

"I like to think of myself as George Washington, Thomas Jefferson, that kind of thing. Enlightenment farmer."

"The *Journals of Ethan Dyer: Writings of a Gentleman Botanist.*" Tony recalled Pauline, Melissa's mother, and her journals. Special paper, colored inks. Did this boy even know? "Has Melissa seen this?"

For the first time, Ethan looked alarmed. "Oh, no! No one knows about this!"

"I need to show you something," Webb said.

Ray raised his head from the wooden bench where he lay and winked at Gladys. "You two want the porch to yourselves?" He reached out an arm and Gladys, grinning indulgently, passed the blunt back to him.

"Let me just get it," Webb said, shaking his head as he headed back into the house.

Ray inhaled deeply, holding the smoke as long as he could. He lay back down flat, holding the blunt out and smiling as he exhaled.

Gladys leaned back against the sofa. Their afternoon cocktail hour had grown to include sesame crackers and a plate of the cheese they ordered through the co-op in Alpine. Today's feature was an aged pecorino that seemed the perfect complement to the crackers and the Shiner Bock.

To Gladys's delight, the enlarged happy hour allowed, almost mandated, a simpler dinner. Rather than face the complexity of the stove, Gladys and Webb could slap together cold-cut sandwiches and chips, and rejoin Ray, who would be stretching on the porch, still savoring the smoke. This arrangement evoked such pleasant domesticity that Gladys was still smiling when Webb returned, bearing a quilt.

Webb unfolded the thing. Peaches and small green leaves. The patchwork cover started in one corner with a single, tumbling peach, then more and more peaches cascading to the opposite corner into a bushel basket.

Alice had taken up needlework when she and Gladys got involved with the library, stitching her way through endless committee meetings. Gladys had never seen this piece, though. The peaches were made up of crescents of cloth, as many as six or seven to a peach, showing colors from deep red to light yellow. She recognized some of the fabric: pastel slips from tablecloths her friend had favored for holidays, and shiny blouses Alice had worn to church with drapey, loose-fitting skirts.

With great care, Gladys stubbed out the blunt and rested it on the big metal ashtray Earl had crafted in high school. She picked up a napkin from the stack next to the plate of cheese and crackers, and she wiped each of her fingers, one at a time. Then she stepped forward and lifted the bottom corner of the cover.

This work had taken years. Gladys stood for a second, studying the fine stitches on the last few patches. She imagined her friend laboring over them in those dwindling moments when she had energy enough to concentrate, strength enough to control the needle. The stitches were flat and even, every curve of fabric lying smoothly up against the next piece.

"There's a sack," Webb said. "With a bunch of thread, even needles."

Gladys studied the cover, tracing the stitchery near the top, where Alice had started the actual quilting. The quilts Alice and Gladys had made together featured quilting stitches that ran in straight lines across length and breadth. The two of them had held to the standard of hand-stitching to secure backing and filler to the patchwork front, but had never attempted anything fancier than diagonal lines or outlining simple shapes.

Alice's quilting here suggested tendrils of fresh leaves springing from new shoots. Across the white backdrop and through the cascading peaches, Alice had hand-stitched in pale green and light brown. She had woven the lines in and out, hardly discernible among the cascading peaches, suggesting the budding branches without drawing notice to the stitcher's artistry.

Webb looked over the edge of the quilt at his wife's friend. "There's no tissue pattern, or any sketching. I thought maybe someone who knows what she's doing could figure it out."

"This is beautiful," Gladys said.

Behind her, Ray was rolling off the bench, pulling himself to his feet with the help of the porch railing. He walked up behind her and reached around to touch the peaches, running his fingers over the finely worked fabric. "We've got the quilting frame," he said. "The big one. It's out in the shed."

"I haven't done any quilting since we moved out here," Gladys said.

"We can set it up," Ray offered. "In the big room."

Webb looked at Gladys.

"You know, I was never as good as she was at it. Once she got started, she did things—you know, sort of freestyle—that no one else could do. Just like those peaches."

"Well, she did know how peaches looked up close," Webb said.

Gladys traced a green line with her finger. "And this . . . I wouldn't ever know . . ."

Ray spoke up. "You can kind of tell, though. There's a pattern. You can see it, if you focus on it." He leaned over her shoulder, traced the same green line, then moved to another one. "See how it repeats? Here?" He pointed again. "And here?"

Gladys turned a little, looked at her husband's animated expression. She smiled. "I'll take a crack at it."

Webb stepped back a little to give himself room to fold the quilt.

"But you've got to know," Gladys said, "I'll never do as well as she did."

Webb nodded, kept folding and smoothing.

Gladys motioned toward the door with her hand so he would put the folded quilt down inside.

When Webb returned, he picked up his beer and leaned against the rail. He sipped. "I'd just like to see the thing finished," he said. "Not leave the thing undone."

Ray lit the blunt again, drew hard, and then passed it to Webb, who nodded his thanks.

Gladys, watching the two of them sharing weed, missed her friend Alice. No one else to tell about it, Gladys thought. She shook her head a little. Would it be possible, she wondered, to work on it by day and unravel it at night? Some Big Bend Penelope, trying to forestall . . . what? Webb's determination to put things in order?

Gladys sighed, reached for the blunt, then set it, still smoldering, back in the ashtray. "I'd better start dinner," she told them, thinking those were the reddest four eyes she had ever seen. She chuckled though, as she turned into the house. How long would it have taken for Webb to show us that quilt, thought Gladys, if he hadn't started smoking pot.

Johnny had waited as long as he could to drop the last one. He would have taken money from the cash register, but there was never much cash there. Even the ATM posed dangers of discovery; the last time he hit it, Siggie bounced five checks and made him put it back out of his salary. That was when Shane introduced him to Freddy Parker and he'd worked out his own supply.

Now, though, sitting in the truck near the city park, the panic was creeping up and he knew there was no choice. He drummed his fingers on the dash, thought about two guys he knew near Godley. He'd run the ATM, then head their way. Just seeing himself in Godley made him feel better.

Johnny slid out of the car, walked behind a tree and relieved himself. He laughed a little about Siggie. She didn't scare him. Not really. He'd slapped her the last time she'd jawed on him about money. Slapped her and roared out in the truck. She'd spent a week at her parents'; they drove her crazy, and, in the end, she needed him as much as he needed her. But it only worked if he had outside money. Shane was right: they needed to get back into business.

Johnny zipped up, cracked his knuckles in the dark night, then shook his jerky hands. He spied the water bottle on the floor when he opened the truck door and the overhead light came on. Hide that, he thought. Before one of the kids got it.

He was holding on to it in case he got a chance with that girl at the counter of the engine parts place in Fort Worth. Take her out for a beer, drop a little of that slimy water in it. Not enough to put her out, just enough to make her agreeable.

Johnny picked up the bottle, started to climb into the truck, then thought better of it and rummaged around instead to see if there was a stray beer. Damn! His hand clattered through the empty cans. I'll get a sixpack, he thought, when I get the cash. Take it to those boys in Godley. Good will.

Climbing into the truck and backing out onto the road cleared his head a little. He headed to the highway, then opted for the Farm-to-Market instead. It was loopy, and he especially liked the dip just outside town where the trees closed in tight and water sometimes reached flood stage.

He crested the hill and pressed hard on the accelerator.

"Straight down! Straight down!" he whooped to the blackening road. He peered into the dark, looking for water. He headed for that knob of asphalt that preceded the lowest point and thrilled to the rush in his stomach. "Four wheels off the ground," he yelled. Even screaming, he knew it was darker than it should be. That's why he was leaning forward. That's what made him think about the lights. Damn!

His right hand fumbled with the switch, but that just kept turning on the blinker. If he didn't hit them soon, he'd miss the bottom. "Fuck it!" he snarled. He put both hands on the wheel and just closed his eyes.

"It's a fort? As in a stockade?" Della set her newsletter proofs down on the covers and looked at him. "I've walked down that path a hundred times; it ends in brambles."

"It only looks that way from our side. I walked back. It's overgrown, but passable. And there's another path, from the road. That's how Ethan gets in."

"And he's growing pot? And Melissa doesn't know?"

"Shhh. Greg's right down the hall."

"Greg is brain-dead, as far as I can tell."

"He is a little mopey," Tony said. He had pulled a magazine off the stack next to the bed, but it lay unopened in his hand. Now he rolled it up and gestured at the window with it. "How much pot do you think six plants produce?"

"I don't have any idea," Della said. "I can't even remember the last time . . . it must have been that time Barbara Morrison puked all over Kat's ficus. Remember?"

He frowned. "When was that?"

"Don't you remember? Kat and Hal would have us all over and we would sit in that back room, all that chrome and glass furniture, with all those plants and that silver wallpaper with green ferns on it?"

"Can't say I remember the wallpaper."

"But you remember the wine and the board games. And the grass."

He nodded. "And the M&M's. And"—he turned to her— "didn't we use the M&M's to keep score for something? Cards?"

"Poker chips," she confirmed. "Though we used to scarf them up so fast, we'd start using popcorn."

"Oh, yeah." Tony smiled. "I remember that now. Barbara sick in the corner, Pauline kneeling next to her with some sort—"

"The tablecloth. She ran into the dining room and came back with a tablecloth for Barbara to puke on. I think that's why it was the last time."

"Oh, yeah."

"After that it was swimming with the kids, or a night at the movies and a drink out afterwards."

Tony looked at her, at the pulled-down corners of her mouth and her wide eyes. Her brows arched in a permanent question. "That was the last time we smoked pot together?"

She nodded, smiling. She lifted her face to him, as if she wanted him to kiss her, as if she had confessed something. Did she know that he used to smoke it at the store sometimes, after hours, with that girl—Cheryl, Shara, something—who worked part-time and went to the junior college? And when he married Suzanne, even before that, when the house in Fort Worth had seemed so empty, he would pull out LPs—ZZ Top, Cream, Grateful Dead—stack them up and listen and smoke till he fell over sideways.

Della's eyes had narrowed and she was watching him, disappointed, probably, that he hadn't kissed her. "That wasn't the last time for you, was it?"

He felt like a thief, as if he had stolen some precious memory from her, but all he had stolen was the belief that he hadn't smoked pot without her. "I used to miss you so much, when we first split up, after Jamie . . . I used to just sit in the dark and work up a little buzz." Now he did lean over and kiss her, lightly, on the tip of her nose.

"I know. I used to do that, too. Not pot, but wine. And I'd play old records. The Eagles. Bob Dylan. Simon and Garfunkel. Even the Beatles." She thought for a second. "Well, I don't begrudge Ethan his little secret, but it's mighty peculiar he planted it on our property."

"Too many people on the orchards," Tony told her.

"And Melissa. Do you think—"

"He says she doesn't know. Asked that we not tell her. Actually, he asked me not to tell anyone. But of course he knows—"

Della nodded, smiling faintly, and he shook his head again. Everyone knows, he thought.

"But you can't tell Melissa," Tony warned. "Or the others."
Della snuggled up against him. "What did he say about her?"
Tony squinted.

"Melissa! What'd he say? Is he worried about Greg?"

"We didn't talk about that," Tony said. "He just told me about
the plants. He resurrected some kind of do-it-yourself irrigation
Ray Hutto rigged up."

"He didn't even ask about Greg?"

Tony shook his head. "I don't think he's worried much about
Greg. You know . . ." He thought back over the conversation.
"Maybe it's being a farmer. Or at least growing up on a farm, an
orchard: maybe you learn patience. How to let things take their
course."

"I can't believe you didn't get him to talk about Greg." Della
propped herself up on one arm, thoroughly awake. "Who else did
you smoke with? Did you smoke with Suzanne?"

"We had sex, too."

"In the backyard?"

"In the hall. In the bathtub. Swinging from the chandelier.
Only one way to erase that memory."

"So you've told me. I might take you up on it," she said.
"Greg's starting to creep me out, always there in the next room."

"I thought you were cool with it."

"I was," Della said. "Because Melissa wanted us to keep an eye
on him. But now he's talking about taking a leave of absence, and she
. . . that's why I thought maybe you'd get something out of Ethan."

"Look, Del, the only ones who know what's going on are
Melissa and Greg and Ethan. And they're not talking."

"No," she agreed. "But you have to try harder, next time."

"You know, if you're so stir crazy, we could spend a night or
two in Fort Worth. The house is just sitting there. The cleaning
service comes every week, changes the sheets, polishes the headboard. It's all ready."

He should have stopped. He could read the whole thing in her
face. She was thinking about Jamie's room, wondering how it
would feel to see it now, fixed up as a guest room after Suzanne
had moved her kids out. He wanted to tell her it was like nothing
at all, that it was just a room, and after a while you didn't even
think about it, but that sounded crueler than saying it would
break her heart.

*   *   *

When he opened his eyes, Johnny remembered exactly how to operate the lights with his left hand, but he didn't turn them on right away. Instead, he closed his eyes again and tried to determine how he felt. He wiggled his fingers and toes, ran his tongue over his teeth and along the inside of his mouth, put his hand out to where the airbag would be if it had gone off.

Then he opened his eyes again. He flipped on the lights, but all he could see were branches. The truck was pointed uphill, it seemed, but had landed on all four wheels. "Christ." His head pounded, but it didn't feel as if he had hit it on anything. With his eyes closed, he reviewed what he had just seen and concluded that somewhere after the dip, he had run off the road, through the brush.

"Well, hell!" he muttered. Running through brush was why he had bought the damn truck. Eyes still closed, he figured it out. It was still night. He was okay. The windshield was intact, the engine had stalled, but the battery light was still on. Just back it up, Johnny thought. The throbbing behind his eyes was killing him, and he was shaking, but nothing would get better till he got to Godley. He had to put the truck in gear.

Easy, Johnny thought, firing the ignition and putting the beast into reverse. The engine throbbed in time to his head, and he released the clutch enough to make the truck rock. But it didn't go. "C'mon," he said. "C'mon, c'mon."

It must have been muddy, must have been wet where he went off the road. Because once the truck unstuck, it rolled easily back toward the asphalt. He thought for a second about checking the tires, but he didn't care, as long as he was rolling. Then he put the thing in first and drove forward, on the road.

"Now the lights," he said aloud. He flipped them on and caught just a glimpse of his own muddy tracks before he revved up to speed. "Heading down the highway," he sang. "Out to see America. Out to see—" He remembered the ATM. Cash. Beer.

There was a place on the road about halfway to Godley. Johnny could see it, the bright lights, the—

"I wet my fucking pants!" he said. He let up on the accelerator, rolled to a stop in the middle of the road. Goddamn it! Why did this shit always happen to him! He wondered if he had pants in the back of the truck, but he doubted it. That bitch was always grabbing laundry.

A new plan took shape. He started a U-turn, got himself horizontal in the road, backed up, inched forward, backed up, inched forward. Underway again, he couldn't distinguish his own shaking from the shudder of the truck. Must have blown a tire, he thought, but that didn't matter. He'd sneak into the house. Change his pants. Sneak out. Go to the ATM. Get a sixpack. Head to Godley.

Maybe he could knock off a piece with Siggie, just real quick, just to keep her from getting too mad. He'd kiss her a lot first. Afterward, she'd fall asleep, and she'd never know when he left.

He overshot the drive, had to back up. Drove slow over the gravel. Killed the lights. Her parents were at the end of the road, but he and Sig were off to the side. He could just pull right up to the front.

Johnny felt his head split, felt his skin zip open, peel back. He couldn't hold the wheel, which wanted to go into the bar ditch. He hit the brake. Damn right wheel! In the ditch.

Johnny knew this part by heart. Just do this, he ordered himself. He flipped open the console between the seats, felt for the bottle. He yanked off the top, poured out the Tylenol—a handful—slammed them into his mouth. Then he reached under his own seat. I'll just sip it, he thought. I'll leave enough for the counter girl.

It was slimy, and sweet-tasting, but not bad. Johnny, in the dark, grinned. He had sweat through his shirt and his pants were soaked, and with the air in the truck off, it stank. He opened the door and slid out. His legs were wobbly, but okay. Siggie's car would be easier to drive.

I'll just walk up to the house, he thought. Change clothes. Do Siggie.

He sipped again. Do Siggie. Change clothes. That was right.

Walk up to the house. Do Siggie. Change clothes. Siggie's car. ATM. Cash. Sixpack. Godley.

He could barely lift the bottle, but his shaking was gone. This stuff definitely, definitely.

Johnny tried a few steps. Their house was half a mile from the road. He must have driven halfway. A quarter mile, he thought.

Then he stopped. He held the bottle up in front of his face, trying to see it in the dark. Shane has more, Johnny thought. Shane has plenty. There's plenty for the counter girl!

House. Siggie. Clothes. Siggie's car. ATM. Cash. Sixpack. Godley.

Johnny smiled, amazed at how great he felt, knowing he had a plan. He turned the bottle up and chugged. Then he walked a few steps more. He could see the house now. Bathed in yellowish light, a safe little island. Maybe he should try the back door.

Johnny stopped in the road. He could feel every stone under his shoes. Even without turning, he could see his truck behind him, tilted in the ditch. The house. The stones. The truck in the ditch. The bottle slipped out of his hands, and he heard it bounce.

Johnny just grinned. Shane had more.

Still, it was a good bottle. Maybe he should get it.

And everything worked out, Johnny thought. Because he was on his hands and knees when he started puking. He puked right there, into the ditch. When I'm done, he thought, I'll just go on to the house. House. Siggie. Clothes. Something.

Chapter 19

Della waited till Kat had left for Fort Worth and Melissa had sent the boys off to Vacation Bible School with Greg.

"My Presbyterian mother's probably rolling in her grave," Melissa said, breezing into the office. "But you have to hand it to the Methodists, they've got summer covered, at least in this town."

Della wondered what the Methodists would think of Greg, if they knew. Even so, they would welcome Trey and Garrett. "The boys seem to be enjoying it. Especially the swimming," Della said. "I doubt your mother would object to swimming and crafts. Or Bible verses, for that matter."

Melissa smiled, and Della felt rewarded for offering reassurance.

"Greg's turned out to be a help," Della said.

Melissa nodded again. "Uh huh." She had seated herself at Pauline's old rolltop and switched on her computer.

"And the boys seem glad that he's here."

"Yeah." Melissa concentrated on her keyboard.

"Soooooo . . ." Della let her voice trail off.

Melissa turned.

"I'm guessing Greg's staying a while, huh?"

"Is that a problem?" Melissa frowned, then registered understanding. "You don't like him at the house."

"Oh, that's no problem," Della gushed, then laughed. "Well, I mean, Tony's a little nervous. He keeps counting my lingerie, makes me sign out my panties, but, hey! What's life without a little fetish control?"

Melissa looked at her. "Then things are fine, aren't they?"

"I'm just trying to . . . we're wondering when Greg's . . . how long he's staying. You know, because of the room and everything."

"You have someone who wants to rent the Hutto house?"

"Not now. But, you know, we need a place for Erica during the peach festival, and we want the rooms here available for guests. All your runners. Big money."

Melissa nodded. "I hadn't thought about that. Maybe Erica could stay over at Ethan's."

"You're pretty confident."

"I'm pretty busy," Melissa said. "I'm sorry, Aunt Dell. Y'all have been great and we've just taken over!"

"No, you've been great, we're merely"—Della waved a hand at their surroundings—"accommodating. Melissa, you're saving Peach Fest."

"I hope not, I hope there're a lot more folks than me."

"But you're the catalyst."

"Yeah. But that doesn't mean my cross-dressing husband gets to live with you forever. I'll talk to him, maybe he can rent by the week somewhere."

"Melissa, honest, that's not what I'm getting at."

"Honest?"

"Honest. Greg's a little depressing, night and day. And it does make me nervous, wondering what he does in his room so much." Della relaxed. "But he can stay forever if that's what you want, Melissa. We're just trying to plan the next few weeks. We've got reservations to take care of."

"Well, I think Greg's staying through Peach Fest. At least, I'm hoping he is; I need his help. And that"—she shook her head, smiling gently—"should not be your problem." The smile grew mischievous. "I guess this means you and Uncle Tony want more time alone, huh?"

Della would never get used to grown-up children who assumed that adulthood allowed them the same invasion of her privacy that she inflicted on theirs. Her resentment, however, yielded to vanity: Melissa found Della and Tony interesting! Della felt herself blush.

"Now you sound like Rita," Della said.

"We just don't want you to be alone."

"Definitely Rita."

Melissa smiled. "Well, I could do worse."

"And I'm not alone, anyway," Della said. "I've got Rita and Kat. And now you!"

"Well, through Peach Fest, anyway." Melissa waved her hand at the desk. "Then it's back to the real world."

"Any plans?" Della asked.

"I'm thinking now about Austin," Melissa said. "Erica's hot to get me on board there, but I may just do consulting. I'm still putting together a résumé. It could take months to find something. And who knows where I'll end up. Maybe back in California. I've still got contacts there. Though no house."

"Is Greg staying in Portland?"

Melissa shook her head. "I don't think he knows. He wants to be close to the boys, he wants to stay in tech development, he wants to live someplace green." She sighed. "Sometimes you don't get all you want."

"But if you try sometimes," Della sang.

Melissa blanked.

"Wrong generation," Della muttered.

"Oh." Melissa nodded. "The Rolling Stones. You're right. My generation is more like, *Trust is just a faded memory.* And now I just want to lie on my back kicking and screaming. I keep wondering what drugs would help me."

Della leaned forward from the sofa, put her hand on Melissa's. "Oh, honey, it'll get better. I promise it will."

Tears made their way down either side of Melissa's face as she stared at Della. "How, exactly, will it ever get better?"

"Well, I don't mean it will be perfect," Della said. What compelled her to reassure? How could things possibly get better for Melissa? "But, look," Della told the girl, "you've already reconnected with Ethan. That could make things better in a hurry. Besides," she said and winked, "you're back in Texas. Everything's better in Texas."

"I wish I believed that," Melissa said.

"Uh, honey, when I say everything's better in Texas, you're supposed to break into a wide grin and nod your empty little head."

That did produce a smile, but only a little one.

"I don't think I'm being fair to Ethan," she said.

Della checked her desire to comfort Melissa on that score as well. "What do you mean?"

"I mean . . . before Greg showed up, I told him we could start dating. Really, I'm kind of relieved we didn't. I'm not ready, Aunt Dell. I don't think I'll ever be ready. I don't want anyone that close to me. Ever!"

"Oh, honey—"

"I think that's why I want Greg to stay: so I can avoid anything closer with Ethan. But, the thing is, I still want him to pursue me. Ethan, not Greg," Melissa said.

Della nodded.

The tears were streaming now. "I want him to be desperately, passionately in love with me. Me. Me. Me. I don't even care what he thinks about the kids."

"Melissa, honey, of course—"

"Oh, I know all about rebuilding my ego, seeing Greg's . . . preference . . . as a rejection, reaffirming my sexuality. Blah, blah, blah. But the thought . . . just the thought of getting really close to anyone . . . Ethan, or any other man . . ." She looked up. "You are so lucky, Aunt Dell. To have Tony. To want the one who wants you. I don't know if I'll ever want anyone else."

"Honey, you have to give yourself some time. That's what I meant, before. I know I want Tony because I'm just old. I've lived longer, I know what's out there. And none of them are as good for me. But it took a while. And a few wrong turns."

Melissa gave a tentative smile. "I'm glad you didn't run after that handyman."

"Well, I did," Della corrected her. "He just turned me around and sent me back to Tony."

"You're even luckier, then."

"Oh, I don't know. Lucky might have been having Tony *and* the handyman hunk."

Melissa just looked at her.

"Oh, spare me. I'm just joking."

"I hope so. You know, there's no reason why you and Uncle Tony couldn't get married while I'm still here with the boys."

"Why would we get married?"

"That's what people do, Aunt Della. When they love each other . . . and one of them isn't a cross-dresser."

Melissa's heartfelt endorsement of marriage pierced Della's

blithe veneer. She leaned forward and put her open hands on either side of Melissa's face. "Uncle Tony and I do love each other, sweetie. But you're going to have to let us set the pace." Della pulled away and sat back against the sofa. "You'll be the first to know. I promise."

She thought for a second. "And, I'll tell you what. Maybe Tony and I will move over to the Fort Worth house for a while. You and the boys can have the Hutto place, and that'll free up a suite here. We'll just bunk there for the race weekend." Della took a deep breath, wondering if relieving Melissa's sorrow was reason enough to play house with Tony in Fort Worth.

"Are you sure, Aunt Dell? You don't have to do that, just be—"

"I'm sure." She grinned. "We're not giving you the place, just a little loan."

"But it solves things for us up to the race, anyway. The kids'll have a room and Greg can crash in the small room. Thanks so much."

Ethan picked up a sandwich from Randi before he headed down to the patch. When he called ahead, Randi had bagged up his gouda and turkey on a kaiser roll, along with a side of slaw and a pack of barbecue chips. She even carried the sack out to him when she saw the farm truck pull up in front of the drugstore.

Now that Greg had shown up, Ethan guessed Randi considered him fair game. It was probably harmless, thought Ethan. Her giggly chatter offered a few moments' diversion in days that had become long and hard since his father had left for the Big Bend. Randi was still dating that optometrist; her conversation couldn't hurt as long as he stayed in the truck and she stayed out of it. You sound like the old man, Ethan told himself. Except that the old man doesn't crave conversation.

More trucks waited at the orchard gate across from the Hutto place: Shane Castleburg's monster and the white Ford bearing the seal of the Sydon County Agriculture Extension Service.

Forget the sandwich, Ethan thought. He pulled the hand brake and jumped down. "Frank. Shane. What's up?"

"Just a plum-pox check," Frank said. "I'm going to grab leaves off your trees here, then the others on this road."

"They look okay, or they did yesterday," Ethan said.

"Probably are. Haven't had any outbreaks here, but they took out whole orchards in Pennsylvania, couple other places. Hard to control, once it starts."

Ethan nodded, pulled off the circle of chain that held the gate to the fence. "Dad's down in the Big Bend," he said. "You get the other fields?"

"This is the first of yours," said Frank.

"You find anything, leave word at the house. Go ahead into the other orchards."

Shane, who had stood quietly, stepped back to let Frank get into his truck. "Good talking to you." He smiled as the agent drove through.

Ethan closed the gate, careful of the metal, hot from the full sun.

"I wouldn't worry," Shane said. "Crop's gone, you're selling anyway. What's a little—"

"What's a little hoof and mouth?" Ethan asked. "What's a little mastitis?"

Shane stood next to his own truck. "Nothing I'm worried about. You know, if Frank thinks there's plum pox anywhere, he pretty much has to go in and examine it. Whether or not you give permission."

"Is that what you were chatting about? Plum pox?"

"Agriculture," Shane said. "I saw his truck from my place down on the river. I can see the whole hill from there."

Don't look over there, thought Ethan as he continued to smile at Shane. "Pretty dull watching."

"Oh, I don't know. I hear Melissa's moving over to that side, her and the kids and that supposedly estranged husband."

"Where'd you hear that?"

"Around." Shane leaned against his truck, eyed Ethan up and down. "You ought to stop and listen to Randi when you pick up that lunch of yours. You can learn a lot at a lunch counter."

Ethan shook his head, opened the truck door. "I'll keep that in mind." He reached for his sandwich, which had been baking on the passenger seat, then closed the door and grabbed a clipboard and a cloth tape measure from the box in the back.

"You know," Shane said, startling Ethan by coming up from behind, "if Melissa's living somewhere like the Hutto place, and there's something illegal going on, that could cause a whole lot of trouble for her." Shane looked at the farm truck, taking in the mud-splattered fender and the weather-beaten white paint. "Or," he suggested, "she could blame that same little problem on that husband she claims she wants to divorce."

Now he rested a hand on the roof of the cab, his palm flat on the sun-blasted surface.

"You know," drawled Ethan, "G. Gordon Liddy used to do that to intimidate people: put his hand in the fire."

"It could go a lot of different ways," Shane continued, keeping his hand where it was. "You gardening on the Hutto place."

"Not much of a crime: gardening." Ethan grinned. He doubted Shane felt much through his calluses.

"It could be less of one, if you were willing to share." Shane slid his hand off the truck.

Ethan nodded toward the orchard beyond the gate, where Frank coasted down a far row of the orchard, stopping a second at each tree to pluck a few leaves through his open window. "I've got work to do. You know: agriculture." Ethan walked over to the gate. "We think of him as some old radio-talk guy. But it turns out, Liddy went to jail."

"Now," said Ray, "here's where you make the curve." He leaned forward and carefully used the washable marker to sketch a shallow turn along the edge of a patchwork peach. Gladys sat at the quilting frame, the quilt stretched out before her like some un-crossed plain.

Poking the needle into the fabric, Gladys felt her way through the cotton top, the batting, and the back. She pulled four stitches onto the needle in the direction Ray indicated, then pulled the thread through.

To her chagrin, Webb rarely joined them while they worked. Gladys thought of it as inching along, but an inch was twelve stitches, not to mention Ray's painful charting of course and her own struggle to match Alice's precision. Meanwhile, Webb tramped along their road out to the highway, or drove himself into the park, hiking the trails above the basin. He checked the plot, filling his backpack with a fertilizer he mixed after studying Gladys's stash of *High Times*. And he tended the less exotic plants in their back garden, staking the tomatoes and battling the slugs that attacked the melons.

Ray, for his part, had become an expert on quilting technology. He took charge of Alice's needles, inspecting them for sharpness and smooth coating, to make certain they would pierce cleanly and produce no additional drag. He polished the hinges and clamps on the frame, and adjusted the height and frame tension as she worked.

Gladys helped Ray with his stretches in the morning, and they all still had happy hour on the porch in the afternoon. Maybe it just takes two husbands, at my age, thought Gladys. Or three adults for any household our age.

When Webb joined them that afternoon, Ray insisted that he survey their progress. Webb stood before the quilt, suspended vertically, now, on the upended frame. "It's coming along, isn't it?" Webb said. He examined the line Gladys had stitched out to the edge, and the way it turned back beneath one of the peaches. He gave a half-smile.

"You planning on taking that to your brothers?" Ray asked.

Webb took a step back from the quilt, then turned to Ray. "Hadn't thought about it. I doubt it, though."

"Oh, you're not still talking about that," Gladys said, leading the way out to the porch. It amused her that they followed so easily, but it no longer surprised her.

"Why not?" Webb took one corner of the porch sofa.

"Well, for one thing," Gladys informed him, settling into her own corner of the old couch, "I'm not ruining my eyes and crippling my fingers on a quilt that's going to be hidden away at some nutty monastery where folks can't even tell you what a masterpiece it is."

Ray eyed the two of them from his bench. "She's got a point. I figured you'd stay out here as long as you could stand it, then get back to your orchards."

"Ethan's listing the place for sale."

"You told us," Ray said mildly. "He hasn't sold it yet, has he?"

"Not that I know about."

"Well, I'm thinking that if you don't go to that . . . brotherhood . . . you could just pull that thing off the market."

"Or not," Gladys said. "Why don't you just sell the place and settle out here with us?" She pointed toward the side of their property. "The folks that own that lot told us they'd sell to us, if we were interested. We'll help you get settled."

"All the pot you can smoke," Ray offered.

Webb shook his head. "You don't . . . I've already told them I'm coming."

"Why?" Gladys asked.

"I just want to do some good," Webb said.

Ray squinted over at his friend. "You don't have to turn over any assets, do you?"

"We've been all through this," Webb replied. "I pay for room and board, offset by the value of my labor. All the labor is valued at the same rate, and most of the brothers earn their way without paying anything."

"Sounds like prison," Gladys said. "They don't charge you to stay there, either."

Webb ignored her comments. "I'm free to maintain my financial investments as I see fit, and I'm free to leave whenever I want."

"And what kind of labor are you figuring on doing there?" Ray asked. "Where is it again?"

"Ohio. And there's another fellowship in Missouri, and one in Iowa."

"And you're going to . . . ?"

"Farm," Webb said. "You know that."

"Webb," said Gladys, "don't you think you do good farming in Sydonia? You raised a family there. You lived with Alice there. What is it you want to do?"

"The brothers help others," Webb said. "You saw the brochure. They operate a school, they feed the needy—"

Now Gladys sat up straight. "Webb Dyer, are you saying there are no needy people in Sydonia? Your neighbors could use free food."

"It's not just free food," Webb insisted. "There's a school, we teach kids how to grow things, how to work, how to—"

"You do that without talking?" Ray asked.

Webb just glowered.

Ray rummaged around in the storage box and pulled out a joint. He studied it a second but didn't light it.

"It just seems so extreme," Gladys said. "Especially the silence."

Webb looked at her and shrugged.

"You're doing it now, aren't you?" she accused.

He gave a faint smile, and Gladys sat looking at him.

"You think Alice would want this for you?" she asked finally.

"Gladys!" Ray was horrified, and still hadn't lit the joint.

Webb's smile broadened. "You know what? I think Alice would tell me to go on and do what I want."

"Shut yourself off from other people, never speak, contemplate your navel?"

"Find a little peace," Webb said, still mild. "You know, what I think would bother Alice is how upset you are."

"Well, I think Alice would be upset, you running away this way. There are people who need you here. Your sons and their children. And . . ." Gladys could not stop her tears, had no idea where they came from.

Webb leaned over, put his hand atop hers. "I won't be far," he said.

"Glad?" Ray said. He started to stand up.

"I'm okay," she hastened to assure him. "Really." Then she turned to Webb. "But I always figured we could count on you, Webb Dyer."

"I'm here, aren't I?"

Now Ray did get to his feet. "Glad, the man drove four hundred miles. He looked after your marijuana. He even got his son in on it. What are you going on about?"

Gladys looked from her husband to their friend. "I just . . ." She felt her lips getting wobbly again.

"I shouldn't have brought that quilt," Webb said.

Ray looked from his wife to his friend and back again. "What the hell is going on here? I'm lighting up."

"Easy for you to say," Gladys said, but it was a weak attempt. She felt foolish. She couldn't say why she was so upset, and now she'd upset Webb and Ray, too. Tension was terrible for Ray's arthritis, stiffened him unbearably. She watched him struggling with the box of kitchen matches, saw Webb looking at her, then following her gaze to Ray, then leaning over to give Ray a hand.

Webb handed it all over to his friend, who struck the match, lit the joint, drew enough to make it glow, then passed it back to Ray.

She watched them smoking, neither one daring more than a glance at her. If Webb had never heard of those brothers, Gladys thought, he would have retired in Sydonia, or moved to Houston or Dallas with one of his boys, and we wouldn't have seen him at all, anyway. Maybe it is that quilt.

She sipped at her tea, clinking the ice in her glass as she set it back down. Webb shot her another glance.

"Oh, cut it out!" Gladys ordered. "The storm's over."

"I figured I'd get one really good harvest, and win the best bushel and the best peach competition," Webb said. "Then, you know how they auction the winners off for the library fund?"

Gladys and Ray both nodded.

"I figured I'd bid ten thousand for each."

"Ten thousand!" Ray stared at him.

"That'd be the highest ever paid for the bushel. And the peach, too, I suppose." Webb spoke slowly, recounting his plans. "Then I'd just pick up and go. Vanish. I mean, you and the boys would know, it wouldn't be a secret where I went. But I'd be gone. No trace. Just leave that little bit of good behind."

"Just make your grand exit?" Gladys asked.

"Then the storm."

"Oh." Gladys got it now. "God ruined your plans."

Webb sighed. "I guess."

"Well, you could still do it," Ray said. "You could sell the place, write the check, and leave town. That would do a lot of good."

"But it wouldn't be my peaches." Webb drew on the joint, and his voice came out a little higher. "I'll write a check anyway, of course. I want the library . . . you know, Alice—"

"Yeah," Gladys said. "You could write a big check. And then move out here."

Webb said nothing; he just looked away. Gladys studied him. Then she thought, *he can't stand seeing me without Alice. Damn it!* Tears again.

"Have you heard from Greg?" Melissa whispered to Della. She had walked over to the shed, where Della was leading a workshop in journal-keeping. Three matrons and a sensitive-looking young man sat at the table with open notebooks before them. Della had provided them with four-packs of colored gel pens, and she stood outside the shed door, watching them through the window as they performed a random listing exercise to get in touch with themselves.

"Who's the guy?" Melissa asked.

Della shrugged. "Potter. On his way to craft fairs in Arkansas. Rita's giving his wife a facial. What's up with Greg?"

"He's usually back by three, or he calls. But I haven't heard from him, I thought maybe someone else got the phone."

"Doesn't he call your cell?"

"Yeah, but maybe he couldn't get through. I double-checked the answering machine, too." Melissa breathed out hard. "Do you think he took them over to Dave's?"

"Why don't you call over there?" Della asked.

Melissa knew what she was thinking. "I'm not worried that he's kidnapped them," she said. "And I've been trying his cell, but he's got it off. I called the church, but everyone's already left."

Della peeked through the window again. "I'm sure he'll show up," she said, but she was already heading back to her journal-writers.

Melissa felt stupid. She was worried about nothing. But the boys were usually home by now, and she had turned so much of their day over to Greg that she couldn't even be sure he had taken them to day camp this morning. Not that she agreed with the ladies that Greg might kidnap them. But this was exactly the situation all the books warned you against. She didn't have anything she should: the kids' fingerprints weren't on file anywhere, their most recent pictures were boxed up, and she couldn't remember what they were wearing.

What made her trust Greg? Would her husband really believe that she would let him stay close to their two young boys once she stabilized her situation? Was he so contrite and concerned for her that he would be her child-care lackey just to worm his way back to her good graces? She tried to phrase an explanation for the police, but words failed.

Melissa jerked open the storm door and stepped into the kitchen. The house was silent. What if Greg had dropped the boys back here and they had run down to the river and fallen in? What if some pervert posing as a guest had greeted them on the front porch and driven away with them? Who were those people at Vacation Bible School, anyway? No one she knew.

She headed back to the office, pulled out the Sydon County directory, one inch thick and graced with a bushel of peaches on its cover. *Fire Department. Poison Control. Police. Sheriff.* A different scenario presented itself.

What if someone found out about Greg? Followed him. Ran him off the road. Beat him senseless.

All the hate crimes she had ever heard about came back to Melissa. Lynched from a lamppost. Dragged behind a truck. Eviscerated with hunting knives and pruning hooks. Trey and Garrett forced to watch. All because their father wore frilly underpants.

She was imagining the police interrogations, the hordes of reporters, the flocks of morbid onlookers reaching out to touch Trey and Garrett as they marched stoically toward their father's grave, when she heard the kitchen door, followed by Garrett's running.

He came straight to her, her youngest, launching himself at the doorway to land against her knees, hugging tight. "Trey broke his arm," Garrett said to her knees. "It was bent and he cried, and now he has a sling."

She let him drag her to the kitchen, where Greg was ushering a dazed Trey toward the stairs. "Tell you what," Greg was saying. "I'll carry you up, and then we'll get you to bed."

"What happened?"

Greg lifted Trey in his arms, careful to position the boy's cast and sling away from his body. "Just a little shoving match," Greg crooned, heading up the stairs. Melissa and Garrett followed.

"It wasn't shoving, it was a fair fight," Trey said after his father set him down on the bed.

Melissa leaned over him, brushed his hair back from his forehead. "How's it feel?"

"I got him," Trey insisted. "Then they pulled us apart. Then when it was time to go, he ran up behind me and shoved me down the steps. On the concrete!"

"Just rest now," Greg was saying.

"On the concrete!" Garrett repeated, reenacting the fall. "On the concrete."

Melissa turned to Greg. "Why didn't you call me?"

"Didn't they call? That teacher, Ms. Emily, said they'd get hold of you, we went straight to the emergency room, I figured you were on the way!" He glanced over at Trey, whose eyes were closed. "We should let him sleep," Greg said.

Melissa pressed her lips together, then motioned to the door-way. "Garrett," she whispered, "why don't you run and tell Aunt Rita and Aunt Della what happened, so they'll know Trey's okay."

Garrett raced downstairs and his parents followed. They faced each other in the center of the kitchen.

"Why didn't you call me?" Melissa demanded once the boy was out of earshot.

"I told you! I thought that Bible school . . . Mel, we went straight to the emergency room and they took us right to x-ray."

"I don't care. You could have called when you were waiting on the x-rays."

"Honey, you're upset! But he's okay, honest. And I was right there, the whole time. And I had to deal with Garrett—"

"What you had to do was call me! I'm their mother. I know how to deal with Garrett."

"I know how to deal with Garrett," Greg said calmly. He walked over to the table, sat at the end, so that he was still watch-ing Melissa. "Garrett was more upset than Trey was. I think when he saw Trey crying, he was really frightened. Trey's just angry be-cause he thinks he won the fight but lost the war anyway. Cowardly attack from behind."

Melissa cut the distance between them by half, but remained standing. "What did the doctor say?"

"That it's a green-spring fracture, should heal just fine. Keep him in the cast solid for a week, after that, he can take it off to bathe and sleep. He gave him a shot for the pain. After that, just Tylenol. No more fighting." He shifted, folded both hands in front of him on the table. "What happened with the luminarias?"

"They're ordered. They'll be here the week of the race. All I need is a sponsor."

"No luck, huh?"

"That's pretty obvious." She scowled. "Who was the other kid? I want to talk with that Ms. Emily."

"We can probably meet with her tomorrow," Greg said. "Maybe we want to keep Trey home a day, anyway. Until we make sure there's no shoving while he's in the cast."

"I'm ready to do some shoving of my own," Melissa retorted. "What the hell kind of Bible school is that, anyway? What hap-pened to turn the other cheek?"

Greg shook his head. "I think you're making more of this than you need to. Kids fight. Even in a church school."

"Yeah, well, you can say that when you're worried sick about your family and no one's called."

"Mel, I'm really sorry about that. She promised me she'd call, otherwise I would have. And for all the excitement, it's not much of an injury."

"But it could have been, falling on the concrete." Her earlier visions ripped through her head. "He could have had a concussion. The bone could have pierced the skin. What if that child had a weapon . . . a knife or—" She stumbled toward the table, sat down so she could rest her head in her hands.

"Hon, he's okay. Honest. They're both just fine."

This was Sydonia. Would her children ever be safe? "Weren't you scared?" Melissa asked.

"Terrified," said Greg. Tears filled his eyes. "I'm just waiting for you to calm down so I can fall apart."

"How you feeling, Johnny?"

The uniform shook him a little, but when he saw it was Vinnie Perez, Johnny relaxed. Vinnie had been a few years ahead of him in school, and was an okay guy. Kind of a goody-goody, Johnny thought, but not the kind to rat out a classmate or pick on younger kids.

Johnny looked down at the covers of his hospital bed and shook his head. "Can't remember how I got here, but I feel fine now."

"Your wife found you in the ditch, face first in your own vomit," Vinnie said. Johnny saw that he was holding a pen and a little pad of paper. Ready to take notes.

"Did she?" Johnny leaned back against the pillows, closed his eyes. "Poor thing."

"She brought you in, somehow. Put you in her car, drove you here."

"Siggie's strong," Johnny said. "I'll give her that."

Vinnie chuckled. "She said it was like lifting those big sacks of grain. Only nastier."

Johnny opened his eyes, looked remorseful. "She's good to me, Siggie. She's been here twice, once with the kids, and she never said a word about it. Not one complaint. I must have stunk up her car something awful."

"Your truck, too."

"What do you mean?"

"I mean, bad tire and all, she couldn't wait to get that thing towed into Fort Worth, get it all cleaned." Vinnie chewed at a corner of his lower lip, tapped the pen against the notebook. "Moved it out before I could even get a look at it."

"I'm a lucky man," Johnny intoned.

"Threw out all the beer cans. No one took a blood alcohol." Vinnie studied his notes. "Not much to report. No telling what made you so sick, nothing to say you were driving the truck, just that you were there, in front of it, in your own puke."

"Could have been a bug," Johnny suggested. "One of those twenty-four-hour things." He glanced at the IV in the back of his hand. "Could be why I'm so dehydrated."

"Could be," Vinnie said. He had one of those thin mustaches that moved as he spoke, making it hard to judge his intention. He peered over the notebook at Johnny. "I think it had more to do with the plastic bottle I found."

"Bottle?"

"Georgia Home Boy," Vinnie said. "Is that your buddy's idea?"

"Buddy?"

"Johnny, it's me: Vinnie. I'm the one who used to pick you up off the playground after Shane and his brothers beat the shit out of you. You drove your truck into the bar ditch on a road you drive a thousand times. You want me to take fingerprints off the bottle? Or you want me to figure there's not enough evidence here and just chalk it up to that twenty-four-hour thing?"

"Vinnie, buddy, take it easy. I don't know what you mean. I don't know what happened the other night. What're you doing checking out our road, anyway? That's private property."

"Not since your in-laws decided to deed it over, let Sydon County carry the upkeep. Nice people, your in-laws. Done a lot for you, haven't they?"

"Vinnie—"

"Johnny, listen to me." Vinnie took a step closer, so Johnny could see the light jumping over the star in the badge on his tan shirt. "Your best friend rolled on Freddy Parker. Now he thinks he's a wise guy, maybe starting a new business while Freddy grows old in jail."

"Who's Freddy Parker?"

"Freddy Parker's the man who slipped you meth and money. Even more important to you, Johnny, Freddy got Shane started. And the second we found Shane in possession, he rolled on Freddy. Can you imagine what he'll do to you, when he decides he doesn't want a partner anymore?"

"I don't know what you're talking about. I don't know anything about any water bottle, either."

"How'd you know it was a water bottle, Johnny?"

"You said—"

"I said a plastic bottle."

"You can't . . . this is chickenshit. I'm calling the nurse."

"You do that, Johnny. But think about this, first. Shane's already been to see you once, make sure you didn't remember anything." Vinnie smiled, inclined his head. "That's what led us to you. Now he'll come back to make sure you didn't tell me anything. How are you going to explain we're charging you with possession?"

"Possession of what? You said there was no alcohol. And the truck's been cleaned."

"Johnny, even my eyeballs tell me the slimy water's GHB. Why a speed freak like you would switch to jib, there's no telling. I don't see you mixing in at raves, so I'm guessing it has something to do with Shane. And money."

Johnny wished he could lift his hand and swear with it. "I'm telling you the truth. I don't know what happened the other night, and I don't know anything about a bottle."

"Well, I'm on my way to call the crime lab. See if your prints are on the bottle. Or your DNA."

"You don't have my DNA."

Vinnie raised an eyebrow. "You were face first in your DNA." He turned toward the door.

"Wait," Johnny said, using his head to motion Vinnie closer. "What do you want?"

Chapter 20

She took nothing but her summer clothes and her cosmetics. "It's just for a few months, maybe less," Della told Kat. "And the house has everything I'll need for furniture and kitchen things. It's all my stuff, too. From when we were married."

"You didn't take any of that when you moved out?" Kat was standing at the closet, handing clothes to Della as she folded them into her big suitcase.

Della shook her head. "Fresh start."

"That must have been one understanding woman he married, to live with all your stuff."

Della took a green dress from Kat and held it up to consider. "You know, I think she was so broke, she was just grateful to him for not having to split the rent. I don't think she cared who had purchased the Cuisinart."

"Yeah," Kat said, "being broke makes you appreciate the little things." The accounting side of Kat's brain kicked in. "You even left the Cuisinart?"

Della smiled. "I wanted a bigger one. You know, with a wide feed tube." She looked around the bedroom. The furniture was castoffs; heavy, dark-wood pieces which had been moved out of the guest rooms in favor of sturdier, lighter wood. The best features here, Della knew, were the double windows, almost floor to ceiling, that gave her a view out the front of the house toward the courthouse.

Della and Kat had flipped for this room, and Della suspected that Kat's generosity now might be related to squatter's rights. Kat never invested her time foolishly.

"Do you ever just think about moving out completely?" Della asked her friend. "It's so far, for you, up to Nick's house."

"Actually, it's not that bad," Kat said. "When I'm working, my appointments are either in Dallas or Fort Worth. And Nick kind of likes spending weekends here, even if I'm busy with guests. You're the one who's looking at a reverse commute."

"Just for a while," Della said. "Till Melissa figures out what she wants to do."

Had it been up to Melissa, she would have moved Greg across the river to the Ladies Farm. Moving the boys to the Hutto house, even the few suitcases and the handheld amusements that had multiplied since their arrival, seemed to take forever, a period of time made even longer by the endless explanations to Trey and Garrett.

"I can get them settled," Greg had offered.

But having missed the arm break, Melissa yielded no spare second of quality time. Even though every second of moving was a second stolen from *Midnight Peaches, a cool race through a hot town.*

"The tag line must be working," she told Ethan, who had met her at Randi's for a quick committee update. "I'm already sick of it."

"That means you're repeating it to a lot of people."

"It sure feels that way."

Randi and Ethan had collected on most of the pledges; even Johnny Urquardt had paid up, according to Shane, who, to the relief of the others, had called in his report. Erica had e-mailed them that morning that sign-ups looked much better; and the luminarias were on their way.

"Rotary's got the lighting organized to the nth degree," Randi said. "Which just leaves assembly."

"Well, there's plenty of free labor," Ethan said.

"There will be the night of the race. And the weekend prior to Peach Fest. But those things aren't coming in till a few days before," Randi said, "and everyone's tied up by then with their own booths."

"I've got volunteers," Melissa said.

"Not the ladies," said Ethan. "They're bound to have guests. Plus, I heard they're doing barbecue dinners."

Melissa took a breath and looked straight at Randi, without glancing at Ethan. "Greg," she said. "Greg and the boys. Kirk Hilgon said he'd help. But Greg will organize it."

"Are you sure he can?" Randi asked. "I mean, he doesn't know anyone, he's new here—"

"He'll have Kirk," Melissa said.

Randi, flushed, looked to Ethan.

Ethan smiled. "That's great. Now our only worries are the weather and the crowd. And if we get the weather, we'll get the crowd."

He saved the rest until they were outside, and Randi had gone back to the fountain. "I guess it's easier to recruit volunteers now that you and Greg are living together."

"We're not living together; just sharing the Hutto house."

"Just roommates."

"Ethan, I know it's not that easy—"

"It is that easy, though. Just not pleasant. You and your husband have moved into the Hutto house." He stuffed his hands in his pockets. "It's so easy, Shane Castleburg choked it out with no problem whatsoever. You'd think literate, articulate adults like the two of us could manage a phone call or an e-mail."

"I'm sorry." Melissa shielded her eyes against the glare reflected off the windshields of parked cars along the square, then nodded at the courthouse lawn. "Could we sit down and talk a moment?"

"If you're not worried about it getting back to your husband."

Melissa motioned toward the courthouse, and they made their way across the street to a bench in the shade. She had dressed in sandals and a sleeveless cotton shift to emphasize her slim shape and browned arms and legs, but now the fabric stuck damply to her back. She wished desperately that her vanity had not prevented her from twisting her hair up off her neck.

"Ethan, I'm sorry. Between the race, and Greg showing up, and the boys, I haven't thought . . . well, I have thought about you. A lot. I really thought by now we'd be . . . you know . . . the way you said." She smiled. "Groping in the car seat, at least."

He smiled back, but there was no humor. "I thought so, too."

They sat side by side, not touching, only slightly inclined toward one another. "I guess you're tied up, too, with your dad out of town."

"It takes a lot of time, tending an orchard that's not bearing fruit."

"Imagine the grit he—your dad—has, year after year, knowing nothing might come of it," Melissa said.

"Yeah. He keeps the faith."

"They're all like that. Your folks, my parents, the Huttos, the ladies." She shook her head. "I don't know how they do it. Stay so loyal, through all that."

"Hard for us to imagine. Especially when we're contemplating how to advance our relationship while you're living with your husband."

"I'm not living with him!"

"Excuse me. While you're living in the same house as your husband . . . and children."

Even in the shade, Melissa felt the heat in her face and the sweat trickling into her eyes. "This isn't a good time," she said. "I'm sorry." She launched a long explanation about Trey's arm, and Garrett's bad dreams; about playground fights and mealtime anxieties. When she finally wound down, she glanced up to find him serious and unyielding, studying her with almost academic curiosity.

Melissa drew a breath. "I'm sorry," she said, but it did not move him. "I'm sorry, I'm sorry, I'm sorry!"

"I know."

"You will never know . . . never understand how sorry."

"What is it you want, Melissa?"

"I don't know." She looked away again, leaned forward to let the scorched air dry the sweat on her back. "It's so soon," Melissa said. "I'm not sure what I want. I thought I had what I want, and now it's shot to hell. I'm not some goddamn orchard, I may never yield, Ethan."

"Yeah, well, I'm not some goddamn faithful farmer. I'm only a real estate investor, willing to take a little chance. But I can't figure out what you are. Except maybe someone who's backing away."

"I'm not backing away," said Melissa. "I'm just trying to . . . maybe put things on hold for awhile."

"Things were on hold between us. What I'm asking is what's on hold with your husband."

"Stop it! If you can't understand . . . this is just logistics."

"You were living in a house with three older women to help you look after your sons. What logistics do I not understand?"

"Greg is the boys' father," Melissa recited. "No matter what he's done or how I feel toward him, his relationship to them is forever. He showed up unannounced and uninvited, and he's not going away." Now she was pleading. "Any life I have . . . any life at all, no matter who with . . . will always include some relationship with him. It's just now sinking in to me, I'm not sure you . . . or anyone, really . . . is going to understand. There's no such thing as starting over, not entirely. You just . . . I just . . . have to go forward. But I'll always be dragging my whole tangled mess of a family with me."

"Only because you want to."

She nodded. "I do want to. Because the alternative—shutting Greg out, battling him every day—that's worse."

"Then stop telling me how sorry you are. If you don't think we should ever go out, say that. And if you want me to wait till after the race, say that."

"I don't think we should ever go out." She knew the difference between sweat and tears. She knew what stung her eyes. "I'm too . . . too . . ."

"Confused? Upset? Torn? Married?" Ethan stood, oblivious to the courthouse crowd returning from lunch.

Melissa sat on the bench, aware of the spectacle. "All those," she whispered. *I just wanted . . . I just wanted . . .* But even she couldn't fill in the blank.

"She must've caught him. So she runs back here, hooks up with her high school sweetheart, and he comes running after." Shane dropped the binoculars, letting them dangle from their strap around his neck while he rocked back in the chair on the little concrete apron in front of his shed.

"Well, now he's got her back, looks like." Johnny had brought his own binoculars, but he could barely see the house, let alone who might be standing on the balcony.

"My guess is, he's done some serious ass-kissing. Like a new car, something like that. That's what they do, when you're married."

Johnny sighed. "Yeah."

Shane jerked his head to indicate the dairy farm behind him. "That's what she does to the old man."

"Got you a house out of it, though."

Shane pulled a cigarette from the pack in his shirt pocket, lit it and dragged. He blew out before he spoke again. "Once the old man goes, we're throwing her out. Me and my brothers."

"You might not be able to," Johnny said. "The old man could fix it so that—"

"Let him try," Shane said. He stood up, dragging again on the cigarette. "C'mon." Shane motioned Johnny inside.

Johnny knew better than to argue with Shane about Castleburg business. He also knew better than to point out that Eli Castleburg was in his mid-fifties and strong as an ox. Shane himself would be middle-age by the time his father died. Instead, Johnny followed Shane to the computer, where Shane pulled up a spreadsheet.

"I set this up so we can just plug in how much we want, and then it'll give us all the amounts. How much GLB, how much sodium hydroxide—"

"I thought we were using lye."

Shane sighed, exasperated. "Lye's for amateurs. This is medical quality."

"Pretty fancy," Johnny said. "We serving it in champagne glasses or what?"

"Listen, pal, we're mixing for some pretty picky customers. I'm taking it to them tomorrow."

"Tomorrow?"

Shane grinned. "They want a sample of our wares." He stood up, cigarette dangling from his lips as he yanked the printout from the printer. "What's the matter?" he asked, exhaling as he waved the cigarette in his hand. "Not enough time to report back to your pal Vinnie?"

Johnny turned toward Shane and managed a smile. "What do you mean?" He held his hands out, palms upturned.

Faster than Johnny could see it, Shane grabbed Johnny's wrist and ground the cigarette onto Johnny's open hand.

"Ow!" Johnny jerked his hand, but Shane held tight.

"What'd you tell Vinnie?"

"Nothing."

In a single motion Shane dropped the printout and scratched at the fresh burn.

"Jesus!" screamed Johnny, finally pulling away. Somehow the paper mocked him, floating to the ground at his feet while he doubled over the raw palm. Pain exploded from its center, and Johnny could not control his own whimpering.

"Here," said Shane gently. "Come on, Johnny, try this."

Johnny looked up to see Shane squatting before him, holding out an ice cube. Still shaking, Johnny unfolded his right hand, bracing it from beneath with the left.

"Just hold it steady now," Shane told him, holding the wrist himself and helping Johnny sit on the floor, leaning against the wall. Shane sat next to him. "You see, Johnny, I'm the only one who looks after you. Believe me," he said, "when Vinnie Perez burns you, he won't be offering any first aid."

"He said you rolled. On Freddy Parker," Johnny mumbled.

"I did the same thing you did," Shane assured him. "Told them what they already knew anyway." Shane gave a short laugh. "Hell, after Freddy's sack of batteries floated into their net, there wasn't much they didn't know. Freddy was fried."

Johnny laughed, more out of relief and gratitude for the ice than anything funny about Freddy Parker.

"He found the bottle," Johnny said. "Vinnie. The water bottle. He said they could match my DNA."

"They can't match shit," Shane said. "Vinnie's watching too much television."

"Maybe they could," Johnny said. "Maybe they send it . . . I puked all over—"

"What'd he want?"

"What?"

"What did Vinnie want, Johnny? From you?"

His hand burned. "To tell them . . . you know . . . who you're meeting."

"Good."

Johnny looked up.

"Good," Shane said again, nodding. He put a hand on Johnny's shoulder. "You wait till we've lined everything up. Then you tell them I'm meeting someone from Austin. Race night. Right across the river, in that little clearing near the Hutto place."

"Call Wade," Webb instructed, when the doctor finished explaining the angiogram.

"What about the others? Ethan?"

Webb shook his head, and he saw Gladys put her hand on Ray's arm to restrain his questions. "We'll call Wade," she said.

He knew he didn't need to tell her about the address book, Alice's address book, in his suitcase, just as he hadn't instructed her to get his wallet when Ray helped him out to the car. Webb glanced at the window, but the heavy shades were drawn. He guessed, though, that it was probably already light, and it had taken most of the night to attach all these wires and inject the drugs that allowed him to breathe again.

The cold jets of air puffing at his nostrils from the tube taped to his face made every breath dry and hard, and his neck and arm ached from holding steady so he didn't dislodge any wires. Even his finger had a clothespin clipped onto it, measuring, measuring, measuring. He thought about the orchard, putting tapes around peaches, and tree trunks, weighing bushels, sorting fruit.

And then you measure again, thought Webb. That's the final one, where they pay you, measure what all that fruit is worth.

He sighed, realizing as he opened them that he had closed his eyes. Now his two old friends were studying him, their gaze shifting back and forth, from his face to the monitor next to his bed. He gave them a little smile, but it didn't seem to reassure them. If they called Ethan he would come. If they called Wade and he called Ethan, Ethan would stay with the orchard.

Tony had advised Della every time he made a change to the house, but she was not ready for the plain white walls and the gleam of the polished wood floors. The straight lines of the furniture—their furniture—described blocks of muted color in the sky-lit great room. Their bedroom, with its massive armoires and scrolled headboard, attested to her youthful stabs at continental elegance, punctuated by the nicks and scratches of family life with two sons.

When she asked, Tony told her that Suzanne had changed the bedspread to a floral print; he had retrieved the old one—an abstract in blues and greens—from the closet after she left. As far as Della could see, the only trace of Tony's ex-wife were two floral shower curtains and a slow-cooker of heroic proportions. "She thought I could use it," Tony explained with a faint smile. "Since she was cooking for her car salesman in New Mexico."

Della looked around the kitchen, opening the refrigerator and examining the contents. "I could make omelets," she suggested. "If you'll run out and get a few things. Omelets with cheddar, rice, maybe some green beans. Or spinach. How about spinach with lemon, garlic? And get some rolls, crusty ones. Wine."

She had addressed the inside of the refrigerator, starting shyly but growing in certainty as she progressed.

"Don't you want to unpack?"

Della shook her head, still looking at the refrigerator. "Let's have dinner first," she said. Her wardrobe had devolved to knits and permanent press; staying packed wouldn't hurt.

Sydonia dominated their dinner conversation. "It's some kind of law of unintended consequences," Della said. "The worst possible kind of unintended consequences. I was only trying to make things better for Melissa, but it turns out Ethan thinks she's reconciling with Greg."

"If I was Ethan, I'd think the same."

"You would?" Della set down her fork. "I was about to say it's because Ethan's never been married or had kids, so he doesn't get it. Melissa could be head over heels in love with Ethan, but she's still got to think about the kids."

Tony shook his head. "You think this is about the kids?"

Della nodded while she chewed and swallowed. "Good cheddar," she told him. "Sharp. Yeah, I think it's about the kids. And doing what she promised about the race."

Tony pressed his lips together, which could only be an invitation for her to press him.

"Come on, what do you think is going on?"

"Why does any guy move back in with his wife?" He grinned, motioned to the breakfast room. "We'll eat omelets for dinner if we think it'll get us laid."

Della shook her head, tried not to look at the stripped-down kitchen. "Greg's bizarre but he's not stupid. You think he believes that living at the Hutto house will get his wife back?" Where were the stacks of magazines? she wondered. The expired coupons and loose buttons that used to find their way to this nook?

"That's why he came here, isn't it?"

"Well, yes. But he also knew it was hopeless. And if he didn't know before he got here, I'm sure Melissa set him straight." She forgot her surroundings. "He parades around in women's underwear, Tony! And he thinks she's going to reconcile?"

Tony shrugged. "I'm just telling you what I'd do. What I did do, when you think about it."

"What you did," Della reminded him, "was pass yourself off as a heartbroken romantic until you found someone to move in and take care of you."

"Wasn't hard to do," Tony recalled.

"I suspect not. It's a lot easier for a middle-age man to find someone than a middle-age woman."

Neither one of them wanted to argue that point. Della felt grateful that they could drop it, continue eating in silence. It was the sort of thing that could happen when you knew someone well. She supposed that comfort was part of what Greg missed. Part of what she herself sought in moving back here, however unsettling the changed surroundings.

That's another thing Ethan doesn't get, Della thought.

Chapter 21

"Rain's unlikely," Greg said. "I went online, just to double-check the legend, and it hasn't rained during the peach festival for eighteen years. Never, if you're talking about bad storms or downpours."

"But that doesn't mean people will show up." They had put the boys to bed in Earl's old room, and now Melissa sat on one side of the round table with her laptop open before her; Greg sat on the other side, with his own computer.

She supposed his office was sending him some work; otherwise, they would never have given him the leave. High-tech's too tenuous to jeopardize a safe job, she thought, just to pursue me. I've got to get my job search in gear. Which means I've got to get this run behind me.

Melissa studied the numbers at the internal-access Midnight Peaches site. "We need two thousand more, rain or no rain. And then another three hundred and fifty to pay for the luminarias."

Greg looked up. He had begun to wear reading glasses, and now the light from his computer reflected off the lenses so that she could not read his expression.

"We'll make it up anyway," she assured him lightly. "Selling them the next morning. Or even keeping them till next year and reusing them, ordering in replicas for Peach Fest."

He ignored her bravado. "I thought you were going to find a sponsor."

"We ran out of prospects," Melissa said. "Or time." She sighed. "Or energy."

"Are you all right?"

"Sure. Just eleventh-hour panic." She thought about Ethan. "Wondering how I'll make it through the next two weeks. Wondering what the hell I'm doing here."

"I doubt you want my take on it."

She smiled, shook her head. Ethan had stopped e-mailing. No jokes. No encouragement. Maybe that's all I wanted from him anyway, Melissa thought. I'm such a fraud.

"How much do you need?"

"What?"

"Money. For the luminarias."

"Seventy-five hundred." She sighed. "Too late now, anyway." She considered. "Well, we could print up stickers or something to tack onto the lanterns. But we've missed the program. They'd have to be doing it out of the goodness of their heart. Or love of Sydonia."

Greg nodded. They didn't talk much after that. She didn't want to ask what he was working on, and she supposed he had heard enough about Midnight Peaches.

"I thought I'd run into Fort Worth tomorrow," he said finally. "Need anything?"

"I'm going myself," she said. "Press proofs."

"You're welcome to ride with me."

She shook her head no. "Thanks, though."

"I thought I'd get those bed tents."

"Bed tents . . . for the boys?"

"You know, like a pop-up tent. You set them up over the bed, turn the bed into a car, or a fort, stuff like that. I saw an ad for them, I thought we could get a house or a car for Garrett, maybe he'd sleep a little easier. Trey, maybe camo or sci-fi. They have these castle shapes."

"Yeah, that'd be good, but it might frighten his brother."

"Maybe there's a sports theme or something."

She nodded. "I could meet you to pick them out. I want some say. It's a good idea though, for Garrett. Give him a sense of security."

"Mel," Greg said. "Just ride along. I'll drop you at the printer's, pick you up, whatever. Then we'll shop. Divorced couples do it all the time."

Divorced couples. She hadn't considered that a category.

It's just the gossip in Sydonia that's got you concerned now, she thought. The gossip, and Ethan saying he was right about reconciling. But Ethan's over. Share a ride into Fort Worth.

Which left no real reason not to have him drive in with her, she thought the next morning as they reached Fort Worth. It doesn't matter what kind of underwear he's got on, Melissa thought. All he's doing is driving and looking at press proofs.

Everything had been developed and proofed online; now she just had to check color and registration, look for obvious flaws.

"Bigger than it looks from the front," Greg said as he pulled into the parking lot.

"Tony says he refers a lot to them," Melissa replied. "They can handle whatever he can't."

"I hope they refer back," Greg muttered.

They climbed to the loading dock, nodding hello to a pressman sprawled in a molded plastic chair and enjoying a cigarette in the shade. The door led into a back hall, which they followed to the pressroom, an icy, high-ceilinged place that vibrated with rumbling noise. The perimeter was punctuated by worktables radiating an eerie fluorescence, outposts of habitation against the huge, black presses: one still, one pounding and shuddering.

Melissa spied her peach-toned program cover from across the room. She and Greg were halfway across the concrete floor before anyone turned and noticed them. Izzy Guerra, who had called about the press run, held up a hand in greeting, then motioned to the cover, an untrimmed glossy sheet hanging from a clip against a light box.

"Get you anything?" Izzy asked when they got close enough to hear.

"Diet Dr Pepper," Melissa said.

"Coke," said Greg.

Izzy handed her a magnifier, pulled the sheet off the clip, and laid it flat. Then he went in search of beverages. An hour and five color adjustments later, Melissa and Greg emerged into sunlight bearing a damp press sheet, a few trimmed and folded samples, and the remains of their sodas. To Melissa, the peach in the logo fairly glistened with ripe taste as it dangled before the abstract runners. As she had assured Tony, it was Della's best work.

Tony, who had stopped by to check on them, had agreed.

"He's a nice guy," Greg said now, as they started the drive to the mall. "Tony."

"Yeah." She frowned. "Don't draw too much comfort there."

"I wasn't—"

"Sure you are. You see them happy together after a long time apart. They've been divorced, involved with other people, he was even married, and yet, after all that, there they are together. It's beautiful. But it's not us."

Greg looked straight ahead. "I didn't say it was."

"I know you; I know what you're thinking. If you just hang in here, the way Tony did, then you—"

"You know," he said, "I may be looking for models, but maybe it's a model for civil divorce, not passionate reconciliation."

Melissa looked out the window, watched the pleasant streets of Fort Worth slip by. "Civil is good," she said finally.

They stopped first at Bed, Bath & Beyond, then moved over to Linens N' Things. "Let's just try the mall," Greg suggested.

"Where did you see the ad?" Melissa asked. By now the asphalt in the parking lot radiated heat and the car interior was brutal.

He shrugged. "I don't know. I think it was before I left."

"In Oregon? And we're shopping in Fort Worth?"

"Well, I figured any place would have them. Isn't there a toy store?"

"Not close by." She directed him to the relative shade of the parking garage, and they entered through a department store. They whipped through the bedding department, where a useless clerk suggested they look around and perhaps they would see what they were asking for. Then they tried children's furniture.

It's futile, thought Melissa. But we're here. Might as well.

They headed for another store.

It was at the fountain, the center point of the mall, that they stumbled across Victoria's Secret.

She stopped.

Greg moved a few steps forward, then, realizing she wasn't with him, turned to see what had detained her. He looked at her, then looked at the store window, crammed with shiny, silky pastel things draped over boudoir furniture and trimmed in feathers and lace.

Melissa stared. Beyond the display, she could see customers, saleswomen. Two men, one alone, probably buying a gift for his wife. Another with a woman.

Melissa watched the couple, able to see only their shoulders and above, catching only the highest arc of their motioning hands. They floated among the racks of lingerie, and Melissa thought first, automatically, how lucky the woman was. His wife, Melissa thought; a girlfriend would never express herself so surely. A man who took her—

But, of course, she could think that only for a second. Then Melissa saw Sexy Sadie, taking her husband on an outing for the frilly things that excited them. Directing him to finger certain satiny ribbons, examine particular bits of virginal lace.

Making their choices with agonizing deliberation, rendering payment in a heated flurry. Rushing back out to the car to consummate the selection. Shopping as foreplay.

Melissa felt sick. It was one more thing, one more place she had lost. Her earlier assumptions so foolish now, not even innocent, glaringly ignorant. She whirled toward Greg.

"Don't look at me. I've never set foot in there." He grinned, crossed his heart. "Honest."

"Well," she said, "now you know it's here." She set her jaw, walked away.

He let her regain control before he caught up with her. They walked slowly, his grin in check. "Truth is," he told her, "that stuff's made for women."

"I thought that was the point."

"Well, almost. It's just that, if a man is going to actually wear it, it's got to be a lot different, bigger, wider. Personally, I got my stuff through catalogs."

"Catalogs for men?"

"Pretty much."

"How'd you ever conceal the anticipation?"

He shrugged, remained impassive. "Actually, it heightened the excitement. Almost doubled it. You know: once when I ordered, again when it arrived."

"How come you talk about it in the past tense?"

"Just habit. I guess part of what I did was because of you and the boys. Hiding the catalogs. Waiting till everyone was out. Now . . . I guess it will be different."

"I guess so," she said, quickening her step. They reached the next store. Melissa focused on the bed tents. "If we can't find them here, we'll have to try online." She gave a short laugh. "Sort of like catalog shopping."

They struck out at the store, then tried Target and Mervyn's before they hit the grocery store on behalf of the Ladies Farm, and headed back.

"So was hiding it part of the excitement?" Melissa asked.

"I thought you never wanted to talk about this."

"It's different now," she told him.

"How?"

"Uh-uh. You answer my question first."

"Keeping it secret was a mess. I don't think . . . I mean, I've thought about it a lot and I don't think I wanted you to find out. It wasn't one of those deals where I secretly wanted to be caught. But I have to tell you—even though this is the worst thing in my life, getting divorced—Melissa, it's a relief that you know. I never thought I'd ever have to hide anything more than a Christmas gift from you—"

"What are you talking about? You were hiding it when we met!"

"I know. I was. But even so, I felt that I was open with you about everything. I know that sounds stupid, but it's as if . . . as if I had cancer or something that I didn't know about yet, so even though it was secret, I wasn't the one keeping it secret." He paused. "So, no, hiding it wasn't part of the excitement. There's your answer. So now you answer mine. What's different now?"

Melissa shrugged. "I guess I've had time to calm down. A little curiosity is natural, don't you think?"

"I'm sure."

"But it doesn't change anything," Melissa said. She recalled the couple in Victoria's Secret, her certainty that she could never be part of that couple, her fury that such certainty meant nothing in the unfolding of a relationship over a lifetime. "It's just idle curiosity."

Tony and Dave called themselves the retreads, holding irregular meetings in Dave's garage after hours. They presided over the distribution of Shiner Bock to the attendees and reviewed Tony's progress toward full membership from his current probationary status. "Saw Melissa and Greg at a press check today," Tony said now, motioning with his half-filled bottle.

"Oh?"

"Came to look at the program. For that run."

Dave nodded.

Tony shook his head, recalling. "I hate to think I ever looked that sad."

Dave gave a short laugh. "I doubt you ever sashayed around in pink nighties, either."

Tony yielded the point with a flourish of his hand, but Dave was squinting through the glass. "That young Ethan out there?"

Dave peered through the window, then leaned over and tapped on it. Ethan, who was filling his tank at the self-serve, didn't respond. Dave reached up and punched the button that lifted the garage door. "Hey! Young fellow! Come on in and lift a cold one!"

"What's the word on your dad?" Dave asked, handing Ethan a beer as he walked in.

Ethan sipped, frowned, shook his head. "Sixty-percent blockage. They're going to do a bypass. Wednesday."

"Wednesday!" Tony said. He hadn't even heard that Webb was sick.

"In Alpine?" Dave asked.

"They're taking him to Houston tomorrow."

"You going down there?" Dave asked.

Ethan looked away for a second. "He thinks I should stay here. But the crop's shot. I thought I'd get there Wednesday morning, early; see him before he goes under."

"Sixty percent." Tony grimaced.

"Wade went out there," Ethan said. "They sent his tests and pictures to Houston. So the surgeons already have evaluated him. They think he's a pretty good candidate, considering his overall health."

"Amen to that," said Dave. "What about the rest of the boys?"

"The others'll meet us in Houston, then we'll take turns staying with him at the hospital, then at Wade's."

"Well, tell him we're pulling for him," Dave said, lifting his bottle. "Those things are getting pretty routine. He'll probably sail right through."

"I imagine it's not quite routine for the patient," Tony said. He looked at Ethan, who had seated himself up on the counter. "You tell Melissa about this?"

"Haven't talked with Melissa much. Maybe you could let her know."

Dave and Tony exchanged looks.

"I saw that!" Ethan glowered, then sipped some more. "She's living with her husband," he said. "Don't you guys think I need to back off a little?"

"Well, now, *living*'s a strong word," Dave cautioned.

Another glower from Ethan, which made Tony laugh. "You kids!" Tony said. "One little setback and you turn and run! Hell!" He nodded toward Dave. "Dave was bringing Rita the Sunday paper for a year before she even divorced her last husband."

"Well, she was separated," Dave said. "Anyway, you don't have much to worry about." He looked back at Tony. "Ready for another?"

Tony nodded.

They had another round. Ethan updated them on how many runners had registered for Midnight Peaches, and how many of them were from out of town. "Closest hotel room now is up in Tarrant County."

Ethan slipped off the counter and walked over to a tire-pressure chart. He studied it while the two others drank more beer and stayed silent. Finally he turned around and looked at Tony. "What'd you mean, I don't have much to worry about?"

"Uh, that was me who said that," said Dave, but Ethan ignored him.

"You really think Melissa is going to reconcile with a crossdresser? With two kids?" Tony said.

Ethan studied his shoes.

"Oh, come on, boy!" joshed Dave. "You're not going to lose out to some man in frilly panties!"

Ethan studied his shoes some more. "So," he said finally, "when Ray Hutto asked me about Greg's wardrobe, he was referring to women's lingerie?"

"You didn't know?" Tony asked.

Ethan, gaze flat, shook his head.

"Now, I can understand that," Dave said quickly. "Girl like Melissa, coming home the way she did. Knowing you from high school and all. How could she tell you a thing like that?"

"Well, it sounds like she managed to tell everyone else." Ethan's mouth was twisted up on one side, but he stayed calm. "Sounds like everyone in Sydonia knows but me."

"Well, now, I wouldn't say—"

Tony gave a little laugh, pointed to Dave and then himself. "The way it works at the Ladies Farm is this: anything you confide in one of them, she tells the others. Usually when they're cleaning up after breakfast, or at lunch if there aren't any guests. Then, you know, Della tells me, Rita tells Dave, Kat tells Nick." Tony grinned. "But it pretty much ends there. I mean, I only brought it up because I figured you knew already. We—you know, Dave and Nick and I—don't talk to a lot of people."

Without a word, Ethan set his empty on the counter and walked over to the refrigerator for another. Dave and Tony watched him gulp about half the beer. Tony admired the way the kid planted his feet wide and lifted the bottle and held it there. Enjoy it, he wanted to tell the kid. Savor it while you still can.

Then Ethan stopped drinking and looked back at Tony. "You think my father knows?"

"That's what he wanted to know?" Della asked. Tony had ambled into the Ladies Farm smelling like a brewery, so Della was driving home. Dave had stayed at the store. She didn't want to ask how Ethan had gotten home. Maybe he was sleeping at the store.

Tony pushed the passenger seat almost horizontal and lay with his eyes closed. His forehead wrinkled, but he didn't open his eyes.

"He wanted to know if his father knew?"

"There was other stuff," Tony mumbled. "He's pretty pissed."

"You're the one pissed," Della said. "When did you start drinking on school nights?"

"It was just a beer or two."

"Just a beer or five, from the smell." Della hated playing the scold. "What else did you tell him?"

"Nothing. What else was there to tell?"

"You said there was other stuff."

"Oh," Tony mumbled. "Just jokes and stuff."

Della glanced over at him and shook her head, but she conversed only with herself. For one thing, she felt sure Melissa didn't tell Ethan because it embarrassed her. It was too personal to share with someone you were trying to impress. For another thing, someone should tell Melissa right away about Webb so that she could offer her help. And, thought Della, so she could explain to Ethan why she had not wanted to share the details of her split with Greg.

Chapter 22

"Comes in handy, being a pilot," Wade told Webb as they settled into the room in Houston.

"I could've ridden in the back of a van," Webb told his eldest. "It's not as if I'm in pain. Or mending from surgery."

"No, that's ahead," Wade said. "That's why we need to keep you strong. What I still can't understand is why you didn't feel bad. How could you not feel anything?"

Webb shook his head with irritation. "You heard the doctor. I felt tired. I felt winded. I just didn't think that was my heart. There wasn't any pain. I was just worn out."

"Worn out with grief," Gladys said. "That's what hurt your heart so. Missing Alice."

Wade hadn't favored Gladys accompanying them to Houston, but his father and Ray had both encouraged her. Evidently she was a proxy for Ray, who was prone to arthritic infirmity, particularly in a place as moist as Houston. She had already made herself useful, instructing Ethan exactly on what to bring with him from the house. But his father didn't need anyone reminding him how much he missed his wife.

Webb, though, just waved a hand at the woman.

"You need to be visiting your children, bouncing grandkids on your knee and helping them put in vegetable gardens and add on to their houses," Gladys insisted.

Webb nodded to acknowledge the advice.

"Clark and I are the only ones with houses," Wade countered, "though we do have a bunch of kids." He smiled. "Mine are pretty much past knee-bouncing stage." He turned to his father. "But it wouldn't hurt for you to share a little worldly wisdom with them, while you're here. They might still listen to you. My opportunity's long gone."

"When you're done there, I want you to come out and help me with Ray. He was doing much better with you there. You got him to do those stretches."

Webb nodded again. Wade hoped this indicated agreement; he didn't think much of his father joining a religious order, at least not the way Ethan had explained it. Particularly not after heart surgery.

To Webb, lying in the bed in Houston wasn't much different, so far, than lying in the bed in Alpine. He hadn't been quite honest about the pain. He did have kind of an ache in his chest. He supposed Gladys was right; he'd grown so used to aching for Alice he hadn't noticed much of a change. It was only when he had been unable to breathe, when Ray had found him lying on the porch, unable even to get up, let alone catch a breath, that he wished he had mentioned something to his friends.

"I'm sorry I scared you," Webb said now.

"We're not scared," Wade said. "Just worried about you."

Webb ignored him and looked at Gladys.

"I know," she said. "But we'll all get over it." She grinned. "What's life without a good scare now and then?" She thought a second. "Anyway, you heard the doctor. You're not in mortal danger; you're just sick, and you'll get better."

Webb waited.

"All I'm saying is, you've been sick without knowing it. So maybe you want to rethink your plans, once you're feeling better. Maybe those were the plans of a sick man. I'm not saying they were," Gladys said. "But you ought to give it some thought."

"Wednesday?" Melissa set her soda down on her desk.

"I don't mean to scare you," Della said. "But I knew you would want to know."

Melissa shook her head. "Ethan never said a word to me. I saw him last week—"

"Well, honey, he probably didn't know last week. If Webb hadn't been in Alpine, they would have done the thing by now."

"Why did they take him to Houston, anyway? Couldn't they do it in El Paso?"

"Wade's in Houston," Della said. "He knew how to get his daddy flown there, and the other boys are flying in. Except Ethan. I think he's driving. Tony wasn't sure."

"So he had a beer with them? Tony and Dave?"

"Uh huh."

"Did they . . . how'd Tony say he looked?"

"Now, you know better than that, Melissa. No man's going to notice if someone's pale, or wasting away with grief. The most I got out of Tony was *hangdog*."

Melissa considered. "*Hangdog*'s pretty descriptive. Did he— Ethan—did Ethan tell them anything else?"

Della breathed out and shook her head. "Well, they talked. And drank beer. And I guess he told them he thought you were going back to Greg."

"I told him—"

"I know. But nobody's—at least Ethan's not—buying it. So I guessed they talked about Greg, since Ethan's really never met him."

Melissa studied her. "Aunt Dell?"

Della nodded. "Oh, yeah. Couldn't let a detail like cross-dressing go by without mention." She reached out, stroked Melissa's heart-shaped face. "I'm sorry, honey."

Melissa nodded. "I should have told him. I started to, once or twice, but I just couldn't."

"I know," said Della. "I guess it's as hard for you to talk about it as it is easy for the rest of us. I'm sorry, too, that I told Tony, and that Rita told Dave."

Melissa shook her head. "I figured that you did. I mean, how can you not tell your husband." She managed a weak smile. "Especially something that juicy."

"Well, I'm sorry anyway. Tony and Dave are both so close-mouthed, it didn't seem like any risk at all. Anyway, I thought I'd better tell you. I'm sure you want to call Ethan before he leaves for Houston."

"Why?" asked Melissa. She gave a short laugh. "I'm sure he doesn't want to talk to me."

*   *   *

Della and Kat pulled up the reservations. "Five are runners," Kat said. "The sixth is an older couple, I thought we'd put them in the Babe." Kat looked at her.

Della nodded. The Babe Didrikson Zaharias was on the first floor, with wheelchair access. It was also the room in which Barbara Morrison had died. More than a year later, Della still couldn't predict her own reaction when they rented out the room. A couple would be okay, as long as they appreciated the place.

"I do wish we'd had the Hutto place ready."

"You mean, you wish you had it free to rent," Della corrected. "We rented it out to Alana and her kosher crew with no problems."

Kat nodded her concession. "This is Pauline's family."

"She's got a place here."

"Really," said Kat, "I wish she'd stay." She had turned back to the computer and was pulling up the grocery list. "Okay, you have the menus?"

"Pull up the file," Della said. "If we fill in the number of servings, it'll calculate the quantities and copy it to the grocery list."

"You're kidding! Who did that?"

"Melissa, of course."

"I am going to miss her."

"Well, maybe she will stay. If she can make up with Ethan." Della made kissy noises.

"If she makes up with Ethan, she'll move to Austin to be near him," Kat speculated. She studied the screen. "Damn, that's sweet."

"Once we get all the recipes keyed in there, it'll be even sweeter."

"How are you with the cookbook, speaking of recipes? You haven't said a word about it."

"Oh, Tony rolled it off the press two weeks ago," Della bragged. "He sent the fancy cover out to a big shop, spiral-bound the whole thing. It's ready to go." She smiled. "I left a copy in the kitchen. You just haven't been home much."

"Neither have you, from what I hear."

"I've made it back almost every day."

"And?"

"And I hate the commute."

"And?"

"You remember when you saw Laurie?"

Kat nodded. Laurie, the severely handicapped daughter whose existence Kat had kept secret for years, lived in Virginia with her adoptive family. Kat had visited Laurie for the first time last year and had gone back to stay with her while her adoptive parents, Tom and Pam, took a vacation. Even now, Laurie did not know Kat was her biological mother.

"Were you disappointed?"

Kat squinted at her friend. "I gave her up because I knew how handicapped she was. Just finding her alive was a miracle."

"I don't mean, were you disappointed in her. What I mean"— Della made a rolling motion with her hand—"is, was it less emotional than it was to think about it? I mean, you know how you get all keyed up about something, thinking about it, planning, and then—"

"Anticipation? Everything's that way, isn't it? Did you just find out Tony's not perfect? Over the long haul, who, ever, lives up to your expectations?"

"Actually," said Della, "Tony's exceeded my expectations. For perseverance alone."

Kat looked even more annoyed.

"I just thought . . . you know, all this time, even after I knew I wanted to reconcile with Tony, I thought the thing I couldn't do was go back to the house. The only reason I agreed was that I thought Melissa needed . . . you know."

"Yeah."

"Anyway, it's just not at all the way I thought."

"The house?"

"The room. Jamie's room."

"How did you think it would be?"

"I thought it would be . . . I mean, I knew Suzanne's two daughters had lived there, I knew it was redecorated, and then Tony painted it over, and put this sleep-sofa . . . but I mean, I thought I . . . I'm the same, inside. And Jamie . . . my memories of Jamie . . . it's like . . . I stood there, then I sat on the sleep-sofa, and"—Della shook her head—"I couldn't shed a single tear. All I could do was think that we probably ought to pull up that pastel carpet and buff up the floors, maybe get a throw rug, sort of neutral, tone on tone. You know?"

"Oh, I like those. All cotton maybe?"

Della gave her friend a laugh, and pushed on her shoulder. "It's like, even his memory is going, I can't get worked up about it anymore. And I . . . it's a big loss, to sit in that room and think about his posters on the walls, and the clothes he used to throw all over the floor and not break down. It makes me feel disloyal. Hard. I miss him. But it's not the same."

"You want to keep grieving?"

Della sighed. "Yes. No. I don't know. I just thought . . . it feels wrong. It feels like I should be in more pain."

"Why? You're living with a man you love, the Ladies Farm is prospering, even Peach Fest is shaping up as a success. You have a son and a daughter-in-law and a beautiful granddaughter. Life goes on." Kat reached over and put a hand on Della's knee. "Maybe you should just let yourself enjoy it."

Ethan tossed the contents of his father's bureau drawer onto the double bed and sorted through the sad pile of briefs and tees. With the exception of an unopened three-pack of solid colors obviously sent by one of his brothers, Ethan could not find anything worth wearing, but he packed it all on the theory that the familiarity of his own clothing would boost his father's recovery. On the same tack, and in accordance with Gladys's instructions, he swept a rung of khaki work pants and denim shirts off their hangers. Ethan left the suit, which he knew his father wore only to funerals and an occasional church service.

Ethan supposed his father had worn his boots to the Big Bend, and hoped the clothes that had gone with him looked better than this sorry mess. It doesn't matter, thought Ethan. I'm driving. I might as well throw it all in the back of the car. He found a large suitcase and began filling it. His father, driving off to the Big Bend for an indefinite stay, had probably taken a small duffel, and a few baskets of produce.

Ethan studied the open closet, noting the neat arrangement of dress boots, bedroom slippers, and an old pair of running shoes. Ethan didn't recall his father ever running, but perhaps he had walked with Ethan's mother, once all the boys had left and they had time to themselves. He knelt down, his face brushing against a woman's bathrobe still hanging in the closet. It didn't surprise him to catch a whiff of his mother's perfume as he reached for the running shoes. Fabric, he had learned, held on to perfume a long time. The phenomenon had taught him to launder his sheets and pillowcases at least weekly, particularly if he didn't have a steady girlfriend.

Ethan pulled back and straightened up, studying the pair of shoes in his hand. Socks, he thought. Almost forgot socks.

Socks, in Webb Dyer's universe, belonged in the bottom drawer, close to feet. The socks—thick-knit white ones—made a mound on the right side of the wide drawer. On the left lay several photo albums, familiar to Ethan from childhood. He pulled them out and leafed through them quickly: a parade of the five boys in front of Christmas trees, a succession of pictures of his father in front of the orchards, his father and Manny, Sr., beaming over bushels of fresh peaches. There was one whole album devoted to the fruit stand his mother had operated, complete with close-ups of fresh peach ice cream and Ethan himself in a baby swing suspended from the metal beams of the sorting shed.

The oldest album began with a black-and-white picture of his mother in a corsage and his father in his dress uniform in front of the courthouse in Fort Worth. Ethan knew the photo; a framed enlargement had sat on his parents' dresser for years. He didn't see it here, and supposed it had accompanied his father to the Big Bend. Ethan closed the album and slipped it under the stack of others in the drawer.

He finished filling the suitcase, thinking about his parents' wedding photo, and their marriage. He liked to tell people who badgered him about settling down that he hadn't met the right woman. He still thought of marriage as something for the future. It had alarmed him, the first time he had dated a divorced woman with a child. He had attributed his squeamishness to reluctance at having sex with someone's mother, but now he realized it was fear of lagging behind that had jolted him. His contemporaries had moved on to marriage, parenthood, and now divorce. They were working on remarriage while Ethan was still trying to figure out what he wanted to be when he grew up.

"Curse of the youngest," he muttered now, carrying the suitcase out to the living room. "Or the chicken-hearted."

Chapter 23

She hadn't been to the house since their last canoe trip, the summer after high school. Melissa drove right up to the front, ignoring the two dogs who ran off the porch and barked steadily as she climbed up the steps. "Ethan!" she called. "Ask your mom if you can come out and play!"

He stepped out onto the porch.

"Still not smiling, huh? I'm sorry your dad's sick. I thought I'd better see if I can help you with anything."

"I'm leaving as soon as I check the orchards," he said.

Melissa sat herself on a wooden kitchen chair that was backed up against the house. "I couldn't tell you about Greg. I'm sorry."

He stood, silent.

"I kept trying, but it just felt . . . I don't know, I couldn't think of a way that didn't sound like there's something wrong with me. And I wanted you to think I was okay." She tilted her head to one side, looked up at him. "I wanted you to think I was hot, actually."

He leaned against the wooden porch support, looked out at the first orchard his parents had planted. "You are hot," he said, finally. "The hottest."

"Yeah, I can tell by your enthusiasm." She shook her head. "I'm sorry. My timing stinks, and I don't want to delay you. I just couldn't stand that you would head to Houston without at least knowing that I'm sorry."

"I think you already told me you're sorry."

"Well, I guess I'm saying that, along with everything else I'm sorry about, I'm sorry I couldn't tell you about Greg."

"You did manage to tell everyone else."

"Not really," Melissa said. "Just Aunt Della and the others when I got to the Ladies Farm. And Erica."

"Erica!"

"Ethan, could you suspend judgment long enough to think about what it was like for me? Finding out my husband of eight years, the man I thought I knew better than anyone in the world, is prancing around in women's undies? Can you imagine that?"

Studying his profile, Melissa could see a small smile work its way into his expression, flickering a second before it disappeared.

It's something, she thought.

"All the jokes you could ever imagine," she said, "I felt like the punch line to every one of them."

"I doubt it's anything you did," he said.

"I know that. But it is, in a way."

Now he turned a little, shaking his head.

"I don't care what anyone says, it's still the case that I'm not enough. Even if he was born that way, there's probably some woman, somewhere, who could make him—"

"Oh, don't be stupid," Ethan said. "You're just working on my sympathy. And believe me, Melissa, I am sympathetic. After Tony told me, after I got over being mad that you told everyone but me, I started to think about how you must feel. And I thought the things you just said: you must feel like shit.

"But Greg's . . . preferences . . . have nothing to do with you. There's no woman meant just for him. Not the way you mean. Of course you're not enough for Greg; you wouldn't be enough for any man. We always say things like, 'You're more than I could ever want,' but what we mean is, 'You're more than I deserve.'

"Believe me, we always want something more. Someone else. Something else. It's not that we can't control ourselves." He gave a short laugh. "Most of us are masters of restraint. Sensitivity. But that doesn't stop us from wanting more." He pressed his lips together. "And if you told the truth, you'd say you want more, too. If you hadn't found this out about Greg, and you just visited and found me here, you'd still come on to me. Not that you don't love your husband. And maybe you wouldn't do anything. But you'd still flash that smile, wear those shirts unbuttoned down the front. You'd still want me to want you."

"I wasn't teasing you," Melissa said. "I might not have known where we were heading, but I was willing to find out, at first. Then, Greg showed up—"

"And you remembered you were married," Ethan said, shaking his head.

"I guess I did."

"Are you going to stay with him?"

"No," Melissa said. "I'm not even sure he wants me to stay with him."

"He came a long way for someone who's not sure he wants you."

"Well, he's sure he's the boys' father. Anyway, my marital problems are not your problem. I just wanted to say I'm sorry. And to see if I can help you. We're still friends. Aren't we?"

"Sure."

"Ethan?" She stood, stepped toward him. "Is there something I can do for you around here? Pick up the mail? Feed the dogs?"

In a ballet of evasion, he turned and stepped sideways without even brushing against her. "It's taken care of. Thanks, though."

She looked at him, thought about the last time they'd taken the canoe up to the Brazos. Pouring their hearts out, figuring how they would go skiing over Thanksgiving. Did it mean anything to him? Did he even remember?

"Trey broke his arm," Melissa said. "Did you know that?"

"Erica told me. How's he doing?"

She shrugged. "Fine, I guess. There's, you know, this undercurrent of playground pushing, I don't know how to . . . raising boys is different, you know, from what I would—"

"My mother said that all the time," Ethan told her. "Trey'll be all right."

No he won't, she wanted to say. *He'll go nuts, run away, explode, implode . . . all because I picked the wrong husband. All because my parents insisted I join them in Mexico for Thanksgiving, and your whole family went to your brother's in Houston.*

"You could do one thing," he said, "while I'm in Houston."

She jerked back to the present.

"I told Erica I'd run with her when she gets in, she needs to check the course at night."

"I can't run a ten K," Melissa said.

"Try a bike," he suggested. He looked at her. "How did you find out? Did you follow him?"

Melissa sighed. "Sort of." She launched into the story: the sports bag, the trunk in the closet, the post office box, the catalogs. She even told him about the online support groups. Melissa sank back into the chair. "But I only lurk. I never log on."

"And he was like that when you met him, but you didn't know?"

Melissa nodded. "That's what he tells me." She shook her head. "He says it's just something he always did, that he doesn't even think about it consciously anymore, that it's just automatic."

"And he doesn't think you should be upset?"

"Oh, he understands I'm upset. He knew I'd be upset, that anyone would be upset. That's why he was so careful to keep it secret. He just doesn't think it can be changed. It's as if I'm upset over his having blue eyes. It's who he is."

"Has he ever tried—"

"Counseling? Psychiatry? Drugs? Hypnosis?" Melissa laughed. "He told me that after I found out, he even consulted someone about an exorcism. And shock therapy, until he found out what part gets the shock."

Ethan winced. "With you there, buddy."

"Even I understood that one. And, in fairness to him, I will say that he was more than willing to continue therapy and marriage counseling."

"But only if you stayed."

"Well, yeah." Melissa frowned. "I think. I don't know, actually. But I don't want counseling on how to save that marriage."

"No?"

"No." She sank back down in the chair. "I can't even imagine—" She studied the porch floor, the wood smoothed and polished, year after year. She thought about all the feet: five boys, their friends, their cousins, their prom dates, their own wives and children, summer and winter, boots and sneakers, oxfords and loafers, sandals and river shoes. There was no chance, now, for her to provide such a homestead for her own family.

"Would you have married me?"

"What?" Melissa steadied herself on the chair.

"Not will you; would you have? If you hadn't gone to Mexico and I hadn't gone to Houston? Would you have met me in Colorado? Would we have made wild, passionate, hot-tub love, vowed to be true? Married, at some point? Summer vacation? Junior year? Would you have transferred to A&M? Lived with me in student housing?"

"What . . . why are you asking?"

Ethan scratched his head, wrinkled his brow. "I'm not sure, but I think that's really why I'm mad. I mean"—he gestured now with his hands—"if we drifted apart, you fell in love with someone else, and you lived happily ever after, I couldn't complain, right? You found your soul mate.

"But this"—now he made a rolling motion—"this . . . we drifted apart, and you fall for this . . . underwear guy—"

"Cross-dresser."

"Cross-dresser," he amended, waving his acquiescence. "Obviously not your soul mate, and I . . . we . . . we could have been together."

"If you hadn't gone to Houston for Thanksgiving?" *Run to him*, Melissa told herself. *Run to him and run away from Greg, as fast as you can. Take the boys. Go somewhere else, anywhere else. Make a new life. He can adopt the boys. You can have another baby.*

"You don't think so, do you?" He looked heartbroken. Sadder than Greg.

Melissa shook her head. "What's a ski trip?" She shrugged. "What's a trip to Houston, or Mexico? We outgrew each other in different places."

"So the answer is no. You were never going to marry me."

Melissa had to laugh. "I was never going to marry you? Ethan! When did you ever want to marry anyone? You just want to stay single and in love."

She braced herself, but he just grimaced and gave a brief nod. "That's what I've been thinking. That I don't want to be married. Even to you. But I'm pissed that you wanted to marry someone else." He inclined his head a little. "And a little pissed, still, that you never mentioned your husband's lingerie."

"Yeah, well, what's a little lace between friends?"

She stretched her legs in front of her, studied her sandaled feet, mourned her failure to establish the family homestead for which she longed. Melissa looked over at Ethan. "I guess I'm back where I started: alone with my boys, trying to remake my life."

"I wouldn't call the Ladies Farm exactly alone. Not to mention Underwear Boy."

She shot him a look.

"Sorry. It's just too easy." He stuffed his hands in his pocket. "You know, I might enjoy this. I mean, now that I'm sure I'm not going to marry you, we can be friends."

"You'll be lucky to marry anyone," Melissa muttered. She stood, made her way over to him. "Look," she said and put a hand on his arm. "You've got to get on the road. Give your dad a hug for me. And let us know how he's doing."

He slipped his arm around her waist and gave her a hug. "You hang in there. I'll be back in time for the race."

Melissa pulled back a little. "That's ten days. You stay and take care of your dad." She patted his shoulder. "Erica and I have got this handled." She paused. "You want to tell me—"

"Just friends, I swear."

"You wouldn't say anyway." She pushed at him a little, and he grinned. Then she headed for her car.

By the time she checked her rearview mirror, he had disappeared from the porch. She wanted to believe that he stood in the shadows, watching her depart. That despite everything, he still yearned. He's right, she thought. I do want more.

"Well, she talked to him," Della said. "But I don't know what happened."

"I thought this was all about letting her take care of her life without our interference," Tony replied. He leaned forward and picked the remote off the coffee table.

"Hey! We're talking."

"I didn't turn it on," he said. Then he grinned. "It's my security blanket. I just like to hold it, especially when you're attacking me. I think we should go to bed."

"I think we should too. I'm due in Sydonia by eight tomorrow. But first we have to settle this."

"Settle what? It's up to Melissa and Ethan. Or Greg."

"Settle that you think I'm attacking you. As if you're afraid of me because I'm angry with you."

"I am afraid." He clutched the remote to his chest in a protective embrace.

Della threw her head back and laughed. "Oh God! I wish I really had that power!"

"So you're not angry?" He gestured with the remote as if it were his hand.

"I am angry, Tony. You and Dave were idiots. Drinking and shooting your mouth off like frat boys."

"Oh, you're so sexy when you play the disciplinarian."

"Now, that does make me angry." But she laughed, because in some ways she liked his teasing, and that made her even angrier. Get a grip! Della thought, but if she possessed any sort of grip it must be what she felt slipping away. "Melissa trusted us with her secret and you told it to the one person she cared about."

"Look, I'm sorry." Now the remote was describing circles in the air. "But it's out. We told Ethan, and now it's their problem. I said I'm sorry, Della. But I can't take it back." Tony shrugged. "Sorry."

Della stared at him.

"What?" he said.

"What?" she repeated. "What? You just mumble that you're sorry and you think that fixes it?"

"Try listening. I said I can't fix it. I'm sorry and I can't fix it." Tony scowled. "I don't know why you're so mad about this, Della, except you know you're partly to blame because you're the one who told me."

"Well, that was a mistake I won't make again: confiding in you."

"Della." He leaned forward, reaching toward her with the remote still in his hand. "If Ethan and Melissa ride off in the sunset together, closer than ever because the two of them face the truth together, you'd still be angry, wouldn't you?"

"That's not . . . you're deliberately making this sound silly. You're trying to trivialize my feelings."

"You just want to fight. Honey, I don't want to fight."

"Stop saying that."

"But you're trying to pick a fight, Della. Why is that?"

"Why . . . what . . ." She stopped. She stood up and stomped away.

"Shit!" His voice echoed down the hall behind her.

Jamie's door was open; she must have left it that way, Tony never did. She walked in and sat on the sleep-sofa. It took only a second for him to follow. He paused in the doorway, then took a seat next to her. "Is this it?"

Della leaned against him so that they were shoulder to shoulder, looking at the room together. "Do you think you could commute to Fort Worth?" Della asked him.

"That's what I was doing, remember?"

"Let's sell this place," Della said. "Neither one of us particularly wants to live here. We can live at the Ladies Farm, in my old room, or over at the Hutto house once the race is over and Melissa leaves. Or we can buy another house. In Sydonia. Or rent an apartment here for when we want to stay in Fort Worth."

"I always thought we'd get a place in New Mexico."

"New Mexico?"

"In the mountains. To get out of the heat in the summer."

"Really?" She looked at him. "Near Santa Fe?"

"North, I thought. Around Taos or something. Robbie and Laura could join us. Or maybe send Katie to spend a little time with Grandma and Grandpa."

"You think we could afford that?"

"If we live at the Ladies Farm, sure. What else are we going to do with the money?"

Della shook her head. "How come you never said anything?"

"How come you never asked?"

"Oh, that's easy! It's because I'm totally self-centered."

"You're just self-protective. Wary of the clinches."

"That too," she said. "So, New Mexico?"

"Or the Big Bend. I didn't think we could manage Wyoming."

"Probably not." Della looked at him. "You know, I didn't think you'd want to sell this place."

"It's just a house, Della."

Chapter 24

Greg and the boys set up their assembly line in the living room of the Hutto house. They had pushed back the furniture and set up folding tables. Boxes of unpacked luminarias lined one wall. Flats of the assembled tin holders were stacked outside, shaded by a makeshift awning Greg and Tony had assembled from a tarp and tent poles. The votives themselves, shipped separately from a church-supply house, were stored in cartons at the Ladies Farm fitness shed, where they wouldn't melt.

After much discussion and a few calls to Ethan in Houston, Erica and her husband, Peter, had taken up residence at Webb Dyer's farm house. "She thought we'd need the extra manpower," Melissa told Greg. "That's why she brought her husband."

Greg nodded, but never took his eyes off the task of snapping the bottom of the luminaria into place. He handed the finished piece to Garrett, who placed it in the flat.

Trey, meanwhile, pulled a flattened luminaria from the stack before him and popped it open, so it was four-sided, without top or bottom. All four sides bore a peach image pierced into the tin so that the lit candles would cast flickering peach reflections all around.

With his arm still in a cast, Trey worked mostly by bracing the piece between body and cast, and pressing. Then Greg reached out to Trey, who passed along the opened luminaria and a solid square of tin. Greg fit the pieces together and passed the result off to Garrett once more.

"I guess it's a good thing we didn't spring for the handles,"

Melissa said, taking the next luminaria from Trey and popping the bottom piece into place. "It'd be next week before we finished."

"How much were they? The handles?" Greg asked.

"A penny."

"Good move," he congratulated her. "You sure Hilgon's coming?"

"Tim and two of his buddies. A whole other team."

"We might get them all done first," Trey said. "If we hurry."

Melissa watched him pressing another luminaria up against his stomach to pop it open. "Trey, honey, why don't you put that on the table and open it there?" She walked around behind him and reached over, showing him what she meant. "Can you try that?"

Trey nodded, followed her lead. She stayed there a second, inhaling the shampoo smell from his hair. "That's good," she told him, stealing a glance at Greg as she straightened up.

His eyes flickered a second, but he turned back to the next luminaria, assembling it and handing it off to Garrett.

"You guys are doing a great job," Melissa said. "I thank you, the runners thank you, even the peaches thank you."

"The peaches!" Garrett giggled. Melissa gave him a hug. "You let Mommy know when you need a break," she instructed. "Meanwhile," she said, motioning to her own stack at the end of the table, "I'll race you."

At the hospital auxiliary booth, Siggie perched on a ladder as her mother and her mother's friend, Sandra, directed her in wrapping the auxiliary banner around the top of the booth's wooden frame. Siggie, having learned from previous years, secured the vinyl first with tacks pressed into the plywood; when both women were satisfied and had moved on, Siggie would go back over the thing with the staple gun.

"This booth isn't sitting straight," Sandra told Mrs. Blanton.

Siggie imagined her mother nodding in agreement but didn't turn to look. The courthouse lawn was as level and well-shaded a festival site as Sydonia could offer. The auxiliary, by virtue of its longstanding participation, had snagged its customary spot on the corner opposite the drugstore. Crowds walking up from the big parking lot behind the bank hit the auxiliary booth first and last.

To Siggie, the slight incline was more than offset by the superior traffic. Siggie looked skyward through the live oaks to where the heat shimmered without regard to the antlike scurry of Sydonians setting up Peach Fest.

She would rather be at the store, where she could stay busy, than here on the ladder awaiting her mother's direction. Her folks didn't ask about Johnny. They had helped her pack the kids off to her sister in Omaha, and her father had helped her call the wrecker to get Johnny's truck to the body shop. But they had said barely a word about Vinnie Perez's visit to them while she was at the hospital with Johnny. And even when she told them Johnny could come home, they didn't ask how he was feeling, or for his version of what had happened. They had closed him out of their lives.

Siggie reached over and tugged the banner a little straighter in response to Sandra's instructions. She was just waiting, really, out here in the sun, for something else to happen. Someone to tell her to start stapling, someone to tell her to climb down off the ladder, someone to fix whatever it was that ate at Johnny. He had promised her that he was done with the speed, and he had cut way back on the beer. She had told him not to bother coming into the store anymore. Her parents didn't even have to ask.

But Siggie knew there would be more. She lifted her stapling gun and shot into the soft plywood.

"The boys are at Webb Dyer's?" Rita didn't look up as she lined the basket with colored tissue, set in two rolled-up T-shirts and two embroidered Peach Fest caps, and then arranged the packages of peach tea, peach coffee creamer, a peach-scented candle, a luminaria, peach bath salts, a peach-colored bath mitt, peach salsa, peach preserves, and six perfectly baked cookies with peach-jam centers.

"That's where they're sleeping," Della said. "That's how Melissa made room for Tony and me." She looked across the kitchen table at her partners. "Kat, can you hand me some more of that green cellophane?"

Kat handed over another roll, returned her attention to addressing envelopes and cards to the recipients of the thank-you baskets. Then she put her pen down. "Trey and Garrett are staying with Erica and her husband? But not Greg?"

Rita arched one eyebrow, lined another basket with layers of peach and dark green tissue.

Della shrugged it off. "I think she didn't want to impose too much on Erica. Greg's such a sad sack."

Rita snorted. "If she didn't want to impose, she'd send Greg over to look after his own sons, so Erica and her husband could concentrate on this race they've got us all working on."

"I'm sure Greg will do his share," Della said.

"I'm more worried about Greg getting his share," Rita said. "Or what he thinks is his share."

Kat set down her pen and exhaled loudly. "Oh, that's not going to happen!" She looked to Della for support. "Is it?"

Della grinned. "Well, they've got Tony and me for chaperones, so I doubt there's much chance. Besides"—she waved a hand over the baskets—"I don't think anyone's got time for anything but the race and Peach Fest."

The three admired their handiwork, the laden baskets glistening under green cellophane, topped with peach-colored bows and effusive notes of thanks. They had even filled a group of smaller baskets for their own guests, most due to arrive the following day. Even now, their occasional housekeeper, Nancy, was upstairs, cleaning rooms.

"I guess it's a good thing Darlene and Earl couldn't make it," Rita said. "We wouldn't have anyplace to put them, anyway."

"You're going out there for the Fourth," Kat reminded her. "We're the ones who still haven't seen the baby."

"He's a cute one, too," Rita bragged. "Much rounder than Tiffany. Calmer, too. Probably because Darlene's a little calmer these days."

"We do settle down," Della observed.

"Well, I always expected Darlene to grow up," Rita said, dismissing her former concerns with a wave of her hand. "You're the one I wouldn't give odds on."

Johnny emptied exactly an ounce out of each bottle. Shane stood over him for the first few, to make sure he did it right, but it wasn't as if Johnny couldn't measure. Or pour. When he finished a case of water, he took it back to the lab, where Shane topped off the bottles with the jib.

Johnny stood and watched for a second. The GHB slid through

the funnel and into the water bottle. You could see it there, bluish slime, drifting through the water until Shane capped the bottle and tipped it back and forth a little. Shane laughed when he caught Johnny looking at him. "Some frat boy's gonna get lucky with this stuff! Rave mania! Mel Low!"

Johnny shook his head. "Don't see this stuff as lucky."

"You puked the first time you got drunk, too, but that didn't hold you back. Hand me that bottle up there."

Johnny gave Shane the next bottle, then stepped back. Just looking at the stuff made his stomach queasy.

"You set for your dance with Vinnie?" Shane asked.

"I need the stuff," Johnny said.

"Hold on," Shane said. "I'll get it in a bit."

"I just don't . . ."

Shane looked back at him. "Don't what?"

"Shane, if I give him the bag, tell him Freddy's boat beached downriver, we found it after the storm, here's the stuff—"

"You give him everything I give you, too," Shane warned. "Don't be playing halfsies with the evidence."

"But what I'm saying is, if I give him the speed, what if he still wants to know about the jib?"

"That's when you tell him you found these bottles in the boat. With the coffee cans stuffed with plastic bags full of speed. Freddy was diversifying." Shane pulled three bottles from the case he had just finished. "And you thought they were just water. So you glugged the stuff down." Shane grinned. "Kicking a habit like yours builds up a powerful thirst."

Johnny took the three bottles.

"Come on," Shane said. "We've got to get finished, get this thing torn down. You hold Vinnie off long enough to get the deal done, we'll be in business."

Johnny headed back to the kitchen table. When he brought the next case to Shane, he asked, "What do you mean, in business? I thought we were just going to do a giant score and then get out."

"That's what I thought, too," Shane said, measuring and pouring as he spoke. "But that was before the RV."

"RV?"

Shane waved a hand in the air. "That's our new rolling factory, buddy. I've got it stashed in Fort Worth. We'll wait till all this cools down, get the thing outfitted and roll on!"

Johnny said nothing.

Shane straightened up, motioned Johnny out of the lab. "Here," Shane said. "Be sure you wear this. The hat, too."

Johnny took the T-shirt and hat from Shane.

"Midnight Peaches," Shane laughed. "Best thing that ever happened to us!"

Webb watched them when he wasn't dozing. The way she nagged him about his stretches, the way he pointed her along the quilt. At first it had seemed pointless, her bringing the quilt on the plane, carrying that sack full of threads and needles. Then, after Ray arrived in Houston, Webb feared Ray was going to build a new frame for her, right there in the telemetry wing. Ray had driven the Avalon from the Big Bend, stopping every hour to stretch, camping nights at remote sites, where he could smoke in peace.

Gladys and the quilt had worked out. The boys, the health people, the grandkids came and went. But Gladys and Ray, fussing at one another, pulling the needle through, holding the thing up for him to inspect from across the room, had become almost the measure of his progress. The first day after the surgery, Gladys had actually spread the thing over his bed, bunched it up under his punctured and taped hand.

The first time he walked down the hall, dragging that IV rig behind him, Gladys had pulled her chair just outside his door, quilting until he arrived back from that terrible trek.

Now they were discharging Webb, sending him home to Wade's place. Gladys and Ray, who had been staying with engineer friends in Houston, were going to stay a week or two more.

Webb wanted to scream at them all. *You don't understand!* he would say. *They opened my heart. They looked at it! On television! They wound tubes through it, handled it. My heart!*

But Webb could not scream. The health people—a blur of technicians, nurses, doctors—moved him around, got him up, down, made him hug a pillow to cough, stood outside the door and cheered him on when he moved his bowels. They measured and weighed, counted and charted, and Webb obeyed their orders. He couldn't remember the last few days before the surgery, during which, they told him, he had grown weaker. But he was weaker now, certainly, and he couldn't resist the command of anyone around him. Webb could not imagine how he could drag this injured heart over acres of peach trees. He could not even imagine walking out to his truck and throwing it in gear.

Gladys and Ray and the quilt were all that connected him to the life when he could do those things.

Meanwhile, thought Webb, Ethan should get back to the orchards. The rabbits would be at the new trees if he didn't maintain the wrapping.

"Well, I'm going," Ethan responded when he showed up that morning. "We'll get you settled in at Wade's this afternoon, I'll take off tomorrow morning." Ethan looked around. "Where're Gladys and Ray?"

"Wade's," Webb said. He couldn't explain about Gladys shopping for new pajamas and slippers, and maybe scouting out a set of TV tables. Ethan might already know those things anyway. If not, Gladys would explain them later. Webb had to hoard his explanations, dole them out only when necessary.

"Look what Erica sent you," Ethan said. From his paper sack he zipped out a white T-shirt. The front of the shirt was emblazoned with a picture, almost a photograph, of a perfect peach pursued by a bunch of runners. Everything except the peach was sort of cartoony, including the title, *Midnight Peaches,* and the line underneath, *A hot race through a cool town.*

"Want to wear it?" Ethan asked.

Webb shook his head no, not wanting to elucidate all the gyrations, not to mention pain, involved in pulling something over his head. Ethan probably understood that one, because he said, "I brought your denim one, that buttons up the front."

Webb nodded.

"We're just waiting now on the doctor to sign the discharge," Ethan said.

Webb nodded again.

"I saw the quilt."

Webb watched his youngest son.

"I can't believe she finished." Ethan shook his head at the recollection.

"Take it with you," Webb directed.

"To Sydonia?"

"Auction it," said Webb.

Chapter 25

"Tomorrow evening, after dark," Johnny told Vinnie.

"You're dropping off the water *and* the jib?"

Johnny nodded.

"Where?"

"Well, the water at the starting line. About two miles, at the bottom of the hill. Then near the bridge. Then the finish."

"And then?"

Johnny licked his lips, looked out the car window. Even this far from the road, he worried about someone seeing them. "Twenty cases. Four places, five cases each."

"Four dealers? Four?"

Johnny shifted, looked at the cop. It was a funny thing, he thought. He never noticed that Vinnie, really, wasn't any bigger than he was. Kind of a skinny little guy, really.

"Johnny? Stay with me here."

"I don't know. He knows. Shane. It's four places; for all I know, it's ten people."

"And the money?"

"In between the bottles."

"What does that mean?" Vinnie looked irritated.

Johnny breathed out hard. "They leave cases of water. Real water."

Vinnie started to smile. "They pick up cases of GHB in water bottles? They leave cases of water?"

"Shane thought . . . you know . . . it looks like it has something to do with the race, no one'll notice. Places sort of near the route, but not on it. And the money . . . it's in those envelopes they printed for the race. With the peach on it. And a brochure inside. So maybe, if someone saw it, they'd think—"

"Yeah, yeah, it has something to do with the race. Twenty cases, twenty-four bottles a case, a hundred dollars a bottle. That's forty-eight thousand dollars, Johnny. You getting half of that?"

"I'm not getting any of that now. You know that." He shook his head, looked out the window. Damn Shane! They should have quit the business when Freddy Parker got picked up. You could always get speed somewhere.

"You're getting to keep your life, Johnny." Vinnie grinned. "Unless Siggie throws you out."

"You think she will?"

Vinnie laughed, shook his head slowly from side to side. "I don't predict what women will do, buddy. I'd recommend some serious kiss-up, though. I'm betting that last round left her pretty pissed."

Johnny cringed at the memory. He still slept in the family room, mowed the grass, sat down for dinner at her folks' twice a week so they could ignore him to his face. And she shut him out of the store, which meant he couldn't get near the cash. She wouldn't even let him near the kids; she had sent them off to her sister.

Johnny sighed.

"You're a lot better off than your partner. If you are a partner."

Johnny closed his eyes, laid his head against the passenger window. Then he banged his head a few times. "He just gives me some of it," Johnny said. "Not much, either. He made me pay him back for those T-shirts, too."

"Oh!" Vinnie nodded. "Your company sponsored the race T-shirts. That's real nice, Johnny. I've got mine right here." Vinnie reached into the back and pulled out his shirt and held it open for Johnny to see. "You did a good thing, there, buddy. All Sydonia is grateful to you."

Johnny shook his head. What did this guy want? He'd already given him Shane, the whole deal, even the cover story Shane had concocted. They'd get four dealers. What did they want from him?

"Where's Shane in all this, Johnny?"

Vinnie made it sound as if he was just wondering. Like, *what do you think about this weather we're having, Johnny?* Like, *I'm just curious.*

"I . . . I'm not sure . . . he didn't say."

"But he's picking up the money, after the race."

"Before the race," Johnny said dully. "Right after they put it down."

"And y'all meet up after the race?"

"He said to meet him."

"You're mumbling again, Johnny. You're supposed to meet him?"

Johnny nodded. Weren't the drugs enough? Did he have to tell it all?

"Come on, Johnny, be a man. Speak up. Meet him where?"

"There's a clearing, near the Hutto place. Close to where I make the last drop."

Shane slipped down to his prefab home while his father and the other old farts were cutting the ribbon in front of the court-house. He pulled on gloves, stepped back through the lab, and started dismantling equipment. Welcome to Peach Fest, he thought.

The beakers, tubing, and the heating mantle went into an Igloo cooler, which he carried out to the truck. The cooler was a weathered, dented model, no longer manufactured, which he had purchased at a yard sale in Arlington a year before. The kind of thing that came in handy sooner or later.

Shane peeled down to his briefs and his flip-flops, and tossed all the rest directly into the laundry. Then he headed back to the lab and started scrubbing. The walls, ceiling, floors, and counters were all laminated sheeting. Shane's preference would be to strip it out and recover the area. But given what Johnny was probably spilling to Vinnie Perez, Shane thought a good scrubbing with a commercial cleaner would have to do. Once the walls and ceiling were done, he sprayed the counters and scrubbed them. Then the sink, twice filling it to the top with a foaming cleanser and releasing the stopper to flush out the pipe. Finally the floor.

Two hours later, Shane backed his way out of the lab, carrying the bucket and scrub brushes with him. He tramped over to the tub in the laundry room and rinsed the bucket and brushes there. Then he peeled off gloves, briefs, and flip-flops, tossed them all into the washer with his other clothes, and headed to the shower.

Shane had a theory. The tendency by people around him to underestimate his intelligence had caused him misery as a child. He could knock other kids down. He could fall and laugh and get up again. But nobody remembered the chemistry set. Or even his ranch management degree, courtesy of TCU. Now, though, that underestimation worked to his advantage. And really, he thought as he massaged shampoo into his close-cut hair, I'm just the same kid with the chemistry set. And, he thought with satisfaction, I still knock other kids down.

Once dressed, Shane walked around to the storage shed that took up most of the prefab. The old farm trucks and the retired station wagon filled most of the space. Along the far wall, his stepmother had installed shelving to contain her husband's life-long accumulation of dairy journals. From that library, Shane had readied a cart full of dusty publications, which he pushed around to his apartment.

He spread magazines all over the lab, stacking them on the counters and stashing them in the cabinets. "Just stuff," Shane muttered, tossing several magazines on the floor and walking over them to give it all a lived-in look. He even pulled articles out and taped them to the walls. "Dusty old stuff."

By the time Shane got into the truck, the Peach Fest Parade of Princesses was probably in full swing. At this moment, the Castleburg Dairy Float, complete with mechanical cows, was transporting nearby Stephenville's dairy queen and her court past the viewing stands along Crockett to the courthouse. Royalty from every stock and produce competition in six counties appeared at Peach Fest; the Peach Court, in return, graced neighboring festivals by virtue of a grueling appearance schedule and very supportive parents. Two of Shane's three sisters-in-law had attracted his brothers when they appeared atop the chamber's Peach Float. Won their talent competitions pants down, Shane snickered now.

He pulled up to the orchard gate across from the Hutto place, left the engine running while he took the cooler from the truck, hastened across the country road, and slipped down through the brush. He remembered pinning Earl Westerman in this plot whenever Earl's uncle had his back turned. Earl scored big, Shane thought, sliding a little over the dry dirt. Darlene.

Ethan kept a few tools behind what was left of the old fort. Shane leaned over, planted the cooler next to the tools, then retraced his steps. When he got back to the truck, he balanced on first one foot, then the other, pulling the duct tape off the bottoms of his boots. The wadded tape and his gloves went into the old Whataburger sack, which he restuffed with the ketchup-y paper. He took care not to dirty his fresh Midnight Peaches T-shirt.

Shane got to the bank parking lot in time to enjoy most of the parade. He deposited his trash in the receptacle next to the booth where he treated himself to a peach ice cream cone. A quick glance over at the hospital auxiliary showed Johnny sniffing after Siggie. Nodding curtly as he passed the unhappy pair, Shane sauntered over to the Midnight Peaches booth to see what he could do to help. "I realize I'm early," he told Melissa, who was handing out race packets as the floats sailed by. He tipped the bill of his Midnight Peaches hat at her. "But I thought I could give you a hand."

Ethan stepped from the blinding midday light into the cool of the restored bank lobby that served Sydonia's Art League. "I'm the one who called," he told the woman who sat behind the table in the front. "This is for the judging."

"Are you Ethan?" another woman asked. "I knew your mother." This woman stepped out from behind the table and helped him pull the quilt out of the black trash liner in which Gladys had placed it. "Here," she instructed, waving him to step back as he held onto two corners. She held the other end, and tilted her head to study the piece.

Other people passed by, moving from the quilts to the water-color landscapes and on to the handwoven baskets and comic figures crafted from peach pits and twigs. Ethan looked at his mother's quilt. The cascade of peaches seemed to move as the light from the bank's celestory windows played over the quilt's surface.

Hints of clouds and blue sky backed the upper reaches of the quilt, while the basket and earth tones grounded the lower corner.

"It's magnificent," the woman who held the other edge said. "I can't believe she finished this, I remember when she showed me the pattern. She was . . . Oh! I'm sorry!"

"It's okay," Ethan assured the woman. "My mother didn't finish it, actually. Gladys Hutto did most of the quilting. Mother did the, um, appliqué."

"Gladys Hutto?" The woman shook her head. "Did this?" She peered at him over her half-glasses. "I quilted with your mother. Gladys . . . she's wonderful . . . but she didn't quilt much. Mostly she just kept the conversation going. She claimed she could barely thread a needle."

"Ray helped, too," Ethan said. "Ray Hutto."

The woman shook her head, then motioned him to gather the quilt up. Together, they suspended it on the wall among the other entries. "Well," the woman told him, as they headed back to the registration table, "this is quite a group project."

Ethan shrugged. Quilting was a social endeavor. His mother had won a lot of quilting competitions, most along with various friends. She used to leave the prize ribbons in the dining room buffet, along with the tablecloths. He could remember finding them, whenever he and his brothers pulled a fresh cloth from a drawer to set the table for a holiday dinner.

Ethan looked across the lobby at the quilt, which rendered the other entries unremarkable. Even from here, the peaches leapt from the wall, dripping color and flavor. The silence of the women at the table as they joined him in studying the quilt confirmed his judgment. It embarrassed him, now, that he had barely noticed the thing while Gladys labored over it at the hospital.

"It was a group project," Ethan confirmed, turning toward the Arts League women. He pictured the ribbons, little prizes fluttering out as they unfolded the tablecloths. "Let me give you their names," he offered. Ethan took the pen from one of the women and filled in the blanks on the official entry form: *Gladys Hutto. Ray Hutto. Alice Dyer. Webb Dyer.*

Business stayed brisk all afternoon at the Barbecue Boys trailer. Dave had hired a team of high schoolers to work the counter, leaving the smokers and carving to Nick, Tony, and Dave. They had restricted their offerings to sliced or chopped brisket sandwiches featuring two sauces: peach brandy and ginger peach. No one in the long, steady line complained.

"You think we'll have enough?" Nick asked, eyeing the brisket slabs as Tony opened the smoker and speared two more for Nick's cutting board. In deference to Nick's medical training, they always let him carve.

"We've got plenty," Tony said. "Earl picked up a special order in Omaha, dropped-shipped us a bunch of cartons."

Nick nodded as if just hearing this, though the four of them—Tony, Dave, Nick and Earl—communicated almost daily via e-mail about their fledgling business. Generally, all briskets went to the Big Bend, where Earl smoked them, basting them in their private-label sauces, and then either shipped them directly to catalog customers, or sent them to Dave for sale at the Quick Stop.

This time, though, they had set the smokers up the previous day, dumped steaming peach chips over the mesquite-wood coals, and started smoking early this morning. Tony nodded at Nick's sauce-smeared Barbecue Boys apron. "You need fresh scrubs, Doc?"

Nick grinned. "I want to know where the nurse is to wipe the sweat from my brow."

Tony, whose clothes were soaked through, shook his head. "I tried to coax Della down here, but all I got was noise about guests and race preparations."

"As if that mattered," Nick said.

Since he had started dating Kat, Nick had become a sometime Ladies Farm resident. His fertility practice, near the Dallas–Fort Worth airport, drew patients from across the Midwest on a high-dollar quest for the one treatment, the one procedure, that would produce a healthy baby. Tony guessed that slicing barbecue at Peach Fest was probably a welcome break.

Tony looked across the square to the stage, from which the show tunes floated, accompaniment for a stream of gymnasts, tap dancers, and budding ballerinas. He frowned, turned to Dave. "How'd they do that before boomboxes?"

"Record players," Dave said. He was used to working without talking. "Bands. Clinky pianos."

Tony nodded, turned back to his own smokers. Then he turned again toward the stage. He pointed. "Is that Ethan?"

"If it is, I'm not saying anything. Rita about tore my head off after our last little party."

"Yeah." Tony gave a half-wave, but Ethan didn't catch it. I hope that rig's still dripping on those plants, he thought guiltily. He hadn't even had a chance to check it this week, let alone pull weeds. So much for looking after things, thought Tony.

Chapter 26

"I promise I'll be back," Shane said to Melissa as he slipped away from the race registration table. Despite several thousand preregistrations, they had been busy all day, signing up runners, taking in checks, and handing out race packets. T-shirt and cap sales had been terrific. Shane attributed this to Erica, the redhead, who had twisted her shirt up to a midriff-baring confection that amazingly managed to display the Midnight Peaches logo in its full-color entirety.

Erica was a ball-buster, though. She took the beer from his hand and dumped it on the ground. She pulled a cigarette from his lips and almost stubbed it out on his chest before dumping it in a water bottle. Shane had just grinned at the water bottle. That's when he excused himself. "I do have some family responsibilities," he told them. "Gotta close up the store."

Almost at the highway, where Crockett resumed its existence as a farm-to-market road, Shane's mother had claimed a corner of cow pasture for a retail store. After her death, Eli had hired a succession of kids and divorcées to scoop out ice cream and pour cream over bowls of sliced peaches. Eli believed that minding the store was far too easy for any of his sons; but the three who had stayed married had provided three willing peach princesses to tend the register. If they held out on one another, Eli didn't care. It kept them out of the dairy profits.

Shane pulled the truck around to the back, where the ice-cream wholesaler delivered Castleburg's private-labeled premium and the produce dealer brought them California peaches. The Castleburgs hadn't produced their own ice cream since Shane's mother died, and they had never grown peaches. Lately, they specialized in milk, dairy cows, and sperm. But the shop, sitting as it did in the automotive gateway to the peach capital of Texas, gave visitors a taste of what they took for homegrown, homemade goodness at a price that could not be achieved by more scrupulous production.

The sisters-in-law had cleaned the tables and cashed out the register. "I'll get the garbage," Shane offered, and they accepted without a questioning glance. Once they got the floor mopped, they could stumble back to the farm, crash, and return by sunrise to serve peach pancakes and coffee with peach-flavored creamer. Peach Fest tested everyone's mettle.

In accordance with Eli's instructions, Marshall, Shane's next younger brother, showed up to escort his wife and sisters-in-law to the night depository and then home. "Too many strangers in town," Eli always said, as if it weren't the strangers' money he wanted escorted safely to the bank.

Shane waited till they had pulled away before he killed everything but the perimeter lights. Then he opened the garage doors to the delivery bay and pulled his truck inside, close to the office. He lowered the door behind the truck, left the other open, and pulled a beer from the fridge in the office. Then he rolled an office chair out to the bay and sat in the darkening heat, smoking and drinking his beer.

"Come on!" Trey said.

"It's time!" said Garrett.

"We can put them out now," Trey insisted, "and come back and light them later."

Greg ignored their plans. "Let's make up Mommy's bed, first," Greg said, amazed that he had coaxed both boys down for a nap. "Then we'll eat our Barbecue Boys sandwiches. Then we'll hose you both down in the Huttos' shower. Put on fresh T-shirts. And then we'll put out the luminarias."

"I want to sleep here some more," Garrett said. He sat himself on the twin bed that until Peach Fest had been his.

"It's time to light the candles," Trey said.

"I mean . . . I mean . . . when it's time to sleep."

"It's Mom's bed, now," Trey said. "And it's not time to sleep. It's time to light the candles." Trey looked at Greg for support.

"Come on, sport," Greg said, holding his arms out to Garrett. "Let's get you fed and showered. And, I promise, first thing Monday morning we'll move you back here and you'll get your bed back."

Garrett wrapped his arms around his father's neck. "When's Monday?"

"I get to use the fire lighter," Trey said, tripping along behind them.

"And me!" Garrett said. "I get to light candles."

"Tell you what," Greg told his younger son. "We're going to give Mom a gift, and you can be the one to give it to her. After you help set out the candles."

"I want to give it," Trey said.

"More than you want to light the candles?" Greg asked.

Trey fell silent.

"Come on, now. I promised your mom I'd have you cleaned up and out of here before Uncle Tony and Aunt Dell get back. They'll need to shower in a hurry, when they get here. They have to get back to the race."

After dinner and showers, he put the boys in fresh Midnight Peaches T-shirts, and straightened the bed while they pulled on shoes and socks. Greg tugged at the sheets, wondering how two boys—who had insisted on sharing their mother's bed rather than taking a bed of their own—could scramble fabric this way. Suddenly he stopped tugging and started to laugh. The boys looked expectantly at him.

"These must have belonged to the Huttos," Greg father told them. He held up a pillow. "Look. Look here." He smiled at them. "Peaches."

"I've got to go drop the water," Johnny told Siggie. He had been at the auxiliary booth all afternoon, arranging and rearranging crocheted dolls and wooden birdhouses on tables around the booth, and hanging rubber-tire horsey swings from the live oaks. Johnny wished someone would configure a tire from an eighteen-wheeler into an adult-sized horsey, and then he could just straddle it under one of the trees down by the river. Somewhere shady, but far away from Shane's place. Maybe at that Ladies Farm, which even though it abutted Castleburg's seemed to Johnny to be a Shane-free zone.

Siggie stared hard at him, then turned back to the stack of doll clothes she was folding for the thousandth time. "I'll be back," he offered. "I just said I'd do this one thing. For the race."

"For Shane, you mean."

"They're the drink sponsor. He's got to close up their store, help with the deposit. I'm helping out, that's all. Jesus! Sig, we're the T-shirt sponsors of the goddamn thing. I've been here all afternoon."

"And you're leaving just at cleanup time."

Sometimes he wanted to slug her, but most times he just wanted her to stop. He wiped his hand over the lower part of his face, rubbing the stubble along his jaw while he tried to think of something that would shut her up. "I'll be back later," he told her. He glanced across the square, to the bandstand and the starting line. "We could stay and dance until the race starts. Grab a little barbecue, huh? I'll meet you back here."

Siggie kept folding doll clothes, but at least she didn't say no. That was something. Johnny stuffed his hands in his pockets and backed away, grinning at his wife just in case she looked up.

He made his way to the truck, which was parked in front of Superior Feed. Siggie's dad had held down the fort while Siggie and her mom worked Peach Fest, and he was long gone. Probably spiffing up to ride in the pace car for the race. Along with the Castleburgs.

At least she hadn't changed the locks, Johnny thought, letting himself into the warehouse. Johnny went straight for the employee fridge, where the old man had probably stashed at least a sixpack. *Jackpot!* he rejoiced. It must have been a case. Johnny put six of the Coors in the truck, then drank a seventh before he mounted up. No use being greedy.

Besides, Johnny thought, reaching back into his pocket. *Besides.* "He-l-l-l-o, Mr. Bean," he said, pulling a pill and holding it up to the light from the truck dash. He'd been waiting till he left Siggie. She had no idea that Vinnie had slipped him a little advance. Johnny opened the second beer and washed his friend down his throat. "Come on, boy, we've got work to do."

All the water was stored in the walk-in refrigerator at Dave's

Quick Stop. Johnny and Shane had delivered it there the other morning and, at Dave's suggestion, had draped the stacked cases with a tarp and tied it down to make sure no one pilfered race supplies. Dave and Rita both were at the store, but Johnny told them not to trouble themselves.

Johnny and Shane had built a fortress of water around the twenty cases of GHB. When he got to the center, Johnny smiled at the markings. Midnight Peaches stickers covered the twenty cases.

"You got enough room in your truck for all that?" Dave asked as Johnny wheeled out the last load.

"No problemo," Johnny sang out as he breezed by. Those peachy little stickers had sent his spirits soaring. He loved peaches.

Johnny followed the list in order. First the starting-line water. Then the GHB near the tracks, a half-block from where they crossed Crockett. Shane had made him write it on his wrist, but Johnny knew it by heart. At the bottom of the hill, he nearly ran over the little fuckers putting out the candles, but he got the water to the water station and the jib in the undergrowth on the bladed spur road.

Five cases, plus the Midnight Peaches nine-by-twelve envelope tucked between the first and second cases. The last place was past the Hutto house, in the brush above the clearing. Johnny, looking over the treetops that descended to the river, smiled. From this height, he could imagine there was no Vinnie, that he and Shane would meet here later and split their biggest payday. He'd buy something nice for Siggie—something that showed her parents he was worth a shit—and maybe a bass boat. Something for the kids, too.

But he would stash most of it. Johnny wouldn't get caught short again.

"Come on, Della!" Tony said. "Share the soap." He stepped into the shower and reached around her.

"Here," Della said. She slipped out from his grip and handed over the bar of soap. There were actually two bars, and two soap holders, two handheld shower heads mounted on opposite walls, and a sauna-type bench that fit two. The Hutto house fostered togetherness. It seemed like ages since they had been alone here.

Tony started to lather her back. Della leaned her head back, let the lukewarm water cascade over the front of her body while Tony massaged soap over her shoulders and neck.

"Mmmmmm," she said. "If we get a new house, we should get a shower like this."

"Like it?"

"Oh, yeah." She had been on her feet, first at the Ladies Farm and then at the race table, all day. She had strung banners and folded T-shirts until she was light-headed. It was hard to know what she wanted more: a shower or a nap.

It was clear what Tony wanted. "Tony," she murmured as she turned to face him, "honey, what I'd love most right now is a nap." Della rested her head against his chest, let the water run over her back and legs. He put his arms around her, squeezing her slippery body.

"Sure?" he asked.

She gave a little laugh, looked down at his hands. "Uh, less sure."

"Well, why don't we think about it?" Tony suggested. He took her hand, put the soap back in it. "You could soap up my chest while we consider it."

Della accepted the challenge, thinking more about his body than their lack of time. Tony was tall, which was always a plus for Della. His shoulders were a touch too narrow for his height, and he had begun to stoop a little. But there was something to be said for a reasonably nice-looking man who still wanted to shower with her.

They kissed and kissed under the stream of water. Then, as they were struggling toward the bed, throwing down towels and shivering and straining in the air-conditioned cool, she gave a thought to Gladys and Ray, who had constructed the double shower off of their bedroom. The thought prompted a knowing half-giggle, low in her throat, which only spurred Tony's enthusiasm.

Later, lying on her back, exhausted, Della considered the shower some more. "It's really amazing," she told Tony. "I mean, that they're so close, they wanted to shower together. Even now."

"You like that shower?"

"Yeah." She turned her head, looked at him. "Don't you?"

He considered. "So if we build a place down here, you want one of these?"

"You know, I think I would," Della said. "I hadn't really thought about it."

"But you like the shower?"

She chuckled. "Yeah." Della propped herself up against the headboard, stuffed a pillow behind her back. "You know, in some ways, I like that double shower better than a whirlpool. Don't you?"

"If you do," he laughed.

"Well, what do you want?"

Tony frowned. "Actually," he started. He propped himself up next to her, dropping a sweaty arm over her shoulders. "I think I'd like an outdoor shower."

"Outdoor?"

"But still double, like this one," he assured her. "Wouldn't that be cool? An outside shower? I mean, even in winter, if we had a good door leading out, from the bedroom—"

Della sat up straighter. "That would be good." She imagined the steam billowing over them on a cold day, the gray sky obscured by their own cloud. She imagined lathering him up on a July afternoon, the water a cool stream dancing in the summer sun. "That would be great, actually. That's fantastic!" She stretched her neck out, kissed the tip of his nose. "You knew what I'd like before I did! You are such a good husband!"

"Think so?" He wasn't smiling at all.

She felt her face grow warm. "Well, yeah." She wanted him to stop studying her. "Don't you think I'm a good wife?"

"No," he said.

She shrank back. "Why not?"

"You're not a wife. You're an ex-wife. I'm an ex-husband."

"Well, that sure puts a chill on a warm, cozy chat."

"I didn't say I didn't like you."

"No. But you said—"

"I know what I said, Della. I said we're not married."

"Tony, that's not how I meant it when I called you a good husband."

"I know," said Tony. "That's how I mean it, though. If you're going to act like a wife, then be a wife."

"Tony—"

"I'd like you to marry me."

"Aren't you supposed to ask?"

"I did ask, Della. And you accepted. That didn't work. Now I'm trying something different. I'm stating my feelings. Non-judgmentally. Factually. I would like you to marry me."

"Very good. Very Dr. Phil."

"You're not stating your feelings."

"No," she acknowledged. "No, I'm not." Della studied the ceiling.

"Though you did say I'm a good husband."

"Yes," she agreed, closing her eyes. "I said . . . I . . . those are my feelings. I stated my feelings." She opened her eyes. "I feel . . . I feel that you are a good husband."

He didn't speak.

"My husband," Della continued. "And I want—" She turned to him, and his eyes were brimming. "I want to be married," Della told Tony. "I want to be married to you."

Shane watched the delivery truck pull into the far bay and listened to the rumbling whistle of the diesel as it cut off. He took one more look down Crockett toward town, but saw only the twinkle of lights against the night. Then he stepped back inside and lowered the garage door before he turned on the overheads.

Shane whipped the tarp off the bed of his pickup and nodded at Kenny, the driver of the water truck, as Kenny approached.

Kenny nodded back. He pulled on his work gloves, then reached over the side of Shane's pickup and hoisted one of the five-gallon bottles onto his shoulder. He had his thumb hooked through the loop on the bottle to steady it. With his other hand, he unscrewed the cap, tilted the huge bottle forward ever so slightly, and poured a silvery stream into a small paper cup. He drank in one sip, swishing it in his mouth before swallowing. Then he dropped the cup on the floor, stomped over to his own truck, and slipped the bottle into the special rack on the side.

I shouldn't have parked so close to the office, Shane thought. He wouldn't have had to carry it over that far. The wide space had once been filled with display racks for the fresh produce and preserves his mother had resold. She'd open the back doors for the farmers to make deliveries, then raise the front doors for customers. The wide space sat empty now. You could put five trucks here, Shane thought.

Kenny stood blinking a second while Shane scrambled over to

pick up the paper cup. "How's Freddy?" Shane asked, licking his lips. He guessed a guy like Kenny didn't mind a few extra steps.

"Holding up," Kenny said. He lifted another of the five-gallon bottles. This time he ran a small stream over his thumb and forefinger, rubbing thoughtfully while he held Shane's gaze. The third bottle got a little more tasting. For the fourth, Kenny actually held the bottle up high in the light and studied it. Shane studied Kenny's biceps.

It had taken hours to empty all those twelve-ounce bottles into the five-gallon jugs. And Shane had no help for that task. And then the risk, storing it behind the old tractors. He'd sat up almost every night, scanning the river and the hill down to the shed.

Kenny snorted a little as he loaded another jug onto the side of his truck. "Kicking in," he said, turning for the next bottle. He stopped for a second, as if to gauge the effect, then nodded slowly without looking at Shane.

Shane wondered how such small sips, even repeated sips, could cause a discernible effect in anyone Kenny's size. But Shane had followed Freddy's recipe. Maybe this stuff got diluted further before resale. If it does, he owes me more, Shane thought, then shook his head to drive the thought out of his head. That kind of thinking got you killed.

"That's good stuff," Shane hastened to assure Kenny. "I followed Freddy's recipe to the last detail."

Kenny turned from the truck and stared at Shane.

He's just a mule. Just a big, dumb mule, thought Shane. Lifting. Carrying. Handing over the money. He watched Kenny securing his truck, rolling down the louvered cover for the rack of water. Whatever Freddy tells him.

Kenny rummaged around in the back of the truck. The money must be back there, Shane thought. He pictured a storage compartment with a false bottom, imagined Kenny pulling back a vinyl mat, lifting the door and withdrawing an envelope. Shane stood next to his own truck and waited.

Kenny slammed the back of the truck shut.

Shane heard a lock click. He frowned. He thought Kenny was supposed to leave water for the Castleburg cooler. The water delivery was the cover. Maybe the water's on the other side of the truck, Shane thought.

Kenny walked toward him and held out an envelope.

"My brother wanted you to have this," Kenny said. He stopped.

Shane stepped forward, reaching. In the second that he saw the gun, he realized that Kenny had offered the envelope with his left hand. That Kenny had never removed his gloves. That the noise in town would obscure any sound and that he was too far from Kenny to splatter anything.

He's shooting me, Shane thought, but he had no control of his legs, no voice to protest, no cover in the open space. The roaring in his ears might have been the gun, might have been the opening of the bay door, might have been the thunder of Kenny's engine, might have been the bay door closing. It might have been the life seeping out of him from the singed holes through the chest of his Midnight Peaches T-shirt.

Chapter 27

"Is that Flops?" Della asked. The barking came from outside, toward the river.

"Sounds like," Tony said. They had showered separately this time, and donned fresh T-shirts and a liberal coating of insect repellent.

"Maybe we ought to keep her here," Della said. "Why don't you call her?"

"Why?" Tony pulled on his socks and running shoes. "She's just chasing rabbits. Birds."

"All those runners," Della said. "People wandering through town. Someone drifts away . . ."

He gave a laugh. "Flops isn't likely to hurt anyone. Rabbit or human."

"She'll scare them, though," Della said. "A big old dog, barking and running at you."

"Ready to lick you to death?" Tony looked at Della. "Okay." He slapped his Midnight Peaches cap on his head. "I'll call her."

"Hurry," Della yelled after him. "We're missing the race!"

From the height of the judges' stand—before which the floats had passed in review just that morning and where, following a thorough grilling of the five finalists regarding their plans for world peace, Miss Peach Fest had been crowned—Melissa watched the runners gather on the street in the hot night. She watched Erica placing the last of her electronic tag monitors at the finish line and stationing human monitors to prevent tampering. She watched Cassie Ellers, triumphant after a busy day at her shop on the square, inspecting the starter's pistol. She watched the sheriff's car lining up as the pace car, its revolving lights augmented by the digital readout of the official time: 000.00.

Melissa let out a long, hard breath. The runners were here. The timers were set. The pace car was in place. They had drawn a crowd. They had made money.

The white race shirts made the runners a globular mass, throbbing with its own excitement in the twinkle of the dance-floor lights. The band, which had a cover of every country hit from the past forty years, had settled into vintage Anne Murray, pleading to have this dance for the rest of their life.

Melissa looked down the race route and saw a flicker in the dark, at the crest of the first hill. As she watched, the flicker grew, side to side along the road. Those were the luminarias, slowly heading her way. Below her, through pauses in the music, she heard the runners call to one another. She supposed they were pointing, whispering. When the music stopped, there was almost no sound at all. Just the flickering path making its way toward the starting line.

Orrin Bell, from the chamber, climbed the steps of the wooden platform and began fiddling with the sound controls. The lead singer for the band thanked everyone for their kind attention and promised to resume play after the race started. He yielded then, to Orrin, who instructed the runners to take their place.

Melissa swallowed hard, watched Eli Castleburg and Burt Blanton, Siggie Urquardt's dad, take the back seat of the pace car. The sheriff rode shotgun, with an older deputy, Carl Ratsinger, behind the wheel.

She barely listened to Orrin. Every instruction and every pause was scripted now. Melissa had written the script. If he departed from it, she did not want to know.

She concentrated instead on the seething T-shirts below, watched them coalesce, then thin to a trail that filled the street for blocks beyond the square. Orrin droned on, thanking sponsors and reminding runners to leave the tags laced on to their shoes until they were removed by race officials at the finish.

She heard clattering on the stairs and looked up to see Garrett throwing himself onto the platform. "We lit the candles," he yelled. "We lit them with fire!"

Melissa put a finger to her lips and reached down to scoop him up. Trey and Greg followed, while Orrin continued without noticing them.

"We lit them," Garrett whispered in her ear.

"I know," Melissa whispered back. She pointed to the illuminated rise in the distance. "I can see."

"Mom," Trey was whispering. "Mom, we want . . . we have—"

"Wait!" she cautioned, putting an arm around her older son and shepherding him away from Orrin. "Get ready!" she warned.

Orrin counted down. At the starting line, Cassie Ellers fired the starting pistol. A cheer rose, a whooshing, low-pitched cheer that faded into a low rumble as the runners chased the pace car.

"It's like they're swimming," Trey said.

Garrett, whimpering, took his hands down from his ears, and looked out over the hypnotic flow of runners. They watched in silence for almost five minutes as thousands of runners surged by.

"Well, they're off," Greg said as the last few straggled through the starting line.

Melissa jumped. She had forgotten he was there.

"And it's a success," he added.

"I guess so," she said. She edged toward the stairs. Now that the race was underway, she wanted to get the final tally and stand at the finish to make sure the tag clipping went smoothly. Greg and the boys stood their ground.

"We have something," Trey said. "Something—"

"I want to do it!" Garrett wailed, snapping alive in her arms. "I . . . me! Daddy said."

Melissa looked at Greg as Garrett slid the length of her body to regain his feet and pull now at his father.

She hadn't noticed that Greg was carrying a package. It was small and square, and he handed it to Garrett without a word.

"Here," said Garrett, thrusting the thing at his mother. "Here."

Melissa took it and unwrapped the loose tissue. She smiled. It was a luminaria, to which Greg had attached wire so that it could be suspended. It would be pretty, she thought, casting a peach-shaped glow over a dining room table, or on a deck.

"Read the note," Trey said. "The note is the gift, too."

"It often is," Melissa assured him, unfolding the sheet that had been tucked in with the candle.

"Here," Greg offered. He pulled his Peach Fest Mag Lite from a pocket and stood behind her, shining the light over her shoulder.

Melissa warned herself to slow down, to read aloud, to show her sons that the sentiment was more important than the gift. But instead of a handwritten greeting, or a crayoned drawing, it was an e-mail. It was from someone named *jackofall* to *gregw,* and it said, *This will confirm our organization's commitment to underwrite ten thousand luminarias for the Midnight Peaches run held in conjunction with Peach Fest in Sydonia Texas. Payment to be made within fourteen days.*

There was more. *Logo in final report. Option to repeat. No competitor to be included in sponsors.* Melissa skipped through it. She turned to look at Greg, who was studying her.

"How—"

Now he grinned. "Jack and I share a secret."

"You—"

"I gave him the means to protect it a little longer."

"Do you like it?" Trey was asking. "Is it a good one?"

Greg shrugged. "It's a good cause; they had the budget for community relations; it doesn't hurt them. They were going to spend it anyway; why not in Sydonia?"

"Do you like it?" Garrett joined his brother's refrain. "Do you like it?"

Melissa looked at Greg. He shrugged again. "It's weapons systems. They were the only company I could think of that hadn't gone bust."

"And he's from ... in ... California? Someone you know there?"

Greg's nod confirmed it all.

"And he's—"

"He's the kind of guy who, when I explained my problem—our problem—to him, knew that he had to help."

"Mom!" Trey again. "Mom, don't you like it?"

"Of course I do!" Melissa told them, kneeling down to hug both boys to her as she acknowledged the horrible, terrible truth. "Of course I like it. I love it! It's from my family!"

*   *   *

Johnny swallowed another tab. He washed it down with another beer. He got up from the folding chair in front of Shane's
place and walked along the river to the spillway. He had to get
back to Peach Fest. He should be dancing with Siggie by now, she
was going to kill him if he left her standing there.

Where the hell was Shane? He was supposed to be meeting
Johnny across the way, but Johnny couldn't see shit. Unless Shane
knew the truth about Vinnie.

Johnny stopped pacing.

He tried again with his binoculars, but even when he wiped the
sweat off his palms, all he could see was the outline of the trees.
He couldn't even make out the clearing.

Damn him, Johnny fumed in the dark. He knew. He set me up.
He told me to meet him so Vinnie could pick me up. He picked up
the money and he's gone with it!

Johnny collapsed back in the chair. He had to think.

His head was pounding and his mouth was dry and bitter.
Shane couldn't get away, even if he didn't go to the clearing.
Vinnie told him there would be someone watching each spot.

But what if it was the other way? What if Vinnie had set him
up? What if Vinnie got him to spill the plan and then turned
around to make a deal with Shane? What if they were up there on
the hill splitting the money, laughing about his taking the fall?

Johnny jumped from the chair. He started for the truck, then
wheeled around and stepped up to Shane's door. He rattled the
knob, but it was locked. Furious, he stepped back a little, then
rammed it with his shoulder. Nothing gave. "Fucker," he muttered. "Fuck. Fuck. Fuck."

This time he stepped off into the yard and ran at it. "Shit!" he
screamed, bouncing back, hard.

Johnny pushed himself back up and seized the chair. He barely
turned his head as he sent it crashing into the front window. "Now,"
he said, stepping back as the chair tumbled into the yard. "Now."

The window frame took several more whacks, but he got
enough of it out that he could crawl through. He saw blood on
the ground, felt things snagging his shirt, but that was nothing . . .
nothing! compared to what he would do to Shane. He stumbled
to the bedroom. It was all there. He took the rifle with the scope,
and the night goggles. "Now," he said. "Now, now, now!"

*   *   *

Ethan and Peter Taloukis sat waiting on either side of the road in the park, the luminarias flickering around them, the volunteers at the nearby water station filling the night with low chatter.

"Of course Erica told me," Peter assured him, straining to sound nonchalant. "It's not that big a deal, is it?"

Ethan slapped at a mosquito, tilted his head back to stare at the stars. "Must have been a big deal to them," Ethan said. "That's why she's here."

"Where does that leave you now?"

"Out," Ethan assured him. "Well away from it."

"You're better off," said Peter, who had counseled and consoled Ethan through breakups in Austin.

"I think we've all reached that conclusion," Ethan said.

"What now?" Peter asked. "Heading back into real estate?"

"Not right away."

"This is a nice town," Peter said. "Erica thinks it's like a storybook."

Ethan chuckled, but didn't reply.

"Come on, pal."

"I don't know," Ethan said.

"Don't you—"

"Wait." Ethan held up a hand in the dark, as if Peter could see it. "Here they come."

The red and blue lights on the pace car flashed through the trees, and they watched it make the sharp U into the park. For the hundreth time, Ethan placed his hands on the monitor, making sure it was properly positioned. It was a small enough task, he thought. Critical but hard to mess up.

The volunteers stood back as the pace car rolled through, then stepped into the road to offer paper cups of water. First came men, five or six of them almost single file, silent and breathing hard. Then serious women. Then the crowd. In a few seconds, runners clad in shorts and T-shirts clogged the park road. Soft crunching sounds rose from the feet of runners crushing discarded cups. They ran in loose clumps, no more than four abreast. They smiled. They whooped. They thanked the volunteers for the water.

Ethan saw a few veer into the brush, probably to take a leak.

Others slowed to a walk to gulp the water without choking. There was laughter, conversation. Middle of the pack, thought Ethan.

Shane had come through with the water. Give him credit, Ethan thought. And without a murmur of protest. All for the privilege of his father getting to ride in the pace car.

Having driven all night to enter a quilt in competition because his father requested it, Ethan recognized the inclination. Bringing his father the ribbon that the judges had pinned on the quilt that evening would provide satisfaction matched only by reporting whatever figure the quilt fetched at the Sunday-morning peach pancake breakfast and auction to benefit the Sydonia library.

Then what? Ethan wondered, turning over Peter's query as the runners passed by his station. Envy stabbed at him, seeing all these people who knew where they were headed, at least for a single evening.

The night goggles made all the difference. When the dog raced into the clearing, Johnny almost jumped off the edge of the spillway. The shadowy, green retriever was the clearest thing Johnny had ever spied in the dark. He had moved the chair down to the river, but there was no point in sitting. Shane and Vinnie would be showing up any second, splitting the money that belonged to Johnny. The money for which Johnny had worked so hard and risked so much.

Johnny pulled another beer from the sixpack in the water and popped the top. They couldn't hear anything from this distance. They were way up on the hill; he was down at the river. He picked up the goggles again and peered through the trees. The retriever was yapping and jumping around the wooden barrier. For a second he worried that the dog might come his way, but then Vinnie popped up from behind the barrier.

"Well, what do you know?" Johnny whispered. "That dog finally sniffed something out." He picked up the rifle and sighted through the scope. "Pow," he said. "Pow, pow, pow."

He giggled. Shane thought he was such a hotshot, but who was walking into the sights now?

Vinnie was squatting down behind the barrier, just his head and shoulders visible as he made friends with the jumping retriever. Johnny focused on the dog, imagined Vinnie's shock when the dog's head blew off. That'd be a lucky shot.

He switched back to the night goggles, adjusted the view so that he saw most of the cleared space. The brush that shielded the place from the road moved in the wind. Shane would step from those black branches in just a second, thought Johnny. Just one more moment, his pockets bulging with cash.

Or maybe he had a sack. That made more sense. Maybe a backpack. Or a briefcase. Some fucking businessman. Screwing his friend.

A blob moved into his field of vision from the lower left. The dog leapt toward the blob, which resolved to a man. A tall man.

He came from the side. Because he knew I'd be down here . . . because . . . because . . . Vinnie told him! That's why Vinnie was there alone! Why Vinnie wasn't cuffing him, just walking toward him, talking. Hadn't drawn his gun. They were both standing to the side, talking, not even guessing that Johnny could see the two of them.

Johnny could see them pointing, moving back toward the side. He's stashed the money, Johnny thought. Right there in the woods. They're going to get it and then they'll circle back here. It was all clear now. For the first time, he saw the whole thing. They'd kill him, Vinnie'd blame the whole thing on him, and he and Shane would split the cash.

Johnny frowned. The others . . . the dealers who had left the money and . . . they were all in on it! It was the only way! The dealers left the money and the cops just watched them. They didn't get anyone! Vinnie and Shane paid them all off! All of them!

He's screwing me! Johnny thought. I did all that lifting and mixing and hauling. Buy this! Do that! And he's paying off cops with my share! Pinning the whole thing on me!

They were walking toward the trees. They were two, three steps away from disappearing. Johnny dropped the goggles and reached for the rifle. He sighted through the scope. The dog was jumping, bouncing around. Vinnie was motioning. Shane was turning, heading . . .

Everything started to quake. Johnny grasped tighter, tighter. The harder he held, the more it shook. They were standing, talking, walking, the dog was jumping. Johnny sighted, closed his eyes and squeezed. He saw them go down, falling or jumping with the rifle. He could not hold the rifle tight enough and he couldn't see anything because sweat stung his eyes. *Shoot again,* he told himself. *Shoot!*

He squeezed. And squeezed. And squeezed.

Chapter 28

In the pace car, the message came through with a crackle. There were two cars near the Castleburg place and both of them headed straight to the prefab. The sheriff told Carl Ratsinger to head for the Dyer orchard across from the Hutto house.

"That's my boy down there," Eli said. "That's Shane's place! You take us—"

"They'll pick him up," the sheriff replied. "We're heading . . . turn here," he told Carl. "I've got a deputy under fire, we're . . . here, stop here, stop!"

Carl braked at the intersection with the unpaved county road, and the sheriff jumped out of the car. "Pop the trunk," he ordered, and Carl complied. "Here." He jerked open the passenger door, pulled Burt Blanton from the car, pressed flares into his hand. "Keep those runners on course. You too, Eli."

They left the two men standing dazed in the center of the road, and tore down to the orchard entrance. The sheriff had donned his vest and unholstered his pistol by the time he slipped into the brush that led down the hill.

We've already missed the start of the race and he's playing with the dog! Della thought when she heard Flops's new round of barking. Annoyed, she headed out onto the deck to locate her husband-to-be. *You promise to marry 'em, she thought, and the first—*The shot, echoing up the river from the opposite bank didn't alarm her. *Stupid kids,* she thought. But, after a pause, three more followed, one banging off a rock with a metallic ping that left no doubt that someone across the river was firing at the hill.

Cell phone in hand, Della clambered down the path to the bench, looking wildly across to her own bed and breakfast. "Tony!" she yelled, knowing this was the stupidest course, the one most likely to get herself killed without helping Tony at all. "Tony!" she screamed again, striking out for the plot.

She crashed along the narrow path, swatting at branches and stumbling over roots and vines that caught her clumsy feet. "Tony!" she yelled, but she could not hear her own voice, could not hear anything over the pounding in her ears. The path narrowed further, curving around the hill over the river. Ahead, she saw movement, something blurred, and then Flops broke through the trees, barking nonstop. Flops without Tony.

"Flops! Oh God! Flops!" The dog leapt around her, barking more. Then she took off. Della couldn't follow into the trees, stuck to the path another twenty feet, sending rocks and debris flying down the hill to the river on her right.

"Hold it!" someone said. "This is the sheriff. Stop right there."

Della took another step, saw the sheriff now, kneeling over a tangle of bodies. "Tony!" she screamed.

Ethan had watched the pace car climb out of the park and cross the bridge. He could still see the car when the siren wailed and it sped off from the runners.

Ethan could see the flashing lights. He knew Sydonia. He knew that when the lights turned to the right, they were heading onto the unpaved county road that intersected just beyond the bridge. They were heading either to the Hutto house or his family's orchard.

The runners had become walkers now. They passed singly or in pairs, talking in low murmurs, sipping from their cups of water, ghostlike in the flicker of the luminarias. Ethan pulled his bike from the trees and walked it across to Peter. "You handle this," he told Peter. "I've got to see what's happening up there."

"What's happening?" Peter asked, then followed the motion of Ethan's hand. He started to ask more, but Ethan swung a leg over the bike and pedaled through the park. "Coming through!" he called as the runners grew thicker. "Coming through on the left!"

Ethan puffed his way up to the bridge, but then the crowd got too thick and he had to walk his bike. Eli Castleburg, half-running in the opposite direction, met him where the park road joined the farm-to-market, almost colliding as he emerged in the night. "What happened?" Ethan asked.

"Shooting," Eli said. The old man had barely enough breath to choke out the word. "Shane—"

"Shane?" Ethan said. "Shane shot—"

"Shots across the river. From Shane . . . Shane's place."

Ethan started to run, pushing his bike ahead of him. *Shane. The plot.* He raced across the bridge.

At the county road, he saw Burt Blanton, waving a flare in the dark. "This way," he kept saying. "All runners this way."

But Burt Blanton was one man in a sea of runners. They engulfed him, and as Ethan broke to the right, some of the runners trickled after the bike.

"This way," Burt Blanton kept yelling. "This way."

Ethan pedaled harder.

Johnny didn't know if he had hit them or if they had hit the ground and were heading his way. He tried to check, but between the shaking and trying to juggle his equipment, he couldn't see anything.

Oh God, thought Johnny. Abruptly, he sat, missing the flat stones and straddling one of the slots so that his seat got soaked. Even so, he didn't move. I need to think, he told himself. The night goggles dangled from his neck, and he clutched the rifle with both hands, above his lap, where it was dry.

That reminded him about the pills in his pants pocket. You can't sit in the water, he thought. They'll get . . . you've got to . . . Ever so carefully, Johnny swiveled on his butt, holding the rifle above his head with his left hand, steadying himself with his right. Then he pushed himself up to a kneeling position. Kneeling on a dry, flat rock on the spillway. That was good. It was nothing, now, he thought, to reach into his pants with his right hand, feel the little packet, the tabs wrapped in the stiff paper.

First, of course, he wiped his hand on his shirt, to make sure it was completely dry. Then he slipped the packet out of his pocket.

Johnny knelt for a moment on the spillway, the water, almost at its summer low point, streaming thinly over the slots between the flat rocks. Now the tricky part: getting the tablets out of the thickly folded square of paper. He lowered his left arm till it was out from his body, the rifle parallel to the spillway. Feeling better balanced, Johnny lifted the packet to his mouth and grabbed a corner with his teeth. Twisting with his fingers as he steadied the thing with his mouth, he got the paper unfolded, but it was facing downward.

Quickly he cupped his right hand under the loose paper, felt three tablets drop into his palm, grabbed for the fourth as it slipped down the front of his shirt and managed to catch it against his belly with his forearm, just above the dangling goggles. *Now! Now!* Still grasping the three in his palm, he slid his sweaty forearm along his shirt, teasing the renegade toward its three buddies. Come on! He jiggled a little as it stuck to his skin, then slid toward his wrist, where it lodged once more between moist flesh and warm T-shirt.

Annoyed at the stubbornness of the thing, Johnny turned his palm up, reaching at the same time with his other hand. But then the other three . . . *Stop!* he tried to scream as he grabbed with his left hand. He slammed the palmful of pills into his mouth, pushed them against his tongue as he reached with his other hand for the lone escapee.

He twisted, trying to stop its descent with his left hand. Too late he understood that one hand at his mouth and one hand clutching at the air around the goggles left no hands to hold the rifle. No hands to stop its clattering against the rocks. No hands to prevent the clicky rattle that accompanied its falling into the Nolan.

Johnny swallowed hard, praying that the pills worked fast, cleared his brain. His soaking pants were nothing to the sweat that poured out of him.

"Shit!" he screamed, then realized he was kneeling on the spillway with no rifle and no idea if Shane was still alive. He peered toward the water, which glinted occasionally when it caught the quarter-moon. *What if . . . what if the rifle . . .* He flopped on to his belly and stuck his hand into the frothy water collecting at the spillway. He tried not to picture what was massed there, lodged up against the stones. He felt stuff—hard, granular stuff, and thick, slimy stuff—bumping around his forearm. Gnats swarmed around his head. The air smelled like summer rot, mossy and too sweet. Somewhere Johnny heard sirens.

He fished around. Then he pulled up his dripping arm and scooted out farther on the spillway and fished again. And again.

Somewhere in there, Johnny felt something smooth and long, something metal. He pulled it up.

Johnny lay on the stones, his slimy, wet arm grasping the rifle. The pills were starting to work, he was starting to feel good about retrieving his weapon. I was smart, he thought. Shane thought he was the smart one, but I was smarter. Shane would be fifty feet downstream by now, but I thought it through; I kept my head and thought it through. I searched above the spillway.

Johnny panted with satisfaction. He could face anything now.

He pushed himself to his knees and crawled backward, his left hand clutching the rifle. He was revving up the truck and tearing around to the Hutto place. He was charging down the hill. He was finishing the job he started, he was taking his money and he was hitting the road.

"Where you going, son?"

Johnny fell flat and clutched the rifle beneath his body. The water streamed through the slots in the spillway, bubbling so that he could barely hear anything else. He was soaked. And the mosquitoes, the gnats, the flies. At least, when he peed, he was already wet, already lying in water so no one could see. Even with the sudden light. No wonder there were mosquitoes.

No one'll know, he thought. About peeing.

"Back up slowly," the voice said from somewhere behind the light.

Think it through, Johnny told himself. Just like the rifle. Slowly, he rose back up on hands and knees, grasping the rifle flat on the stones of the spillway.

"Slowly, now," the voice ordered.

Johnny thought about the water flowing on beyond the spillway. He could slip in and slide out of the light, float away around the bend. But here's where you have to be smart, he told himself. Here's where you've got to think through to the next step. You can't get to your truck. Your truck's right here, just a few feet away. You just have to get past the guy with the light.

Surprise is your best weapon, Johnny counseled. Picture it first. Visualize. He liked that. Visualize. One swift, smooth move. All the strength from those pills.

He had backed up almost to the bank of the river.

"Stand up. Slowly. Put your hands—"

Johnny sprang. From a crouch, he whirled around, fully extended, raising the rifle as he turned. He refused to be distracted by the trickle of water from the barrel, refused to be slowed by the light. He was charging forward, wet rifle in position, when the deputy shot.

When he heard the first shot fly by his ear, Tony looked up. Then something hit him hard and he was flat on the ground and there was a huge weight across his chest. Still woozy, he heard the deputy on the radio, calling for help. Someone had shot at them from across the river, right at the moment the deputy ordered him to take Flops and leave the area. Immediately.

Now there was someone else barking orders. And Flops, just barking. And Della.

"Tony," she was saying. "Tony!" Then, "Oh no! Oh my God!"

I don't think I'm . . . Something was very wet, very sticky.

And then that voice again, the man. "Dead."

I'm not dead, thought Tony, and he felt the weight, the pressing on his chest, just roll away.

Then Della took his hand. He knew her hands, felt them lifting his own hand to her lips. "Honey!"

"I don't think I'm—" He stopped, amazed at his own voice. "I'm okay, I think."

"You're covered with blood."

"From—" Tony's head throbbed, but he was not remembering, really remembering. "Him." Tony struggled to speak. "Him. He pushed me down. He screamed." Tony tried to shake his head, but that blinded him with pain. "He . . . help . . . a phone . . . a radio," Tony recalled. "Twitching. Shaking. His blood."

Chapter 29

When the runners who followed Ethan realized that there were no luminarias on their new route, they knew they had left the racecourse. But they were middle-of-the-pack runners, and they were far enough down the road that they had killed their chances of a personal best. The Sydonians among them assured the others that the road was only a shallow curve that would meet the race route up ahead.

The runners pounding the bladed dirt road by the light of a thin moon made a lot of noise and stirred up clouds of dust. Ethan expected them to turn around, but he did not stop to direct them, and when he slid his bike to a stop and headed into the brush, several of the runners overtook him. They were looking for the party.

The deputies posted at the top of the hill recognized Ethan. Once they let him pass into the brush, they were unable to stop the dozens of runners who, whooping with joy at the adventure, followed him. The deputies yelled, but by the time they dug the bullhorn out of their trunk, the runners were crashing through the brush, trying to follow the beam of Ethan's official Midnight Peaches Mag Lite.

The better-equipped runners flipped on their own flashlights and, when they hit the clearing, they stopped in confusion about the destination. Nervously, they looked up the hill, where the pace car still flashed red and blue in the dark.

Ethan headed straight to the cluster of officers next to the remains of the fort. He could hear more sirens from across the river and the buzz of the runners milling around the clearing, but his eyes locked on the boot-clad legs that lay still on the ground.

Ethan's brother Tommy had been in Scouts with Vinnie Perez. They had gone to Philmont, hiked through the mountains of New Mexico in a driving rain with their provisions on their backs. Vinnie, Tommy had recounted, had carried enough dry socks for their entire patrol.

As he muscled through the knot of people standing over Vinnie Perez, he heard the rest. Johnny Urquardt had shot Vinnie with Shane Castleburg's rifle. And Shane had been found dead at the Castleburgs' retail store. Tony and Della sat on the ground next to Vinnie's body, Tony covered with blood and both of them staring at Vinnie's body. Someone had covered Vinnie's face with a deputy's hat.

The sheriff rose as Ethan approached.

"Ethan!" Della said. "Tony must have hit his head. They're— the medics are coming."

"You know anything about this?" the sheriff asked.

Ethan glanced down at Vinnie, and around at the circle of faces, before locking on to Della's steady gaze. "No sir," said Ethan. "Not a thing."

It was dawn before the sheriff pulled the stakeout on the cases of water bottles hidden in the brush around Sydonia. By that time, the runners, who had trampled every square inch of the clearing, had been herded back up the hill and on their way to the finish line.

The sheriff's deputies had confiscated a rake, a hoe, and a variety of hand cultivators, along with a pile of equipment suitable for making GHB. After opening a few bottles, his deputies suspected, and he concurred, that the twenty cases of water actually were twenty cases of water, but they had sent it all to a lab in Fort Worth for confirmation.

They knew Johnny had shot Vinnie from the spillway, and they knew that Shane had been shot with a gun that had not been located. The sheriff doubted that a search of the Urquardt home would reveal much, but they would try. They would try Freddy Parker, too, but with Vinnie and his informants dead, they had no leverage.

Vinnie had left a mother and a father in Houston who wanted

to hear that their son was a hero. Eli Castleburg had lost a son, the probable victim of his own poor choice of friends. And Siggie Urquardt, as Burt Blanton had assured him, was far better off without her useless husband.

The runners had milled about on the hill long enough to have trampled over any other evidence. The deputies had pulled the remains of cannabis, probably growing on the hill, but who knew how long it had grown there.

They had questioned all the ladies at the Ladies Farm, their significant others, and their guests. They knew nothing. Tony Brewer, who had been checked and released at the emergency room, and sent home with his ex-wife, knew nothing. They had searched Shane Castleburg's place, trashed by Johnny Urquardt, and they found nothing.

Someone had formulated GHB with industrial chemicals purchased by Johnny Urquardt and stored at his in-laws' feed store. There was no GHB left in Sydonia, and there was no money. Vinnie, Johnny, and Shane were dead, and the sheriff had no other witnesses. It was near noon, and he had promised a statement to the media.

Perhaps Vinnie Perez had been duped by Johnny Urquardt, and then, under fire, had protected an innocent citizen out chasing his dog. Perhaps Johnny, with or without Shane, had made and sold GHB to some other party. Perhaps some other party had sneaked into Sydonia and shot Shane. If you assumed that Johnny Urquardt had made and sold the drugs, then killed his partner and the investigating officer, you could file the case unless new evidence turned up somewhere else.

There was no more evidence in Sydonia. No one left to prosecute. Any way you looked at it, the sheriff concluded, it was a drug deal gone bad.

"Vinnie Perez saved my life," Tony said at the memorial service. Vinnie's mother and father, petroleum chemists who now lived in Houston, sat in the front row of the Sydonia High School auditorium, flanked by their other children. "All of you who have spoken so eloquently about Vinnie's childhood, his high school years here in Sydonia, I envy you. I only knew him for a second. It was the most important second of my life. And one of the finest in his."

Tony cleared his throat, sipped from his glass of water. He looked out at the crowd that overflowed into the halls and the cafeteria, and wondered who was left on the streets of Sydonia.

"A criminal . . . a criminal shot at us from across the river. And Vinnie"—his voice wavered—"Vinnie pushed me flat to the ground—so hard I knocked my head and got a concussion—and he covered me. And I lived. And he died.

"Mr. and Mrs. Perez, your son . . . your son walked into a dangerous place, and when life was at its most dangerous, your son was fearless. And I will be glad every day of my life that Vinnie— Vincente Perez—was here. All of us are grateful that we knew him, even for a second."

Once the doctor gave the okay, Gladys and Ray helped Webb pack, and Gladys drove Webb back to Sydonia in the Avalon while Ray caught a flight back to the Big Bend with a friend of Wade's. "He'll be all right on his own for a few more days," Gladys assured Webb as they sped along the interstate.

"I imagine he'll be glad to get back to his routine."

"His drugs, you mean," Gladys said. "Where he feels safe."

"Not a bad thing, that stuff," Webb said. "Easily cultivated. Makes me want to give up peaches."

"You are giving up peaches." Gladys kept her eyes on the road, but she knew Webb was frowning. "I want you out there," she continued. "Soon as you get the late crop in. That's what we agreed."

"Ethan's still working on a buyer," Webb reminded her. "It might be sooner than you think."

"You know, he's a good boy," Gladys said. "To hang around Sydonia till fall." She paused, then said it all. "And not to tell anyone, with all that going on. That must have been hard."

They turned off the interstate and onto the farm-to-market. They were an hour and a half from Sydonia, and Gladys felt herself straining forward, wanting to see the live oaks at the courthouse and to walk in the clearing below her old home.

"It shows the wisdom of backup," Webb said.

Gladys knew what he meant. "Thing is, now we have to find some other place."

"Well, there are the orchards," Webb said. "But I put in a little more backup out west."

"What does that mean?" Gladys glanced over at him.

"I put in a few other plots."

"Where . . . where—"

"Outside the park," Webb said. "I started looking for some of those other springs, the ones people wouldn't think of for swimming. Buggy, too. Don't go without spraying yourself down."

"Oh, yeah," said Gladys. "That's my main concern."

"I left . . . you know, in case anything happens . . . in my trunk, under the spare, there's one map. And the other—"

"Good God, what a mind!"

"Listen, now," Webb said. "Another is in a little metal match holder under the mulch around that plum tree of yours. The one to the far right."

"So you planted two more plots? When did you do this?"

"Three. Now, down by your mailbox where you've got those rocks around that little cactus garden?"

"You put a map in the cactus?"

"No, in a rock. One of those fake ones. On the left side, as you face it. Right under the little prickly pear. Not the big one, the little one."

"Gotcha," mumbled Gladys. She thought about Webb, stomping through the Big Bend, exploring springs, studying sunlight and drainage.

"It was while you were quilting. I couldn't . . . you were working so hard. I never meant for you—"

"Well, I'm glad I did it. That quilt made five thousand dollars for the library. Know who bought it?"

"Ethan didn't say."

"Ethan didn't say to you. You didn't ask. It was Tony Brewer. Della's husband. Actually ex-husband. But they're going to get married again. So he bought it as a wedding gift. Now aren't you glad you asked me to quilt?"

"It's just . . . I never dreamed it would be that much work for you. When I saw—"

Now Gladys laughed. It felt like ages since she had laughed that way. "You mean," she asked, tears running down her cheek, "you mean, you thought, all these years, you thought I could quilt like Alice and just chose not to?" She shook her head, remembering her friend's patient coaching and steadfast encouragement and her own feeble attempts at fine needlework.

"I guess I never thought that much about it." He turned toward her. "I'm sorry now, I guess. I thought the least I could do was plant your backup a little closer to home, return the favor, sort of."

"Don't you ever be sorry, Webb Dyer," Gladys said. The laughter had stopped, but the tears still shone on her cheeks. "Finishing that thing was a privilege for me. It was one more thing for Alice. Gave me one more chance to work with her. There was a lot of pleasure in it."

"I guess I meant I'm sorry about Alice," Webb said. "I never told her I knew the difference, that even I could tell how good she was."

"Sometimes, Webb, you do have to speak up."

They had convinced Melissa to stay through the auction, which had been postponed a week. Now, though, she stood in front of the Lexus, the two boys buckled in the back.

"You call when you get home," Della instructed.

"Call every day," Rita pleaded. She stuck her head in the car for more good-bye kisses. "You boys, you call every day and let us know what you saw. Where you've been."

Melissa turned to Della, and Della drew the girl to her. "You come back whenever you want, you hear?" Della breathed deep to catch the scent of Melissa's hair, the warmth of her skin. For a second it connected her to Pauline and their time as young parents, all their children playing together in someone's backyard while they played Trivial Pursuit in the family room.

But now, Melissa was taking her own family back to Portland, to work out some sort of accommodation with her cross-dressing husband.

Melissa laughed. "You come see us, Aunt Dell." She looked at the others. "All of you. When the heat gets too much, and you want someplace nice and cool and green. We'll make room."

They waved her on her way. Rita, Dave, Kat, and Nick headed back into the house. "I'll be along," Della called to them. Tony had to go to Fort Worth, and she wanted to walk him to the car.

"She'll be all right," Tony said, putting his arm around her. "She's pretty smart. She did save Peach Fest."

"Despite everything," Della agreed. "I'm not worried. Just curious to see how it all plays out: Greg taking an apartment,

Melissa going back to the house. It's still going to be tough. She'll start dating, or he will. Then what?"

"Look who's talking!" Tony said. "If you want to worry, worry about poor Ethan Dyer."

"Now, Ethan really will be all right," Della said. "He'll get the orchards sold, he'll get his dad moved out to the Big Bend, and then he'll find something he wants to do."

"In a monastery?"

They had walked around to the carport at the side of the Ladies Farm. Behind the house, they could glimpse the Nolan, thin and slick and green until they got more rain. Still shaded from the morning sun by the cottonwoods and the steep, far bank.

"It's not really a monastery," Della said. "At least, not according to Melissa. It's a place for him to stay while he sorts things out . . . more like a nonsectarian retreat. With chores."

Tony shook his head. "If he wants chores, he should hold on to the orchards."

He leaned back against the side of his truck, pulled Della to him, his hands on her waist. This would be their first day apart since Johnny Urquardt had shot at him, and, no matter how silly it seemed, she didn't feel quite ready to kiss him good-bye and send him off to work.

For a second, she recalled Vinnie's parents, who had made a point of thanking Tony for his kind words. *Losing a son,* Della had tried to tell them, *losing a son is like—*

But, of course, there had been no way to tell them.

Della rested her forehead in the center of his chest. He had enough of an adjustment without her concerns. "Listen," she said.

"Hmmm?" He didn't seem to be in any hurry.

"You call, too," she instructed, looking up at him. "When you get to the store."

"Sure." He kissed her forehead, and she pulled away and motioned to him to get in the truck. Tony grinned. "I usually do, don't I?"

She nodded, smiled, bit her lip. It would be a good thing for Tony, Della thought, if she could hold back her tears until after he drove away.

So Tony got into the truck and backed out from under the carport and drove up the drive and into the street and headed for the square to pick up the farm-to-market to Fort Worth. Della walked around to the front of the Ladies Farm, where she could barely make out the pickup as it stopped at the light where Travis met Crockett.

It's okay to cry now, she thought; but she remained dry-eyed. There was a calm, she found, that came from the certainty that this moment—this very moment—was the finest of her life. That knowledge was everything she had hoped.